SOFIA

Titles available in this series

Yannis
Anna
Giovanni
Joseph
Christabelle
Saffron
Manolis
Cathy
Nicola
Vasi
Alecos
John
Tassos
Ronnie
Maria
Sofia

Greek Translations

Anna
published by Livanis 2011

SOFIA

Beryl Darby

JACH

ISBN 978-0-9574532-6-5

Printed and bound in Great Britain by
CPI Group UK Ltd., Croydon, CR0 4YY

First published in the UK in 2015 by

JACH Publishing
92 Upper North Street, Brighton, East Sussex, England BN1 3FJ

website: www.beryldarby.co.uk

For Jackie Evans, one of my first and most loyal readers who has become a good friend

Family Tree

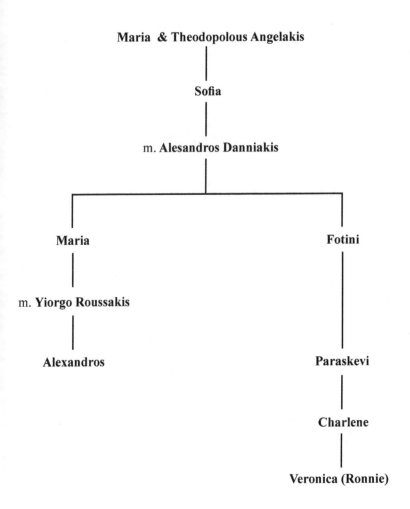

Maria & Theodopolous Angelakis

Sofia

m. **Alesandros Danniakis**

Maria

Fotini

m. **Yiorgo Roussakis**

Alexandros

Paraskevi

Charlene

Veronica (Ronnie)

Author's Note

Once again I have used the pretty village of Kastelli for the setting of this book.

I have no knowledge of the history of the large house that has fallen into disrepair or the owners, past or present.

The story is a product of my imagination. The family I have accommodated there and their activities are entirely fictitious.

Any resemblance to the true history or any of the people who ever lived there is entirely coincidental.

2012

The kebabs arrived and Kassianae helped herself, turning them over to select the couple she thought the choicest. She gnawed away at them, scorning the knife and fork that had been placed on the table, and taking sips of her whisky at intervals.

A plate of diced apples and oranges were brought and again Kassie used her fingers to help herself. Finally satisfied she sat back in her chair.

'Another little drink to help wash that lot down wouldn't come amiss,' she said, looking pointedly at John, and he signalled that another whisky should be brought over.

'Would you like a coffee?' he asked and Kassie looked at him scornfully.

'Why would I want coffee? I can drink coffee at home at any time.'

John smiled and shook his head. Two neat whiskies had already disappeared in quick succession, yet she appeared as sober as he and Nicola.

Kassie leaned back in her chair and belched again, banging her flat chest with her hand. 'That's better,' she announced. 'Now what is it you want to know?'

Winter 1910

Alesandros Danniakis sat in his room in Aghios Nikolaos and consulted his notebook. He had started work at the tax office when he left the High School, the job arranged for him by his father who had worked there all his life. Gradually, due to working assiduously, he had moved up from being an errand boy to being trusted with a counter position where he received the money from the collectors who travelled around the villages.

He understood how the tax system worked and when the opportunity arose he applied to be a travelling collector. It had been a profitable move. He would visit a farmer and tell him, quite correctly, that he owed five hundred drachmas in tax to the government. It was rare for a farmer to have that amount to hand and Alesandros would offer to make up the difference from his own savings and call again in a month for the balance.

What the farmer did not know was that he had a year in which to pay the full amount and he could pay by instalments. Alesandros took advantage of his ignorance and when he called a month later for the balance owed to him the farmer would offer him a few more drachmas. Alesandros would sit with the man, explain that having paid the government on the farmer's behalf the outstanding money was now owing to him, and he would be charging interest until such time as the debt was cleared.

Over the years he had accepted olive, apple, lemon and orange trees as payment of the interest. Once the fruits had been harvested he would return to the farmer and ask for his share of the income from the produce. In this way the farmer was never free from his debt and Alesandros was becoming a wealthy man.

Today, he decided, he would visit Driros, Kourounis and Perambela and ask the farmers for the money he was owed from the autumn apples crop as some of the trees belonged to him now. From there he would travel back to Kastelli and ask Theodopolous for his outstanding debt. Theodopolous had a regular income from the cottages he rented to the villagers who grew the fruit and vegetables for the village and travelled to Neapoli for the market there each week. He was a conscientious landlord and never hesitated to complete the necessary repairs to keep the cottages in good order. If his tenants were unable to pay their rent he would accept a chicken or vegetables rather than the cash.

Alesandros hoped the man would be unable to pay. If that was the case he could relieve him of an olive tree. Olive trees were the most rewarding source of additional income as everyone needed the oil and the townspeople were willing to pay a high price to satisfy their consumption. Once he started to request his share of the olive harvest Theodopolous would soon find that the only way he could settle his monthly arrears was to relinquish another tree.

Alesandros closed his notebook. He would ride his donkey to Perambela, then on to Kastelli, call at Driros and finally return to Aghios Nikolaos where he would pay a further instalment of the farmers' tax in to the office.

Sofia sat at the table with her friend, Tryphaine, playing noughts and crosses.

'I've beaten you again, Phaini.'

'That's because you always start first,' complained Tryphaine.

'You start this time, then,' smiled Sofia, and helped herself to another biscuit. She was not competitive when she played games with any of her friends and it did not concern her if she lost continually. 'Have another biscuit.'

Tryphaine placed her elbows on the table and sighed. 'I shouldn't eat biscuits. I'm getting fat.' None the less she took a biscuit from the plate.

'You're not fat,' remarked Sofia scornfully. 'Compared to Olympia you're skinny.'

'She can't help her weight. Her mother says she hardly eats anything, but has something wrong with her.'

Sofia raised her eyebrows, but did not reply. Olympia had visited her house and as usual Sofia's mother had produced a plate of biscuits for the girls to share. By the time Sofia had eaten one Olympia had managed to eat three and had no compunction about eating the remaining two.

'Do you think it will snow again tonight?' asked Tryphaine. 'We could ask some of the other girls to join us and have a big snowball fight.'

'Provided the boys don't want to join in. They can throw further than us.'

'We'll tell them they're not invited.'

'We told them that last time and they took no notice. The inside of my cloak was wet where Lambros put snow down my neck deliberately.'

Tryphaine grinned wickedly. 'I think that was his way of telling you he likes you.'

'Well, I don't like him. It took Mamma three days to get my cloak properly dry, and then it rained and it was wet again.'

'At least you don't have to work out in the fields when it's raining,' observed Tryphaine. 'Some days my cloak and boots are still wet the next day when I put them on.'

Sofia nodded. She knew she was privileged. Her father did not work in the fields. He had olive, apple and orange trees. When the fruit was ready his wife and daughter joined the other villagers and picked until all the trees were bare, but he did not expect his wife and daughter to be out in all weathers like the villagers who tended the fields.

'You must get awfully cold,' said Sofia solicitously.

'Frozen,' replied Tryphaine glumly. 'I don't mind the work in the summer, but I hate it in the winter.' She shrugged. 'We all do.'

'We rely on you and we're grateful. If you didn't provide us with vegetables during the winter we'd starve.'

Tryphaine looked at the plate of biscuits again. 'I'm sure your Mamma would manage to cook nice meals for you.'

Sofia pushed the plate nearer to her friend. 'I don't want any more. You finish that one.'

'You're sure?' she asked as she took the biscuit off the plate. Her mother only made biscuits at Easter and Christmas, having spent most of the day out in the fields and after cooking a meal for her family to eat in the evening she had little inclination to spend another hour of the day making biscuits.

'Next time Mamma makes biscuits I'll ask if you can come and watch,' offered Sofia. 'Then you could make some biscuits as a treat for everyone.'

'Do you know how to make them?'

Sofia nodded. 'I know how to cook most things. Mamma shows me and sometimes she lets me make the dish. If I forget to add something she reminds me. She says I have to know so that when I'm married I will be able to cook properly.'

'When are you getting married?'

Sofia laughed. 'Not for ages yet.'

'Are you betrothed to someone in the village?'

Sofia shook her head. 'Not that I know of. Mamma and Pappa have never mentioned anyone to me.'

'You're probably promised to the son of one of your father's friends or a cousin.'

'I don't think so. I haven't any cousins anyway. What about you?'

'Mamma says I am going to marry Nikos. He and his parents are invited to the house sometimes and Nikos and I sit and look at each other.'

'You don't talk?'

'What is there to talk about? He's spent his day out in the fields the same as I have.'

'Do you like him?'

Tryphaine shrugged. 'I don't dislike him.'

Sofia thought about the boy her friend was destined to marry and was thankful that she had not been promised to him. He sat with his mouth open much of the time as if he was unable to suck enough air into his lungs and when he spoke it was with a nasal twang.

'He works hard,' she said and Tryphaine nodded.

'That's what my Pappa says. He says if your husband works hard and provides enough food for your table you have nothing to complain about.'

Sofia nodded. Surely there must be more to being married than providing food. Her parents talked together, often laughing and joking and her father would slip his arm around her mother's waist and hold her to him. He always thanked her for the meal she had cooked and said he had enjoyed it. There were times when she had sensed that her father was worried and he had talked quietly to her mother, seen her squeeze his hand and tell him they would manage somehow.

'I'd better go,' said Tryphaine and rose from the table. 'Mamma may think I'm staying to eat with you and then she won't save anything for me.' She said the words, hoping she might have an invitation to join them for their evening meal.

'I'll see you tomorrow, then.' Sofia rose as well. 'If it snows we'll see about having a snowball fight.'

'I hope it does. If it snows I won't have to go and see if there are any onions worth collecting.'

Tryphaine pulled her cloak around her shoulders and Sofia opened the door, closing it quickly as Tryphaine left to ensure the warmth stayed in the house. She sat back down at the table and rested her chin on her hands. She would like to continue with the embroidery she was doing on a blouse for her mother, but it was to be a surprise for her for Christmas, and it was too cold upstairs to sit and sew. Her fingers would be blue and numb in no time and she would be unable to stitch evenly.

She found Tryphaine's words about getting married disconcerting and hoped she would not be told in a few years' time that a village boy was to be her partner. When she and her mother were alone she would ask her mother if any such arrangement had been made, that was if she could find the courage.

Alesandros blew on his fingers to warm them as he shifted the donkey's rein from hand to hand. It was colder than he had realised. If he was going to ride to Perambela it would be sensible to call on Makkis at Kourounis and see if he could collect the money owing for his apple crop from him also.

He kicked the donkey's flanks, encouraging her to trot a little faster. When he reached Drakos he would stop at the taverna there and have a glass of wine to warm him through before taking to the trail that led to Driros. Another glass of wine at Driros would sustain him for the ride to Perambela and he should arrive as Elias and Marina were having a mid-day meal which he hoped he would be invited to share.

By the time he reached Kastelli it would be late afternoon and Theodopolous should be at home. Anyone with any sense would be snug indoors on a cold day like this as soon as they finished any essential jobs outside. He cursed himself as a fool for setting out to collect his debts on such a cold day, but by the look of the sky it could have snowed by the following morning.

There was no way he could make the journey if there was snow on the ground. The donkey would lose her footing and he could easily become lost if the trail was not visible. This could be his last opportunity to visit the four farmers for a number of weeks and he wanted what was due to him. He hoped none of them would be able to pay him in full and he could arrange to relieve them of another tree.

They were so foolish. He considered they were his 'bad debts' as they never seemed to have more than a few drachmas to hand. If they put some money to one side every week, as most of the other farmers did, they would have enough to pay their taxes when he called and not have to take advantage of his offer to pay on their behalf. Each time they gave him a tree as payment for the amount they owed and the interest he had charged they were reducing their income. They very quickly became caught in a downward spiral of debt that they would never be able to clear. With a little astute juggling of his personal finances he was able to pay the tax they owed to the government in instalments and increase his own income at the same time.

The taverna owners never seemed to have a problem paying their taxes and he was grateful as they had nothing to give him apart from a free meal or a drink. He accepted those as his due, but they would certainly not add to his income in any way. He needed enough money to approach an affluent father and ask for his daughter's hand. Provided the man had sufficient money he would have already built a house as a gift for his daughter when she married, but Alesandros was wise enough to know that he would have to prove he had a healthy amount of money of his own put aside. He had no one in mind, but he knew he should make provision for care in his old age. He was not getting any younger and soon his choice would be limited to widows or middle aged women who had never had a suitor. It was time he asked around to ascertain if one of his colleagues from the tax office had a suitable daughter or niece.

Two glasses of wine at Drakos, one complimentary and the other paid for, warmed him through and he turned off on the trail that led to Driros in a happier frame of mind.

Christos was truculent when he arrived. There had been a glut of apples that year and he had not received as much as he hoped from the sale of his crop. Alesandros commiserated with him. He knew the amount the farmers had been paid for their apples and although not knowing how many kilos his tree had produced he had worked out what he considered a reasonable sum that should be paid to him.

Alesandros was adamant that he would not accept a lepta less than the full amount and finally Christos counted out the drachmas and received a receipt in return. Annoyed that he had needed to spend so much time cajoling the man into paying, Alesandros left hurriedly, swinging his arms to bring some warmth into his body, wishing he had been able to add another apple tree to his growing orchards.

He rode through Kastelli, knowing that word would reach Theodopolous that he was in the area and continued on to Kourounis. Theodopolous was becoming a problem and he did not wish to spend the remainder of the day arguing with him about the amount that he owed.

Makkis scowled when he opened his door and saw Alesandros standing there. 'I would have thought it too cold for you to be venturing out,' he remarked.

Alesandros shrugged. 'Cold or not, the government expect their taxes paid on time and I expect my loans to you to be paid on time also.'

'Well, you've wasted your time coming to me. We had a fire shortly before the crop was ready and I lost most of my apple trees. I've nothing for you.'

Alesandros shook his head sympathetically. 'That's too bad. I'll not press you for money you haven't got, but you realise I will have to add the amount to the debt already owing to me. That will also increase the interest you owe. If you're still unable to pay the money the next time I call then we'll have to come to some arrangement. You have orange and olive trees, I believe.'

Makkis nodded. 'Thankfully they were spared by the fire.'

Alesandros smiled. 'Then I hope you will have a bountiful crop and make some money from both. I would be willing to take an olive tree or a couple of orange trees as settlement.'

'I'm sure you would.' Makkis spoke bitterly. 'Then you'd be asking me for even more money, claiming your share of the crop income.'

Alesandros spread his hands. 'I would only claim what was due to me. I'm an honest man. If you made enough money you could always buy them back from me for the same amount as I originally claimed. I would not put my price up.' Alesandros knew that it was most unlikely Makkis would ever have enough money to buy back any trees. 'That's a fair offer.'

Makkis nodded. 'I'll think about it.'

Alesandros replaced his hat on his head and wound his scarf around his neck. There was no point in wasting any more time with the man today. The next time he called he was sure he would find it more profitable. He stamped his feet and rubbed his hands together, it had not been very warm in Makkis's cottage.

As Alesandros hitched his donkey to the post outside the cottage in Perambela a savoury smell greeted him and his stomach rumbled in anticipation. He had chosen his time of arrival well. It was obviously going to be their meal time.

Marina opened the door and ushered him in, offering him a seat by the fire. As he sat she removed the pot that had been hanging over the fire and simmering gently.

'You'll stay for something to eat?'

'I'd be very grateful.'

Marina nodded. However grateful the man might be he was not having any of the goat stew she had prepared earlier. She would save that for her and Elias to eat later. She had made enough for it to last them for three days and she knew if Alesandros joined them she would be lucky to have sufficient for another meal.

Whilst waiting for Elias to appear, Marina went into her scullery and returned with a loaf of bread, olive oil, salt, onions and a small slab of cheese. She placed the food on the table along with a plate and knife and Alesandros's face fell. He had been hoping for something delicious from the cooking pot.

Elias arrived, closing the door swiftly behind him as the wind blew an icy draught across the room. He frowned when he saw Alesandros sitting in his chair by the fire.

'I hadn't expected to see you on a cold day like this,' he observed.

'Business has to take precedence over the weather. How are you doing Elias?'

Elias shrugged. 'Not as well as I had hoped. The apple crop was a failure.'

Alesandros raised his eyebrows. 'Really? What happened?'

'Trees were blighted by a parasite.'

Alesandros shook his head. One man had suffered from a glut of apples, another had lost his trees due to a fire and now Elias was claiming his crop had been damaged by a parasite. He knew each farmer was lying to him as he had the figures the assessors had produced. It was from these assessments that the amount of tax owed by each farmer was calculated.

'That's bad news. Have you managed to get rid of it?'

'I think so. The trees are looking a good deal healthier now.'

'I'm pleased to hear it. How are your oranges? Have they been affected?'

Elias hesitated. He could not claim that all his trees were suffering from a parasite. 'They seem healthy enough at the moment.'

Alesandros took his place at the table, tore off a large piece of bread, poured olive oil over it and sprinkled it with salt before helping himself to half of the slab of cheese. Elias made no comment about the sparseness of their meal, knowing why Marina had not served the goat stew that he had been anticipating all morning.

'Well,' said Elias eventually. 'That has filled the inner man. Have you had enough Mr Danniakis? If so we will have to talk business. I imagine that is why you have paid us a visit.'

Alesandros nodded. 'I was hoping you would be able to pay

me my share from the apple crop and also reduce the interest you owe me.'

Elias spread his hands and shook his head. 'Sadly I am in no position to do so. I had hoped for a good year to be able to extricate myself from your debt, but it was not to be. I can only offer you another apple tree and hope the crop is profitable next year.'

Alesandros shook his head. 'I cannot take the chance of accepting another apple tree. How can I be sure it is healthy? I think an orange tree would be a fairer offer.'

Elias sighed. 'I'll have to hope the frost doesn't affect them.'

'I will hope so also. Now, here is your receipt for an orange tree and here is the amount that you owe me to date. I have included the amount I expected to receive for the apples.'

Elias took the two pieces of paper. They meant nothing to him. He could count money, but numbers on a piece of paper were meaningless. He pushed them into his pocket without bothering to look at them and Alesandros felt annoyed with his own honesty. He could have written an extortionate figure as interest and the man would not have queried it.

'I'll be on my way, then. I have another call to make. It feels like snow out there and I would like to be back in Aghios Nikolaos before it begins to fall.'

Elias and Marina rose from the table, making no attempt to prolong Alesandros's visit. As Elias closed the door he turned to his wife with a smile.

'He obviously believed the story about the parasite. At least we have enough put by to pay the rent now.'

Marina frowned. 'But you've had to give him an orange tree.'

Elias shrugged. 'I had no choice. It was pay whatever he asked in cash or give him a tree.'

Sofia looked up from her sewing as a knock came at the door. Her mother did not move from the weaving loom and her father nodded to her, indicating she should see who was outside.

'It's Mr Danniakis, Pappa.'

'Then ask him in, girl. Don't leave him on the doorstep on a day like this.'

Alesandros walked across the room and took the seat beside the fire that Sofia had vacated. She drew the heavy rug across the door to keep out the draught and stood by the table. If her father was going to ask Mr Danniakis to have some refreshment she would be expected to bring it.

'Cold out there,' observed Theodopolous. 'I was glad to get back inside. I don't envy you the ride back to Aghios Nikolaos. I reckon it will have snowed by tomorrow.'

Alesandros nodded. 'That's why I decided I should go around and collect some of the money that is owing to me. I might not get the opportunity to do so again for few weeks and you know what you farmers are like.' He winked and tried to speak jovially. 'If I don't arrive on time you've always had an unexpected expense and have no available money.'

'That's very true,' observed Theodopolous. 'Bring our guest some wine and biscuits, Sofia. He needs something to warm him before he makes his return journey.'

Obediently Sofia decanted an amount of wine into a carafe, collected glasses from the shelf, placed some biscuits on a plate and took them through to the living room. She poured a glass of wine for her father and another for Mr Danniakis before offering the tax man a biscuit from the plate.

Alesandros downed the wine in one mouthful and held out his glass for it to be refilled whilst he took a biscuit. He took a bite and then crammed the rest of the biscuit into his mouth.

'These are very tasty.' He helped himself to two more.

Theodopolous nodded. 'My daughter is becoming a good cook.'

Alesandros raised his eyebrows and looked at the girl. 'How old is she?'

'Thirteen years, near enough.'

'Very accomplished for her age. I'm sure you're proud of her.'

'Naturally. She's very adept with her needle as well. Show Mr Danniakis your work, Sofia.'

Blushing, Sofia picked up the blouse she had been stitching and held it out for inspection.

'Very neat.' Mr Danniakis smiled at her. 'You'll make some lucky man a good wife one day.'

Sofia's blush deepened and she went to stand beside her mother at the weaving loom. She wished the man would go. She wanted to return to her place by the fire and continue with her sewing.

Alesandros turned to Theodopolous. 'Now, we must talk business. How was your apple crop this year?'

'Not bad, but I didn't get as much as I had hoped.'

'Are you trying to tell me you cannot pay me my share?'

Theodopolous spread his hands. 'It's a difficult situation. I had the money from the apple crop, but my daughter needed new boots for the winter and a new cloak. She's a growing girl. My wife made her cloak, of course, but I had to go to Neapoli and purchase the wool.'

'So you used my money from the apples?'

Theodopolous shook his head. 'No, I used the rent from the cottages for the purchases and had your money put to one side. Unfortunately we had a very high wind and two of the cottages lost some of their roof tiles. I had to use the use the money from the apples for the repairs.'

'Didn't you charge them for the repairs that were needed?'

'The damage was due to the wind. I could not hold them responsible for that. Since then the ground has become too hard to dig and the farmers have been unable to harvest much of their winter vegetable crop and take it to the market. I have had no money from them for three weeks. They have given me whatever vegetables they could dig up, along with a couple of chickens, milk and eggs. I accept them in place of their rent, but it means I have no money coming in.'

Alesandros frowned. 'I think we need a serious discussion, Theo. Your debts are mounting. You owe me the money I paid for your outstanding tax last year along with the interest. For the last three years you have been unable to pay your debts and I have accepted apple trees. You owe me for my share of the apple crop and again you say you have no money.'

'It is quite true. I would be only too happy to pay my debt to you if I had the resources. As it is we are going to struggle through the winter months.'

Alesandros looked around the room. It was hard to believe that the man was as penniless as he claimed. The walls were hung with rugs to keep the draughts out and the warmth in, rugs were spread over the flag stones on the floor, on the dresser there were china plates and glass ware. They could hardly be struggling financially if they had enough flour for the girl to make biscuits.

'So what do you suggest, Theodopolous? How are you going to manage to pay me all that you owe?'

'Another apple tree?' suggested Theodopolous.

Alesandros shook his head. 'An apple tree will nowhere near cover the cost. I will have to ask for olive trees and hope that when the crop is harvested this year you ensure you have enough put aside to pay me my share.'

Theodopolous frowned. 'Olive trees are a valuable commodity. I only have fifteen.'

'Fifteen? There are more like forty in the grove.'

Theodopolous nodded. 'That's true, but they do not all belong to me. When my father took land from the villagers to build this house he gave each household an olive tree as compensation. When the crop is harvested Pappas Symeon works out the amount each family is entitled to and shares it amongst us.'

'So I should be collecting an olive tax from the villagers as well as yourself.'

Theodopolous shook his head. 'It was agreed with the farmers that my father would pay the tax for the villagers. I am responsible for all the tax.'

Alesandros looked at the man in disbelief. No wonder Theo never had any money if he was paying tax on twenty five trees for which he received no income. 'You owe me a good deal of money. One olive tree would reduce your debt a little. If you signed over five trees to me you would be free of last year's debt, except for the amount owing for the apple crop, of course.'

'Completely free?'

Alesandros nodded. 'You will owe me nothing until after the olives have been harvested. You will then owe me my share for the yield from the five trees that belong to me and the amount outstanding for the apple crop. Hopefully the olive crop will be lucrative and you will be able to put some money to one side.'

'What about my tax?'

'At the moment the government charges you tax on the rents from the cottages and also from the produce of your orchards. The less you own the less tax you have to pay. I will be responsible for the tax on the olive and apple trees that I own.' Alesandros did not mention that he had no intention of declaring to the government the various trees he owned around the countryside, but he would honestly deduct the tax from the amount the farmer was calculated to owe.

Theodopolous sighed deeply. 'I can see no other way out of this dilemma. In my father's day the government did not charge such an extortionate rate of tax. He was able to pay his dues and still have money in his pocket.'

'It is not my doing,' Alesandros assured him. 'If I had not been willing to help you to pay your taxes the government would have stripped you of all your trees by now. You are fortunate that you are dealing with me and also have the cottages.'

Theodopolous nodded and placed his mark on the piece of paper that Alesandros handed to him. He could not read, but had to trust that he was only giving the man five olive trees in exchange for his debts. If it was not so cold outside he would have asked Alesandros to walk up to the church with him and ask Pappas Symeon to vouch for the transaction.

'Another drink before you leave?' asked Theodopolous. 'I would ask you to stay and join us for our evening meal, but in view of the weather I think you would be wise to start your journey back to Aghios Nikolaos very soon. You would not want to be stranded in Kastelli for an indeterminate amount of time.'

Alesandros understood that the man was not being solicitous; Theodopolous had no wish to have to offer the tax collector accommodation for days at a time if it did snow and the trails became impassable. Alesandros filled his glass and tossed the comforting liquid down his throat with a satisfied smile. He might well stop again on his way back to Aghios Nikolaos for another glass or two to keep out the cold.

By the time Alesandros reached Limnes snow was beginning to fall, large soft flakes that settled on the bushes. Alesandros urged the donkey onwards. He needed to reach Drakos before the weather worsened and hid the trail. Once he had left Drakos and started back towards the coast it was likely that the snow would turn to sleet or rain. Although it was tempting to stop in the village for another glass of wine, common sense prevailed. It would be wisest to reach Aghios Nikolaos as soon as possible. His head bent down and his shoulders hunched, he resolutely continued on his journey.

He was a few kilometres from Aghios Nikolaos when the snow turned to sleet, then to rain which finally ceased. A strong wind was blowing from the sea and seemed to be penetrating every pore in his body, making him feel colder than when it had been snowing. He shivered intermittently and wished he had thought to carry a bottle of wine with him. Before returning to his lodgings he determined to stop at the taverna and have a brandy to ward off a chill.

Once he reached the field where he tethered his donkey he

hurriedly removed the saddle, ensured she had water and fodder, and threw a blanket and a waterproof cover over her back. If she had any sense she would stay inside the shelter until the morning.

Alesandros hurried down the path, the saddle over his arm, and pushed his way into the taverna. There were few customers and he was able to move close to the fire where he nursed his brandy in both hands; sipping slowly and savouring the warmth it brought to his half frozen body. It was with reluctance that he finally left and walked along to his lodgings.

Alesandros sat at the table in the living room of the house where he rented a room. He had removed his wet cloak and hung it on the hook behind the front door. Having changed into dry trousers and jacket, he hung the damp clothes on the peg behind his bedroom door. After an initial feeling of warmth from being inside and away from the elements, the chill of his room began to penetrate, despite the oil stove that gave out a meagre heat, and he had collected his papers and cash box and moved down to the living room. It was warmer there than in the small room in the roof where he had his bed and few personal possessions. He had no complaints; the amount he paid in rent covered his food and his washing so a cold bedroom could be tolerated. With his papers spread before him and his notebook to hand he calculated the amounts still outstanding from the farmers he had visited that day. As he worked he ran his fingers along his luxuriant moustache, partly from habit and also to ensure the ends were twisted together to form a point.

Christos had paid the money due from the apple crop and Alesandros added that to his cash box and locked it securely. Makkis owed for the apples, but Elias had settled his debt by signing over an orange tree to him. Spread across the Lassithi area Alesandros now owned a total of twenty two orange trees and twenty eight apple trees, along with the five olive trees he had persuaded Theodopolous to part with. Theodopolous was a problem. The man seemed to have no grasp of finance at all. The next time he visited he would have to sit down with him and explain that he must save some of his income, even if it meant repairs to the cottages had to wait.

Alesandros rubbed his hands together, partly for warmth and partly from pleasure. Provided the trees remained healthy and the annual crop was good he could consider himself a wealthy man. He placed his papers together tidily and moved the oil lamp to one side. 'I've finished working on the table, Stassa. You can use it to lay out our meal as soon as it suits you.'

Stassa nodded. She was loath to move from the fire, knowing Alesandros would swiftly take her place. She knotted her shawl firmly around her shoulders and rose from her chair with a sigh. The cold weather made her joints ache and she hoped Alesandros would decide to have an early night so she could lift her skirt and rub her knees with liniment to give her some relief.

Alesandros placed his papers and cash box on the floor beside his chair and swiftly moved over to the fire. He spread his hands out to the welcome heat, relishing in the comfort it gave him. He would ask Stassa for a hot brick to put in his bed tonight as his toes still felt numb. He looked enviously at the large bed in the corner and wished he had a proper fire in his bedroom.

Stassa ladled generous helpings of chicken and vegetables from the pot on the fire into bowls and placed them on the table along with a loaf of bread. Reluctant though he was to move away from the fire, Alesandros was hungry and he took his place at the table with alacrity.

Lambros folded his newspaper and joined him. 'Cold day to have been out around the villages,' he observed.

Alesandros nodded agreement, his mouth full. 'It was snowing by the time I reached Limnes as I rode back.'

'Don't know why you travel around when you could sit in an office during the winter.'

'I prefer to be outside. All you see in an office is four walls.'

Lambros smiled. 'Don't have time to look at the walls. Too busy concentrating on the type setting.'

Lambros worked for the local printers where the weekly newspaper was produced. It was his job to set each individual letter into the holder ready to be printed. It was a skilled job. The letters had to be placed in back to front so that when the printing took place they were the correct way round and the spaces between the words were even.

'And then you bring your work home with you.' Alesandros pointed to the newspaper that Lambros had folded and left on his fireside chair.

'Like to check for errors. I'm only responsible for three pages, but the trainee we've taken on is still making mistakes. This is the trial print so if I find he has made mistakes there's still time to correct them before the whole run is printed off.'

Alesandros nodded. He was pleased he did not have such a repetitive job. Lambros was their most accomplished type setter, having worked there since he was a boy. He earned a regular salary each week, but he would never become a rich man.

'That's what I mean there's always someone looking over your shoulder. Travelling around I can work the hours to suit me. Tomorrow I'll only be going in to the office in Aghios Nikolaos to pay in the tax I collected today, after that I can do as I please.'

Stassa frowned. That could mean that Alesandros would spend most of the day sitting beside the fire in the living room. She had no objection to the man, he was always polite and if she asked him for any help he gave it willingly, but she preferred to keep to her regular routine. Each morning she would tidy their bed and sweep the living room floor before she took her basket and visited the local shops for meat and vegetables. She had planned to boil up the bones from the chicken, make some herb dumplings and add some more vegetables to make a nourishing soup. Once that was done she wanted to make a start on crystallizing the oranges she had bought two days ago. The remains of the loaf could be toasted over the fire as a filling addition just before she served their meal.

If Alesandros planned to be there at lunch time she would have to make some more bread and take it to the baker to place in his oven. She was bound to meet a neighbour who would wish to stop and gossip in the warm bakery, and it was doubtful that she would be able to make a start on crystallizing the oranges before the afternoon. That was when she had intended to sit beside the fire and turn the cuffs of a shirt that Lambros wore to work. After a while no amount of scrubbing on her part was able to remove the printing ink that invariably ended up on the cuffs by the end of each week.

'Will you be here for lunch?' she asked and was relieved when Alesandros shook his head.

'I thought I would get something at the taverna. Gives me a chance to have a chat with my colleagues.'

Alesandros was relieved that the weather had not worsened over night. Over the mountains in the distance he could see the dark snow clouds, but down by the coast the sky was grey. The fishing boats had left as usual, making dots of bright colour on a grey sea and he was thankful that he had never contemplated becoming a fisherman.

He walked into the tax office, removed his still damp cloak, and sat at a desk where the clerk had a ledger open before him and was assiduously copying figures onto a sheet of paper.

'Good morning, Alesandros. What can I do for you?'

'Morning, Christos. Yesterday I managed to visit some of the farmers in Lassithi who still owe their taxes.'

Christos frowned. 'It was no day for travelling up there.'

'I found that out to my cost. It was snowing as I returned, but the journey was worth it. I managed to extricate a little from each of them as they had received their money for the autumn apple crop.'

Christos pushed the ledger to one side and searched for another from beneath his desk. 'You're very conscientious, Alesandros.

You've had considerable success with some of our most difficult farmers.'

Alesandros shrugged aside the compliment. He had been allocated some farmers who were well into arrears with their taxes and paying interest to the government and due to the system of payments he had worked out it made him look extremely successful as a collector.

'Best to get their money before they've spent it.' He pulled a sheet of paper from his pocket. 'Here is where I visited and this is the amount each one paid me.'

Christos scanned the list of farmers and raised his eyebrows. 'Their apple crop must have been good this year.'

'So the assessors said.' Alesandros made no mention of the various excuses he had been given. The money he was handing over was from the tax the farmers had paid him earlier in the year. 'They were pleased to be able to pay their outstanding debt. I'll probably have to visit a couple of them again after you've entered this and checked everything is paid to date.' He pulled a bundle of notes from his pocket and placed them on the desk before Christos, settling back whilst the man counted off the appropriate amount to coincide with Alesandros's reckoning.

Satisfied that the money agreed with the total Alesandros claimed, Christos opened the ledger and began to search for the page where the details of the tax for each farmer was recorded. He always found it gratifying to be able to rule a line under a name and write "paid" and the date. Half an hour later he looked up at Alesandros and smiled.

'As you said, only two still owing us. They have three more months before we have to start penalising them and charging interest.'

'I hope that won't be necessary. I'll make sure I visit them again once the weather has eased. Next week I'll make some calls along the coast. I should be able to get to Mardati and Pirgos without a problem. Now, would you care to join me at the taverna for some lunch and a glass of wine?'

Christos shook his head. 'Thanks, but my wife has put some lunch up for me.'

Alesandros sighed. It was time he was married. He had visited a prostitute once, but after looking at her drab room and the soiled bed the desire had left him. Who had visited her before he had arrived? He could end up with some horrible disease. He determined that until he found a respectable woman to marry he would continue to relieve his needs himself.

'That's what I need; a wife to look after me properly. You wouldn't know of anyone suitable I suppose?'

'Xene could be looking. She's been a widow a good while now.'

'How old is she?'

Christos shrugged. 'I'm not sure. My wife might know. I'll ask her tonight and let you know the next time you come in.'

Alesandros nodded. 'Nothing definite, you understand. This is just an enquiry. I could find someone eminently suitable next week, so I wouldn't want the widow to rely on me approaching her.'

Christos smirked. 'She could have her sights set elsewhere and wouldn't appreciate an approach from you. I'll speak to my wife and see what she can tell me about Xene.'

Alesandros lifted his cloak from the back of the chair. It still felt damp. If he could find a place close to the fire at the taverna he might manage to dry it out a little more. 'I'll see you in a few weeks, Christos.'

The clerk nodded and pulled the ledger he had been working from earlier back in front of him. Alesandros was certainly a reliable employee. Many men would not have ventured up into the hills to collect taxes that were due and ensure they were paid into the office on time.

Sofia rubbed the frost from the inside of her bedroom window and peered out. There had been a sparse covering of snow the previous day when she awoke, but by mid-day it had melted. Now everywhere was white, without a speck of grass showing and the tree branches bowed down by the weight. It had snowed quite heavily during the night and by the look of the dark sky there would be more to come during the day.

She wrapped a blanket around herself and walked barefoot down the stairs, careful not to trip on the trailing ends. She hoped her mother was already up and had placed more logs on the fire to warm the room and also to heat some water for her to wash her hands and face. She would have to wear her cloak and boots when she visited the outhouse and there was certainly no heating in there. She was more fortunate than the other villagers; at least she had some privacy and was not open to the elements whilst she completed her toilet needs.

Both her parents were up. Her father was placing logs by the side of the fireplace and her mother hanging a pot of water over the flames.

'Boots and cloak, Sofia,' her mother said sternly and Sofia nodded. If she tried to make a quick run across the yard as she did when it was raining she would probably slip over. She pulled open the back door of the house and could see the footprints where both parents had visited the outhouse earlier and then another line of footprints leading to and from the wood store.

Shivering, she clutched her cloak tightly to her, and made her way cautiously across the yard. She hoped her father would light a fire in her bedroom and she would not have to depend upon the oil stove to keep her warm whilst she dressed. She would be happy to carry some logs up during the day to keep it burning. It would also mean that her mother could have the stove close to her weaving loom when she sat and worked during the afternoon.

Her immediate needs catered for she removed her cloak and boots and returned to the living room, wrapping her blanket around her shoulders again and standing before the fire. Thankfully she had not needed to rise during the night and use the bucket so she would not need to venture outside to the outhouse again until later in the day. No doubt she would be expected to accompany her mother to the well for some water and she shivered at the prospect.

The rope would be cold and stiff and it would take twice as long as usual to haul the bucket up and tip the contents into their containers. They would have to walk back slowly carrying the pails. If they slipped and dropped them the water would spill and they would need to return for more.

Feeling warmer, Sofia made her way up to her bedroom and began to dress hurriedly. Replacing the blanket on her bed, she did not remove the woollen undergarment and blouse she had worn during the night, but added another blouse and her bolero. Two underskirts beneath her winter skirt would keep her legs warm and whilst she was indoors she could wear her house shoes, made from wool and with leather soles.

As she sat on the side of her bed to don her house shoes she heard someone knocking on their front door and hoped it was not Tryphaine arriving to ask her to go out and throw snow balls so early in the day. She stood by her bedroom door and heard a boy's tremulous voice. With a sigh of relief she picked up her comb and ran it through her hair, removing most of the tangles that had come from nowhere during the night, and tied her head scarf firmly in place. She could hear her father speaking sternly and then the front door closed and there was silence.

Sofia straightened her bed covers before making her way back downstairs to the living room. Her mother was heating milk for her over the fire, but there was no sign of her father.

'Where's Pappa?' she asked.

Maria straightened up, lifting the pan of warm milk and set it on the table. 'That boy Stratos has got himself into trouble again.'

Sofia raised her eyebrows. Stratos always seemed to be up to mischief of some sort. 'What's he done?'

'Decided to throw snowballs at Pelagia's window. He said he wanted her to think it was snowing hard. Trouble was he didn't realise he had also picked up a stone. It broke her window. Your Pappa's gone to see about repairing it.'

Sofia nodded. It was obviously an accident, although Stratos had been foolish as usual. Pelagia was unlikely to think it was snowing hard when lumps of snow landed on her window.

'Apparently he had done the same at some of the other cottages before he was chased away. Lucky he didn't break more windows. Drink your milk whilst it's still warm, then we'll have to go for the water.'

Obediently Sofia crumbled some stale bread into the liquid and began to spoon the mixture into her mouth.

As Sofia had thought, the rope at the well was stiff and it took the combined strength of her and her mother to wind the bucket down into the water and back up again when it was full. The exertion had made her thoroughly over-heated and Sofia wished she had not placed so many clothes on that morning when she dressed.

Sofia and her mother began to walk back to the house carrying two full buckets each. If they used the water sparingly it would last them the whole day and leave a little to be heated for her father to shave the following morning. The enforced slowness of their pace quickly removed the excessive heat Sofia had found uncomfortable earlier and she shivered, slopping water from her bucket as she did so.

'Careful,' her mother warned her. 'We don't want to make another trip.'

'I need to rest a minute. You go on.' Sofia placed her buckets on the ground and pushed her hands beneath her armpits to restore their warmth. At first the cold handles of the metal buckets had felt like fire on her hands, but now her hands felt numb.

'Don't tarry too long,' her mother warned her, 'Or you'll feel colder when you start to walk again.' Maria spoke without slowing her stride.

'We should have brought some rags to wrap around the handles,' remarked Sofia.

Maria did not answer her daughter. She should have thought about some rags for around the handles herself. It would have prevented the metal from cutting into their hands. Usually the journey to and from the well was speedy enough for neither of them to notice the weight, but today their errand had already taken twice as long. She turned her head to see if her daughter had picked up the buckets again and was following her and as she did so her feet went from under her.

Maria fell hard, the snow doing little to cushion her fall, and the buckets spilling their contents around her, soaking her cloak and skirt.

'Mamma, are you hurt?' Sofia called anxiously.

Maria took a deep breath and shook her head. She should not have turned to look for Sofia. Now they would have to make another trip to the well. Two buckets of water would not be sufficient for the day. She pushed the empty buckets to one side and stood up. As she put her weight on her left foot she winced with pain. She had obviously twisted her ankle as she fell.

Picking up her buckets she smiled wryly at Sofia. 'You take your buckets up to the house and then come back to help me. Take care how you go. We don't want any more water spilt.'

'But you're soaking wet, Mamma. You ought to come back and put on some dry clothes.'

'I can do that later. Off you go.'

Obediently Sofia continued towards their house and Maria tried a cautious step. Her ankle was painful, but no doubt walking on it would help and the pain would soon wear off. Slowly she limped towards the well, gasping each time she placed any weight on her left foot. She now felt cross with herself. She had lost two buckets of water, her clothes were wet through to her skin and she had hurt her ankle.

By the time Sofia returned, bringing some old rags with her to wrap around the handles of the buckets, Maria had managed to fill one of her pails. She leaned against the wall of the well, taking the weight off her damaged ankle, perspiration beading her forehead.

Sofia looked at her mother in concern. 'What's wrong?'

'I hurt my ankle when I slipped over. You'll have to carry both the buckets.'

'You start to walk back and I'll fill the other one and catch you up. I put another log on the fire whilst I was there. It had died down and you'll need to have the room warm to dry your clothes.'

'Your father's not back yet, then?'

Sofia shook her head. 'I would have asked him to come back with me had he been at home.'

'Whatever for?'

'He could have carried the buckets and we would have been home more quickly.'

'That's not man's work,' replied Maria scornfully.

'I know, but if I had told him you'd had a fall he would have come to help.'

'Good job he wasn't there, then. He would have been the laughing stock of the village. A man carrying the buckets of water whilst his wife and daughter walked alongside him! I'll start to walk back and you follow when you've filled the other bucket. Take care. I don't want to have any more wet clothes to dry.'

Maria took a couple of steps forward and stopped, breathing heavily. 'I really have hurt my ankle, Sofia. Take the buckets home and then come back here bringing a stick for me to lean on.'

'You could lean on me and I could come back for the buckets later.'

'Do as you're told, girl. I'll come to no harm waiting here for you.'

Sofia wrapped the rags around the handles of the buckets and lifted them off the ground. Her shoulders felt sore after struggling with the stiff rope of the well on her own to bring the bucket up to the surface.

'I'll be as quick as I can, Mamma.'

'Just don't spill the water,' warned Maria.

Sofia hurried back to the house as quickly as possible with the heavy buckets. She placed them in the scullery and went outside to the wood pile. It took her some minutes of rummaging amongst the uncut logs to find a branch sturdy enough to take her mother's weight. As she tried to haul it to the door she realised just how heavy it was. Biting her lip in exasperation she picked up her father's axe and began to chop the wood in half. Finally satisfied that her mother would be able to manage the improvised crutch she picked up some more rags from the scullery to wrap around the rough bark.

She had no idea how long it had taken her to complete the errand, but when she reached the well her mother was shivering, her lips blue with the cold.

'Come on, Mamma. I need to get you home as soon as possible so you can get warm again. If you stay out here much longer you'll end up with pneumonia.'

'I don't think I can walk,' protested Maria.

'Yes, you can,' insisted Sofia. 'I've wrapped some cloth around the stick and if you lean on me as well you'll be able to manage.'

They made slow progress along the village street and Sofia looked in vain at the cottages as they passed by to see if she could attract some attention and additional help. Many villagers had closed their shutters again once they had seen the snow. By the time they reached the door to their house Sofia felt her back would break with the weight her mother was putting on her with every step and was thankful they lived in the centre of the village and not at the far end.

Once inside Maria was able to use the backs of the chairs to help her get to the fire. Sofia tossed her own cloak to one side.

'Give me your cloak, Mamma, and then start to undress. I'll get some towels to dry you and then you can wrap a blanket around yourself until you are properly warm.'

Maria looked doubtfully at Sofia. It was many years since her daughter had seen her without her body fully clothed. 'I'm sure that isn't necessary. I'll just take off my top blouse and skirt.'

'Everything, Mamma. Until your fingers are warm again you won't be able to feel which clothes are dry and which are wet. I also need to get your boot off and you can't sit on a chair or the bed if your skirt is wet.'

Reluctantly Maria began to undo her bolero, her numb fingers finding the fastenings difficult to deal with. Sofia placed three towels on a chair and pushed her mother's hand out of the way.

'Let me do that. You're getting the laces in a tangle.'

Maria stood obediently as Sofia removed her bolero and three blouses before wrapping a towel around her shoulders. Once having undone the belt at the waist of Maria's skirt the top skirt and two under skirts were easy to remove.

'And your drawers, Mamma.'

Maria felt herself flushing. 'I don't need to take those off.'

'Yes, you do. They're wet. Pull them down and hold the towel around you. Once I've dried your back you can sit on the bed and I'll take off your boots and drawers.'

Sofia rubbed her mother's back with the rough towels, finally placing one on the bed and allowing her to sit down.

'Now lift your feet up and let me get those boots off. I hope your ankle hasn't swollen too much. I'd hate to have to cut them.'

Maria let out a cry of pain as Sofia pulled her boot from her injured foot. Ignoring her mother's distress, Sofia removed the other boot and then her mother's drawers. She handed her mother a dry towel.

'There you are. You can continue to dry yourself whilst I have a look at your ankle.'

Already Maria's ankle was swollen and there was a purple bruise running from above her ankle and over most of her foot.

'Are you properly dry?' asked Sofia and Maria nodded.

'Then stand up for a moment whilst I put a blanket round you.'

'I can't sit here with nothing but a blanket around me,' protested Maria.

'Of course you can. I'm going to warm up the remains of yesterday's soup for you to drink, then I'll bring you a dry blouse and skirt. Once I've done that I'm going to ask Theophalia to come and have a look at your ankle.'

'You're making such a fuss,' muttered Maria. 'I just had a fall and twisted my ankle.'

Sofia placed her hands on her hips. 'All right, then, Mamma. Once you are dressed again I will lend you my cloak and you can walk up to Theophalia and show her your ankle. Is that what you want?'

Maria shook her head. 'No, I can't, but I still think you're making a lot of fuss over an ankle.'

'What's happened here?' asked Theo as he took in the scene at a glance, Stratos cowering behind him.

'Mamma slipped over when we were collecting the water. She's hurt her ankle. Theophalia says it's a sprain and she should be able to walk on it without any pain in a few days. She's placed a cold bandage on it and I have to renew it when it gets warm.'

Theo walked over to his wife where she was lying on their bed, a blanket still wrapped around her. 'You certainly mustn't go out again whilst the snow is on the ground. You're fortunate it is only a sprain and not a break.'

'Sofia was very good, Theo. She carried all the water home and then came back to help me. When she realised how bad my ankle was she insisted on going up to Theophalia's cottage and asking her to come and look at it. She insisted I took off my wet clothes and she rubbed me down so briskly that I thought she would take the skin off my back.'

'Wet clothes?' Theo looked at the sodden cloak that hung on a wooden chair before the fire. 'Why were you so wet?'

'I spilt the water all over me and the snow melted, of course and made me even wetter.'

'Are you warm now?'

'Oh, yes, but I was very cold earlier.'

Theo bent and placed another log on the fire. 'Stratos, come here boy, by the fire and get some warmth into your body.'

The small, boy, his teeth chattering with the cold and his thin legs sticking out from his short trousers came forward gladly. With his unruly mop of dark curls, grey eyes, pointed chin and large prominent ears, he was the butt of the village boys' jokes.

Maria looked at him and clicked her tongue. 'The poor boy looks frozen half to death. What have you done to him, Theo?'

'As a punishment for breaking Pelagia's window I made him help me hold the window in place whilst I replaced the glass.'

'You should have sent him home to get his cloak and boots first,' she remonstrated with her husband.

Theo's mouth set in a grim line. 'He has no cloak or boots. Sofia, where are your old boots that you have grown out of?'

'In the storage room, Pappa.'

'And your cloak?'

'Mamma put that in her cupboard. She plans to unpick it and use the wool.'

'Go and get your boots, Sofia. They are no use to you any longer and Stratos needs something more than wooden clogs on his feet.'

Sofia looked at the little boy who was still shivering despite the warmth of the fire. She guessed her father's intention and knew she also had a bolero that no longer fitted. 'I'll get them,' she said.

Theo opened the cupboard where his wife kept the wools and cotton she used for her weaving.

'It's rolled up at the back,' Maria advised him. She did not want him rummaging through everything and getting her skeins tangled.

Theo pulled it out and held it up against Stratos. 'It's a bit long for you, but a bit of string will hold it up so you don't trip over it.'

Stratos nodded. He did not know what to say. When Theo

had ordered him to accompany him back to his house he thought the man was going to beat him for breaking the window, now he seemed to be giving him a warm cloak and pair of boots. He had never possessed either before.

Sofia handed her father the boots and he indicated Stratos should sit down and try them on. They were too big for the boy, but Theo went into the scullery and returned with some rags that he stuffed into the toes and then tied the boots firmly around Stratos's ankles.

'That will save them from slipping off your feet. As your feet grow you can take the rags out. Provided you look after them they should last you for a few years.'

Stratos nodded again. 'Thank you, sir,' he managed to stutter.

Sofia held out the bolero. 'He can have this as well. It's too tight for me.'

Theo placed it over the boy's grubby shirt, realising he had only one other beneath it. It was a wonder the boy had managed to live through twelve winters if he was always so poorly dressed.

'Do you have any other shirts at home?' he asked.

'One, it's in the wash.'

'Now, Stratos, you have been a very naughty boy. Tomorrow you are to go to Pelagia and offer to collect some water from the well for her and also go to the shops for anything she needs.'

Stratos hung his head. 'Yes, sir. Thank you, sir.'

'And,' continued Theo, 'When you have completed those tasks you are to come here and do some errands for me. If you are kept busy you won't have time to get into trouble.' He tied the string tightly around Stratos's waist and bunched up the cloak so the boy would not trip. 'Off you go now and see if you can be useful to your grandmother.'

As Stratos closed the door behind him Sofia looked at her father in amazement. 'Why did you give Stratos my old boots and cloak?' she asked.

'Because he did not have any,' replied Theo simply. 'You are a very lucky girl. You have warm clothes when you go out; he does not.'

'You shouldn't have made him stand outside in the cold,' remonstrated Maria.

'I didn't. He stood inside. I had no need of his help, but I wanted to make sure he was still there when I finished the job. The boy needs care. His grandmother does her best to look after him, but there's no spare money in the house for new clothes.'

'I thought his father was working in Neapoli and bringing money back to the village.'

'He is, but it's difficult for him. All the time he could walk there and back each day it was no problem, but when he broke his leg he was unable to work for some weeks and then he found trying to walk to Neapoli and back each day was impossible. I understand he has a room in a lodging house, but after paying for that and his food there's little left over to bring here.'

'Do they have enough to eat?' asked Sofia. She did not know what it was like to be hungry.

'Probably not,' answered her father. 'In the summer when the fruit and vegetables are plentiful they probably eat quite well, but at this time of the year there's little growing wild they could make use of.'

'What are you going to ask Stratos to do tomorrow when he comes?' asked Maria.

'For a start he can bring some logs in for the fire. Then he can shovel the snow away from the back door and make a path to the outhouse. Whilst he does that I can chop some more logs and then he can stack them.'

'I used your axe today, Pappa. I hope I haven't blunted the blade.'

'Why did you use it? There are plenty of logs chopped.'

'I had to shorten the branch I took up to the well for Mamma to lean on. It was the only suitable one I could find and even then it was too long and heavy.'

'Provided you didn't chop your fingers off there's no harm done. I can soon sharpen it again.'

Sofia was relieved that her father had not scolded her for using the axe. He took a great pride in keeping the blade razor sharp and she and her mother were forbidden to touch it for fear of cutting themselves. They were also forbidden to touch his shotgun that he kept in the corner, although he used it rarely to shoot a rabbit.

'I'll get some bread and cheese for our lunch. The bread is a bit hard so it will have to be toasted over the fire. There's a little soup left from yesterday that you can have, Pappa and then I'm going to make a chicken pudding for our meal this evening,' Sofia announced. 'Mamma had planned a chicken pie, but that would mean taking it up to the baker for him to put in his oven. By the time I had carried it back it would be cold.'

'Just do what you can, Sofia. I'll not complain about a bit of stale bread.'

Theo drew back the rug and opened the front door as someone knocked again. Tryphaine stood there, well wrapped up and with a broad smile on her face.

'Is Sofia able to come out and play snow balls?' she asked peering into the room.

'Sofia, Tryphaine has called for you to go out and play.'

Sofia entered the living room from the scullery. 'I'm sorry, Phaini. I can't come out. Mamma has hurt her ankle and I'm needed here.'

Tryphaine's face fell. 'Oh, I was looking forward to throwing snowballs. It's no fun on your own.'

Sofia shook her head. 'Not today. If Mamma's ankle is better tomorrow I'll come out and play then.'

Tryphaine looked towards the bed where Maria was still huddled beneath the blanket. 'Oh, is there anything I could do?'

'No thanks. Mamma is fine, but it hurts her to stand on her ankle so I have to get a meal ready for tonight.' Secretly Sofia was quite pleased to have a good excuse for not going outside again.

Tryphaine shrugged. 'Oh, well. I'll come by tomorrow then. I hope your ankle improves quickly Mrs Angelakis.'

Theo closed the door and pulled the rug back over the door. 'You could go out if you wanted, Sofia.'

'I've had enough of the snow for one day, Pappa. I'd rather stay here in the warm. When I've prepared the pudding I can sit by the fire and sew.'

Maria's ankle had healed within a week, but she had developed a harsh cough that caused her to press her hand to her chest. Theophalia visited and ordered Maria to stay in bed, but the cough persisted and both Sofia and her father were worried. Finally Theodopolous walked to Neapoli and asked the doctor to visit his wife. Doctor Andrianakis said he was not due to visit Kastelli for a further two weeks, but Theodopolous persisted and offered the doctor in excess of his usual fee for a visit to a patient's house.

Doctor Andrianakis arrived the following day and tethered his donkey to the window railings. Sofia had been watching for him and hurried to open the door.

'Do come in, Doctor. Pappa is waiting for you.'

The doctor nodded. Theodopolous had already paid him to make the house call so he was not concerned whether the man was there or not. He placed his medical bag on the table and removed his cloak. Maria sat propped up in bed; her breathing was shallow and laboured.

Doctor Andrianakis took Maria's pulse and listened through his stethoscope to her chest. 'She has bronchitis,' he announced, removing his cigarette from the side of his mouth. 'She should stay in bed and be kept warm. A light, but nourishing diet of meat broth, a couple of glasses of red wine during the day and a small glass of brandy at night will help her to sleep. She should spit out any mucus that she coughs up and until her coughing has eased it is advisable for her to sleep sitting up with a piece of warm cloth on her chest.'

Theodopolous gave a sigh of relief. He knew his wife was suffering from more than a cold and he had dreaded the doctor would diagnose pneumonia. 'How long will it be before she recovers?' he asked.

Doctor Andrianakis shrugged. 'I cannot say. It will have to run its course. I'll call in again when I make my next visit to Kastelli and hope there will have been an improvement.'

'A glass of wine, Doctor, before you ride back to Neapoli? You would be welcome to share our mid-day meal with us.'

The doctor shook his head. 'I'll not refuse a glass of wine, but then I should leave. I need to call at Fourni as I am in the area.'

April 1911

Whilst her mother was ill Sofia had taken over the running of the house, doing the shopping and preparing the meals, ensuring her father had a clean shirt every other week, along with the blouses and petticoats she washed for herself and her mother. She had even washed the sheets from her parents' bed when the weather improved and she was able to put them out in the yard to dry.

Maria still coughed when she exerted herself and Sofia insisted that her mother should only do the cooking and her weaving. Despite the arrangement Sofia found that most days she was preparing their evening meal due to her mother having had a coughing fit and needing to take to her bed for an hour. For the first time Sofia realised how difficult it was to keep the house clean, along with the other essential household chores. Each day the yard had to be swept, the rugs picked up from all the rooms and the floors swept. Every other day the living room and scullery floors had to be scrubbed along with the front step and once a month the windows needed to be cleaned. She had always taken the bread to the baker and done the shopping before her mother had fallen over. Now she had to complete those essential jobs before she could think about any cooking, cleaning or washing.

Theo had taken Stratos under his wing and arranged that the boy should collect water from the well each morning to save Sofia the task. For this he gave the boy five lepta a week, on the strict understanding that he did not get into any mischief. Each week he visited the cottage where the boy lived with his grandmother and checked with her on his behaviour, giving her two drachmas and saying it was for the work her grandson did for him.

Despite Stratos collecting the water, thus saving Sofia a daily chore, her father realised that the work the girl undertook each day was wearing her out. She had lost weight and looked continually tired, although she never complained. It would soon be Easter and the rugs would need to be taken down from the walls and the house cleaned from top to bottom. It was too much to expect of her, even if Maria was able to make the soup and biscuits that were an essential part of the celebration.

Theo considered the villagers carefully. Whom could he approach and ask to come to the house a couple of times each week to do the heavy work? Stratos's grandmother was too old, as were a number of the other women, the others were either too young or had children that needed their attention. Finally he decided he would ask Kassianae. She had two children, but if her mother was willing to look after the girls for a couple of hours twice a week she was the solution to his problem.

The olive crop had been harvested and Alesandros was in possession of the list of the number of barrels of oil each farmer had produced and the amount they had been paid. Now the weather had improved he would certainly make the journey up to the Lassithi plain and collect the money owed in taxes. His earlier visits to the farmers who lived along the coast, had been, on the whole, successful. There was only one who had needed to settle his debt with an orange tree; and that in Alesandros's eyes was a successful settlement.

On visiting the tax office he made for Christos's desk, hoping the man would have some news regarding his widowed neighbour. If she sounded suitable he would ask Christos to arrange a meeting between them, but he needed to know if she owned her house. He was not prepared to pay rent to a grasping landlord and never know from one day to the next if he would be asked to leave to make way for the landlord's family.

Alesandros handed over the money and the list of farmers who had paid him and sat patiently whilst Christos checked the amount in the ledger and wrote "paid" beneath each man's name.

'They've not had a bad year,' Christos observed. 'The cold weather came after the apple crop had been harvested and before the olives were ready.'

Alesandros nodded. 'They were fortunate. I'm planning to visit the Lassithi area next week. I hope that will be as successful.' He replaced his papers into his bag and stood up to leave, turning back at the last moment. 'That other little matter we spoke about, the widow along your road. Did you manage to find out anything about her from your wife?'

'Not a lot. She appears to be clean and respectable. Her mother lives there with her.'

'Is it her mother's house?' Alesandros was prepared to accept that arrangement as when the mother died her daughter would automatically inherit the property.

'Her mother owns that one and three others. If you want to hang around for a while she could be in shortly. She told my Anna she was planning to bring her mother in today so she could settle up the tax she owed.'

Alesandros nodded. 'Good idea. If I like the look of her I'll ask you for an introduction. I'll buy a newspaper and take a seat over there.'

Within minutes Alesandros had returned, a newspaper beneath his arm, and he took a seat at the far side of the room. It would give him a clear view of the door and he would see exactly who was entering. After reading a few lines Alesandros would look up and around the room to ensure he had not missed the arrival of the widow and her mother.

He acknowledged with a raised hand the arrival of two other tax collectors that he knew and hoped they would not come over to talk to him when they had completed their business. Once the widow and her mother had arrived he planned to walk over to the desk where they were sitting and pretend he had mislaid a paper. That way he would be able to get a good look at her.

Finally his vigil was over. A stooped woman entered, the door opened for her by a younger woman whom he assumed to be her daughter. Alesandros looked at the swarthy woman and gave an involuntary shudder. Her hair grew low down on her forehead and also along her top lip. They walked to the nearest desk and sat down before the clerk.

'I've come with my mother so she can pay her tax.' Her loud, shrill voice cut across the room surprising Alesandros. 'I've had the figures checked by the priest and he says it's all in order. All she has to do is hand over the money and make her mark.'

The clerk recoiled back from the volume of her voice and Alesandros wondered if her mother was deaf and that was why she was talking so loudly. He folded his newspaper and walked casually towards the desk. He would at least take a closer look at the woman. As he passed Christos he raised his eyebrows and Christos indicated with his thumb that they were indeed his neighbour and her mother.

'Excuse me,' Alesandros halted beside them. 'I believe I may have left a paper here when I was dealing with my accounts.'

The woman looked at him and frowned at the interruption. She was even less attractive when she did so, her thick eyebrows meeting in a straight black line. 'There was nothing on the desk when we arrived,' she announced loudly. 'If you're trying to push in we were here before you.'

'Not at all. I am merely looking for my misplaced paper. Maybe I went to a different desk.'

'Then go and look elsewhere.' She turned back to face the clerk.

'I didn't see any paper on the desk when we arrived,' the older woman confirmed, her voice as strident as her daughter's, although an octave lower.

Their voices sent a shudder through Alesandros. He could not live with people whose voices set his teeth on edge and spoke so loudly all the time, even if he had been prepared to accept her unfortunate looks. He walked over to Christos's desk.

'Is that the widow and her mother?' he asked quietly and Christos nodded.

'Are they both deaf?'

Christos shook his head. 'I don't think so. They don't seem to have any trouble hearing Anna or myself if we speak to them.'

'Why do they talk so loudly, then?'

Christos shrugged. 'Just their way, I imagine. Do you want me to introduce you?'

'No, I was thinking of someone a little younger and I wouldn't want to live with two women in the same house.'

'Up to you. If Anna or I can think of anyone else I'll let you know the next time you come in.'

'Thanks. In the meantime I'll keep my eyes open as I go around. One of the farmers might have a suitable unmarried daughter.'

Alesandros left the office, the shrill voice of Xene still ringing in his ears. Thank goodness he had been able to see and hear her before he had asked Christos to introduce them.

Alesandros sat outside a taverna, taking advantage of the spring sunshine. He had ordered a glass of wine to accompany the calamari dish that was to be his lunch. He sipped the wine slowly as he decided how to spend the remainder of his day. He had no wish to return to his lodgings, having spent more than enough time there during the cold winter months in the company of Stassa whilst Lambros was at work. There was little conversation between them and Stassa had given him the impression that he was in her way whilst she did her cleaning and he had retreated to his inhospitable bedroom on a number of occasions.

He opened the newspaper again. Having bought the paper he might as well read it. He could then leave it behind when he left the taverna and no doubt someone would pick it up gratefully. To his dismay there was nothing in the paper that he had not already read in the copy that Lambros brought home each week. He folded it neatly and pushed it to one side as his calamari arrived. He would take his time over the meal and then walk along the path by the sea. The heat from the sun would soon diminish and he would be happy to return to his lodgings.

Provided the following day was as pleasant he would be able to enjoy his ride to Lassithi. Christos would no doubt argue over the amount of tax that was due for his olive crop, Makkis still owed for the apples and he would have to be firm with the man and insist he paid his debt in full or sign over some more apple trees to him. Elias should be able to pay his dues provided he had been prudent and set aside some money; it was Theo who would no doubt be a problem. With a sigh, Alesandros paid his bill and walked away from the table, ignoring the shout from the proprietor that he had left his newspaper behind.

As Alesandros had surmised the day dawned with a slight mist over the sea which would burn off quickly once the sun had fully risen. He took his cloak with him as a precaution; however good the weather down by the coast, once up into the hills there could be a dramatic change in the temperature.

On reaching Driros he knocked on the door of Christos's cottage and received no reply. The man was no doubt out in his field at the back, preparing the ground for the vegetables that would reach fruition in the summer months and he would take to the market to sell. Alesandros tied the donkey to the gate post and made his way on foot around to the rear of the house.

Christos was bent over planting beans at regular intervals, the stakes for their growth already in place.

'Good morning, Christos,' Alesandros hailed him from a distance.

Christos straightened up and scowled. He had been expecting the tax collector to visit him now the weather had improved, but he had hoped that by working out at the back he could legitimately claim that he had not heard him knock.

'I'm busy,' he announced.

'I can see that.' Alesandros halted a few paces away, not wishing to be accused of damaging anything Christos had already planted and also being assaulted by the garlic that would be on the man's breath. 'Better weather to be out and about now.'

'Can't complain.'

'I trust your olive harvest was good this year.'

Christos shrugged. 'Not as plentiful as I'd hoped.'

'Really?' Alesandros raised his eyebrows. 'I thought the figures given to me were higher than last year's.'

'By the time I've bought the new seed and plants for this year there's not much left.'

'Enough to pay me, I hope. I wouldn't want to have had a wasted journey.'

'Some, maybe.'

'Shall we go inside and settle up?' suggested Alesandros.

Christos shook his head. 'I told you. I'm busy. No doubt you're going round to the other farmers. Call on me on your way back when I've finished planting the beans.'

'It won't take more than a few minutes of your time.'

'If I stop now I'll need to wash and wait around whilst you count the money and write on one of your bits of paper. I need to finish planting my beans by the end of today. The weather won't hold at this time of year. It could be raining tomorrow.'

'Unfortunately collecting tax does not stop when it rains, unlike planting beans.'

'Then come back when it's raining.' Christos bent down and continued making a hole and inserting a bean.

Alesandros sighed in exasperation. He could not force the man to stop planting. 'I'll be back later, then; and I'll expect the amount you owe in full.'

'I'll see what I've got,' muttered Christos.

Alesandros stood and watched Christos for a few moments, then turned on his heel and walked back to the cottage. He was fairly certain that Christos would have the money waiting for him when he returned and he was not prepared to accept any excuses.

Makkis, at Kourounis, was equally unwelcoming.

'I paid you for the apples the last time you were here,' he insisted.

Alesandros shook his head. 'When I came before you told me you had lost your trees due to a fire. According to the assessor there was no fire and you were paid for two hundred kilos of apples. That means you still owe me my share of the sale along with the tax. You now owe the tax on your olive harvest and interest to me for a late payment. It would be to your advantage to settle up in full now, rather than get deeper into debt.'

'I'm sure I paid you.' Makkis wrinkled his forehead as if to remember.

Alesandros spread his hands. 'If I have made a mistake I apologise. To settle the matter show me the receipt I gave you.'

'Receipt?'

'The piece of paper where I wrote down that you had paid the tax on your apple crop and paid me at the same time.'

'I don't keep odd scraps of paper.'

'Well you should. They can be important. I have no copy of that receipt to say you have paid, so unless you can produce yours I have to tell the office that the amount is still outstanding.'

Makkis opened the door wide enough for Alesandros to enter. 'I'll see what I've got.' He knew he had the money set aside to pay, but he preferred to see it sitting in the box beneath his bed. A piece of paper in its place meant nothing to him.

Alesandros followed him into the living room and sat down at the table, waiting whilst Makkis scrabbled about in the cupboard beneath his bed. Finally he placed a box on the table and glowered at Alesandros.

'No doubt you want to check it for yourself. The priest counted it out for me so if it isn't correct he's the one you need to speak to.'

Alesandros consulted his figures and began to count out the money slowly. 'That's the tax for the apples.' He pushed the notes to one side and wrote out a receipt which he handed to Makkis. 'Put that safely in your box. It's worth as much to you as money. If I did make a mistake and call a second time you could show me that and I would have to leave without you paying me as much as a lepta.' He counted off some more notes. 'This is my share from the apples.' He wrote on another piece of paper and handed it over before placing the money into his pocket.

'Now, the olives. I hope there will be enough left to pay the tax in full.' Painstakingly Alesandros counted out the money and was gratified to find the amount was correct. He looked at Makkis and smiled. 'You seem to have got yourself well organised this year. Here's the receipt for the olives, and remember, keep these receipts safe. You wouldn't like it if I came again in a month's time and asked you for this amount again.'

'You'd not get it,' growled Makkis, as Alesandros placed the tax money into his shoulder bag.

'Provided you still had those receipts you'd be within your rights to refuse me. I have copies of them, so I don't think you need to worry. Any chance of a glass of wine before I continue on my journey?'

Makkis shook his head. 'Can't afford wine when you rob me of my income to pay tax. Glass of water?'

Alesandros nodded. He was genuinely thirsty, but would have much preferred a glass of wine. If he reached Perambela close to Elias's meal time he might well be offered a glass, along with some bread and cheese. If not, Theo was bound to tell his daughter to fetch wine and biscuits for him. The man knew his manners.

He did not see Makkis take the bottle of wine from the cupboard, take a long swig and make a rude sign in his direction as he mounted his donkey.

Marina opened the door of the cottage at Perambela to him and a look of consternation came over her face. 'Elias,' she called, 'Mr Danniakis, the tax collector is here.'

She stood to one side, allowing Alesandros to enter the living room. Elias sat before the small fire, his leg resting on a pile of cushions.

'What's wrong?' asked Alesandros. 'Have you had an accident?'

Elias shook his head. 'Gout,' he announced morosely.

'What caused that?'

'No idea. Comes on without any warning. I've had it for near enough a week now. Too painful to put my foot to the ground.'

'Have you spoken to the doctor?'

Elias nodded. 'Says it happens when my blood is too rich or not rich enough. How am I supposed to know if my blood is rich? If it is rich where has it got the money from? I'm a poor man.'

'I don't think he means rich in terms of money,' frowned Alesandros. 'I think he means how healthy your blood is. What has he given you as a remedy?'

'There's nothing he can give me. He told me to rest and stay off my foot. That's all very well, but how am I supposed to go about the work in the fields? Marina can plant, but she can't do the heavy digging.'

'Maybe one of the local lads would be glad of a bit extra and could help you out.'

Elias shook his head. 'I can't afford to pay anyone.'

'You have the money from your olive crop, and you should have some put aside from the winter oranges.'

'We'll need all of that to live on until I can get about again.'

'You mean you can't pay me the tax you owe? What about my share from the apple crop? That's still owing to me. Now there are the oranges. You signed a tree over to me on my last visit, remember.'

'I'll pay you that, but I can't pay anything towards the olive tax. If I'm up and around the next time you call I'll try to settle up then.'

Alesandros frowned. 'Does that mean you want me to pay the tax on your behalf and charge you interest?'

Elias considered. 'No, let it stand as owing at the moment. I don't want to have to give you any more of my trees.'

'Very well. I'll start to make out the receipts whilst you get the money.' Alesandros looked pointedly at Elias's elevated foot. 'Marina.'

Elias's wife came in from the scullery and Elias beckoned her close and whispered in her ear. With a nod of her head she left the room and Alesandros hoped she had been asked to provide some bread and cheese for him, along with a glass of wine. She returned moments later with a clay pot in her hand and passed it to her husband.

Slowly Elias drew out some money and handed it to Alesandros. 'Is that enough?' he asked.

Alesandros counted it and shook his head. 'I need a bit more, Elias. There's enough there for the apple crop, but you said you'd settle up for my oranges as well.'

With a deep sigh Elias inserted his hand into the pot again and withdrew some more notes. Satisfied that he had been paid sufficient, Alesandros counted the notes out before the man, filled in the receipts and handed them to him.

'It's just the olives you owe for,' Alesandros assured him. 'Keep that receipt safe and I'll come along in another month and see if you can pay the tax on the olives.'

'It will depend how quickly this gout goes away,' replied Elias morosely.

Alesandros thought it was unlikely he would be asked to stay for a meal, but he decided to ask for a glass of water and hoped it would miraculously turn into wine.

His request was relayed to Marina and she carried a glass in for him. 'It's fresh,' she assured him. 'I drew it from the well myself this morning.'

Alesandros drained the glass and smacked his lips. Marina took the empty glass from him and set it on the table. He realised he was not going to be asked to stay any longer and walked to the door, Marina close on his heel.

'I'll see you next month, Elias,' he called back as Marina closed the door behind him.

'Make sure he gets on his donkey and rides away,' ordered Elias and Marina peered out of the window.

'He's gone,' she announced.

'Thank goodness for that. I was beginning to get pins and needles sitting there with my foot up.' Elias rose and tossed the cushions back onto the bed. 'Good job you saw him hitching up his donkey and warned me or I'd have been hard pressed to think of an excuse not to pay the olive tax.'

'But you'll have to pay it at some time, Elias.'

'I know, but if we do well with the vegetables during the summer we'll be able to put a bit of extra by.'

Marina shook her head. Her husband was always optimistic about their future.

Alesandros left Elias and Marina feeing reasonably satisfied. He had managed to extricate most of the money that was owing to him, but now he had to tackle Theodopolous. He hoped the man might have the money for the olive crop waiting for him; at least the amount owing to the tax man. He would deal honestly with him and only ask for the amount of tax that was due for Theo's share. Provided that was forthcoming he would be able to pay the balance that was Theo's responsibility immediately. He would be happy to wait for his own share of the income as that would incur interest from the man and be to his advantage.

His donkey safely tethered, Alesandros knocked on the door and twirled the ends of his moustache into their sharp upward points. If it drooped it made him look miserable, whatever his mood. When Sofia answered him a look of consternation crossed her face.

'I'm not sure if Pappa will be able to see you today. He's supervising the cleaning of the water cistern.' Was she supposed to ask the man in, despite the absence of her father?

'I'll walk along and speak to him. How is your mother?'

'Considerably better, thank you.' Sofia waited until he had turned away before she closed the door. She pulled a face at her mother. 'That was the tax man. Should I have asked him to come in?'

Maria replied without looking up from her weaving. 'No reason for him to come in if your Pappa isn't here. Your Pappa will ask him back if necessary.'

Theodopolous was leaning on the wall that surrounded the water cistern. There were a number of men from the village there, some on the steps leading down to the water holding buckets. A couple of men stood on the lowest steps, barefoot and with their trousers rolled up, using a net to skim the leaves and twigs close enough for them to reach and tip into a waiting bucket. As the bucket became full it as handed to the man further up, who in turn passed his bucket up to be taken to the top and emptied.

Alesandros stopped beside him. 'How often do you have to do this?' he asked.

'It all depends on the weather. We can't clean it during the winter months as the steps become slippery. As soon as the farmers need the water for their crops we have to make sure the outlets are not clogged up where the debris has sunk to the bottom and the best way to do that is to remove any leaves and twigs that have fallen in.'

'Is it necessary for you to stay here to watch them? I had hoped we could conclude our business today.'

Theo shook his head. 'There's really nothing for us to settle. I have a few drachmas put aside, but nothing like the amount you will want.'

Alesandros sighed in exasperation. 'However little you are

able to pay is to your advantage in the long run.'

Theo shrugged. 'You cannot have what I do not have.'

'Could we go back to the house and go over the figures?'

'We can, but it won't produce any more money in my box.' Theodopolous turned to the boy who was standing watching the men whilst they worked. 'Stratos,' he called, 'If there's any problem come and fetch me.'

Stratos nodded. The only problem he could envisage was if one of the men slipped into the dirty water and no doubt by the time he had alerted Theo to the event the man would have been hauled out and be the butt of his companions' humour.

Alesandros looked at the cottages as he accompanied Theo back to his house. They all looked in good repair, the roofs sound, the window frames, shutters and doors painted as protection from the weather. He hoped they were paying the full amount in rent to Theo.

'So, Theo, how are things with you?' asked Alesandros as he seated himself at the table.

Theodopolous spread his hands. 'I'm no better off than the last time you called. I needed to buy the paint for the cottages.'

Alesandros nodded. 'I noticed they looked very smart as we passed, but they looked almost as good the previous time I was here.'

'Until you looked closely. The sun is more of a problem than the rain. When it's hot the paint cracks and the wood beneath shrinks. The first time it rains everyone complains they have a leak or cannot open or shut their doors. It makes sense to give them another coat of paint in the spring and again in the autumn. Saves more expensive work later.'

'Did you pay for the paint?'

'Of course. The cottages are my responsibility.'

Alesandros nodded. 'Are they all paying their rent regularly?'

'One or two are a little behind, but they'll catch up now they're able to take their produce to market in Neapoli.'

Alesandros sighed. 'Over the years they have increased the price of their produce in the markets. You know yourself that taxes have increased as prices have risen. When did you last increase their rent?'

Theo looked at him in horror. 'I cannot increase their rent. If they have a problem paying me now it would only make the problem worse.'

'I've told you, you should charge them interest when they fall into arrears. They probably have more money than you.'

Theo gave a mirthless chuckle. 'That's possible, but they also have their expenses. They need to buy seed and plants and farming equipment, along with their food and clothing.'

'So have you managed to put aside any money towards the debt you owe me?'

'I had to use the rents for the Easter celebrations. That was essential. I'm planning to start saving again now and I think I may have a solution to my problem.'

Alesandros raised his eyebrows and Theo continued.

'If I gave you my remaining olive trees that would clear my debts and I wouldn't have to pay tax on them in the future. It could give me a fresh start.'

Alesandros considered the offer. He was sorely tempted. 'If I took your remaining trees you would still have to pay tax on the ones belonging to the villagers. I'm not prepared to pay tax on trees that don't belong to me.'

'The tax on the fruit trees is not as great as on the olives. I should be able to manage that each year and the tax for the olives would come from the cottage rents.'

'Provided the villagers pay their rents,' Alesandros observed.

Theo nodded eagerly. 'Could we come to some arrangement?'

Alesandros pulled his receipt book from his shoulder bag. 'If you're quite sure that is what you want, Theo.'

'It would be the solution. I could manage quite happily if I didn't have to pay the olive tax.'

Alesandros did not point out to him that without his olive trees he would not have the same amount of income and still be responsible for the villagers' olive tax. 'I'll call again in a month and see if you are able to settle some of your arrears.'

Sofia answered the door and informed him that her father was chopping logs, but he was welcome to come in and she would tell him that Alesandros had arrived. Maria was seated at the weaving loom and Alesandros went over to bid her good day.

Maria smiled at him. 'Yes, it is a good day. I feel so much better now the sun is shining and there is some warmth in the air.'

'I think we all feel like that when spring arrives. Of course, once we have the full heat of the summer we will all be complaining that it is too hot.' To Alesandros the room was over heated and he could feel perspiration gathering under his armpits. He took a seat as far away from the fire as possible and began to remove papers from his shoulder bag whilst waiting for Theo to make an appearance.

Sofia returned, bearing a carafe of wine and a plate of small honey cakes. 'Pappa said to bring you some refreshment. He will be in shortly.'

'Thank you, my dear. I seem to remember that when I last visited you had made the biscuits. Have you also made the cakes?'

Sofia shook her head. 'Mamma made these. I had some other jobs that needed to be done.'

'I am sure they will be just as delicious.' Alesandros smiled up at her and Sofia blushed as she poured him a glass of wine.

The back door closed and Alesandros returned his attention to the papers which he spread out before him.

Theo appeared, picking at his hand and squinting at it. 'Sorry to have kept you. I needed to wash and I seem to have a splinter. I thought I would be able to pull it out, but it's in deeper than I realised.'

'Do you wish to remove it before we talk business?'

Theo shook his head. 'Sofia can get it out for me later.' He poured a glass of wine for himself and sat down across the table from Alesandros. He held up his hand as Alesandros was about to speak. 'I know you've come for the taxes and I'll be quite honest and tell you now I haven't got the money and I can't pay.'

Alesandros frowned. 'You've been paid for the olive crop. I have the figures here. You owe me the money for five trees and you owe the tax on the ten you own and those belonging to the villagers.'

Theo nodded. 'I know, but I haven't any money to pay at the moment. Provided there are no urgent repairs needed to the cottages I'm hoping to save up some of the rents ready for your next visit.'

'So what have you spent the olive money on?'

Theo spread his hands. 'It was most unfortunate. My wife became ill and I had to ask the doctor to call outside of his usual monthly visit. I had to pay him, of course, and that took most of the olive money.'

'I'm sorry to hear that Maria has been ill. Has she recovered now?'

Theo nodded. 'She had a bad bout of bronchitis. It was a chapter of accidents.' Theo related to Alesandros how Maria had slipped over whilst carrying the water buckets, hurting her ankle and soaking herself to the skin, resulting in a chill that went to her chest and turned to bronchitis. 'She has to be careful now not to do anything too strenuous. Sofia has been so good. She insisted on doing all the cleaning and heavy work until she was in a state of collapse herself. I've arranged for Kassianae to come in to scrub the floors and clean the windows.'

'How long do you plan to employ the woman?'

'I'm really not sure. Certainly until Easter is over. There is no way Sofia could manage to take the rugs down on her own and beat them. Maria will be able to manage most of the Easter cooking, but she certainly isn't fit enough yet to do the cleaning.'

As if on cue Maria coughed, a deep, harsh sound and she pressed a hand to her chest, the other holding the weaving shuttle. Sofia was immediately at her side offering a glass of water. Maria took a few sips and a deep breath.

'Do you want to lie down, Mamma?'

'I'd like to get some more weaving done first. I'll continue until I cough again; then I'll have a rest.'

Alesandros turned back to Theo. 'So you are saying you are unable to pay me anything at the moment?'

'That's so.'

'You realise you'll end up owing interest.'

'It can't be helped. If I could change the leaves on the trees into drachmas I would pay you willingly. I am relying on the villagers having a good year and paying their rent on time.'

'What about their arrears from the winter? You said they had not paid you rent, but given you produce.'

'One is as good as the other. If they pay their rent in money I buy our food. If they pay in produce I don't have to buy the food.'

Alesandros sighed. The man was abysmally ignorant about business. No doubt the villagers had given him five or six eggs and he had accepted them as a full week's rent, rather than a token and a promise of the balance later.

'So what are you suggesting, Theo?'

Theo frowned and began to pick at the splinter in his hand again. 'I have little choice. I will have to sign over some more olive trees to you.' Theo spread his hands despairingly. 'What can I do? It was not my fault that my wife was ill.'

'I know, I know, I'm not blaming you, Theo, but I am worried. You were unable to pay your taxes last year and I paid them on your behalf. You owe me the interest along with my share from the olive crop. Now you are saying you cannot pay your tax again this year.'

Theo shook his head sadly. 'I try to save from the rents, but there always seems to be something essential that needs to be done. During the snow Vassilis's chimney collapsed and broke a couple of tiles. That had to be repaired. Pelagia set her cottage alight when she neglected to watch over her cooking. She panicked and ran outside calling for help. Fortunately the flames were put out before there was any real damage done, but I had to repaint the inside walls for her.'

'Surely she should have paid for that.'

'Vangelis used her blanket to smother the flames along with a bucket of water. She had to replace that and she certainly couldn't afford to pay for both. I also had to repair her window that was broken.'

Alesandros sighed. 'You are too good hearted, Theo. You should insist they pay their rent in full and on time.'

'I cannot take from them what they have not got.'

'Then charge them interest. They would soon find the money if they knew they would have to pay you more the following week.'

'I wouldn't know how to work that out. Most of them pay their rent on time provided they have the money available. No one deliberately tries to cheat me.'

'No, but they take advantage of you. You believe their excuses. Is the government going to be lenient and sympathetic when I explain why you haven't enough money to pay your tax? Of course not. They will immediately start to charge you interest and their rate is twice the amount I charge. They know that once you see how much the bill is accumulating you will find the money to pay.'

'Are you able to help me again? Just until I am able to get some money together.'

Alesandros leaned forward and spoke seriously. 'Theo, I cleared the debt you owed me last year by accepting five olive trees. Are you suggesting I should do the same again?'

'It would certainly help me.'

'It would help you this year, but what about next year? The time will come when you have nothing left with which to clear your debt.'

'If I have nothing left the government won't be asking me for any taxes.'

'They will still ask for the tax that is due on your fruit crops and the villagers' rents and I will be asking you for interest on any loan I have arranged with you. I have arranged to visit Perambela in four weeks time. I'll call on you and we can discuss the situation further. Of course, if you can pay me, that will be an end of the matter.'

Theo nodded. He doubted very much that he would have the money to pay the next time Alesandros called. Having to use the olive crop money to pay the doctor had been a necessity. Even if he saved every lepta from the rents it would take him almost a year to accumulate that amount again. There was the additional expense of Kassianae and also Stratos. The boy had certainly mended his ways and was beginning to put on a bit of weight now his grandmother had a little more money for food. He could not expect his daughter to go back to dealing with all the household chores and he felt responsible for helping Stratos's grandmother until such time as the boy was able to go out and earn some money of his own by working for the farmers.

'I'm grateful, Mr Danniakis.'

Alesandros rode back to Aghios Nikolaos feeling his day had been successful. He had managed to extricate most of the money that was owed to him. Elias still owed his olive tax but he hoped when he called in a month's time the man would have enough to pay him. It was Theo who was his continual problem. Alesandros had paid the tax due on the five olive trees he owned, although not declaring they now belonged to him, and deducted the amount from Theo's tax bill. It was unfortunate that the man's wife had been ill and the doctor summoned, but the government would not accept that as an excuse to reduce or cancel his bill.

Alesandros stopped in Driros during his journey to Perambela and Christos frowned when he saw him approaching.

'What are you here for? My taxes are paid up to date.'

'I've not come to ask you for any money,' smiled Alesandros. 'This is just a friendly visit as I'm passing through.'

'No tax collector is a friend of mine.' Christos turned his back and continued to mound up the earth around his potato plants.

'Crops doing well?'

'As well as can be expected at this time of year.'

'I'm pleased to hear it.' Alesandros walked back to his donkey, there was no point in lingering and hoping he would be invited to partake of a glass of wine.

The cool reception he had received from Christos decided him not to call on Makkis. It was unlikely the man would be any friendlier. He would continue to Perambela, hope Elias had recovered from his gout and would have the money for the olive tax ready for him. Then he would have to tackle Theo.

Marina invited him in to their cottage and Alesandros was relieved to see that Elias was not there.

'Your husband has recovered?'

Marina frowned. Elias had not been ill; then she remembered. 'Yes, oh, yes, much better now, thank you.' She blushed in confusion. 'I'll call him for you. Have a seat.'

Alesandros sat down at the table and hoped it would not be too long before Elias put in an appearance. He planned to arrive in Kastelli when the family should be partaking of their mid-day meal and they would be obliged to ask him to join them. He heard Elias in the scullery and his spirits rose; the man could be bringing him a glass of wine.

Elias entered the living room, a small pot in his hands. He tipped the contents onto the table.

'I know you've come to collect the tax for the olives. This is all I have.'

Alesandros counted out the notes and coins carefully and consulted his accounts. 'This is almost half the amount you owe.'

Elias nodded happily. 'We've been very frugal over the weeks and I've managed to save up a bit.'

'Still not enough,' Alesandros shook his head sadly. 'I cannot keep on visiting you in the hope of receiving a few drachmas.'

'Would an apple tree make up the difference?'

'You told me they had suffered from a parasite last year.'

'I've managed to clear that. They're healthy now; in full leaf. I have hopes of a good crop.'

Alesandros pretended to consider. He knew the man had lied to him about a parasite attacking his apple trees the previous autumn. 'Well, provided they are healthy now I suppose I could take a chance and accept another.'

'And my debt will be cleared?'

'Until the next apple harvest. Make sure you put some money aside from it, Elias. The government will want their tax and I will be claiming my share for the trees I own.' Alesandros wrote out the receipt and handed it over. 'If you keep your money in that pot I suggest you put the receipt in there also. It's a valuable piece of paper for you. Don't throw it away by mistake.'

Elias stuffed the paper into the bottom of the pot. Once Alesandros had left he would replace the money he had removed before carrying the pot into the living room. His wife would not be pleased that he had signed away another apple tree, but it was better than facing her wrath when he said there was no money to pay their rent or contribute to the Easter celebrations.

May 1911

Alesandros mounted his donkey and set off towards Lassithi in good spirits. He was in possession of the figures the farmers owed in tax and, provided they paid, he should return with a sizeable amount of money to clear their outstanding accounts and a substantial sum for himself.

During the previous month he had visited the farmers along the coast and all but one had paid their dues. Whilst in the area he had visited various tavernas in the hope of finding an acceptable young woman to be his bride. It really was time he thought seriously about marriage. He engaged the taverna keepers in conversation and tried to draw information from them about the locals.

'That meal was very good,' he complimented Miltiades. 'Does your wife do the cooking?'

'No, my daughter.'

'Your daughter?'

'My wife looks after the children during the day and Eva does the cooking. In the evening my wife comes to help me and that means Eva's at home when Stavros finishes work. The arrangement works well.'

Alesandros's hopes faded. Miltiades's daughter was already married with a family.

'I'll definitely have to eat here again,' he said to Miltiades. 'My compliments to the cook.'

Miltiades grinned, showing yellow, crooked teeth. 'Thanks. I'll tell her.'

It appeared that whichever taverna Alesandros patronised there was no unmarried daughter who would be suitable for him to consider as a wife. His hopes had risen when he was in Kavousi and an attractive girl had emerged briefly from the scullery area, waved to the owner and disappeared again.

'Is the young lady your cook?' he asked.

The owner shook his head. 'That's my daughter. My wife does the cooking at home and Litsa brings it down to me in her break. She's a good girl.'

'What work does she do?'

'She cleans the church. Keeps it spotless.'

'That's a full time job for her?'

'She'll spend all day polishing the candlesticks. The priest says he doesn't know how they would manage without her.'

'She sounds a treasure.' Alesandros made a mental note to visit the church and have a second look at the girl. 'Some man will be very fortunate when he makes her his wife.'

'Not likely to happen,' replied the taverna owner morosely. 'She's stone deaf. Has been since birth. Can't talk properly, more like noises than words.'

'How sad. Surely, one of the local lads who have known her since she was a child would recognise her worth and be prepared to overlook her disability.'

Yiorgo pursed his lips. 'They wouldn't take a chance that any child they had wouldn't be afflicted in the same way. All they do is cat call after her or try to take advantage of her if the opportunity arises.'

Alesandros shook his head in commiseration. No one married into a family where there was any history of a physical defect. 'I'd like to think she was able to find a suitable husband. She's very attractive to look at.'

'Are you making an offer for her?'

'Me?' Alesandros was genuinely shocked and embarrassed. Had his interest been so evident? The man must be desperate to get his daughter married if he was prepared to ask a perfect stranger without preamble if he was interested. He shook his head quickly. 'I don't think my wife would be very happy if I did.' He flushed as he told the lie.

'Didn't realise you were married. By the way you spoke you sounded sympathetic, and that's what she needs. Sympathy and understanding.'

'I'm sure she receives both from the priests.'

'Yes, but they're not going to marry her, are they?'

'Maybe they would know someone, possibly in the same sort of situation, and they could be introduced to each other. Now, I must pay my bill and be on my way.'

Alesandros wanted to remove himself from the awkward situation as quickly as possible. He did not want Yiorgo asking for details of his mythical wife.

Yiorgo wrote something unintelligible on a piece of paper and held out his hand. 'Five drachmas.'

Without demur Alesandros handed him the money, despite thinking he had been overcharged. He would not frequent that taverna again.

Riding towards the Lassithi Plateau Alesandros's thoughts once again turned to marriage. He knew there was no one suitable in Driros, most of the inhabitants were elderly and any younger ones were already married. He debated about riding on to Neapoli on his return journey. There were some tavernas on the outskirts of the town and it was just possible he could find someone acceptable.

As he rode into Kastelli he was surprised at the hive of activity at the cistern. Children were milling around and peering over the edge, being pushed away by their parents. All around the cistern the path was a sea of mud.

'What's going on?' he asked Theodopolous. 'Has someone fallen in?'

'Part of an outlet tunnel has collapsed. No one realised until the farmers unblocked the outlets to irrigate their spring planting. There was only a trickle of water coming through a couple of them, despite the cistern being almost full. We all thought the openings were blocked with winter debris. One man tried to unblock an opening with a stick, but it didn't do any good.'

'What are you doing about it?'

'We had to call in a man from Neapoli. He knows about cisterns. He looked at the irrigation channels and removed any debris that was in them, but still the water did not run through. He reckons they're blocked down in the cistern and the only way he could find out and do any repairs was by removing most of the water. Manos made us a rudimentary cross piece so we could let down buckets and bring them up full; saved the men from going up and down the steps and making a bucket chain. It's taken us almost a week to get the water level down low enough for Mr Benediktos to go down and have a look. The crops can't complain about lack of water this year!'

Alesandros peered over the edge. On the far side of the cistern from the steps a man was crouched in the water levering a large stone out from the wall.

'Is that safe? Suppose the whole side collapses?'

'He's on a rope. We'd pull him up. The man's an expert. He knows what he has to do.'

Alesandros looked sceptical. If the side of the cistern collapsed the man would be buried, probably killed by the falling masonry.

'He had a look inside the channels and removed any debris that had accumulated. But he says he's pretty sure that part of the roof has collapsed,' explained Theo. 'We're hoping it's just a couple of blocks towards the front. Once they've been removed the sides can be strengthened with cement. When the cement has set we'll have to hope that it rains otherwise we'll have to gradually refill the cistern from the well water. We don't want to do that if we can avoid it. With the summer coming we'll need our fresh water.'

Alesandros nodded. 'You're obviously busy at the moment. I'll ride down to Perambela and call on you on my way back.'

'He's just about ready to inspect the damage.'

Curiosity overcame Alesandros and he decided he could easily spend a little longer in Kastelli. He watched as a length of wood, one end wrapped in a cloth and soaked in oil, was slowly let down so the man could reach it. A box of matches was thrown to him and he caught it deftly. He struck a match and held it to the cloth which flared up momentarily and then the flame died, leaving a charred end. A ripple of comment went through the watching villagers. The man struck another match and this time the cloth caught alight properly, sending up a sheet of flame.

Cautiously the man lowered himself back down into the knee high water and inserted the flaming torch into the hole and looked around. He pushed it in as far as his arm would reach and then wriggled his body in a short way. Alesandros held his breath. Suppose the man became stuck in the narrow opening? Finally the man eased himself back and emerged, the torch still alight in his hand. He dipped it into the water where it sizzled and sent up a plume of smoke.

Slowly the man walked across the slimy bottom of the cistern until he reached the steps and climbed out. He tossed the torch and soaking box of matches on the ground and undid the rope that was knotted around his waist.

Theo moved over to his side and Alesandros could not hear their conversation. He wheeled his donkey around on the slippery mud and continued on his journey to Perambela. No doubt Theo would tell him the extent of the damage the man had found when he returned to the village later.

There was no answer when Alesandros knocked on the door of Elias's cottage. He tethered his donkey and walked to the rear of the building. Some distance away he could see Elias and Marina working in the fields. He cupped his hands around his mouth and hailed him. After calling three times and receiving no response he began to walk across the field.

Elias immediately called to him. 'Get off my land. You're trampling my crops.'

Alesandros looked down. He could see nothing growing where he stood. He beckoned Elias to come over to him; wiping his hands down his trousers Elias complied. He had hoped that by ignoring Alesandros's shouts the tax collector would go away.

Before Alesandros could say a word Elias shook his finger at him. 'You should know better than to walk across a field. If you've damaged my crops I'll be asking for compensation.'

'I'm sure I've not damaged anything. Had you looked up when I first called you I wouldn't have needed to step onto your field.'

'Why have you come anyway? If you're after the remainder of my tax you're too early. Come again at the end of the summer when I've had a chance to sell some produce, provided it hasn't been damaged by trespassers, of course.'

Alesandros sighed. 'I told you I would call again in a month. Why didn't you tell me then that it would be too early? It would have saved me the journey.'

'How am I supposed to remember when you're going to turn up? Seems like yesterday to me that you were last here.'

'So you have no money set aside for me?'

'That's right; and if I don't get back to my planting I'll not have any the next time you call.'

'You realise the interest is mounting up?'

'To your advantage. No doubt you'll find another apple tree acceptable to settle the debt.' Elias turned and began to walk back across his field.

'If you're willing to part with another apple tree we could conclude the transaction now,' Alesandros called after him.

'I'm busy,' Elias shouted back over his shoulder and continued on his way.

Alesandros shrugged. The man was impossible. If he cleared his debt now he would be able to keep all the money he made from his summer produce and even have some savings ready for when his next tax payment became due. Alesandros mounted his donkey and road away. He doubted if he would have better success with Theodopolous, but he was intrigued to know the outcome of the damage in the water cistern.

The villagers had dispersed. The excitement of watching the man investigate the collapse was over. He had returned to Theo's house where water was heated for him to wash and he changed into his spare dry clothing and was now riding back to Neapoli.

'So, Theo, what's the outcome? I saw you having a discussion, but I realised you had more important things on your mind than dealing with me.'

Theodopolous looked at Alesandros miserably. 'As he thought there's a collapse in the roof of one tunnel that will need to be cleared before he can repair it. No point in clearing the blockage and not making the repair. It will only happen again.'

'How will he do that? He hardly fitted into the opening.'

'It will take time. He'll go down and remove all the loose brickwork. That should enlarge the hole enough for him to be able to get inside properly and remove the fallen bricks.'

'Do you believe him? He's not trying to make out the damage is worse so he can increase his bill?'

'He offered any one of us the chance to climb down with a torch and have a look for ourselves. Vassilis declared himself brave enough and came back confirming the second blockage. He reckons some of the other outlets need attention as well.' Theo sighed deeply. 'It's going to cost a considerable amount of money to put right.'

'Suppose you repaired the one that is damaged and left the others?'

Theo shook his head. 'Mr Benediktos said it would only be a matter of time before there would be further collapses and other outlets would be blocked. The farmers who rely on it to irrigate their fields would have to spend hours each day collecting buckets of water. There's also the problem with the rain. If the water rises too high during the winter months the far ends are unblocked. No point in unblocking them if the water can't get through. During a very wet winter the top overflow opening wouldn't be able to cope with the surplus water and the cistern would overflow.'

'So where are you going to get the money from? Would the government help you with the repair?'

'It doesn't belong to them; it belongs to the village. As the head man of the village it is my responsibility. I was wondering if you would be able to help.' Theo looked at Alesandros hopefully.

Alesandros frowned. 'I imagine the costs are going to far exceed the money I can expect to receive for the olive crop next year.'

'Probably for the next few years.'

'What about the villagers? They are the ones who use the water; surely they should pay for the repair.'

'I'm going to tell them that I will have to increase their rent by a drachma a week to add to whatever capital I can raise.'

'About time you increased the pittance they pay you! I'd need some firm figures before I could consider lending you any money towards the cost. If it's too much for me where will you go for help?'

'I'd have to go to a bank.'

Alesandros frowned. 'Do you have enough collateral to satisfy a bank?'

'What's collateral?'

'Goods they could seize if you defaulted on your payments. You haven't any olive trees now.'

Theo sighed deeply. 'I'd have to offer my house. It's all I have and it's destined to be Sofia's when she marries. I'd like to know she was married to someone who made a good living, like a teacher or doctor, not one of the local boys.'

'I suggest you dispose of Kassianae's services. That would save you money.'

Theo shook his head. 'Her mother's a widow. If I did not employ Kassianae she would not be able to pay the rent for her mother's cottage so I would be worse off.'

'She could move in with her daughter. That would free up the cottage and you could rent it to someone else.'

'Who would want it? There wouldn't be any land for them to farm so how would they pay the rent?'

'They could keep chickens out the back.'

'Other villagers keep chickens. We have a plentiful supply of eggs and poultry. We don't need any more.'

Alesandros shrugged. That was Theo's problem. 'When do you expect to know the cost of the cistern repairs?'

'Benediktos said he would return next week. He has to find out the cost of the waterproof cement that is needed, along with the bricks and calculate the amount of time it will take him to do the repair. He said he wouldn't be able to give me a completely accurate costing. He might find more damage than he anticipates, then he would need more bricks and an extra bag of cement.'

'And more time to complete the job, no doubt. I'll give your proposition of a loan some thought and come back in ten days. It's obviously going to be a very large amount you need and there's no guarantee I would have that much available.'

Alesandros rode away deep in thought. He must consult his book of outstanding tax debts and chivvy the defaulters into paying up. If Theo was putting his house up as security for the loan it was an opportunity not to be missed. The man would never have enough money to repay him, of that he was certain, and the house was far larger and more strongly constructed than anything he would have been able to afford to build. It was the kind of house that any bride would be pleased to find she was living in; if only he could find a suitable woman.

He decided to forgo his visit to the tavernas on the outskirts of Neapoli. He was thinking hard. If the house was intended to be the dowry for Theo's daughter and he became the owner, what was to stop him from asking for the girl's hand? She was attractive and accomplished, very different from Xene. He permitted himself a smile at the memory of her shrill voice.

His little book yielded dividends. Five farmers still owed some olive tax and two owed for an apple crop that belonged to him. He discounted Elias from his calculations. He would get nothing from him until the end of the summer; then he would be insistent that he was paid up to date. The other men would be worth a visit and there were other collections he was due to make. If he delayed paying those into the tax office he could easily make up the arrears at a later date. Provided the sum needed by Theo was not too extortionate he should be able to manage to finance the repair with a little adept manipulation.

'So, Theo, do you have any figures for me? Did Benediktos come back to you as he promised?'

Theo handed a sheet of paper across the table to Alesandros. The figures meant nothing to him. He just knew it was a lot of money.

Alesandros scrutinized the figures carefully. 'I see Benediktos is quoting an amount for each day he works. How many days does he think it will take him?'

Theo shrugged. 'It depends what he finds. He said it could take him three or four days or a week or more; and that's provided it doesn't rain. That's why he's quoted for each day's work, rather than the finished job.'

Alesandros nodded. The man was no fool and he wondered who he had asked to work out the prices for him.

'Father Symeon seemed to think it was reasonable under

the circumstances,' added Theo. 'I asked him to be here when Benediktos called. He understands figure work.'

Alesandros looked over the figures once again and made some notes in his book. 'I tell you what I propose. I'll loan you the money for the cost of the cement and bricks. Benediktos gets his money when he has finished the job satisfactorily. That way I won't be charging you interest on the full amount of the loan until you've actually received it all. If you have managed to repay any of it to me in the meantime I'll take that into account. Does that sound fair?'

'It sounds fair enough to me, but Benediktos may not be agreeable to wait for his money until he has finished. He might think we won't pay him.'

'We'll pay a visit to Father Symeon this afternoon.' This was Alesandros's way of inviting himself to stay for a meal with the family. 'We can discuss my proposal with him and if he agrees he can write it down. You can have a copy, you can give one to Benediktos, leave one with Father Symeon and I will have one. That way there can be no misunderstanding. I'm sure Benediktos will take Father Symeon's word that the money will be forthcoming.'

Alesandros looked at Theo and pointed his finger at him. 'I'm not giving the money to you, Theo. I don't trust you not to use it for some other purpose that you suddenly decide is more urgent, like renewing a cottage roof. I'll put it into Father Symeons's hands and Benediktos can ask him when he needs it. I shall want a receipt for all the money that is spent. I don't want to find there's money used that can't be accounted for.'

'I'm sure Father Symeon will be scrupulous in his book keeping. All the villagers trust him.' Theo rose from the table, a relieved man. 'I'll ask Sofia to bring us some wine and I'm sure she will have no problem providing you with some lunch.'

'Just remember, Theo, if you are unable to repay me I will be taking your house.'

Alesandros returned to Kastelli the following week. There was no longer any activity around the water cistern and the muddy ground had dried out. Alesandros tethered his donkey to Theo's window railings and knocked on the door. To his surprise Maria answered his knock rather than Sofia.

'Theo isn't here,' she informed. 'He's at a meeting with Father Symeon.'

'Church business or is it about the cistern?' asked Alesandros.

'The cistern. That's all anyone talks about at the moment.'

'I'll walk up to the church and ask if I can be included in their discussions.'

Maria looked at Alesandros in surprise. Why would the tax collector be interested in a meeting about the repairs to the water cistern?

Alesandros walked across the paved courtyard of the church and pushed open the door quietly. There was no one inside and he stood there, admiring the spotless brass and intricately carved wood. Considering it was a village church it was a substantial building that was capable of housing a number of people and certainly larger than the one he occasionally attended in Aghios Nikolaos. He closed the door behind him and walked around to the back. There was probably a small room there where the men would be gathered.

To his surprise they were sitting outside on wooden chairs, Father Symeon and Theo side by side and the villagers in a semi circle in front of them. Theo looked up and nudged the priest, who raised his eyes and nodded to Alesandros. Theo offered his chair and Alesandros shook his head, standing behind the priest and the villager enabled him to look at the papers the priest held.

Father Symeon's eyes swept across the men who were listening to him. 'It may be necessary for someone to go down and help Benediktos. Is anyone willing?'

'I'll go down,' offered Vassilis and no one argued with him.

'Once he has removed some of the loose bricks from the entrance he will place some wooden supports along the sides. When he considers it safe he will commence work on the repair. Are there any questions?'

'How are we supposed to water our crops whilst all this is going on?'

Father Symeon looked at Theo, who rose and addressed the farmers. 'You'll have to use the fresh water from the well and carry buckets to your fields. I know it will be time consuming, but that is all I can offer you.'

'The women won't like that. We'll be at the well all day.'

'You must be considerate. Allow the women to get their water first thing in the morning and if they come for some more water later in the day allow them to go ahead of you. There must be no arguing between you about who has had the most water. The important thing is not to waste it. We do not know how much is stored in the well and if that should run dry the whole village will be without fresh water.'

'How will we know if it is running dry? We can't see down it.'

'I'll speak to Benediktos. He may be able to tell us how we will know.' Theo did not want to admit that he was as ignorant as the villagers about the depth of the well.

The men muttered and grumbled between themselves; already they were tired of the time consuming job of hauling buckets to their fields.

'Have you any idea when the cement will be delivered?' asked Alesandros.

'Benediktos said he would make the arrangements. It could be here next week.'

'Have you given him the money for it?'

Father Symeon nodded. 'And before you ask I insisted he gave me a receipt. He assured me the cement was on order from Heraklion and it will be delivered as soon as he has paid for it.'

Alesandros just hoped the man was honest and would not

disappear now he had some money in his pocket.

Theo and Alesandros watched the priest walk back into the church. Theo shrugged. 'He means well, but he knows nothing about repairing a cistern.'

'And you do?'

'No, but I'm willing to listen to Benediktos and follow his instructions. Father Symeon tried to argue that he only needed to place a coat of cement over the existing brickwork. Benediktos said he was not prepared to do that as sooner or later any loose bricks would fall and crack the cement. Eventually they would fall down into the channel again and we would then be calling him back and accusing him of shoddy workmanship. Father Symeon wasn't happy, but Benediktos said we could always find someone else to do the job.'

'Why is Father Symeon concerned about the cost? He isn't paying.'

Theo sighed. 'Some of the villagers complained that I had increased their rent to help with the overall amount and asked if Father Symeon could help them. He said the cistern was the responsibility of the whole village and as such the church would make a donation and make sure the costs were kept to the minimum.'

'How much is Father Symeon going to donate?'

'I've no idea. It could depend on how much it has finally cost when the repair is finished.'

'Well, let's hope he gives a sizeable amount.'

Stratos had been following the two men down the road and now he tugged at Theo's sleeve. 'Can I help Benediktos?' he asked eagerly.

Theo smiled and placed a hand on the boy's shoulder. 'You can be his personal assistant. You can be at the top of the well and collect anything he needs and lower it down to him. If Benediktos says there is a problem you'll run up to the house to fetch me. I don't want to spend all my day down there just standing around.'

Stratos beamed. 'I'll tell my grandma I'll be helping. She said I was to keep away and not be a nuisance to Benediktos.'

'Your grandma is quite right. You mustn't get in his way. You do as I say and you'll be no trouble to him.'

Stratos ran up the road to the end of the village and Alesandros looked at Theo questioningly. 'Who's the boy?'

'A young scamp who used to get into more trouble than you would have thought possible. He helps his grandmother with her vegetable garden, but there's not enough there to keep him occupied all day. The villagers were complaining that he was a nuisance. After a spate of broken windows I decided I would have to take him in hand.'

'Why didn't you speak to his father? He should have dealt with him.'

'His father is a widower and works up in Neapoli. He visits occasionally and gives his mother some money for his son. The boy really only has his grandmother and he took no notice of her scolding. I handed out a few practical punishments to him and then gave him a permanent job as a water carrier. Maria isn't strong enough to carry buckets of water as she used to, and Sofia can't be expected to make two or three trips each day along with her other duties.'

'Do you pay him?' asked Alesandros. Was this another expense the man had incurred that ate into the money he should be saving towards his taxes?

'Of course. If I didn't he probably wouldn't be reliable. I give him five lepta a week.'

Alesandros calculated rapidly. Less than three drachmas a year; he could hardly claim the amount was extortionate.

'I give his grandmother two drachmas a week to help with the boy's food and clothing. I'm sure part of the problem was that he was hungry. Now she has a little extra she's able to buy some meat or cheese to add to their diet. He's become quite a well behaved youngster now.'

Alesandros frowned. Three drachmas a year had suddenly become nearly three drachmas a week; a hundred and fifty drachmas a year that the man was giving away.

'If you spoke to one of the farmers would they consider employing him now he's more reliable?

Theo shrugged. 'Maybe, when there's a lot of fruit and vegetables to be picked for the market, but their own children usually help them.'

'Do they pay them?'

Theo looked at Alesandros in surprise. 'Of course not.'

'So why do you pay this boy just to bring you a few buckets of water?'

'It's a way of making him feel responsible; that he's doing something worthwhile and appreciated.'

'Well I hope you're not planning to pay him anything for helping Benediktos with the cistern.'

Theo smiled. 'He won't really be needed, but it will ensure that he keeps out from under Benediktos's feet and placate his grandmother.'

Two weeks later Alesandros rode into Kastelli. He had money with him to hand to Father Symeon for the cost of Benediktos's work and he had hoped to see the man working. To his dismay the area around the cistern appeared deserted. He rode on to Theo's house, hoping the man would have a reasonable explanation for the delay.

Theo shrugged. 'It can't be helped. The cement was later arriving than Benediktos had predicted. He paid us a visit, but refused to remove any of the brickwork until the cement had arrived. He said he needed to put the bricks back in place as quickly as possible and prop them up otherwise some more could become loose.'

'So how much longer do you think it will take before he can do the repair?'

'He said Tuesday.' Theo spread his hands. 'A farmer took a

message in to Neapoli on Saturday to say the cement was here and he promised to come as soon as he had finished the job he was working on.'

'No doubt he'll want his money as soon as he's finished.' Alesandros nodded. 'I'll come up during the morning. Do you have any money for me, Theo?'

'Me?'

'You said you had increased the villagers' rents to help pay towards the repair. I was expecting you to put that to one side so you could start to repay me.'

'I did have until the cement arrived.'

'That was paid for,' frowned Alesandros.

'The cement was, but not the man who brought it here from Heraklion. The journey had taken him all day and he was planning to stay overnight in Neapoli and return to Heraklion the following day. I paid for his journey time and lodging from the rent money, although I suspect he slept the night in his cart.'

Alesandros clicked his tongue in annoyance. No doubt the man who had made the delivery had already been paid by Benediktos, but Theo, being gullible, had accepted his story and paid a second time.

'Why didn't you ask Father Symeon to pay him?'

'I did; but he said he had given you a receipt for the cement money and he could not add to that.'

Alesandros felt annoyed. Obviously the priest did not trust Alesandros to reimburse him. He shrugged. There was nothing he could do about that now.

'Is the cement stored safely under cover?'

'Father Symeon allowed the man to leave it in the back room of the church. It will be quite safe there.'

'I'll have a word with him and leave the money for Benediktos, then I'll be on my way. I have other calls to make.'

'I'm sure you'll find him at the church. To the best of my knowledge he is not needed at anyone's bedside at the moment.

You can leave your donkey here. It's no trouble.'

Alesandros found Father Symeon straightening the rows of chairs in the church. 'I don't know how it happens,' he shook his head in puzzlement. 'I straighten them in the morning and when I come back in later there are always some out of line again. What can I do for you Mr Danniakis?'

Alesandros looked at the number of cats who were sprawled in patches of sunlight or asleep beneath a chair. If the priest kept the cats out of the church he would probably find his problem with the chairs was solved.

'It's about the cistern repair.'

'It is taking longer than we had anticipated.' Father Symeon shook his head sadly.

'So I understand. I also understand that the church is willing to make a contribution towards the final cost.'

Father Symeon smiled. 'I have approached the Bishop and he has agreed the village should be helped from church funds.'

'Has he agreed an amount?'

'Oh, no.' Father Symeon looked shocked at the idea. 'The church is only contributing. If the Bishop made a donation now he could find he had funded the entire job.'

'You have the figures that Benediktos gave you. Surely he can work out a percentage that would be fair?'

Father Symeon shook his head. 'It could come to considerably more than Benediktos thinks or considerably less. The Bishop is adamant that we have to wait for the final bill before we decide how much can be spared from the church finances.'

Alesandros frowned; he knew full well the church could probably have afforded to pay the entire bill and thus relieve Theo and the villagers of the burden.

'Already Theo has had to make up the difference in the amount calculated for the cement.'

'So I understand,' replied Alesandros drily. 'I would have thought you could have paid that small amount from the church funds without having to ask the Bishop for permission.'

'Theo was quite happy to pay when the shortage was made known to him.' Father Symeon smiled complacently.

'I will leave the outstanding money due to Benediktos with you. I trust, if there should be a short fall due to my calculations, the church would be willing to make up the difference on this occasion, as a temporary measure, you understand.'

Father Symeon held out his hand, but Alesandros shook his head. 'I need to count it before you and receive a receipt. If we could go into the room at the back to complete the transaction.'

'Of course.' With a last look at the chairs Father Symeon led the way and Alesandros was tempted to push a couple out of line.

On returning to collect his donkey from outside of Theo's house Alesandros was surprised to see Sofia standing with a bucket of water in each hand, looking apprehensively at the animal. She smiled in relief when Alesandros approached.

'Please can you move him? I want to go into the house and he's standing across the steps.'

'He is a she,' remarked Alesandros dryly and watched as the girl blushed. 'She won't hurt you. She's scented the water and would probably like a drink. You should have given her a push and said "move".

'I didn't like to. I thought he, I mean she, might bite me.'

'She doesn't bite. Here,' Alesandros took a bucket from Sofia and held it up for the donkey to drink noisily. Sofia looked at him in annoyance. She would have to throw the water between the stones in the outhouse now the donkey had been drinking from it. What a waste of fresh water.

'I thought a village boy brought the water up to the house for you. Why are you collecting it?'

'Stratos brings us four buckets in the morning, but today Mama and I have been washing Pappa's shirts and our blouses, so we needed more.'

The donkey withdrew her head and shook it, sending droplets

of water into the air. Alesandros placed the half empty bucket on the ground. 'Give me your hand and scratch her between her ears. She likes that and she'll wrinkle up her lips as if she's smiling at you.'

Tentatively Sofia allowed Alesandros to take her hand and place it on the donkey. As he had said, the donkey drew back her lips and looked as if she was smiling.

'I won't be frightened of her again if she's tethered here.' Sofia picked up her buckets,

'Don't walk behind her. Always stay where she can see you. If she feels threatened from behind she'll kick out.'

'I'll remember. Thank you, sir.' Sofia picked up the buckets and hurried up the two steps to the front door. She had been embarrassed to admit that the gentle donkey frightened her, but each time she had tried to move around to reach her front door the donkey had moved with her, effectively blocking her way.

Alesandros smiled as he followed Sofia into the house. Fancy a country girl being afraid of a donkey.

'I've handed over the money to Father Symeon and I have a receipt.' Alesandros waved the piece of paper in front of Theo. 'That means you will be liable for the interest on the whole amount as from today, Theo. Make sure you save some of the rent money.'

Theo smiled and nodded. 'Will you not stay and eat with us? It will only be a simple meal, but you're welcome.'

Alesandros appeared to hesitate. 'Well, that's very kind of you. I'll accept gladly.'

Theo called to his daughter. 'Sofia, bring some wine for our guest. He'll be staying to share our mid-day meal.'

Sofia clicked her tongue in annoyance. Doing the washing had taken up most of the morning. Her mother had planned to cook up some pasta, adding some tomato paste, onions and cheese, along with some lettuce leaves for their evening meal and make do with some bread and cheese for their mid-day meal. Now she would have to walk up to the baker and hope the loaf she had made and delivered to him earlier was cooked. She could not offer yesterday's bread to a guest.

Checking that her bodice was fastened demurely, she carried in two glasses of wine and returned to the scullery for a carafe. It was doubtful that either man would be satisfied with only one glass. 'I won't be long, Pappa. I need to go up to the baker. I'll serve our meal as soon as I return.' She turned to Alesandros. 'Will your donkey let me past?'

Alesandros smiled. 'I told you, push her side and say "move".

No sooner had Sofia closed the front door after herself than she was back inside.

'You can't have been to the baker and back so quickly.' Theo observed.

Sofia shook her head. 'The donkey won't let me off the steps.'

'I'll move her for you.' Alesandros took another mouthful of wine and set his glass down on the table. He stood on the top step and took the donkey's bridle firmly in his hand. 'Move,' he commanded.

Dutifully the donkey moved two paces back and Sofia slipped past gratefully.

'Could you tether her at the side window, please? Then she won't stop me going in and out.'

'No reason why I can't. I didn't realise you'd be afraid of her.'

'I'm not used to donkeys.'

'Don't the villagers have donkeys?'

Sofia shook her head. 'They use hand carts to carry their goods to market. They push them up the hills and stand on the step at the back when they go down.'

Alesandros untied the donkey's rein and led her to the side window where he refastened her. He looked after Sofia as she hurried along the road. He had never taken very much notice of the carts he had seen in Aghios Nikolaos or Neapoli. He would have to look and see if they had somewhere for the driver to stand when going downhill.

Sofia was relieved when she returned from the baker and saw the donkey was no longer blocking the steps. Despite having stroked her and been assured that she was smiling when she curled back her lips, Sofia felt very nervous of the large teeth that were then exposed. If you saw a rat it was easy to drive it off with a well aimed stone, but a donkey was a different matter.

Alesandros arrived early in Kastelli. He wanted to meet Benediktos and also to watch how he tackled the repair to the cistern. It appeared that most of the villagers were curious also. They were clustered around the cistern in small groups, the men asserting that they knew exactly how the repair should be done and they would have been quite capable of doing it themselves.

Alesandros tethered his donkey to the railings and before he knocked Theo had opened the door.

'I thought you were Benediktos arriving. He should be here at any time. We could sit inside where it's cool and have a glass of wine whilst we wait for him.'

Alesandros followed Theo into the living room. Despite the fact that it was a pleasant spring day a fire burned in the grate and there was a pot hanging from a tripod.

The men had consumed two glasses of wine each by the time Benediktos arrived. Stratos was walking beside him and when they stopped at Theo's house he took the donkey's reins and tied them to the iron work. From a pannier Benediktos began to unload his tools, handing a large spade to Stratos and carrying the lighter items himself.

Theo hurried out to greet him and asked if he wanted the cement to be brought down from where it was stored at the church.

'Might as well. The bags are heavy. They'll need a man to each corner and have to be handled gently. You don't want to break a bag and lose half your cement on the path.'

'I'll tell them. Whilst they're bringing the bags down some of the others can be bringing up the water.'

'They're not to start mixing it until I say I'm ready. I need to remove the loose bricks and get an idea of how much work there is to do there. No point in having it ready and sitting around going hard. I'll not be able to use more than one bucketful at a time.'

Benediktos removed his boots and rolled his trousers up as far as he was able before climbing carefully down the irregular stone steps and into the water.

'Do you want a rope?' Theo called down to him and Benediktos shook his head.

'Shouldn't do.' He waded carefully through the water until he reached the channel opening. He removed some of the bricks at the entrance and tested the others to ensure they were firmly in place before he wriggled his head and shoulders into the opening.

'I wish he was on a rope,' muttered Theo. 'If that lot collapses on him he could be trapped.'

With his arm outstretched Benediktos began removing the debris he had left in there after his first inspection. Bricks, rocks and general debris began to fall into the water that remained in the cistern. Finally he removed his head from the opening and called for a torch to be lowered down to him.

'I'll take it to him,' offered Stratos, kicking off his boots and rolling up his trousers in imitation of Benediktos. He placed a box of matches safely into his trouser pocket and holding the torch aloft began to descend the steps nimbly. He handed it to Benediktos and then struck a match to light the rag that was wound around the stick.

Benediktos pushed it into the opening and looked again. There was more debris further down that he would need to remove or the water would not run freely even after the repair. He handed the torch back to Stratos and stretched his arm in again. He wriggled further into the hole and was able to touch the rubbish with his hand, but not able to get a firm enough grip to pull it out. He tried to move further into the opening, feeling the sides pressing on his shoulders as the tunnel narrowed. Again he could touch the offending blockage with his hand, but not remove it.

Struggling, he pushed himself back to the entrance and untied the trowel he had attached to his belt. Again he entered the opening and moved forwards as far as possible, scraping whatever debris he could towards him with the trowel. Slowly he moved backwards and pushed the stones and pieces of brick into the water before taking the torch from Stratos and holding it inside to see if he had cleared the obstruction. To his annoyance he could see a brick that was obviously just out of his reach and effectively blocking half the channel.

Standing back in the cistern Benediktos stood and scratched his head. 'How big is the outlet at the other end of the tunnel?' he asked Stratos. 'Is it bigger than this?'

Stratos shook his head. 'No, it narrows when it gets to the ditches.'

Benediktos looked at Stratos speculatively. 'Would you be willing to go inside that tunnel and get a brick out for me? I'm too big to get close enough.'

Stratos hesitated. He had no wish to go inside the dark tunnel. It could be his misfortune for it to collapse on his head, despite Benediktos having no such qualms about his own safety.

'Can I take the torch with me?'

'You can take it in to have a look, but you'll need to return it to me before you start going right in. If you dropped the torch you could set yourself on fire.'

'So I'll be in the dark?'

'Only for a short while. You're not afraid of the dark, are you?'

Stratos shook his head. He was not afraid of being out in the open when it was dark, but being inside a tunnel was a different matter. 'I'll have a look,' he said. 'It might be too far in for me to reach.'

'See what you can do,' urged Benediktos. 'If you can't get it out I'll have to remove a good deal more of the tunnel.'

The torch grasped firmly in his hand Stratos crawled inside

the tunnel. The flickering light gave off menacing shadows from the irregular walls and he felt his heart beating rapidly. When he could no longer make his way forwards on his knees he laid down and tried to push himself forwards using one elbow and holding the torch well ahead of him. He could see the offending brick a short distance ahead of him and tried to bring his free hand up to grasp it. However hard he tried he was unable to do so whilst holding the torch at arm's length. Reluctantly he began to crawl back towards the entrance where Benediktos was waiting for him.

'I can see it, and I should be able to reach it.' Stratos handed the torch to Benediktos and crawled back into the tunnel.

Now he had no light with him Stratos made his way forward gingerly. He seemed to be going far deeper into the tunnel than he had previously. Finally he could no longer be on his knees and he laid down as he had before and pushed himself forwards on his elbows, continually feeling the way in front of him until he touched the brick with his fingers. He wriggled forward a little more and grasped it firmly, pulling it closer to his body, and began to crawl rapidly back towards the entrance.

He emerged, shaking from head to toe, but with the brick grasped firmly in his hand. Benediktos took it from him and clapped him on the shoulder.

'You're a brave boy. Many men would have refused to go in there.'

'Can you do the repair now?'

'I'm going inside again to check there's nothing else causing an obstruction. Provided it's clear I can ask the men to start mixing the cement.'

Benediktos crawled inside as far as he was able, examining the sides and the way ahead of him with the torch. The brick had fallen from the roof and would need to be cemented back into place or the others would eventually become loose, fall, and block the tunnel a second time. There was no way he was going to be able to reach it and he would have to ask the boy to go in on his behalf.

Stratos stood patiently waiting for Benediktos to emerge. 'Is it clear?' he asked.

Benediktos nodded. 'We'll take a break and arrange for the cement to be mixed. Are you willing to help me again?'

Stratos nodded eagerly and Benediktos continued. 'I need you to go back into the tunnel with the brick and a small pot of cement. You'll have to find the hole with your hand and then half fill it with cement. Once you have done that you can push the brick up into place and the extra cement will spread around the sides. You then put a bit more cement over the brick and make it as smooth as possible. Do you understand?'

'I won't be able to see what I'm doing,' protested Stratos. 'I can't carry the torch if I have to use both hands to cement the brick and put it in place.'

'I'll come in behind you with the torch and give you as much light as possible. Once you have found the hole for the brick you'll really be able to do the rest just by touch.'

Stratos looked at Benediktos doubtfully. He had never tried to cement a brick into place.

Benediktos and Stratos waded across the cistern to the steps and climbed up to where many of the villagers were gathered watching the proceedings.

'Why did you send the boy in?' asked Theo.

'I needed someone smaller than me to get in a bit further to remove an obstruction. When the cement is mixed he's going in to do a repair for me, then I should be able to manage the rest.'

'Will you be finished today?' asked Theo anxiously.

Benediktos shook his head. 'I'll have to give it a week for the cement I put in today to set hard. Then I'll come back and give it a second coat. Give that another week and I'll check again. Provided it's dry and no more rubble has fallen you shouldn't have any more problems. You could then start to refill the cistern and check the flow through the outlet.'

'So how much will we be paying you?'

'I told you, by the day. I've made three journeys here and plan two more. That will be five day's work.'

Alesandros frowned. 'Two of those days you only came up to look at the structure and give advice. You didn't do any work.'

Benediktos looked at him reproachfully. 'That was the equivalent of work. I could have been elsewhere earning money and you couldn't have repaired it without my knowledge.'

'That's true,' Theo reassured Alesandros quickly. He did not want any argument over the price they were paying or the man could walk away and leave them with a useless cistern.

Alesandros shrugged. No wonder Theo never had any money if he did not bargain and try to negotiate a cheaper price. To his knowledge on the two days that Benediktos claimed to have worked previously he had left shortly after mid-day and probably gone to another job where he would claim a full day's pay.

Benediktos waited for Alesandros to challenge him. He had his answers ready for requesting a full day's pay each time he had visited, there was the time it took him to travel from Neapoli and working barefoot in the cold and dirty water of a cistern was not pleasant.

'Right, then, we'll get some cement made up and then my assistant and I will go back down and fix that brick.'

Stratos grinned with delight at being called Benediktos's assistant. 'How will the brick stay up in the roof until the cement is set?' he asked, suddenly having a vision of having to lie in the tunnel holding it for some hours.

'We'll take a stout stick down with us and I'll show you how to wedge it up. I don't want you going down into that tunnel when I'm not here, so it has to stay there until I come again.'

Stratos nodded. He had no desire to go into the dark tunnel without Benediktos behind him holding a torch.

Theo and Alesandros watched, along with most of the villagers as the boy crawled inside followed by Benediktos. It seemed an age before Benediktos finally wriggled out, swiftly followed by

Stratos. Benediktos entered the tunnel again whilst Stratos stood patiently waiting. Eventually Benediktos emerged and handed Stratos the empty bucket.

'You can give it a rinse out over by the steps. Take it up and ask the men to mix another bucketful. Give me a shout when it's ready. It will be too heavy for you to carry down the steps.'

Stratos obeyed and finally called down to Benediktos that the cement was ready. Vassilis carried the bucket half way down the steps to where Benediktos met him. Holding the handle of the bucket with both hands Benediktos negotiated the stone steps carefully, his back against the wall. Once Vassilis had climbed back up Stratos scampered down the steps and followed Benediktos over to where he was preparing to work.

'Can I help?' he asked eagerly.

'I doubt I'll need you again this week, but I will on my next visit.'

'Can I stay and watch?'

Benediktos shrugged. 'If you want. It's not very exciting.'

Stratos stood in the dirty water and moved his head from side to side, trying to see exactly how Benediktos was repairing the brickwork inside the tunnel. He could hear the trowel scrape on the side of the bucket and then the slap of the cement as Benediktos threw it onto the wall, but it was impossible to see past the man's shoulders and into the darkness.

By the time Benediktos emerged the watching villagers had lost interest and drifted away. He smiled at Stratos and handed him the empty bucket.

'Rinse it out over by the steps. We don't want any cement residue going into the tunnel. When you get back up make sure you wash your hands thoroughly. There's lime in the cement and it will make your hands rough and sore. Rub a bit of olive oil into them tonight; that will help.'

Stratos obeyed and finally climbed up the steps with the clean bucket to join Benediktos who was talking to Theo.

'I've done as much as possible today. The boy did a good job with the brick and I've put a first coat of cement on the sides and roof as far in as I can reach. I'll be back tomorrow to replace the loose bricks at the entrance. Then I'll return the following week and check for any problems and put another coat on.'

Theo took five drachmas from his pocket and placed them in Stratos's hand. 'I reckon you've earned that,' he smiled.

Stratos looked at the money in surprise. 'What do I do with it?' he asked.

'Whatever you want. Buy something for yourself when the pedlar comes through next.'

Stratos looked at the money again. 'I'll give it to Grandma,' he said. 'She'll know what to spend it on.'

Benediktos smirked. If he had brought an assistant with him he would certainly have asked for more than five drachmas for his services.

Benediktos visited Kastelli twice more, completing the cement work and the next week checking it was sound and dry. Declaring himself satisfied he informed Theo that the cistern could be refilled with water.

Theo shook his head, 'I'll not tell them yet. The only way to refill it would be with the fresh water from the well. We can't use too much of that during the summer. At the moment I'm limiting the farmers to thirty buckets a day each. That's about all they can manage by the time they've carried it to their fields and watered the crops. Another few months and we should get some rain. The cistern will soon fill up then and where the water runs down from the surrounding hills the well will be replenished.'

Benediktos shrugged. He was not concerned with the refilling of the cistern. He had completed his work and been paid. As he rode out of the village to return to Neapoli he heard Stratos calling after him.

He stopped and frowned. 'What's the problem?'

Stratos suddenly seemed shy and lost for words. 'Can I come with you?' he asked finally.

'Come with me? Whatever for?'

'I'd like to work for you and learn how to do repairs,' answered Stratos eagerly.

'What about your father? What would he say?'

'My Pappa is somewhere in Neapoli. He hasn't been down to see us since my Name Day. Grandma wouldn't mind. She's always saying I should find some useful work to do and make some money.'

'How old are you?'

'Pappa said I would be thirteen by my next Name Day.'

Benediktos nodded slowly. 'Well, I'll tell you what; I'll come back to Kastelli next year and if you still want to come with me and work I'll speak to your Grandma. How would that be?'

Stratos's face fell. 'Can't I come with you now?'

'I can't just turn up at my house with you. There would be nowhere for you to sleep. Besides, your Grandma would be worried that you had run away. No, I'll need to talk to her and assure her that you'll be looked after properly.'

'Promise you will come back next year?' asked Stratos anxiously.

'I promise,' Benediktos assured the lad. To have a young apprentice to train up would not be a bad idea. The boy obviously had no idea about money, so would work happily for his keep and a few drachmas in his pocket.

June 1911

Alesandros rode to Kastelli and tethered his donkey to the side window railing, remembering with a smile how frightened Theo's daughter had been when the donkey had refused to move for her. He knocked on the door and Sofia answered and asked him in. She looked nervously over his shoulder to see if the donkey was tethered near the steps. Theo was sitting in his chair, the rhythmical noise of Maria's weaving lulling him to sleep.

'Hello, Theo.' Alesandros greeted him heartily and Theo's eyes shot open.

He struggled to his feet. 'What brings you here, Alesandros? It isn't time to collect tax or money from crops, is it?'

'I hoped you might have some rent money to start to reduce the interest you owe me.'

Theo shook his head. 'Alesandros, I do not have the money to repay you at the moment. I have tried to save money from the rents, but there are always expenses that I had not expected. After the apple harvest I should be able to make a payment.'

'Don't forget that some of those trees belong to me. I will expect my share. I suggest you ask Father Symeon to look after all you are paid and that way you can pay me and reduce some of the outstanding interest. Have the villagers been paying their rents to you regularly?'

'It's been difficult for them. Due to the lack of water that is available their crops are not as good as usual. One or two are a little behind.'

'Then insist they pay you up to date.'

'I cannot.' Theo sighed. 'They blame me for increasing their rent and for not letting them draw more water from the well and filling the cistern.'

Sofia entered and placed a plate of biscuits on the table. As she returned to the scullery Alesandros looked after her. She had certainly matured during the last few months. Why was he looking elsewhere for a wife when there was such an attractive young woman in Kastelli? With a little bit of careful manoeuvring he should be able to make Theo agree to him marrying his daughter,

'You offered me your house as security,' Alesandros reminded him. 'The other alternative would be for you to sign over the ownership of the cottages.'

'If I sign the cottages over to you I will have no income at all. I will be a beggar. I cannot do that to my wife and daughter.'

'If you had taken a loan from the bank they would demand that you relinquish your property to them.'

'I know. I wanted to avoid that dilemma. To borrow the money from you was cheaper than from the bank and I expected to have enough saved to repay you a sizeable amount.'

Alesandros looked at the distraught man before him. Despite being the wealthiest man in the area Theo had never managed to have the full amount for his tax and been forced to borrow. As the interest had accumulated he had given away his orchards and olive trees, now he finally admitted he had only property with which he could settle his debt. Alesandros did not want the responsibility of owning the cottages, but he would certainly like to live in the large house and be the head man of the village due to his status.

He leaned forwards and spoke quietly to Theo. 'Is your daughter betrothed?'

Theo shook his head. 'We had arranged for her to marry a distant cousin. Sadly he died whilst he was still a boy and I know of no one else who would be suitable. She is young yet, there is still time to find a suitor for her.'

Alesandros tapped his fingers together. 'I have a suggestion to make. I will marry your daughter.'

'You?' Theo looked at Alesandros in surprise. 'You want to marry my Sofia?' He shook his head.

'You have to sign property over to me to settle your debts. You do not want to part with the cottages as they are now your sole income. That leaves only your house. What am I going to do with it? I am not married so I would sell it. If I married Sofia the property would eventually go to our children,' explained Alesandros patiently. Sofia was certainly attractive. It would be no hardship to be married to her.

'She is too young,' protested Theo, 'and you are more than twice her age.'

Alesandros shrugged. 'I'm mature enough to make excuses for her youth and inexperience. You say you have no one else suitable in mind. If you have lost your house the only choice you would then have would be one of the village boys and she would become a farmer's wife. I suggest we have an agreement. Your daughter becomes my wife and the house would not only be her dowry, but the full settlement of your outstanding debts. If it is agreeable to you I suggest we are married next spring. That will give you enough time to prepare your daughter for marriage and to accept me as her husband.'

Theo looked at the man in front of him. He was certainly respectable, far better educated than him and also had a good deal of money. His daughter would be assured of a comfortable married life; if only there was not such a large age gap he would have welcomed Alesandros as a son-in-law.

He sighed. 'I'll speak to Maria.'

Sofia was worried. There was something going on between her parents that she did not understand. They would talk quietly between themselves; breaking off from the conversation as she entered the room. Her mother would look up from her weaving, frown and shake her head and her father would gaze at her with tears forming in his eyes. Was she ill and they did not like to tell her the bad news?

Theo counted out the money that he kept in the box beneath the bed. He could count to ten and made small piles on the table. He had eight piles and some change left over. He scooped the piles together and placed them in his pocket. He would pay Father Symeon a visit and ask the priest how much money he had and if it was sufficient to pay Alesandros.

Father Symeon looked at Theo sympathetically. 'There is nowhere near enough here. The amount needed to repair the cistern was over one thousand drachmas. You have eighty drachmas.'

'How much is the church willing to contribute?' asked Theo anxiously.

'I have been authorised to pay two hundred drachmas from the church funds. You still need ten times the amount you have with you to settle the debt to Alesandros.'

Theo sighed. There was no way out of his dilemma. He would have to tell Sofia that she was going to marry Alesandros.

Sofia looked at her father in disbelief. 'I am to be married to the tax collector? I don't want to be married, and certainly not to him. He's an old man.'

'Sofia,' Theo took her hand. 'It was not my wish for you to marry him. I would like to see you with a young man who has a respectable income from his work. The village boys are not suitable for you. I have to ask you to make this sacrifice for your mother and myself. I owe Alesandros a great deal of money. I have no way to repay him except by giving him our house. He has agreed that if you become his wife he will cancel all my debt to him. If you refuse to marry him he will take the house and sell it. He says he has no use for it unless he has a wife.'

'Sell our house?' Sofia looked at her father in horror. 'Where would we live?'

'In one of the cottages. He has assured me he will not dispose of the house if you are his wife. It will eventually belong to your children.'

Sofia wrinkled her nose in distaste. 'I do not want to have his children.'

Theo patted his daughter's hand. 'I realise this has come as a shock to you. Talk to your mother. She will explain your duties as a wife.'

Tears filled Sofia's eyes. 'I don't want to get married, Pappa. Please don't make me.'

'It will not be until next Spring. You will have become used to the idea by then.'

Sofia shook her head; her tears falling freely and she took a rag from her pocket and wiped her eyes and nose. Tryphaine was marrying Nikos in the autumn and seemed to have accepted the arrangement and even be quite excited at the prospect. She could not envisage being excited at becoming Alesandros's wife.

Maria regarded her daughter anxiously. Sofia's eyes were red from weeping; she no longer smiled and went about her duties in the house automatically. If only Theo had been more sensible with his money the situation would not have arisen. His father had left him a sizeable sum when he died and Theo had paid for him to have a lavish funeral with a Mass said for him for the following ten years.

Still with a considerable lump sum and money coming in from the rents and crops, Theo had taken it upon himself to provide the Easter lamb for the village and a box of candles. Whenever a villager married he gave generously at their wedding and at the Christenings that followed over the years. He took his responsibilities towards the villagers seriously. Repairs were done to the cottages without any charge, and if the occupants were unable to pay their weekly rent he would happily take a chicken or some eggs as recompense.

Had he put money aside to pay the tax he would be charged at the end of each year he would still have had enough money for them to live comfortably, but Theo liked to gamble. Two or three evenings during the week, and every Saturday, he would visit the taverna to play backgammon or cards. The stakes were never high, but by the time Theo had treated every man there to a glass or two of wine and lost consistently throughout the evening he would return home with at least five drachmas less in his pocket than he had started out with.

Maria had tried remonstrating with him, but he had smiled and told her not to worry. There was always money for food to put on their table, new boots were bought whenever necessary and he gave her a gold necklace on her Name Day. He assured her that the small amount of gambling he took part in amounted to next to nothing and he was convinced that sooner or later he would hit a winning streak, winning all his money back and more from his compatriots.

Maria did not remind him that the money for the food and often for their new boots came from her selling her weaving to the travelling man who passed through the village purchasing the woollen and cotton cloth from the women. Over all the years they had now been married Theo had not been blessed by a winning streak. She could not fault her husband's kindness and generosity, his willingness to please and help those less fortunate, but she wished she understood numbers. That way she could have kept account of the money coming in and hidden some of it away so that when Alesandros called his bill would have been paid.

Maria called Sofia to come and sit beside her at the weaving loom. Sofia obeyed, thinking her mother was going to demonstrate an intricate pattern to her. Sofia laid her shuttle aside and turned to her daughter.

'Sofia, it breaks my heart to see you looking so unhappy.'

Tears filled Sofia's eyes. 'I don't want to marry Alesandros, but I don't want us to be turned out of our house by him.'

'I do not believe Alesandros is a bad man. He tried to help your Pappa by lending him money, but when you lend money you need to have it repaid. Your Pappa understands that and he has done his best. He also knows this is a good marriage for you.'

Sofia bit her lip. 'He will want to do things to me.'

'Alesandros is not a young man. He should not make excessive demands on you. You may find it distasteful at first, but you will come to accept it as your duty as a wife. Once you are pregnant you will have a good excuse to refuse him.'

Spring 1912

Sofia sat with her hands folded demurely in her lap. During the summer Alesandros had paid a number of social calls on the family.

He had smiled at her, patted her hand and called her "my dear", but she felt no more for him than she would for one of the old men in the village who did the same. She was reconciled to her forthcoming marriage now, but had no interest in the preparations, despite her mother's encouragement.

On this occasion, Alesandros greeted her as usual and then said he must talk over arrangements with her father. Thinking Alesandros had tax matters to discuss she retired to the scullery after bringing in wine and ascertaining that Alesandros would only be staying for a little refreshment as he wished to be back in Aghios Nikolaos before nightfall.

She was surprised when her father called her urgently within a few minutes. Concerned that the wine she had served had soured she hurried into the living room, a worried frown on her face.

'Yes, Pappa? Is it the wine?'

Theo shook his head. 'No, you need to know the arrangements Alesandros proposes for when you two are married.'

Sofia compressed her lips and sat obediently.

Alesandros turned his chair so that he could view Theo, Maria and Sofia at the same time.

'As you know, Sofia, when we are married I will be moving

in to live in this house. I have suggested to your parents that they begin to make arrangements now to move elsewhere.'

Sofia's hand flew to her mouth. 'You cannot turn my parents out,' she remonstrated.

'I am not proposing to throw them out on the street. As I understand it, Kassianae works here to enable her to pay the rent on her mother's cottage. We will not be employing Kassianae so she will not have the extra money for the rent. To solve the problem her mother can go to live in their cottage. That will leave a cottage empty where your parents will be able to live.'

Sofia shook her head. 'There is hardly room in Kassianae's cottage. She already has two children.'

'I'm sure they will be able to find space for her.'

'But why? Why have my parents got to leave their home?'

'For the simple reason, my dear, that it will no longer be their home. It will be our home. I wish to have time alone with my wife.'

'Why do you need time alone with me?'

'We need to get to know each other. I will be out each day and when I return in the evening I will expect a meal ready for me and my wife available to chat with me. I am not forbidding you to see your parents or spend time with them during the day, but I do not want them here when I come home or during the weekends. That is our time to spend together.'

Sofia looked at her parents. What did they talk about during the evenings? Her father either went off to the taverna or fell asleep in his chair. Her mother would continue with her weaving during the summer months and she and Sofia would sit by the fire and sew during the winter. Their conversation consisted entirely of sewing or cooking and she did not think Alesandros would be interested in either subject.

'Nikos moved into the cottage with Tryphaine and her parents once they were married. Why can't you move in here with mine, Alesandros?' Sofia was surprised at her own daring in challenging him.

'I do not think it a suitable arrangement for a newly married couple to be continually in the presence of other members of the family. Your parents will still think of you as a child and expect you to do as they say. I will be your husband and I will expect you to be guided by me. This can lead to conflict. I wish to avoid that.'

Sofia felt helpless. She could not refuse to marry Alesandros or their home would be gone forever and she would find herself living in a small cottage until she finally married one of the village boys and he would then add to the over-crowding.

Nor could she refuse the overtures Alesandros would surely make to her. It would be his right as her husband to have his sexual demands fulfilled whenever he wished. He had voiced his reasons to be alone in the house with her logically and she could not claim that he was forbidding her access to her family.

Sofia gave Alesandros a cold look. 'I will prepare your refreshment,' she said stiffly and returned to the scullery. She was shaking with both rage and grief. How dare he turn her parents out from their home?

Alesandros continued talking to her father. 'I suggest you apprise Kassianae of the situation this week. That will give her ample time to arrange for her mother to move out and for you and Maria to move your belongings into her house.'

'But my weaving loom,' protested Maria. 'It is too large to fit into a cottage. There would not be enough space, besides it would have to be taken to pieces to go through the door.'

'Your loom can stay here and you can work on it as you wish during the week whilst I am away from the village. I do not want you working on it during the evenings when I am home or at the weekends.' Alesandros turned to Theo. 'In many ways the arrangement is to your advantage. I will be responsible for any repairs needed on this house and you will only have to maintain your cottage.'

'And those of the villagers,' added Theo morosely.

'You will have the rents they pay you each week. That should be sufficient for you to live on and do whatever is necessary. Had you taken my advice and insisted the tenants paid you on time you would probably not find yourself in this difficult position.'

Theo frowned. 'I will still have to pay the tax for their olive trees and the orchard harvest.'

'Then, as I have told you before, you must save some of your income so you have the full amount of money when I present you with the bill from the government.'

Theo let out a deep sigh. He had never managed to save any of his income in the past and he was not likely to be able to do so in the future. He had bought the lamb for the Easter celebrations and supplied the candles as usual this year and wondered if Alesandros realised that would become his responsibility in future. His daughter would have to be provided with a wedding feast that was lavish enough to fit her status, and although all the villagers would contribute dishes they had cooked he would still have to ensure there was plenty of wine.

Sofia had sat on her parents' bed with a fixed smile on her face trying to look happy when the villagers brought her their gifts and sang the traditional wedding songs to her. Many of them had not been inside the house before and looked around curiously, surprised at the sparseness of the furnishings. Kassianae had always told them of the comforts the house held; she had obviously exaggerated.

Sofia had dressed carefully in the new blouse and skirt that her mother had made for her, grateful that no angry spot had developed on her face over night as happened occasionally. Now she sat with her mother waiting for Alesandros to arrive in the village.

Sofia looked around the bare living room. She had insisted that her parents removed the wall hangings, their bedding and the china plates and glasses of which her mother was so proud.

'What is Alesandros going to say when he finds so much is missing?' asked Maria.

Sofia shrugged. 'He owns the house, not your possessions.'

'Without the rugs and wall hangings the house will be cold in the winter,' observed Maria. 'We certainly have no use for all of them in the cottage.'

Sofia smiled. 'I know, but if Alesandros wants them back he will have to buy them from you or pay you to weave some more, and make sure you take whatever you want in the way of utensils.'

'What about the bedding? I should have left some for you.'

Sofia shook her head. 'I have no intention of sleeping in your bed. I will make this clear to Alesandros. We will use my room upstairs.'

Maria pursed her lips. 'I don't think he will be very happy about that.'

'Then he can sleep down here – alone.'

Maria looked at her daughter. She would never have believed that the quiet, biddable girl would become so determined and intent on making Alesandros's life uncomfortable, whatever hardships she had to suffer as a consequence.

The sound of a lyra and drum beats came to Sofia's ears. Alesandros had arrived. She watched him walk past the house; he had no companions with him and the celebrations, compared with those for Tryphaine and Nikos were muted. Sofia knew that would not stop the villages from partaking their fill of the feast and dancing with joyous abandon. She gave a deep sigh. The dreaded time had come.

Sofia followed in his wake, the villagers showering her with flowers and myrtle leaves for good fortune, but she hardly noticed. At the church she stood with Alesandros and completed the ceremony, responding to Father Symeon without showing any sign of emotion.

It was with a feeling of satisfaction that Sofia performed her wedding dance perfectly, whilst Alesandros stumbled and missed some of his steps. As they moved close together he gave a slight shrug.

'I am sorry. I have never been a dancer,' but Sofia made no acknowledgement of his apology.

Their dance completed, Sofia and Alesandros led the way back to the large house, the villagers following behind and the musicians now playing vigorously. At the door Sofia smeared honey in the shape of a cross on the three sides of the wooden frame, urged on by the villagers. She performed the ritual of kicking farming implements inside with her right foot whilst smashing a pomegranate, although it seemed a foolish act to her as Alesandros was not a farmer.

The villagers crowded inside after them and Panayiotis was placed on her lap. Sofia had not expressed any preference regarding the sex of her first child, but had agreed that Alesandros would probably want a boy; most men did. She endured the boy's wriggling and his feet kicking at her shins whilst the traditional songs wishing her happiness, good fortune and many healthy children were sung with gusto. As the afternoon wore on the villagers drifted away and the women could be seen passing by carrying laden dishes up towards the church.

'It is time we returned to the square,' Sofia informed Alesandros. 'They cannot start the feasting without us.'

'Could you not make up the bed before we leave?'

Sofia looked at him and raised her eyebrows. 'The bed is made up. I put a new clean sheet on today.'

Alesandros looked pointedly at her parents' bed in the corner of the living room.

'We are not sleeping down here,' Sofia said firmly. 'That is my parents' bed and I would not feel at all comfortable using that.'

'They are not using it. There is no reason why we should not.'

Sofia stood up and looked at her husband of a few hours. 'If you wish to sleep down here you may. I will be sleeping upstairs in my old bedroom.'

Alesandros looked her in surprise. He had not expected her to show such spirit.

Alesandros drank sparingly and did not join in the dancing. He watched Sofia as she danced with the other women and girls, admiring her neat footwork and elegant grace. As she danced the villagers approached her, pinning money to her skirt and blouse and a few walked over to Alesandros and pushed some notes into his pocket.

Sofia's mother joined her in a sedate dance and Sofia took the opportunity to speak to her quietly.

'I am going around to the back of the church. Come with me. If anyone asks we are going to relieve ourselves.'

Maria looked at her daughter in surprise, but followed her unquestioningly. Once out of sight Sofia hurriedly began to unpin some of the money from her skirt and pushed it into her mother's hands.

'Give that to Pappa. Alesandros does not need the money.'

Maria pushed the folded notes into her bodice. The money was usually given to the bride and groom to enable them to buy any household articles they needed, but Maria knew she had left sufficient utensils in the house for Sofia.

Maria frowned. 'Your Pappa may not accept it. He is a proud man.'

Sofia shrugged. 'Put it into his box when you have the opportunity. He will not know it has come from me.'

'Has Alesandros mentioned the missing rugs?' asked Maria.

Sofia smiled. 'I don't think he has had a chance to realise how bare the house is now. He wanted me to make up your bed before we left the house. I told him I was sleeping upstairs and he could sleep wherever he wished.'

'Sofia! You should not speak to him like that. He is your husband now.'

'My husband he may be, but he will find I am not prepared for him to dictate to me. If I disagree with him or do not want to do something I will tell him. This is a marriage of convenience,

Mamma, not from love.'

Maria shook her head. She hoped Alesandros would not be violent towards her daughter if she persisted in her wilful ways.

Sofia continued to dance until finally Alesandros approached her. 'It is time we left. Everyone is enjoying themselves. We will not be missed.'

'I, too, am enjoying myself.'

'Sofia, I realise you are delaying being alone with me. Sooner or later the villagers will notice we are staying far longer than is usual for a newly married couple and start to gossip.'

Sofia sighed. However long she stayed at the gathering the time would eventually come when she had to leave and return to the house with only Alesandros as company.

They walked back along the road in silence and Alesandros opened the door for her to enter. 'I suggest you go and prepare yourself for bed. I will come up to you in a short while.'

Thankfully Sofia hurried up to her room. She was grateful that she would not have the embarrassment of undressing before Alesandros. She would feign sleep when he joined her and hope he saw fit not to disturb her.

Alesandros looked at the still figure in the bed. He removed his outer garments and slipped onto the mattress beside her. He groped for her hand and felt her stiffen. She was obviously not asleep as she was pretending.

'Sofia, I know you are not asleep. I wish to speak to you.'

Sofia did not reply.

Alesandros persisted 'Sofia, I know you did not wish to marry me. You are very young and probably do not feel ready for the role of a wife yet. I am not going to impose myself on you tonight as I realise you have had a busy day and no doubt you are exhausted. We will talk in the morning when we are both rested.' He squeezed her hand and released it, turned his back on her and settled himself comfortably.

Sofia opened her eyes and cast a glance in his direction. His breathing was already becoming rhythmical. At least she was to be spared from any unpleasant indignities that night.

When Sofia woke she saw Alesandros had already left their bed; hurriedly she dressed and went down to the living room. There was no sign of him. She re-laid and lit the fire that had gone out over night due to lack of attention before they had retired to bed and once the kindling had taken hold she placed a pan of water on the tripod to warm through. Taking two buckets from the scullery she walked up to the well. Since Stratos had left the village to work for Benediktos she had collected the water for the house each morning as she had in the past.

She called at the cottage where her parents now lived and knocked on the door. Her father answered and smiled in pleasure when he saw his daughter.

'I've brought some water for you,' Sofia explained. 'I'll bring it in, collect your empty buckets and use them for my water.'

'That is very thoughtful of you. Your Mamma has a struggle to carry one bucket nowadays.' It had not occurred to Theo that he could easily collect two buckets of water. Going to the well for the water was a woman's job.

Maria raised her eyebrows at her daughter and Sofia shook he head. 'I cannot stop, Mamma. I have left some water warming over the fire.'

When she returned to the house Alesandros was sitting at the table. 'Is the water that you are heating for me to use to wash and shave?' he asked

Sofia looked at him. 'It is courteous to say good morning before asking a question,' she said coldly and Alesandros had the grace to blush.

'I am sorry. Did you sleep well?'

'Yes, thank you. The water is for you. I'll bring a bowl. Whilst you are shaving I will make some coffee.'

Alesandros nodded. 'Whilst we drink the coffee we will sit and talk,' he announced. 'There are a number of things we need to discuss. I am not going out until later today so we have plenty of time.'

Sofia's heart sank. She had expected Alesandros to ride off on his donkey and she would have the day to herself. Her mother could have come to use the loom and she would be able to forget for a few hours that she had a husband.

Alesandros smoothed his moustache into the upward ends that he favoured and took a seat across the table from Sofia. He gazed at her earnestly.

'I spoke to you briefly last night when we were in bed. I do not believe you were asleep. I think you heard my words.'

This time it was Sofia's turn to blush. 'I'll not resist you, Alesandros. Mamma has told me what to expect.'

Alesandros nodded. 'I'm pleased to hear it. I would not want to force myself upon you, but that will be for later. We have other things to discuss now.'

Sofia looked at him in surprise. She had expected the consummation of their marriage to be the most important thing on his mind.

'You had hot water prepared for me this morning and I was grateful. I will expect that every morning. Once a week I will expect you to have enough hot water ready for me to be able to take a bath. Whilst I am shaving I will expect you to make me a small parcel of rusks and olives to take with me. I am not always in a village where I am able to get something to eat at mid-day. Each day when I return I will expect a meal ready for me. How you occupy yourself during the day whilst I am away is not my concern.' Alesandros took some notes from his pocket. He counted off a number and placed them to one side. 'That is money that I have to pay in at the tax office,' he explained. 'I will be placing it in the drawer beneath the wash stand and it is never to be touched. It does not belong to me. At night the doors to the house will be locked. I do not want to find I have been robbed.'

Sofia was about to say that there had never been a robbery in the village and realised that if any money did go missing Alesandros would automatically assume she or her parents had taken it. She would certainly not lay a finger on any money he placed in there.

He waved some notes at Sofia and placed them on the dresser. 'That is for you to buy whatever you need for our meals. I don't expect you to waste it. You have ample there. The remainder is my money.' He placed the notes back into his pocket.

Sofia looked at the pile of notes. She had no real idea how much goods cost at the shops. Her mother would give her a note from the pot on the dresser when she sent her shopping and when she returned she would place any notes or coins she had received in change back into the pot. If the shop keeper had declared she had insufficient with her for her purchases she would return later to pay the balance.

'From my money I will buy you your new boots and winter cloak as you need them. If you need to buy weaving or sewing materials ask me to bring them back for you from the town. They will be less expensive than those the pedlar brings around. Whilst we are talking about weaving; where are the rugs from the floor and the wall hangings?'

'They belonged to my parents. They have taken their possessions with them as was their right.'

'I would have expected them to think of your comfort. The house will be cold during the winter.'

Sofia shrugged. 'I am sure my mother would be willing to sell some of them back to you.'

Alesandros nodded slowly. 'And the china plates and glasses?'

'My mother had purchased those over the years. She has left me enough plates and glasses to serve you your meals decently.'

'No doubt we will be able to manage for a while.'

'If you wish to buy more you have the money the villagers gave you at the wedding feast.'

'That is true. You also had money pinned to your clothing. Where is that?'

'Still pinned to my skirt. I was too tired to bother with it last night.'

'You can unpin it later and give it to me.'

Sofia was about to argue that the money belonged to her when she realised that is actual fact it belonged to both of them. If Alesandros wanted to use it to purchase plates and glasses she had no right to object, and she had no idea what she would need it for. She felt a sneaky pleasure that she had been able to pass some to her mother.

'I do not want to hear that you have complained about my treatment of you to your mother or anyone in the village. I'll not treat you harshly or raise a fist to you. If you have a problem you come and tell me. We will talk about it and solve it together. On Sunday, when we have attended church, I expect you to walk back to the house with me, holding my arm and with a smile on your face. I hope that in a few months when you realise I am not an ogre your smile will be genuine.

'Now, to our other business. Your mother will be coming to check our sheets at the end of the week.' Sofia felt the heat rising to her face. 'I suggest we retire upstairs for a while now and you allow me to perform a husband's duty. Once that is done I will ride to Aghios Nikolaos, pay in the tax money and collect my belongings.'

Sofia waited until Alesandros had risen from the bed, dressed and left the room. Her legs felt stiff and her thighs ached. She was thankful that her mother had warned her there would probably be some blood on the sheets. This would confirm to Alesandros that she was a virgin and to her mother that the consummation had taken place.

Alesandros had been gentle with her. He had run his hands over her naked body and complimented her on her beautiful proportions, kissed her cheeks and neck, before stroking and kissing her breasts. She had lain there submissively as his attentions became more intimate and had finally entered her. She had cried out, but the experience was not as painful as she had expected.

Now she examined herself carefully. She felt bruised and tender, but also relieved. The ordeal was over. Her mouth was dry and she wished she had some water up in the bedroom and not have to wait until she had dressed before going down to slake her thirst. She hoped Alesandros would leave the house soon as she wished to remove her clothes and wash her body. She was loath to undress before Alesandros; he might think she was inviting him to return upstairs with her.

When she entered the living room Alesandros was sitting at the table and he nodded to her. 'I was waiting for you to come downstairs so I could tell you I am leaving now. Upon my return I will tether the donkey up by the orchard, so you need have no fear of her trapping you in the house.' He smiled briefly. 'I am sure you will soon become used to her. I will not be asking you to attend to her, unless, for any reason I was unable. She needs fresh water every day and when there is no grass available she needs a bale of hay within her reach.'

Sofia nodded silently. If, for any awful reason, she had to attend to the donkey she would ask her father to accompany her. He could have a stout stick with him and beat the donkey back if she came too close.

Alesandros stood up and placed his bag over his shoulder. 'Remember, your money for any shopping is on the dresser. When you hear me riding towards the house in a short while I expect you to open the door and wave me on my way. I plan to be back home well before dark and I'll be looking forward to the meal you have prepared for me.' He leaned towards her and touched his lips to her cheek. 'I think we can have a happy life together, Sofia.'

Sofia waited until she heard the donkey approaching, then

opened the front door and waved dutifully to Alesandros. He raised his hand in return and she watched until he had rounded the corner before closing and locking the door. At last she could strip off her clothes and wash her soiled body.

Alesandros arrived back in Kastelli with two large sacks slung across his donkey in front of the saddle. He tethered the donkey to the front window ironwork, removed the sacks and opened the door. Maria was sitting at her weaving loom and he greeted her cordially.

'Good afternoon, Maria. Finish whatever you are doing,' he waved his hand towards the loom. 'I have to take the donkey up to the orchard.'

Maria bobbed her head at Alesandros. 'I'll be at a convenient place to stop in a few minutes, Alesandros.'

Hurriedly she finished the line of weaving and fastened the threads securely. Sofia came from the scullery bearing a pot which she handed to her mother.

'Don't let Alesandros see you taking it home. He doesn't need to know you are sharing our food.'

Maria held the pot beneath her apron. 'Thank you, Sofia. I'll no doubt become used to having less time to weave and manage to have a meal prepared before I come over.'

Sofia shook her head. 'You can't keep running backwards and forwards to the cottage to check on your cooking. It's no hardship to me to prepare a little extra. Sooner or later Alesandros will realise that it makes sense for you to return here and live with us.'

Sofia glanced at her daughter doubtfully. How her daughter was going to persuade her husband to allow them back into her home she had no idea.

Alesandros carried his sacks up the stairs and called down to Sofia. "I'd like some hot water ready to wash when I have unpacked. Is there an empty trunk where I can store my clothes?' he asked.

Sofia placed a container of water over the fire and mounted

the stairs. Surely he could have looked in the other room to see if there was a suitable trunk in there. She opened the door to the spare room that had always been used for storage.

'There's one in here. Do you want to take it through to the bedroom?'

'It would be more convenient to have my clothes to hand in the mornings and not have to dress in the storage room.'

Alesandros dragged the empty trunk into the bedroom and began to unpack his clothes from the sack, handing them to Sofia to fold. She noticed that he had five shirts and three pairs of trousers. He threw one of the shirts on the floor.

'That shirt needs to be washed,' he announced.

'I'll do it tomorrow,' answered Sofia. She was not prepared to spend the evening washing his shirt when he had others that he could wear. She would add one of her blouses and ask her mother to bring over any washing she had. There was no need to waste hot water.

His unpacking completed Alesandros returned downstairs carrying a large, leather bound book and two boxes. Sofia followed him, carrying the soiled shirt in her hand. He placed the Bible on the dresser along with the larger box and turned to her.

'That book is a Bible. The same as Father Symeon has in church. Treat it carefully and with respect. I will read chapters from it to you on occasions. It could help you to understand more fully whatever Father Symeon has preached during the service. The other box holds a camera. I will explain how that works to you a later date, but please never touch it without my permission.' Alesandros stepped closer to Sofia and took her hand. 'Here is a gift for you. It is a wedding present and also for your Name Day.'

Sofia looked at Alesandros in surprise. Her mother had made her a new blouse and skirt to wear for her wedding and her father had given her a new pair of dancing shoes that she had all but worn out having danced for so long at the wedding feast. She had not expected Alesandros to give her anything.

'Thank you,' she said, gasping in surprise when she opened the box and saw the heavy gold chain inside. 'Thank you, Alesandros. I have never had anything so beautiful before.' She slipped it over her head feeling the warmth of the gold beneath her fingers.

'It is not for you to wear every day,' he stipulated. 'You can wear it to church on Sundays and show it off.'

'May I wear it tonight?' she asked and Alesandros nodded.

Sofia hesitated; then placed a chaste kiss on Alesandros's cheek. Most of the village women had gold necklaces that they wore to church on Sundays or whenever there as a special celebration. Her mother had one for each year she had been married to Theodopolous and had worn them all at Sofia's wedding, claiming later they were so heavy they had made her neck ache.

Sofia felt a pang of guilt. Because Alesandros had seized her father's house in repayment of a debt she had automatically thought of him as a wicked man. So far he had talked to her quietly and reasonably and had given her no reason to object to his behaviour.

Sofia found the work in the house arduous. Each morning she delivered two buckets of water to her parents' cottage and returned to the well to draw two more for herself. She wished Stratos was still in the village and she could ask him to carry the heavy buckets for her. She straightened their bed, lifted the rugs from the floors and swept away any dust that had accumulated, deciding whilst she did so on the meal she would prepare for Alesandros and her parents. Each day she had to make a batch of bread, and again made sufficient for her mother to collect a loaf from the baker later. Having delivered the dough, she would call at the shops or one of the cottages and purchase whatever she needed in the way of poultry or vegetables.

Maria would arrive and sit at the weaving loom, whilst her daughter scrubbed the front steps, swept the yard, washed clothing and prepared a meal. By the time Sofia had completed her daily duties she had no time left to scrub the floors or clean the windows as Kassianae had done previously. Before her mother had been ill they had shared the chores, usually completing them during the morning and giving her the afternoon free to either spend with the village girls or sit and sew. When Kassianae worked for them Sofia once again had time to spend as she pleased.

Alesandros sat at the table, piles of notes before him that he counted carefully and made a note of their totals in his book. He placed the usual amount on the dresser for Sofia and the remainder into his pocket. He looked around the room. He needed a secure place in which to hide his savings.

A shaft of autumn sunshine fell across the table, speckled with dust and cobweb. He looked up at the window in surprise.

'Sofia, when did you last clean the windows?' he asked.

'Kassianae did them before you told her to leave. I have no time for cleaning windows.'

Alesandros frowned. 'Your mother is here each day. Surely she could help you, or do you just sit and gossip together?'

'Mamma has to complete her own cleaning and make a meal before she comes here. Once she arrives she works all day at her weaving. She is trying to get at least three blankets finished before the traveller arrives in the village so he will buy them from her. I do as much as I can in the way of cleaning each day, but by the time I have made the bread, shopped, done the washing and prepared a meal there is no time left for anything else.'

Alesandros nodded and said no more. Sofia returned to the scullery. At least he had noticed the windows were dirty. She would clean them next week, but he would not get a hot meal that evening. She would claim that cleaning the windows had exhausted her and left her without time to prepare and cook a meal.

Maria remonstrated with her daughter. 'What will Alesandros say when he finds you are giving him only a cheese salad and bread for his supper?'

'I shall tell him I am so exhausted that he should be grateful that I had placed any food on a plate for him. I know what I'm doing, Mamma, but it will probably take a little time.' Sofia sat down beside her mother and took up her embroidery. 'I am entitled to have some time to myself. I am not his slave. He cannot make me work all day.'

Alesandros accepted his meal without comment.

'I've cleaned the windows,' stated Sofia.

Alesandros nodded. 'I noticed. They look a good deal better.' He spread a newspaper out on the table beside him and read whilst he ate. 'There is considerable dissent in Europe,' he announced. 'I thought we should know if the countries have settled their differences. When I have read the newspaper report I will tell you what it says.'

Sofia shrugged. She knew nothing about Europe and was not interested. Her arms and shoulders ached due to the unaccustomed cleaning. She listened dutifully when Alesandros read from his Bible to her, but she often had little understanding of the chapter and by the following Sunday she would have forgotten the content completely. He could have read the same chapter time and again to her and she would not have realised.

Finally Alesandros folded the newspaper and pushed his plate away from him. Sofia collected the plates and carried them into the scullery, washing them in the bucket of murky water she had used to clean the windows and giving them a quick rinse in some clean water. She would throw the dirty water down between the stones in the outhouse the following day. There was no shortage of water in the village, but she made her buckets of water last for as many jobs as possible to avoid having to collect more.

Alesandros had lit an oil lamp as darkness fell and he looked up as Sofia re-entered the living room.

'Sofia, we need to have a discussion,' he announced.

Sofia sat down dutifully and waited to hear what he had to say.

'I realise that you are unused to caring for the house on your own, but maybe you could organise your time a little better so you are able to complete all the jobs that are necessary each week. I noticed the chimney on the oil lamp needs to be washed. If it is not clean the lamp does not give sufficient light.'

'I'll do them tomorrow,' she said sulkily.

'There are other things that need to be done also. Our bed sheets need to be washed. They have not been changed since we were married. They are still stained.'

Sofia flushed. She knew she should have changed their sheets, but after showing them to her mother to prove their marriage had been consummated it had seemed sensible to leave the sheets on the bed in case she marked them again during the subsequent days, then her monthly time came and occasionally she inadvertently soiled them.

'I intended to wash them last week, but it rained,' she defended herself.

'It only rained one morning.'

'You needed your shirt washed.'

'Today it has not rained.'

'Today you wanted the windows cleaned,' she replied quickly. 'When my parents lived here the washing was done regularly. My mother would wash whilst I made the bread, went shopping and prepared a meal. One person cannot do the work of two people.'

'So that is why our meal was a simple salad and cheese this evening?'

Sofia nodded. 'I made the bread and did the shopping. I then cleaned the windows and by the time I had finished there was no time to make a cooked meal.'

'Had you thought about it yesterday you could have prepared two meals. We would have eaten one and the other would have been ready to cook for today.'

'I did not know I was going to spend most of my day cleaning windows!'

'It is something for you to bear in mind for the future when you know you have a time consuming cleaning job that needs to be done.'

Sofia looked at her husband mutinously. 'I shall be spending most of my day tomorrow washing sheets, so our meal may well be salad and cheese again.'

Alesandros shook his head. 'This is what I mean about organising your time. Tomorrow you could wash the lamp chimneys, change our bed sheets and prepare two meals. The following day you can wash the sheets and the meal is ready without the need for you to spend time on preparation.'

Sofia nodded. 'Very well.'

Alesandros smiled and patted her hand. She really was very biddable and obedient.

Sofia changed the sheets and prepared two meals as Alesandros had instructed, washed the glass chimneys to the oil lamps, but did not dust the dresser or sweep the rooms. She wondered if Alesandros would see there were still crumbs on the floor beneath the table and what his reaction would be when noticed them. She served the chicken pieces that she had boiled up with a plate of spaghetti and tomato sauce and Alesandros had eaten it appreciatively, complimenting her afterwards on the flavoursome dish.

'Thank you, I'm pleased you enjoyed it. I have some chicken left and some dumplings made. That will be for our meal tomorrow, so I will have time to wash the sheets.'

'And the chimneys for the oil lamps? Have you cleaned those?'

Sofia nodded. 'They took time as they have to be washed and dried carefully so as not to break them.'

'Did you refill the lamps with oil?'

Sofia looked at him blankly. 'Pappa always refilled the lamps and trimmed the wicks. I thought you would do them.'

'It is not a difficult job. I am sure you could manage it.'

Sofia sighed. If it was such an easy job why didn't Alesandros do it himself? She knew the oil in the lamps was low and she did not want to go out to the yard in the darkness and draw more oil from the barrel. She hoped they would flicker out whilst

Alesandros was still sitting by the fire and he would be forced to replenish them himself. 'I am very tired, Alesandros. When I have washed the plates I am going to bed. I can refill the lamps tomorrow.'

'An early night will do neither of us any harm. I will follow you up.'

Sofia gritted her teeth. She really did feel tired, her shoulders and upper arms still ached from cleaning the windows and she knew what Alesandros had in mind if he also wanted to retire to bed early.

Alesandros did not follow Sofia up immediately. He examined the wash stand with the drawer where he placed the tax money. It would be a simple job to add pieces of timber to the front, back and sides leaving a hollow space between. He could pull out the drawer and his personal money could be slipped down into the space beneath.

Sofia scrubbed at the sheets diligently and then filled the lamps with oil. She still did not sweep the floor or dust anywhere and Maria looked at her with disapproval.

'The floor needs sweeping,' she remarked. 'Shall I do it for you?'

'No,' Sofia shook her head. 'I am leaving it deliberately until Alesandros notices and mentions it.' She sat down beside her mother and took up her sewing.

Maria frowned. 'He'll think I haven't taught you how to look after a house properly.'

Sofia smiled. 'I know what I'm doing, Mamma. You continue with your weaving. When it gets colder I think Alesandros will be asking for one of your blankets. Make sure you ask him for more than the pedlar pays you.'

'I could give you a blanket. You insisted I took all my spare ones to the cottage with me.'

'You are to do no such thing.' Sofia looked at her mother in horror. 'If Alesandros wants a blanket he must pay for it. He has to realise that he may be living in your house for nothing but he has no right to any of your possessions. Please, trust me, Mamma and do as I say.'

Winter 1912

Alesandros rode into Aghios Nikolaos and entered the tax office. He waited his turn and eventually took his place before Christos and handed the man the money and the relative paper work.

'On time as usual, Alesandros. Quite a distance for you to have to travel each week.'

Alesandros nodded. 'I may not be as regular once the winter sets in. If the snow blocks the trails from Lassithi I hope the manager will understand.'

'That reminds me; the manager said he'd like to have a word with you. He's in his office so when we've finished up here can you go and see him? He'll think I didn't give you the message otherwise.'

'Of course.' Alesandros hoped no one had complained about him paying their tax in instalments or charging them interest on a loan.

Yiorgo rose from behind his desk and shook hands with Alesandros. 'Have a seat. I understand you are living in Kastelli now?'

'I married a young lady who comes from there.'

'So I was told. Bearing that in mind I think it would be to your advantage to change your collection area.'

Alesandros heart sank. If he had to pass over his debtors to another man it was possible that his lucrative scheme, although within the law, would be exposed and looked on adversely by the tax office.

'I realise it is somewhat unorthodox to change the collector in each area,' continued Yiorgo. 'A regular collector becomes known. If you agree to the proposal you will continue to be responsible for those in the Lassithi area whom you visit now. I know some of them have been difficult in the past and you seem to be making headway with them. It would only be the coastal areas that were handed to someone else.'

Alesandros gave a sigh of relief. No one that he called on ever wished to pay their taxes, but with the system he had devised no one was ever penalised. Generally the money he was chasing was his own where he had paid their tax and now wanted repayment of the loan he had allowed them along with the interest.

'I'd like to hand a few other difficult farmers over to you. It would mean you travelling to Milatos and Anogia areas, but you'll be in the vicinity. Would you be happy to take on the extra responsibility?'

Alesandros nodded. 'I don't see any problem.' He would welcome some more slow and reluctant payers. He would offer to ease their situation by paying on their behalf and charge them interest on the amount he loaned. He needed to add to his savings that he had stored in the drawer of the wash stand.

'Good. That's settled then. The office for those collections is in Neapoli. I believe there was a problem in the past at Neapoli when not all the collection money was paid into the system by one of the clerks. You will call at the office and a clerk will check your figures against the amounts each person has paid. Once your collection figures have been agreed it will be your responsibility to take the money to the bank in Neapoli. Is that agreeable to you?'

Alesandros shrugged. 'If that is their system I have no problem with it'

'It should be to your advantage. You can collect your wages each week from the Neapoli office and you would only have to make the journey down to Aghios Nikolaos once a month.'

'I'll certainly appreciate not having to make the journey down to Aghios Nikolaos each week, particularly when the weather is bad,' smiled Alesandros. 'I warned Christos that I might not be so regular if we have snow up on Lassithi.'

At first the collections had taken him considerably longer than previously. He had to make himself known to the new farmers and agree their accounts with them. They were suspicious and insisted they visited the village priest for him to confirm that the amount Alesandros claimed they owed was correct. It was only after they had reluctantly agreed the figure they owed that Alesandros was able sit down and explain his offer of a loan to enable them to clear their debts and make a fresh start.

Now he was extremely pleased he did not have to make the journey from Kastelli to the coastal villages to collect the taxes and then visit Aghios Nikolaos each week to deposit the money. It was still cold and often raining, but the journey back from Neapoli to Kastelli was easier and quicker. He also knew that when he arrived home Sofia would have a hot meal waiting for him and there would be a fire to warm himself and dry his clothes.

Sofia waited until Alesandros had eaten his meal, feeling certain that he would refuse her request.

'Alesandros, I need some kindling for the fire.'

Alesandros raised his eyebrows. 'Are you asking me to fetch some in for you?' He looked at the pile of logs beside the hearth. 'You have plenty here.'

'When the fire is low first thing in the morning I need small pieces of wood to encourage it to blaze before I place a log on. A log would put it out and I would have to remove all the debris and re-light it. I would never manage to get that done and your water heated by the time you wished to wash and shave. I am asking you to chop some for me.'

'Chop some wood?'

Sofia nodded. 'Pappa always chopped the wood. It is a man's

work. I am not strong enough to do it; besides, I do not have an axe.'

'So ask your father to chop some for you.'

Sofia shook her head. 'I cannot do that. He has his own logs to chop and if he chops wood for the villagers they pay him. I cannot expect him to do it for nothing. All you have to do is buy an axe and then you could chop some for me each week.'

Alesandros regarded Sofia gravely. 'I am a tax collector. I am not a farmer.'

Sofia shrugged. 'Very well. I'll ask Pappa to chop the wood and you can pay him each week.'

'How much does he charge?'

'That depends upon the quantity he chops. I suggest you ask him at the weekend. I have enough wood to last me until the beginning of next week.' Sofia smiled. 'You could also ask him to trim the wicks to the oil lamps and make sure they are filled.'

'And no doubt I would have to pay him for that also!'

'It's only fair. You leave the donkey up in the orchard on Pappa's land. You do not pay him any rent for that. You cannot expect to have everything for nothing.' Sofia rose from the table and gathered the plates together. 'If Pappa does some work for you it is only right that he should be paid.'

Alesandros gazed after Sofia speculatively. She was right, of course. Had her father asked him to take a parcel or message to someone in Aghios Nikolaos he would have expected to have been paid for his trouble. He also knew that at some time the outhouse would have to be cleaned out to ensure there were no blockages between the stones that would start to smell or be the cause of germs. If Theo was working for him in other capacities he could ask him to do that unpleasant job and also to adapt the washstand to meet his needs.

Sofia watched her father nailing the wood to the washstand and asked why he was doing it.

Theo shrugged. 'Alesandros has asked me to place wood all round. He says it wobbles sometimes and he is afraid the hot water will spill. I never noticed it wobbling.' Sofia gave the washstand a push. It certainly seemed sturdy enough, but if Alesandros wanted to waste money on a silly job like that it was his problem.

As the weeks wore on the weather turned colder and wetter and Alesandros suggested they move down to the living room and slept on the large bed there.

Sofia looked at him in mock horror. 'I have told you, Alesandros, I cannot sleep in my parents' bed. It would not feel right.'

'I was cold last night and we are hardly into the winter. Even with the oil stove upstairs the room is still cold. I think it is time you started to light a fire up there.'

Sofia shrugged. 'If you are cold ask my mother if you can buy a blanket. I believe she has finished those she plans to sell to the pedlar. Once he has bought them you would have to wait until she had woven another.'

Alesandros glanced at her sourly. Whatever they seemed to need appeared to have to be bought from one or other of Sofia's parents. He had collected most of the tax owing for the apple crop from the outlying villages, but the amount he was able to place amongst his savings was not as great as in the past. He had expected that as he no longer paid rent for his lodgings in Aghios Nikolaos he would be saving money.

He had taken the donkey to the blacksmith; had her hoofs trimmed and new shoes fitted, but he had budgeted for that. He had agreed to buy the wool and pay Maria to weave a new winter cloak for her daughter and had his boots mended. He had found it necessary to remove a couple of notes from his secret store to pay Theo for chopping wood that week and he was certainly not happy about that.

Whatever the weather tomorrow he would have to go and visit those farmers who still owed him interest on their tax payments and insist they paid their debts to him.

Sofia swept the crumbs from beneath the table. She was not sure if Alesandros had ignored them or not noticed, but she could not bear to see them there any longer. She dusted the dresser and mopped the floor before sitting down beside her mother at the loom.

'Mamma, my course is two weeks late.'

Maria smiled at her. 'That probably means you're expecting. Have you told Alesandros?'

Sofia shook her head. 'Not yet. I thought I should wait a little longer to make sure.'

'You must be careful for the next few weeks. No heavy lifting. No more bringing pails of water to me each day. Make sure yours are only half full. You must not strain yourself inside.'

'I'll remember, Mamma.' Sofia smiled to herself. She did not particularly want a baby, but it was working in perfectly with her plans.

Maria and Sofia heard Alesandros ride past the house on his donkey.

'Time to leave, Mamma.'

Maria looked at her daughter in surprise. She did not usually urge her to leave and Alesandros was always willing for her to tie off the end of the wool before she left. To Sofia it seemed an age before her mother finally picked up her cloak and left the house. She hoped Alesandros had not seen her returning to the cottage or her plan would go awry.

Swiftly Sofia lay down on her parents' bed. As she heard Alesandros open the front door and enter the room she kept her eyes closed and breathed quietly.

'Sofia. Sofia, what is wrong? Are you ill?'

Slowly Sofia opened her eyes and gave a little gasp. 'Alesandros, I did not expect you home so soon.'

Alesandros regarded her anxiously. 'Are you feeling ill?'

'No,' Sofia sat up and brushed her hair back from her face. 'I just felt so tired I had to lie down for a minute. I must have fallen asleep. I'm sorry.'

'If you were that tired why didn't you go to bed?'

'Mamma left early and I only meant to lay down for a moment or two. I didn't expect to go to sleep.'

'What have you done that has exhausted you so much?'

Sofia shrugged. 'I don't know; maybe it was scrubbing the floors.' Sofia knew she had only mopped them, but she also knew Alesandros would know no different.

'Scrubbing the floor has never made you so tired before. Maybe you are sickening for something. Would you like me to go and ask Theophalia to visit?'

Sofia shook her head. 'No, she would consider it a fool's errand to visit me just because I was tired. I feel better now I've had a rest. Thank goodness I prepared your meal earlier.'

Whilst eating their meal Alesandros kept glancing covertly at his wife. There seemed nothing wrong with her appetite. Maybe she had slept badly the previous night and that accounted for her tiredness. Every so often she would refuse his overtures, claiming to be tired. If she had slept during the afternoon she would not have that excuse tonight. His hopes were dashed when Sofia finished washing their plates and announced she was going to bed as she did not feel quite right.

Sofia gave a wry smile when she rose the next morning feeling nauseous. She guessed this was a sign that she really was pregnant, but she also saw it as retribution for claiming to be slightly unwell. At least she would have a good excuse for a few months to refuse Alesandros and she would make sure that he realised she was unable to manage the house without help.

She ran her hands over her stomach; it felt no larger than it had in the past. She would have to ask her mother how long it would be before she would need to let out her skirts and she would be advertising her condition to the villagers.

Alesandros lay down beside her and lifted his nightshirt. He slipped his hand between her legs and pressed himself hard against her. Sofia clamped her legs together.

'No, Alesandros.'

'Sofia, it has been almost a week. I made allowances for you earlier as you claimed you were tired, but now I have to insist.'

'If you insist, Alesandros, you could regret it. I realise now that the reason I am so tired and feel unwell on occasions is because I am pregnant. I am sure you would not want me to lose our child just because you cannot control yourself.'

Alesandros let out his breath with a hiss. 'Are you sure? Is this an excuse to refuse me and in a few weeks time you will say you are sorry, but it was a mistake?'

'I'm quite sure, Alesandros. I would not lie to you about such an important issue. My course was due three weeks ago and each morning when I rise I feel sick.'

'Surely, if I am gentle it will do no harm.'

'If I should have a damaged child due to you poking around inside me I would find it very hard to forgive you. Every woman wants to have a healthy child. Think of Olympia. She is only capable of doing simple tasks and no one in the village would consider marrying her.'

Alesandros lay there, he desperately wanted his wife, but he did not know enough about pregnancy to argue with her and insist he had his way. He moved his hand from between her legs and groaned. Now he had experienced the delights of a marital status he was loath to relinquish them.

Sofia spoke to Doctor Andrianakis when he paid his next visit to Kastelli. After describing her symptoms he confirmed that she appeared to be pregnant. He gave her advice regarding eating well and avoiding undue exertion, all of which Theophalia had already told her, and said he would check on her progress when he called on the village again the following month.

Sofia felt extremely well, except for when she first rose in the morning. By the time Alesandros had shaved and prepared to go off for the day the nausea had worn off, but she did not tell him. During the morning she made the bread and prepared a meal, but did the minimum amount of housework, deliberately leaving it undone so Alesandros would notice. During the afternoon she would sit with her mother and spend her time stitching the first small nightdress ready for when the baby was born.

Alesandros did notice that the house was dusty, the floors unwashed, the shutters dirty and the bed not changed. Sofia walked around slowly and deliberately whilst he was in the house, sometimes leaning against the dresser or the wall and rubbing her stomach gently before taking a deep breath and continuing with serving their meal or clearing the table.

Finally she sat across the table from him and let a tear run down from her eye. 'Alesandros, carrying a baby is making me so tired. I cannot manage on my own. Could you ask Kassianae to come back to work here?'

Alesandros patted her hand. 'Don't be upset, my dear. I know you are unable to look after the house as you did, but I am not complaining.'

Sofia shook her head. 'You are not complaining now, but I am sure you will be in a couple of months' time. I can see for myself how dirty and neglected the house is becoming.'

'Can't your mother help when she is here?'

'Mamma comes to do her weaving, not to do my housework. I have told you before; one person cannot do the work that two used to share between them. If you paid Mamma to come in and clean whilst I was preparing food she would probably accept, but she cannot give up her weaving and work for nothing.'

Alesandros frowned. 'I'll think about it. I am already paying your father to do work. I'm not sure if I could afford to pay your mother also.'

Sofia said no more. She gave Alesandros a wan smile. 'I will do my best,' she said. She had sewn the seed, now she would wait a couple of days and tackle Alesandros again.

Sofia sat in the chair before the fire, her stomach supported by her hands and deliberately pushed out to make her look larger than she was.

'Alesandros,' she spoke tentatively. 'I have been thinking about what you said.'

Alesandros raised his eyebrows. 'Said about what, my dear?'

'About not being able to afford to pay my Mamma to come and help me in the house. I have had an idea. If Mamma and Pappa came back here to live you would not have to pay either of them. Pappa would chop the wood and see to the lamps and any other jobs you wanted and Mamma could do some of the cleaning whilst I cooked.'

Alesandros turned her suggestion over in his mind. It made sense; he would not have to pay either of them for their services if they were living in his house. They would no doubt bring their possessions back with them and the rugs could be hung back up on the walls to prevent the draughts that seemed to enter through the smallest crack. He would not have to buy them back to ensure the house stayed warm during the winter.

'They would need to pay for their food,' he said finally.

Sofia nodded. 'That would be no problem. They have to buy their food now.' She did not admit that on most days she prepared enough for her mother to take a meal back to the cottage with her.

'I'll speak to your father on Sunday. He may not be agreeable.'

Sofia shrugged. 'In that case there is nothing lost.' She knew her father would not refuse. She had discussed the suggestion at length with her mother who had promised to talk to Theo and persuade him to accept the offer.

Sofia was delighted to have her parents back in the house with her. They allowed Alesandros to have the first hot water each morning for his shave and had arranged that they would bath on Friday evenings. Theo and Maria would go into the scullery together and could often be heard laughing. On Saturday, when Alesandros took his bath, Sofia always waited until he had dressed and returned to the living room before she went to the scullery for her turn in the tepid water.

Theo had immediately busied himself with cleaning the windows and re-hanging the rugs, whilst Maria replaced her own cooking utensils in the scullery, appreciating anew the amount of space she had around her after the tiny cottage.

'I never thought Alesandros would allow us to come back and live here,' she said to Sofia when they were alone. 'How did you manage to persuade him?'

Sofia gave a mirthless laugh. 'I believe Alesandros is very fond of me, but the thing he loves most of all is money. I made sure the house became neglected and insisted I was too tired to cope with the work now I am expecting. When I asked if we could employ Kassianae to work here again he said he did not think we could afford her. He suggested you did the work instead of your weaving. When I told him you would expect to be paid he discarded that idea. I waited a couple of days and then suggested you and Pappa moved back in. He was obviously delighted that Pappa would no longer charge him for chopping wood and maintaining the oil lamps.'

'Your Pappa would have done that for you without asking for payment,' Maria chided her daughter.

'I know, but it was all a part of my plan. He thinks I am very obedient and do as I am told by him. I knew it was no good begging him to allow you back and the baby arrived just at the right time for me to use it as an excuse. I know how to manipulate him and get my own way. I had to convince Alesandros that I needed help and that the help would have to be paid for. He gives me a generous amount for our food each week, but I'm sure if I asked him for any more he would refuse and say I needed to shop more carefully. He begrudges giving Father Symeon a drachma each week after the service. He says it is money being spent out for nothing as the priest is too old to do his work properly any longer and he should be replaced with a younger man.'

Maria shook her head. 'You are a bad girl, Sofia.'

'No I'm not.' Sofia answered indignantly. 'Alesandros had no right to make you leave this house. I certainly didn't want you to spend the winter in that cottage. You don't want a return bout of bronchitis.'

Maria shuddered. 'That was a bad experience. I don't know how you managed to do all the cooking and cleaning and look after me.'

'You were no trouble. It was making you stay in bed that was difficult.' Sofia smiled. 'That was when Pappa decided to ask Kassianae to come here to work so it proves to Alesandros that one person is unable to manage everything on their own. I certainly couldn't have made the Christopsomo on my own. I needed you to help me.'

Maria smiled happily. She enjoyed cooking, although she always gave Sofia credit for the meal they ate in the evening and claimed she had only done the cleaning. 'You'd helped me make it in the past so you knew what ingredients to use.'

Sofia nodded. 'I knew what needed to go into the bread, but I didn't know the quantities. I could have put in too many nuts and not enough fruit, or the other way around. Besides, when I have the baby I'll not have the time to be forever cooking and cleaning.'

'Have you spoken to Theophalia?'

Sofia nodded. 'She thinks it will be in July or the beginning of August. Poor Phaini, she's so envious. They've been married six months longer than me and she's not had any sign.'

'There's plenty of time for her. Your Pappa and I had been married for over two years before I started you.'

'That's what I keep telling her.' Sofia sighed. 'She says that's all she thinks about when Nikos takes her.'

Maria shook her head. Young girls were far too open and frank about their marital lives these days. When she was first married she would not have dreamt of mentioning the intimate relationship between her and Theo to anyone, least of all to any of her friends.

'Maybe now it's the winter and Nikos is not working so hard they will have some success.'

'I hope so. It would make her so happy. Have a look at my stitching, Mamma. Is it neat enough? Are you sure this nightdress will be big enough for a baby? It looks so tiny.'

Maria took the small garment from Sofia's hands and held it up. 'It will probably be too large at first, but babies grow quickly. Have you had to let out your skirt?'

Sofia nodded. 'It began to feel too tight last week. I'm glad Alesandros used his camera after we had been to church on Christmas Day. I didn't look so fat then. I still don't know how a box takes a picture, although he has explained it to me. He says it costs a lot of money to take pictures and he will only do so on special occasions.'

Maria nodded. 'That's sensible of him. Why would he want to take a picture of us every week?'

'Why does he want to take one at all? I felt very stupid standing there smiling at a box. He sees us every day, but he insists on putting the photographs on the dresser between the plates. He told me he would show me how to use it, but I am not allowed to touch it unless he is with me. What does he think I am going to do with it?'

Maria shrugged. 'It might break if you dropped it.'

'Why should I drop it? I don't drop the plates or glasses. What's so special about a thing called a camera?'

'It probably cost a good deal more than a plate or glass. Just for once do as your husband tells you, Sofia.'

'I don't plan to touch it. I'm not interested in it. If I was I would disobey him whilst he was out.' Sofia tossed her head. 'If I really wanted one myself I would ask Pappa to buy one for me, I certainly wouldn't ask Alesandros. I was surprised when he bought the wool and asked you to weave a new cloak for me.'

Maria clicked her tongue. 'There are times, Sofia, when I think you judge Alesandros harshly. I have never heard him speak sharply to you, and he seems truly pleased that you are carrying his child.'

'All men like their wives to have children. It's a prestige thing. If I had not conceived he would probably have found another woman somewhere who could carry his offspring.'

'Sofia!'

Sofia bent her head and hot tears began to fall onto the nightdress she was sewing. 'I'm sorry, Mamma. I just feel that there is something missing.'

Summer 1913

Sofia looked down at the tiny girl she held in her arms. She was thankful the ordeal was over. Theophalia had said it had been easy, but it would be a considerable time before she was able to forget the feeling of being ripped apart inside as the baby gradually forced her way down the birth canal and into the world. She had woken in the early hours with a pain low down in her abdomen and risen to use the night bucket.

She had returned to her mattress, hoping she had not disturbed Alesandros, and tried to go back to sleep. Just as she began to drift off the pain came again and she bit her lip. The baby was endeavouring to be born. She lay there, wondering whether she should go downstairs and ask her mother to go for Theophalia or wake Alesandros and ask him to dress and walk up to Theophalia's cottage; finally deciding she would wait a little longer. Theophalia had told her that until the pains followed each other in quick succession there was no reason to think that the birth was imminent.

Sofia fixed her eyes on the window. Once the sun rose people would be up and about and the only person who would have had their sleep disturbed would be her. It seemed only minutes before she felt Alesandros stir beside her and she realised she had fallen asleep. Gingerly she sat up and began to rise to her feet. The pain had hit her then with such ferocity that she had groaned aloud, a wave of dizziness passed over her and she had collapsed onto her knees beside the mattress.

'Alesandros,' she whispered. 'Fetch my Mamma. The baby has started.'

Alesandros opened his eyes and looked at his wife, kneeling beside their mattress. 'Are you sure?'

Sofia nodded. 'The first signs came during the night.'

'Why didn't you wake me?' Alesandros rose from the mattress and pulled his shirt over his head.

'I didn't want to disturb you.'

Alesandros grunted as he fastened the belt on his trousers. He pushed his feet into the shoes he wore in the house during the summer and hurried down the stairs. If Sofia was having the baby now he had no wish to be around to witness the event.

Maria was already up and had water heating on the fire when he entered the living room.

'Sofia needs you. The baby,' he announced without preamble.

Without a word Maria climbed the stairs to the bedroom where Sofia was still on her knees beside the mattress.

'How long has this been going on?' she asked.

'I had some pains in the night.'

Maria nodded. 'I'll get some towels to put on the mattress, then you can get back into bed. We'll see how you go before I send for Theophalia.'

Sofia nodded. She was frightened now and did not want her mother to leave her alone in the room. Maria rummaged in one of the trunks in the storage room and returned with an armful of old towels and cloths. She spread them on the mattress and urged Sofia to lie back on the bed.

'I'll empty the bucket, then make you some warm milk. Your Pappa can start heating water and Alesandros can go up to Theophalia and ask her to come down to see you.'

Sofia nodded in acquiescence. 'You'll stay with me, Mamma?'

'Once I have the men organised and your milk I'll come and sit with you. You're not that far yet or you'd have had more pains by now.'

It had seemed an interminable time to Sofia before her mother returned and settled herself in the chair beside her and even longer before Theophalia had finally arrived at the house. Theophalia had felt her stomach and nodded in satisfaction.

'The head is well down. There should be no problem. I'll come back in an hour or so and see how far you've got.'

'Aren't you going to stay with me?' asked Sofia anxiously.

'You don't need me at the moment. It can take a while for the baby to get properly started. There's no point in me sitting here watching you. Your mother's here if you need anything.'

Maria sat beside her daughter. 'There's nothing to worry about. Alesandros and your Pappa are downstairs. If Theophalia is needed urgently one of them will call her.'

Sofia reached for her mother's hand and closed her eyes. All she could hope for now was a healthy baby. Maria looked at her daughter's pale face. She hoped the birth would be easy for her and she prayed that the baby would be perfect and that Sofia did not haemorrhage.

Sofia looked down at the wizened face and the pursed lips. 'Is she alright? She looks ugly, like an old man.'

'She's perfect. Give her time. She's had an ordeal, fighting her way out from you. By the morning her forehead will have smoothed out and you will realise she's beautiful. Give her to your mother to wash whilst I take care of you, then when you're both washed your husband can come and have a peek at her, then you must rest.'

Sofia nodded. She did feel incredibly tired.

'You're to stay in bed until I've visited you tomorrow. Use the bucket and change your cloths frequently to avoid soiling your mattress. Your Mamma can deal with the baby when she needs to be changed.'

'What about feeding her?' asked Sofia anxiously.

'When I've finished washing you she can suck at your breast.

You won't have any milk yet, but it will comfort her and encourage your milk to come in. If she wakes in the night just put her to your breast for a few minutes and she'll go back to sleep.'

Alesandros stood at the foot of the bed and regarded Sofia and his baby daughter. 'I've been told there is nothing wrong with her. Is that so, Sofia?'

Sofia nodded. 'She doesn't look very pretty at the moment, but Theophalia says she'll look different in a few hours. Her skin will have lost its redness and wrinkles.'

'I hope so,' he remarked dourly. 'We will call her Maria.'

Sofia smiled with pleasure. 'After my Mamma.'

'It is traditional. If you have a girl next time she can be called Fotini after my mother.'

Sofia looked down at the little bundle in her arms. Little Maria was not yet an hour old and Alesandros was talking about her having another child. 'We'll have to wait a while,' she cautioned him.

'I understand that. I also understand that you need to rest so I will leave you. I will try not to disturb you later when I come to bed.'

'Don't you want to hold her?' asked Sofia.

'I am unused to babies. When she is a little larger, maybe. I will ask your mother to come back up to you.' Alesandros twirled the ends of his moustache and Sofia heard him returning to the floor below. She felt disappointed at his evident lack of interest and a tear crept down her cheek. Were all men uninterested in their children until they were large enough to take to church and they could show them off to the neighbours?

Alesandros had watched his mother-in-law hurrying up and down the stairs with the water that Theo continually heated over the fire. He felt excluded and useless. This was his child being brought into the world, yet whenever he asked what was happening he was told everything was proceeding according to nature's plan. Now having seen the baby he felt disappointed.

When he had been told it was a girl he had expected to see a pretty little baby lying in Sofia's arms. As it was her face was red and wrinkled and she had hardly any hair.

He sighed deeply. He would probably have to place his hand beneath the drawer in the wash stand and extract some more of his hidden money. He had already bought a gold necklace for Sofia's Name Day and to celebrate the birth of their first child. When the girl was christened the villagers would expect a feast as lavish as the wedding feast had been and this time he was the one who would have to pay for it.

Sofia sat downstairs, a cushion placed behind her back and Maria in her arms. She had washed and dressed her carefully in the nightdress she had sewn specially for this occasion. She just hoped she would still be dry when Father Symeon took her in his arms to place a cross on her forehead and name her. It would be embarrassing if there were damp patches on his cassock when he handed her back.

She had asked that Tryphaine and Eleni's oldest daughter, act as the child's godmothers and Alesandros had not objected. He said that if Tryphaine was to be a godmother her husband, Nikos might as well be the godfather. Sofia had not argued, although she thought there were other young men in the village who would have been a better choice.

Father Symeon arrived and for the first time Sofia noticed that he was feeling his age. He seemed somewhat confused about his role in the proceedings and it was not until Theo had taken him to one side and spoken quietly to him that he had approached Sofia with a beaming smile and said he was there to christen her baby.

Maria was passed to Tryphaine and Father Symeon began the traditional christening service. When it came to naming the baby he looked at Tryphaine.

'What did you say her name was? Sofia?'

Tryphaine shook her head. 'The baby is to be called Maria.'

He placed a hand behind his ear and Tryphaine repeated herself more loudly. 'The baby's name is Maria.'

Sofia held her breath until he had completed the naming ceremony. Once named by the priest there was no way a name could be changed and she desperately wanted the child to be called Maria after her mother. She was relieved when Father Symeon handed the baby back to her and she was able to hold her safely; she had not been convinced that the priest would not drop her. Alesandros came and stood by her side.

'I will accompany the villagers up to the church square for the merry making. As soon as I have thanked them for attending I will return.'

'There is no need, Alesandros,' Sofia assured him. 'You may stay there as long as you like. Theophalia says I have recovered well. It is quite alright to leave me alone.'

'I think it very unlikely I will wish to spend too long in their company watching many of them become drunk.' Alesandros shook his head. 'When I go to Neapoli next I will have a word with the Bishop about Father Symeon. He really is becoming incapable of fulfilling his duties.'

Sofia enjoyed being a mother. She loved to watch the tiny baby's face whilst she fed her. Baby Maria showed such concentration on the task and would regard her mother with an intense look whilst sucking busily.

Maria was always happy to cuddle her granddaughter and Theo would stand and look at her, a pleased smile on his face. Alesandros never asked to hold his daughter. When he arrived home he would look at her and stroke her face gently with one finger, then give her the finger to grasp in her tiny hand. There was no way that Alesandros would admit that he was actually frightened of handling a baby.

The first Sunday Sofia was able to go to church he walked with a proud smile on his face and accept the compliments from the villagers on his family. On their return to the house he insisted Sofia stood outside with Maria in her arms whilst he took two photographs.

'Why do you need two?' asked Sofia.

'It is a complicated procedure,' explained Alesandros. 'Inside the camera is a roll of film. It allows me to take eight photographs. When the film is used up I have to remove it and make sure that no light gets into it. If a part of the film is damaged by light the picture will not come out; it will be black. If I take two photos each time I hope one will be acceptable.'

'Would you like me to take a photograph of you holding Maria?' she asked.

Alesandros shook his head. 'When this film is finished and I have taken it from the camera I will show you how to use it. Film is expensive. It is not difficult to take a photograph, but better that you practise without a film. Once I am certain you are capable of using it properly I will allow you to take a photograph.'

As Maria thrived Alesandros began to take more notice of her. When he spoke to her she would smile, wave her hands and kick her legs. When she finally held her arms up to him, obviously requesting him to pick her up, Sofia was delighted to see that he did so after only a slight hesitation.

'I am sorry I was unable to give you a boy. Maybe you would have liked a boy child more than you like a girl,' remarked Sofia.

Alesandros shook his head. 'I do not dislike her, but I have no experience of babies. I would not want to hurt her accidently by being clumsy.' Alesandros sat down in the chair, his daughter resting comfortably in his arms. 'Now she is a little larger I feel more confident.'

'I hope you will now hold her for a while each day. She needs to know you are her Pappa, not a visitor to the house.'

Alesandros nodded. He did not feel completely at ease handling Maria. He hoped it might soon be time for Sofia to feed her and he would be relieved of the slightly damp bundle.

'I spoke to the Bishop in Neapoli today. I explained that Father Symeon was aging rapidly and his duties seemed to be a burden to him.'

'What did the Bishop say?'

Alesandros shrugged, forgetting momentarily that he held Maria in his arms. 'He promised to send a younger man to visit and assess the situation. Apparently you cannot relieve a Pappas of his duties just because he has become old and a little infirm. If the visiting priest thinks there is a problem the Bishop will ask him to come and assist Father Symeon.'

'Will Father Symeon accept help?'

'I have no idea. I imagine it will be done very tactfully.' Alesandros shifted Maria from off his knees. 'I think you should change her clothes. She is making me quite wet.' There was indeed a dark patch on Alesandros's trousers.

Sofia smiled in amusement. 'It is impossible to keep such a small child dry all the time. When you hold her in future place a towel across your knees like I do. Give her to me and I'll change her cloths.'

Alesandros relinquished Maria thankfully and moved to the table where he began to make notes in his book. His visit to the Bishop appeared to have been fruitful and the new farmers he was calling on should be quite profitable to him. He had spent time with two of them explaining how the loan system worked and then left them to think over his proposition. He felt quite certain that when he called next they would accept his offer. He rubbed his hands together. All in all it had been a successful day and he felt confident about approaching Sofia when they retired to bed.

Sofia shook her head. 'No, Alesandros. It is far too soon. You have to understand that it takes a woman some considerable time to heal inside. Remember how tired and weak I was whilst I was carrying Maria? How would I manage to look after her properly if I felt like that again?'

'You have your mother here. She could help.'

'I know she would. When I was expecting Maria my Mamma did all the cleaning and I only did the cooking and was able to rest during the afternoon whilst she did her weaving. As Maria becomes older she will need to be watched continually to ensure she comes to no harm. Besides, I am feeding Maria. Just suppose I became pregnant again – what would happen to my milk? It could make it dry up and then how would I feed her?'

'How long do you expect to feed her yourself?'

Sofia shrugged. 'I cannot say. It will depend upon when Theophalia says she is ready to have a little egg yolk or some breadcrumbs in milk. Once she is capable of digesting those she can begin to have some mashed vegetables and I will gradually stop feeding her just with my milk. You have to be patient, Alesandros.'

Alesandros sighed. He saw other mothers working in the fields whilst they were pregnant and later with the baby tied to their back. Maybe Sofia was not as strong and healthy as she appeared.

Autumn 1913

When the villagers filed into church on Sunday they were surprised to see an unknown priest sitting to one side. They murmured and muttered together, whilst Alesandros sat with a knowing smile on his face. It had been some weeks since he had spoken to the Bishop and he was beginning to think the man had forgotten that a priest was to visit Kastelli and assess the situation.

Father Symeon rose up and before he started the service he waved his hand towards the unknown priest. 'This is, is, Father, er, Costas, who is passing through Kastelli and asked if he could join us. I am sure you will all welcome him.'

Father Constantine acknowledged the introduction with a nod of his head. He did not correct Father Symeon over his name. There was no need to embarrass him before his congregation. If his only problem due to age was forgetting names there was little to worry about. He listened attentively as Father Symeon stumbled his way through the familiar service, losing his train of thought and the attention of the villagers.

The children became restless, many of them slipping off their chairs and crawling around between the legs of those sitting near them. Their mothers became agitated, trying to order them back to their seat in a whisper, or tapping them on the shoulder and indicating they should be quiet and return to their chair. A couple of men edged their way towards the door and left quietly.

Father Symeon appeared not to notice that anything was

amiss and rambled on regardless for further minutes, then stopped abruptly in mid sentence. He stood speechless, totally disorientated, and Father Constantine took advantage of the moment and rose rapidly to his feet.

'I would like to thank Father Symeon for allowing me to join the service in his church today. Now it is over I would like to meet with you as you leave and thank you all personally for attending. If Father Symeon would like to lead the way to the door?' He indicated with his hand that the priest should start to walk towards the exit without waiting for the final blessing.

Still looking bemused Father Symeon walked from the altar and down the aisle where the doors of the church were opened for him. He stood to one side, accepting the gifts of produce or money that was either pressed into his hands or placed at his feet. He thanked people and shook their hands, whilst Father Constantinus looked on.

The villagers gathered in small groups, waiting for Theo and Maria to begin the walk down the road towards their house. It was traditional that they should lead the way and everyone else should follow at their own pace. Father Constantinus moved away from the door and waited for the villagers to leave. He saw Theo and Maria, followed by Alesandros and Sofia, walking slowly down the road. A number of villagers came up to them and doffed their hats before speaking a few words and moving back to their family.

Father Constantinus greeted those around him, complimenting them on their pretty and well kept village, but watched carefully to see which house the leading couple entered. He was not surprised when he saw them open the door to the large, stone built house on the corner of the main road. He strode leisurely down the road and knocked on the door.

Sofia answered him, expecting to see one of the villagers there with a request for her father and was totally taken aback when he saw Father Constantinus.

She bobbed her head in obeisance and smiled. 'How can I help

153

you, Father? Do you need directions to the next village?'

'May I come in for a short while? I'll not detain you for long and interrupt your meal.'

'Of course.' Sofia stood to one side and Father Constantinus entered the living room. Theo and Alesandros immediately rose from the table and Maria looked out from the scullery. She placed the lid on the saucepan of food she had been about to serve and picked up a bottle of wine and glasses.

She took them through and placed them on the table, receiving a nod of approval from Theo. He poured three glasses and handed one to Father Constantinus. 'To your good health, Father. Would you care to stay and partake of our mid-day meal?'

Father Constantinus shook his head. 'That is very kind of you, but I have told Father Symeon that I will dine with him before I return to Neapoli. I just wish to have a few words with you. Who is the head man in the village?'

Alesandros was about to say that he was when Theo spoke up.

'I am,' he said firmly. 'We realised Father Symeon was beginning to feel his age and my son-in-law was the person who mentioned the problem to the Bishop in Neapoli. He travels there frequently, whereas I only make the journey a couple of times each year.'

Father Constantinus nodded. 'The Bishop asked me to come to Kastelli and participate in the service and then report back to him. It is evident that Father Symeon has some problems.'

Theo frowned. 'We are all very fond of him. He has been the Pappas here since I was a boy. I wouldn't want him to think we were turning him out of the village.'

'Of course not. I am fairly confident that after I have spoken to the Bishop he will agree that Father Symeon just needs someone here to assist him, but he will not be deposed. Time will take its course, and when the need arises there will be someone who knows the villagers who will be able to step into his shoes without a problem.' Father Constantinus emptied his glass and refused the refill that Theo offered him. 'Thank you, but I must return to Father Symeon. If I am away too long he may think I have returned to Neapoli without even bidding him farewell.'

'Should he have forgotten you are to share his meal you are welcome to return to us,' smiled Theo. 'Maria is sure to have cooked more than enough.'

Little Maria was sitting up unaided and when laid on the floor or mattress she would try to roll over onto her stomach. She would stand on Alesandros's legs and push herself up and down, making a lunge for his moustache as she did so. Sofia watched her daughter's progress with pride. As Theophalia had predicted the redness and wrinkles had disappeared rapidly and she was now a beautiful little girl with her dark hair beginning to curl. Very soon she would cut her first tooth and the gummy smile she gave to everyone at present would change.

Sofia still refused Alesandros, making the excuse that her milk was needed to feed Maria, although the little girl was happily eating soft food additions to her diet. She had seen Alesandros look at her speculatively as she spooned some mashed potato mixed with chicken gravy into Maria's mouth and knew that she would not be able to avoid his attentions for very much longer.

Alesandros sat on the side of the mattress. 'Sofia, you have made a number of excuses to avoid me exercising my rights as your husband. I have accepted them and not forced myself upon you, but now I am going to insist that you start to accommodate me again. Maria is no longer solely dependent upon your milk for her nourishment.'

Sofia looked at Alesandros intently. 'I appreciate how very patient you have been, but I'm frightened, Alesandros.'

'Frightened? Why should you be frightened? You have had one child. You know what to expect.'

Sofia nodded. 'Maria is so perfect that I am frightened that if I had another child there could be something wrong. I would rather have just one perfect child than a dozen with defects.'

'If anything like that happened it could be dealt with.' Alesandros dismissed the idea and Sofia shuddered. She knew what he meant when he said it could be dealt with. Any baby that was born with obvious disabilities rarely lived more than a few hours. Theophalia knew how to extinguish a tiny life by pinching the nostrils together and placing her hand over the infant's mouth.

'I am not getting any younger, Sofia. I regret now that I left it so late in my life to get married. By rights I should be thinking of arranging marriages for my children and looking forward to grandchildren, not still planning to have children of my own.'

'Maybe in another few weeks, Alesandros.'

Alesandros shook his head. 'No, tonight, now, and I will not accept any more excuses.'

Sofia sat on her mattress with a pillow behind her back whilst she fed Maria her early morning milk. She felt slightly nauseous after suffering Alesandros's attentions the previous night. She told herself it was ridiculous and her imagination. Even if he had made her pregnant again she would not have morning sickness yet. She determined to visit Theophalia later in the day and ask her advice. She was certain there were ways of avoiding becoming pregnant or of disposing of an unwanted addition to a family provided you acted quickly enough.

By the time Sofia took Maria down stairs Alesandros was ready to leave for the day and her mother was heating more water ready for Maria to be washed and changed into clean and dry clothes. As she stood on the doorstep to dutifully wave Alesandros on his way Nikos came running down the road waving his arms wildly.

'Mr Alesandros, wait, I need to speak to you.'

Alesandros waited impatiently. The man was probably going to ask him to purchase something in Neapoli that he was unable to buy in the village.

'Mr Alesandros please can you call on the Bishop and tell him the bad news. Father Symeon has collapsed.'

'Collapsed?'

Nikos nodded. 'I was passing the church on my way to the fields when I heard a strange banging noise. I opened the door and a number of the chairs were knocked over and Father Symeon was lying amongst them. I offered to help him up, but the priest did not reply so I ran up to Theophalia. She came back with me and told me to come down and ask you to inform the Bishop.'

'What about Doctor Andrianakis? Shouldn't I ask him to come down?'

'Theophalia only asked for you to speak to the Bishop.'

Alesandros placed his hat more firmly on his head. 'Of course. I'll ride to Neapoli directly and make my other calls later.' It would take him almost an hour to ride to Neapoli and it was doubtful that the Bishop or one of his designated priests would arrive in Kastelli much before mid-day.

'Is there anything I can do to help?' asked Maria.

'If you have a spare blanket you could help Theophalia put it under him. He's lying on the stone floor.'

Maria opened the chest and took out the blanket that was on the top. She had not long finished weaving it and had planned to sell it to the travelling man when he passed through the village, but the needs of Father Symeon came first.

Sofia washed Maria and waited anxiously for her mother to return. When she did so her face was grave.

'Nothing can be done for Father Symeon. The men have carried him into his house and he looks peaceful.'

Sofia crossed herself. 'He's dead?'

Maria nodded. 'Theophalia thinks he was dead before he hit the ground. Poor man. He had no chance for absolution before he died.' She began to rummage in the cupboard. 'I know the candles are in here somewhere. I'll take them up to the church and if anyone doesn't have one to light I can give them one of these.'

Sofia frowned. 'As a priest he should not have had any sins

on his conscience. Maybe that was why he was taken so quickly. Does Pappa know?'

'I went up to the orchard and told him. I imagine the whole village knows now. Nikos agreed to stay and toll the bell. I spread the word as I went up and Theophalia and the men will have told others.'

'What will happen now?'

'No doubt the Bishop will send someone down to take the funeral service tomorrow.'

'No, I mean who will be our village priest? We cannot all walk to Driros on a Sunday, particularly when the weather is bad.'

'I expect the Bishop has someone in mind to take over Father Symeon's duties. It may be that pleasant young man who was here a few weeks ago.' Maria placed a bundle of candles on the table and pulled a black blouse from her trunk of clothes, slipping it over the one she was wearing.

Sofia sat her daughter on her lap and proceeded to spoon a mess of milk and breadcrumbs into her mouth, avoiding Maria's waving hand as she tried to seize the spoon, and wiping away the mixture as she dribbled it from the corners of her mouth. Sofia felt unreasonably annoyed. Father Symeon would choose to die on the morning when she had planned to speak to Theophalia. Now the village woman would be too busy washing and laying out the priest to have time to chat to her.

'Have you some black material, Mamma? Alesandros doesn't have a black shirt and I'll have to make something to slip over Maria's clothes.'

'I hope your father can still fit into his. If he can't I'll have to slit the sides and tell him to keep his jacket on. I won't have time to make him a new one if I'm going to help you make one for Alesandros.'

Sofia smiled gratefully. The shirt needed only to be roughly made, but she knew it would take her most of the day. She would then have to make a second one, properly stitched, that Alesandros could wear to work each day. She was not at all sure how long everyone would wear black. The priest was not family or they would have been in mourning for two months or longer, but he was considered to be their spiritual father so it was possible they would have to wear black for a year. She sighed deeply.

'There's some material in the chest. Help yourself when you're ready. If I'm not back remember to use one of Alesandros's shirts for the size and cut it too large to allow for sewing. If it's too big you can always add a few stitches.'

Father Constantinus performed the funeral service for Father Symeon and the church was full. All the villagers attended, and even the tiniest children were dressed in black despite only having had one day's notice. Most of the clothing the villagers already possessed where they had been kept after a family member had passed away previously. The shirts and blouses had been taken from trunks and cupboards and put to air outside during the day, hoping the musty smell would dissipate. Black arm bands had been hurriedly stitched for the men to wear over their shirts or jackets.

Father Constantinus stood at the church door ready to speak a few words to each villager as they filed out and promised to call on them during the week so he could get to know them better and begin to remember their names. Theo and Maria were the first to exit as always and Father Constantinus shook Theo's hand.

'It is good to see you again, despite the sadness of the circumstances. May I call on you this afternoon?'

'Certainly. You will be very welcome.' Inwardly Theo groaned. He always fell asleep after their meal. He hoped he would have time for his afternoon nap before the priest arrived.

The priest had provided bread and wine for everyone and went amongst them with a sombre face giving his condolences to each person as sincerely as if Father Symeon had been a family member. When everyone was finally seated he blessed the food and drink asked everyone to partake of refreshment and listen to the few words he wished to say.

'Villagers of Kastelli, I share with you the sad loss of Father Symeon. He was a fine example to all of us who embrace the church and many of you will have known him all your life. You will feel his loss as keenly as if he was a member of your family or a close friend. The Bishop has asked me to take over his duties and I will perform them to the best of my abilities. I know I cannot take Father Symeon's place in your hearts, but I will do my best to serve you all. If you have any problems my door is always open to you and my ears ready to listen. With the aid of prayer all problems can be solved.'

Father Constantinus did not add that he had prayed that Father Symeon would soon be considered unable to perform his duties satisfactorily and he would be chosen to replace him in Kastelli. He had plans to move the village forward. It had been a backward rural community long enough.

Once the villagers had departed Father Constantinus ate a little bread with salt and olive oil and made sure there was no wine left in any of the bottles. He hoped Theo Angelakis would ask him to join his family for an evening meal. If he was to cater for himself he needed to buy some supplies as Father Symeon's cupboard had only the barest necessities. The meal he had shared with the priest a few weeks earlier had been very acceptable and he made a mental note to ask Theo if the priest had employed a housekeeper.

He wandered around the empty church. High up in the roof there were cobwebs and the glass in the top windows let in hardly any light as they were so dirty. The tiles on the floor needed to be scrubbed, there was mud from the villagers' boots that had not been removed by sweeping, but the silver and brass was spotless. During the coming week he would make the journey to Neapoli and apprise the Bishop of the neglect he had found. He would explain that he would be unable to clean the whole church unaided and ask for a sum of money to pay for someone to help him. Ideally he would like to have someone permanently to keep the church clean. He was not averse to sweeping and occasionally dusting, but he was not prepared to scrub the floor and clean windows.

Now Father Constantinus sat easily in Theo's living room. Upon his arrival Alesandros had marked the chapter he had been reading and placed the Bible on the dresser, making sure the priest saw his actions. Maria had stopped her weaving out of courtesy and held her granddaughter in her arms whilst Sofia offered the priest wine and biscuits before sitting beside her mother at the weaving loom.

'So,' said Theo, 'What brings you to my house?'

'Primarily I have come to you for advice. You know everyone who lives in Kastelli.'

Theo smiled. Was the priest going to ask for the local gossip?

'Over time the church has become neglected. I am not blaming Father Symeon; he had become old and infirm in his service to you all. I am not blaming the parishioners. The neglect would have happened so gradually that it is doubtful you would have noticed. I am a fresh pair of eyes. There is a good deal of cleaning that needs to be undertaken and I am hoping you can advise me whom I should approach. I do not wish to insult anyone, but if there is a woman who would appreciate a little extra income each week I could ask her to clean everywhere thoroughly and then ensure the standard of cleanliness is maintained each week.'

Theo nodded. 'I will speak to my wife. She knows the women far better than I do.'

'The next thing is a housekeeper. Did Father Symeon have someone clean and cook for him?'

'Not that I know of. He looked after himself.'

Father Constantinus raised his eyebrows. That explained the dirty pots he had found. 'He did his own cooking? There is hardly any food in his cupboard and none that could be used to make a meal.'

'He would shop each day for his needs. He said he enjoyed cooking and it gave him the opportunity to be out and around in the village; occasionally he would eat at the taverna. More recently someone would take him a meal and he appeared grateful.'

'I'm sure he was. A good meal at the end of the day is always appreciated.'

Theo leaned forward; he knew exactly what the priest was hinting. 'You will be welcome to join us in our meal this evening as your cupboard is somewhat bare.'

Father Constantinus shook his head. 'I could not impose on you. I only came to ask for your advice.'

'It is no imposition. It would be fine introduction to our village if no one was prepared to offer you a meal. We will expect you this evening. It will also give us time to talk further regarding the cleaning of the church. My wife may have thought of a woman who would be suitable by then.'

'In that case you make it impossible for me to refuse your hospitality.' Father Constantinus rose. 'Thank you for your time. I will not interrupt your afternoon further, but see you this evening.'

Everyone gave a sigh of relief as the priest left the house. Theo could continue with his afternoon nap, whilst Alesandros finished reading the chapter from the Bible. Maria could continue with her weaving and Sofia could take her daughter upstairs and lay her down on her mattress to sleep. She needed to finish off the black shirt she had hurriedly made for Alesandros to wear to the funeral that day and sewing was impossible with Maria in her arms.

Sofia and Maria discussed the additions they could make to their evening meal so Father Constantinus would be impressed. They knew that by the following day everyone would know he had eaten with them and they would want to know exactly what dishes he had been offered. Maria decided that the pasta and chicken dish she had prepared earlier would be sufficient for five if Sofia would make some dolmades. There was plenty of bread and Maria looked at the apples that had been harvested and stored a few weeks ago. She selected those that were without a blemish, polished them on her apron and placed them in a bowl on the table beside the cheese.

Maria had heard Father Constantinus ask about a cleaner for the church and wondered if Olympia would be willing to take on the additional duties. The girl was very overweight and usually had a vacant look on her face. She would use any excuse not to go to the fields with her parents and if she did go she worked slowly, stopping frequently for a rest. She was much happier sitting inside the church and spending the day cleaning the silver and brass and might well find that keeping the church clean would be more to her liking and was well within her capabilities.

Father Constantinus ate heartily and helped himself liberally from the carafe of wine that had been placed within his reach. Finally satisfied he sat back and belched.

'Thank you, ladies. That was a most enjoyable meal.'

Maria and Sofia bobbed their heads in acknowledgement of the compliment and began to clear the dishes from the table. Maria had spoken to Theo about Olympia and she guessed that whilst she and Sofia were busy in the scullery the suitability of the girl would be discussed.

'So why do you think I should approach the parents of this young lady, Olympia and ask if they would be willing for her to become my church cleaner?' asked Father Constantinus.

Theo chose his words carefully. 'She is not the most attractive young woman in the village and a little slow in her thinking. She does not enjoy working in the fields. She has a problem with her weight and bending is obviously uncomfortable for her. She stops frequently and straightens up to regain her breath. Her father becomes somewhat impatient with her. She is much happier sitting all day polishing the silver and brass. I think she could manage to scrub the floor provided you were willing to give her the whole day to complete the task. Dusting regularly should be no problem, provided she could reach without having to climb a ladder.'

Father Constantinus nodded slowly. By the sounds of things the girl would do exactly as she was told and could well end up taking a pride in her work if he praised her frequently. 'I don't imagine that dusting and polishing would occupy her whole week. Would she be willing to keep my house clean and tidy and do some cooking for me?'

Theo shrugged. 'I cannot answer for her. You would have to speak to her and her parents.'

Listening to the conversation Alesandros was reminded of the deaf girl Litsa who took a pride in cleaning her local church.

'If you direct me to their house I will call on them tomorrow. That doesn't solve my other problem, though. I need someone able to climb a ladder and removed the dust and cobwebs from the roof. The windows also need cleaning and they are too high to reach from the ground.'

'You should have asked for volunteers at the end of your service today. Father Symeon always asked for young men to go in and clean the church. It was always thoroughly cleaned before Easter.'

'Was it cleaned again later in the year?'

Theo shrugged. 'Father Symeon only ever asked the villagers for help the week before Clean Monday.'

'I think it needs attention a little more frequently than once a year. Once I am satisfied that the initial work has been done it would just be a question of ensuring it stayed presentable. If I saw a cobweb in the roof I would ask someone to remove it; if the windows needed cleaning I could ask someone to wash them.'

'It would just be a case of you taking one of the young men aside and asking him if he would be willing. I can't see that would be a problem provided you didn't always ask the same man.'

Alesandros sat in a chair at the table and listened to the conversation. The question of cleaning the church could well have waited until the following day. The priest had obviously used it as an excuse to cadge a meal from the family.

'There is one other thing I would like to discuss with you. Do the village children receive any schooling?'

'Schooling?' Theo looked at Father Constantinus in surprise. 'They are farming families. Why do they need schooling? What use will that be to them when they dig the fields or harvest their crops?'

'I am concerned about their future. Having looked at the village records I see there has been quite a considerable increase in the number of births that have taken place over the last twenty years. Soon there will not be sufficient farm land to provide a profitable occupation for the young men. They need to be able to look at other occupations.'

Theo frowned. 'What else would they do?'

'If they had some education, could read and write, manage their numbers, they would have the opportunity of finding other employment. They could become shop keepers, clerks, teachers, maybe enter the church.'

'We have three shop keepers, the baker and the iron worker. We have no need for anything else.' Theo looked at Father Constantinus suspiciously. 'It could give them ideas above their station. Has the Bishop asked you to indoctrinate the young men and persuade them to enter the church?'

Father Constantinus shook his head. 'Times have moved on from when you were a boy. In the towns there are schools, run by men who have been trained how to teach and educate the young. They are even admitting girls to them.'

'Whatever for? The girls need to know how to cook and run a home, bring up a family, not read and write.'

'It is beneficial for them to understand how to count their money. When they go shopping they need to know they have been given the correct change, how much they should charge for their services.'

Theo reddened slightly. 'What kind of services?'

'Dress making, cleaning, laundry work, but that is beside the point. I want to start a school for the boys here in the village.'

'A school? Where would it be and who would run it? The only person with any learning is Sofia's husband and he's busy each day. He's a tax man.'

Father Constantinus looked at Alesandros as if seeing him for the first time. 'Then you know the value of education,' he smiled. 'I would run it from the church, just a couple of mornings or afternoons each week. I obviously have enough education to be able to teach youngsters to a certain level. I thought about becoming a teacher, but decided my first duty was to God. I believe he has sent me here to better the lives of the young men and women in Kastelli.'

Theo sat there nonplussed. They had no need of a school, but how did one argue with a priest? He shrugged. 'Well, I suppose there is no harm in you showing them how to write their name and numbers.'

Father Constantinus leaned forward. 'There is just one small problem and I hope you will be able to help me. I understand that you are the head man of the village and well known for your kindness and willingness to help the villagers. I will need some money initially. Not a lot; just enough to provide them with paper and pencils. Once they have become proficient with their letters I will teach them how to read from the Bible.'

Theo smiled to himself. So that was the reason for the priest's call. He wanted money.

'Surely the church has sufficient funds to buy paper and pencils?'

Father Constantinus nodded. 'Of course, but I would have to apply to the Bishop. That takes time. I would have to prove to him that the materials were necessary and I cannot do that until I have had a chance to educate the youngsters and I am able to show him the result of my work.'

Theo sighed. 'How much will these paper and pencils cost?' he asked.

'I am sure that twenty drachmas would be sufficient initially.'

'Twenty drachmas.' Theo turned the sum over in his mind. And finally shook his head. 'It could be a complete waste of money. Suppose no one attends your school? What will you do with all the paper and pencils then?'

'I would not rush off tomorrow and purchase them. I plan to talk to the villagers first and persuade them that it is in their own interest for their sons to attend the classes. Once I know I will have a few pupils I will purchase whatever is necessary. I will also charge the parents a drachma a week and I should be able to repay you within a year.'

Theo chuckled. 'What makes you think the villagers have a drachma to spare each week? I can't see them being willing to *pay* you. They would prefer their son to be out in the fields working rather than sitting in a room being shown how to write his name.'

Father Constantinus's face fell. 'So you are not willing to help me?'

'I didn't say that. I said the villagers would be unwilling to pay you to teach their boys. I'll give you twenty drachmas for the pencils and paper. If the villagers refuse to send their sons to you I will expect it to be repaid to me.'

Alesandros shook his head in despair. No wonder Theo never had the money put aside for his taxes. He was far too willing to give his money away. Alesandros approved of the idea the priest had to start a school to educate the boys, but the villagers should be willing to pay for the privilege. His father had paid for him to attend High School and not regretted his investment.

Father Constantinus beamed with delight. 'Thank you. I can assure you it will be money well spent. A bit of education can make a tremendous difference to a young man's life.'

Spring 1914

Once the villagers had recovered from the initial shock of Father Symeon's death their lives returned to their regular routine. They no longer stopped each other and discussed his sudden demise or stepped inside the church each morning to say a quick prayer before hurrying about their business. Father Constantinus was now accepted as their village priest, and although they were all still a little wary of the newcomer they did not actively dislike him.

Each Sunday he exhorted his congregation to have patience and understanding. The men should have patience with their wives' short comings and the women should be understanding of their duties and comply with their husbands' demands. He reminded them that if there was anger and disagreements in the house it would reflect upon the children and they would grow up miserable and unhappy. At the end of his sermon he would look solemnly at the men and remind them that the sins of the father's were visited on the children.

Maria considered his words. Was Theo's gambling a sin? Was that why they had been forced to give their house to Alesandros and spend a miserable few months living in a cottage? Surely the good deeds her husband accomplished should mitigate his one small fault.

Sofia reflected on his words. Did the sins of the fathers also mean the sins of the mothers? Was she wrong to have gone to Theophalia and asked for her help? She was certain that Alesandros would be extremely angry if he ever found out.

She had explained to Theophalia that she did not feel ready to cope with another child yet and was there an herbal concoction she could take that would prevent her from conceiving.

Theophalia had looked at her in surprise. Usually the married women came to her asking for something to help them conceive. Tryphaine was a regular visitor each month. It was only a wayward youngster, normally after having had a scare, who would come to her and ask for a contraceptive medicine.

'How old is your little Maria now?' asked Theophalia.

Sofia looked puzzled. 'Most of a year. Alesandros has the date she was born written down.'

Theophalia frowned. 'There is no reason why you should not have another child. Your body has had plenty of recovery time.'

'I'm still feeding her a little.'

'That will make no difference. Sometimes that will stop conception occurring.'

Sofia tried to smile. She could not feed the little girl forever. 'I'd just like to be certain that I won't start another for a few months. I want Maria to stop soiling her clothes at night before I have another load of washing to deal with each day.'

Theophalia shook her head. 'Nature has a way of making up its own mind when we are to have our children. I can give you something that will act as a preventative for a while.'

'Thank you, Theophalia. That will be a weight off my mind.'

'I cannot guarantee that it will be effective, accidents do happen. I'll make you up a supply for three months.'

Sofia nodded eagerly. 'Then I can come and ask for some more if I still feel unready?'

Theophalia shook her head. 'I'd not recommend you to take it for any longer than three months. You could find yourself unable to conceive when you do finally decide you are ready.'

Sofia bit her lip. She loved Maria dearly, but was not sure if she actually wanted to have another child. 'How much do I owe you?' she asked.

'Ten drachmas.'

Sofia pulled some notes from her apron pocket. She would have to be frugal with her food purchases this week. She could ask Alesandros for a couple of extra drachmas, saying she had purchased some extra washing soap ready for Clean Monday, but he would want to know exactly what she had bought that had cost her ten drachmas.

Sofia felt miserable. Despite taking almost a spoonful of the evil smelling herbal concoction she had purchased from Theophalia each day her monthly course had not arrived. She would wait until the end of the week and then visit Theophalia again. There might be something more powerful that she could give her.

She removed the sheets from their bed and took them outside in the yard, giving Maria a small bowl of water to splash around in whilst she scrubbed and pounded the soiled linen. When hers and Alesandros's bedding was clean she would wash her parents' sheets and rinse Maria's soiled clothes through in the water afterwards. She planned the week in her head. The sheets today, clean their bedroom thoroughly tomorrow and wash Maria's soiled clothes properly. The following day she would wash the shirts and trousers belonging to the men and begin to clean the living room whilst her mother boiled and coloured the eggs.

During the week she would also need to find time to wash the windows and beat the rugs and wall hangings. Not everything could be left to be done at the very last minute.

Sofia emptied the cupboards in the dresser and piled the plates and bowls onto the table and pulled the end of the heavy dresser away from the wall, refusing to allow her mother to help her. The dresser was heavier than she had realised and she could feel her stomach muscles pulling.

'You just keep Maria safely out of the way, Mamma. I can manage.'

Maria clicked her tongue. 'You should have asked your father and Alesandros to pull it out before they left the house.'

Sofia shrugged. 'It would have disrupted their morning routine. They would have had to wait whilst I removed everything and then I might not have had time to clean behind it today. I would have had to ask them to put it back, pile everything up on it and then do it all again tomorrow.'

There were copious amounts of dust and spider's webs behind the dresser and Sofia brushed them away conscientiously. The dresser should really be pulled out more than once a year; likewise their mattresses should be beaten more frequently. She would certainly ask her father and Alesandros to take them out to the yard the following day and bring them back in later.

She ran a wet cloth over the tiles and began to push the dresser back into place. One of the legs stuck on the damp tiles and jerked to a halt, sending a painful shudder through her. She tried to move it again, but just did not seem to have the strength. She would have to leave it until the men returned.

Sofia finished dusting the dresser and brought a bowl of water in from the scullery. 'I'll wash all the plates and dishes. We'll need the table for our meal so I'll make sure I can put them straight back inside once the men have pushed the dresser into place. That will be another job done.'

A couple of hours later Sofia felt the need to visit the outhouse and gave a sigh of relief when she saw her course had started. She had a week without having to please Alesandros and she need not take the herbal mixture that was so unpleasant. At least Theophalia's medicine appeared to have worked.

The coming of Father Constantinus had made a difference to the lives of the villagers. He had suggested that Despina should purchase a cart and take her goats' milk around to the cottages rather than waiting for the villagers to come to her. It made sense. She could milk the animals first thing in the morning, deliver the milk and then be free for the remainder of the day to work out in the fields with her husband.

Despina went to Theo and asked if he would be able to lend her three hundred drachmas for the purchase of a cart. Theo demurred. He did not have that amount of money to hand. He spoke to Alesandros who agreed with alacrity.

'I will lend her the money,' he said. 'She will have to repay me and I will expect interest until the debt is finally settled.'

'I'm sure she would be willing to let you have the milk without charge.'

'And how many years would it be before I had received all my money back?' Alesandros shook his head. 'No, it has to be a formal agreement. We will meet with Father Constantinus and he will explain to her that I will expect her to repay me five drachmas each week. As she pays the amount of interest owing will reduce until her debt is cleared.'

Theo tried to work out how much interest Alesandros would be charging, but it was beyond him.

Father Constantinus looked at the figures Alesandros presented to him and shook his head. 'I cannot recommend that Despina accepts this agreement. If she pays interest on the amount that is outstanding each month by the time she has repaid the loan she will have paid you more in interest than the original loan. She will never be free of her debt.'

'It is the same as a bank would charge.'

'But you are not a bank. I suggest you agree to loan Despina three hundred drachmas and she has to repay you three hundred and seventy five drachmas. A set figure.'

Alesandros looked at Father Constantinus sourly. 'If she knows that is the final amount she has to pay me she may well only pay five or ten drachmas each month. To know that interest is building up is an incentive to pay.'

Father Constantinus smiled sadly at Alesandros. 'It would be to someone like yourself who understands finance, but Despina does not have the ability to grasp the concept. If you are agreeable to charge her a total of seventy five drachmas interest I am willing to draw up an agreement between you stating how much she will repay each month until her debt is cleared and she can place her mark. Any more than that and I would have to speak to her and tell her to save up her money until she could afford to buy a cart.'

Alesandros sighed. He knew it was impossible to argue with the priest.

Father Constantinus looked after Alesandros speculatively as he left. He knew exactly which sermon he would preach on Sunday and he hastened to look up the appropriate passage in his Bible.

"Beware! Be on your guard against greed of every kind, for even when someone has more than enough, his possessions do not give him life."

The farmers were urged to take their produce to the village shop where they would be paid for their goods and the shopkeeper would charge the villagers accordingly. 'It is no different from taking them to the market in Neapoli,' Father Constantinus explained. 'It will be more convenient for the women. If they forget something it is easier to go back to the shop than find out where you are working and ask you to return to your garden so they can buy some tomatoes or courgettes.'

Manos refused to comply with Father Constantinus's ideas. 'If I wring the neck of a chicken today and it hangs in the shop for a week it will be covered in maggots. If anyone wants a chicken or a rabbit they must come to me. They'll see me kill it and know it's fresh.'

The idea Father Constantinus had for a school for the boys was rejected out of hand by the farmers. They declared their sons were needed to help them on the farms during the summer months and could not spend the time doing something useless like learning their letters. One did suggest that the younger children, those too small to be able to work, were sent to Father Constantinus. He could keep them safe and out from under their feet for a couple of afternoons.

Father Constantinus shook his head. 'The idea is not for me to look after your babies. I want to give your boys some useful knowledge that will help them when they become adults. If Mr Alesandros gives them a loan they will be able to read the agreement for themselves and sign it with their name. They will not have to rely on me to tell them what is says and work out how much the loan will have cost when the interest has been added. It will give them independence. They will be in a position to negotiate the terms with Mr Alesandros.'

Still the villagers hesitated. During the winter months their boys could be spared for a few hours, particularly if it rained. They certainly could not attend if they were needed to pick apples or harvest the olives. Father Constantinus had an idea that he would be made use of to keep their sons out of mischief during the winter days, but nonetheless he determined to try again to persuade the farmers to send their boys on a regular basis to receive a rudimentary education.

Theo gave his wife a gold necklace on her Name Day in August and Alesandros did likewise when Sofia's Name Day arrived in September.

'It is a shame that we are only celebrating your Name Day and not an addition to our family as we did last year. Have you not had any signs?' The boy Alesandros longed for had not appeared.

Sofia shook her head. 'As yet I have had nothing. I would tell you if I was expecting again.'

'Maybe we should try a little harder.'

'Maybe you are trying when it is the wrong time,' she replied quickly. 'When I say I am too tired you still insist.'

'Every day you say you are tired,' protested Alesandros.

Sofia nodded. 'That is true. It is tiring keeping the house clean and doing the cooking whilst looking after a small child.'

'Other women seem to manage.'

Sofia shrugged. 'They must have more stamina than me. Thank

you for my necklace, Alesandros.' Sofia slipped it over her head. It did not feel as heavy as the other two he had given her, but it was difficult to judge as she usually wore both his previous gifts to church on a Sunday.

'We seem to have had a good crop of apples this year,' remarked Theo to Alesandros. 'I reckon we'll be picking for two more days yet.'

Alesandros did not comment. If all the farmers had a good crop the price of apples would drop and the tax the farmers were charged would be less. It was more beneficial to him when a tax rose and the farmer was unable to pay the full amount he owed on time.

'I'll see how the others in the area fared when I make my rounds next week.'

'Little Maria helped, didn't you?' Maria was now walking unaided and she held on to her grandfather's knee. 'She picked up the rotten ones and put them in the basket for Despina's goats.' Theo smiled benevolently down at her.

Sofia smiled at her daughter. 'She thought it was a game. Mamma couldn't believe the state of her when she brought the bread and cheese up for the workers. She wanted to bring her home and give her a bath, but I said she might as well stay and have a bath later. It won't hurt her to get dirty.'

'I hope you kept her well away from the ladders.'

'Of course I did. She was with me and I was sorting the apples with some of the other women. If we found a rotten one we put it on the ground near her. The basket for Despina was right next to me so she didn't stray from my side.'

'Provided she doesn't pick up one with a wasp inside.'

Sofia sighed. 'Alesandros, we all made sure that there was no wasp in any of them that Maria had. If we saw one with a wasp we threw the apple as far away as possible. We none of us want to get stung.'

Alesandros grunted. He had never picked apples and had no desire to do so. He did not like the idea of his wife and child working like the common villagers, but it was traditional that everyone helped pick apples and harvest olives.

Sofia was almost certain that she was pregnant. Her monthly course was three weeks late. The potion Theophalia had given her had obviously worked as Maria was now sixteen months old, but Theophalia had refused to provide her with a further supply.

'I've told you, no more than three months. You've managed to make it last longer than that. I suppose you stopped taking it when you bled.'

Sofia nodded. 'I saw no point in taking it then. I was obviously not going to become pregnant.' She did not admit that she had taken a little less than Theophalia had instructed and managed to make the herbal contraceptive last for five months rather than three.

'Well I'm not prepared to give you any more. Now you must let nature take its course.'

Now, within two weeks of being without her daily dose she felt sure she was expecting again. She felt nauseous each morning when she rose and her breasts were tender. At least Maria would be nearly two years old and able to climb off her mattress during the night to use the pot provided for her use.

As Sofia walked down the stairs, holding Maria's hand so she would not fall, she heard Alesandros talking to her father.

'The weather is holding well. I thought you could make a start on cutting the grass in the orchard.'

Theo shook his head. 'Not this week. I'm still making the raki. It won't hurt for the grass to wait another week. It will give it a chance to recover from where it was trampled down by the apple pickers.'

'It ought to be cut as soon as possible. Our mattresses and pillows need to be re-stuffed. The remainder can be stored in the old sheep shelters. Once you've cut it make sure you stack it well away from where I tether my donkey. I don't want her eating it. There's plenty of fresh grass for her to crop.'

'I'd best make sure the shelters are waterproof before I cut. No point in putting it in there and then finding the roof leaks.'

Alesandros twirled his moustache and took a final look in the mirror he used whilst shaving before relinquishing his place at the washstand to Theo.

Theo had peered into the container that held the olive skins and stones that were slowly fermenting and becoming alcohol the previous evening and licked his lips. It was time to start to drain off the clear liquid into storage jars and the village men could come to sample it, comparing it with the batch made the previous year. Once he had finished making the raki he would have no excuse to delay him cutting the grass in the orchard.

Theo finished shaving and rose to his feet with a sigh. 'I'd rather be making raki than cutting the grass. I'll have to sharpen my scythe before I can make a start.'

'I'm sure you would,' remarked Maria. 'It won't take you long and you know you'll enjoy being up in the orchard for the day.' His wife tried to placate him.

'More like a week. Have you seen how long that grass is? It would help if Alesandros tethered his donkey in a different place each week,' grumbled Theo. 'That would help to keep it under control. I'll bring a couple of sacks back with me so you can make a start on the mattresses next week.'

Still muttering beneath his breath Theo went out to the yard and put a sharp edge to his scythe. He tested the edge frequently with his thumb until he was satisfied he could do no better. He opened the back door and took his jacket from the peg. He did not really need it, but it was more decorous for a man in his position to walk along the main street wearing a jacket rather than being in his shirt sleeves. Once he reached the orchard he would remove it and hang it on a convenient branch.

Theo mopped his brow and took another mouthful of water from his leather bottle. He had managed to cut about a quarter of the long grass in the orchard and it was lying in untidy piles where the sun would dry out the moisture before he gathered and stacked it. He propped his scythe up against the trunk of a tree and wandered over to the old sheep shelters. He pushed at the walls and they seemed sound, then went inside and looked up at the roof to see if any chinks of daylight could be seen. They both appeared to be weatherproof and he gave a sigh of relief. He really was getting too old for climbing about on roofs.

Theo returned home, pleased with his day's work and delighted to be able to report to Alesandros that there were no repairs needed to the sheep shelters.

'I'll cut some more grass tomorrow and by the end of the week I should be able to start gathering and storing it.'

Alesandros nodded. He was not interested in the progress of farm work. If he asked Theo to cut the grass he expected it to be done without a problem.

'I'm planning to go down to Aghios Nikolaos this afternoon,' announced Alesandros when he had finished shaving. 'I thought I would bring back a fish. I'll get it straight from one of the fishermen and now the weather is cooler it should still be fresh when I get home.'

Sofia smiled. She liked fish and the last time they had eaten it Maria had been anxious for every mouthful. Fish was a treat as the only time they ever ate it was when Alesandros rode down to Aghios Nikolaos. The villagers bought from the fish man who would arrive in the village with his cart, call out to announce his arrival and stand brushing the flies off his fish whilst his customers gathered around and selected those that still had the brightest eyes and least offensive smell. No one knew if the fish had been freshly caught or was left from previous days.

Alesandros placed his rusks and olives safely into his bag,

chucked Maria under the chin and placed a kiss on Sofia's forehead. She no longer cringed when he did this, but accepted it with a good grace.

Sofia and her mother discussed how they would serve the fish Alesandros proposed to bring back to Kastelli with him. 'We ought to have something else ready that we can heat up,' cautioned Maria. 'He may not bring a fish if he doesn't think it is fresh.'

'Shall I make some dolmades?' offered Sofia. 'We can cook them today and if we don't need them they will be there for tomorrow's meal. I can take Maria with me when I go to pick the leaves. That will keep her out of your way whilst you get on with some weaving. She'll probably think she's helping by putting anything she finds in the basket.'

Maria smiled at her daughter. 'She's no trouble to me. Are you feeling alright? You look rather pale and weary.'

Sofia shrugged. 'I'm a bit tired. Maria woke me up twice in the night and I had a job getting back to sleep again afterwards.'

'You could go up and have an hour's sleep now if you wanted. I can watch Maria.'

Sofia shook her head. 'No thank you, Mamma. I doubt if I would go to sleep and then I'd just feel guilty that I was lying down up there for no good reason whilst you were working.'

'Have some milk when Despina calls. That will help you.'

Sofia agreed dutifully. She doubted if a glass of milk would have the same desired effect as the herbal medicine, but it would certainly do her no harm. Pulling out the heavy dresser seemed to have been effective the previous time she had thought she was pregnant. She wondered if she could find an excuse to pull it out again.

Theo raked the cut grass, turning it over as he did so to enable it to dry thoroughly. He had cleaned the cellulose from his scythe and sharpened it again. Although he had grumbled to Maria about the chore he took a pride in his prowess with a whetstone and there was no one in the village who could accomplish a sharper edge to their cutting tools than him.

He placed his rake beside a tree and reached for his scythe. Somehow the handle became entangled with his jacket that was hanging next to it and he was unable to catch it. The scythe fell to the ground, neatly slicing through Theo's trousers and his leg. For a moment he looked at it aghast, then the autumn sunshine disappeared and his world turned black as he collapsed on the ground, the blood spurting from the severed artery.

Sofia took her daughter's hand and picked up her basket. 'We'll walk up and see Grandpa and collect some vine leaves on the way back. Would you like that?'

Maria smiled. She was always happy to be outside in the sunshine rather than inside the house where she was expected to sit and play with her rag doll or the odd shaped pieces of wood that her grandfather had made for her whilst her mother cooked and her grandmother sat at her weaving loom.

They walked slowly along the road towards the orchard, stopping to speak to the various neighbours they met and Maria lifted up her arms to be carried. She was not truly tired from walking, but she knew they would reach the orchard more quickly if her mother carried her and her grandfather would stop whatever he was doing to play with her.

Sofia shook her head. 'I'm not carrying a big girl like you yet. After we've seen Grandpa I'll carry you for a while.'

Reaching the orchard Sofia looked for her father. He was nowhere in sight and she peered cautiously inside the sheep shelters before lifting Maria into her arms and beginning to walk over the rough ground.

'Pappa,' she called. 'Pappa, where are you?'

Sofia was half way down the orchard when she saw her father lying on the grass and hurried towards him. Had he hit his head on a low branch? Was he taking a rest? Surely, even if he were asleep he would have heard her calling him.

As she reached him she could see the blood pooling around his feet and the flies settling on it. With a horrified gasp she set Maria down and touched his forehead. 'Pappa. Pappa, speak to me. What has happened?' She received no response and his eyes had a dull and lifeless look.

The flies retreated in an angry swarm, only to settle back again as Sofia stood up. She seized Maria in her arms and stumbled back across the uneven ground as fast as she was able. Upon reaching the pathway she broke into a run towards the outlying houses of the village.

'Help me,' she called, hoping someone would hear her and open their door. She needed Theophalia and she lived at the far end of the village. Maria began to cry, unhappy at the way she was being bumped up and down as her mother ran.

Perpetua looked out of her doorway and saw the distressed young woman. 'What's wrong, Sofia?'

'Please, look after Maria for me,' she gasped and thrust her daughter into Perpetua's arms. 'An accident. I need Theophalia.'

Maria let out a wail and Sofia ignored her. Struggling for breath and ignoring the pain in her side she continued to run down the path, past her own house and arrived at Theophalia's cottage where she hammered on the door.

Theophalia opened the top half of her door and frowned. 'What's wrong, Sofia? Is it Maria?'

Sofia shook her head. 'Pappa. In the orchard. Come quick.' The words came out in staccato sentences as Sofia clutched her side, hoping the pain would subside.

'Has he had a fall?'

'He's bleeding.'

Theophalia picked up her bag that she used for emergencies. It held cloths to staunch blood and herbal remedies that could help with pain. She followed Sofia back along the path to the orchard, having to hurry to keep pace with the girl and unable to ask her for more details of her father's accident.

Sofia ran across the rough ground, heedless of turning her ankle, hoping she would see her father sitting up. He was lying exactly as she had left him, but the flies seemed more numerous than ever, their buzzing filling the air.

Theophalia took in the scene at a glance. 'Go over there,' she ordered and waved her arm to send Sofia away. The flies rose into the air momentarily and resettled.

Sofia walked away a couple of steps and watched as Theophalia took her father's pulse and shook her head. She ripped open his trousers to expose the gaping wound and Sofia turned away and was violently sick. She did not see Theophalia cover his face with his coat so that his sightless eyes no longer stared up at them.

Theophalia rose and placed her am around Sofia's shoulders. 'There's nothing I can do, Sofia.'

'Can't you bandage his leg? Stop the bleeding?'

Theophalia shook her head. 'It would have happened very quickly. Even if I had been here with him when the accident happened it is unlikely I could have saved him.'

Sofia's face went white and she swayed on her feet. Theophalia pushed her to the ground. She did not want the girl to faint. 'Put your head down between your knees,' she ordered. 'You'll feel better in a few minutes.'

Sofia was not sure if the buzzing she could hear was inside her head or from the flies that seemed to be everywhere around them. 'Pappa,' she moaned.

Theophalia held Sofia's hand as they walked slowly back up the path to the village. She would accompany her back to her house and break the news to Maria as gently as possible. Then she would have to visit Father Constantinus and he would toll the bell so all the villagers would know that a death had taken place. After that the men would carry him back to his house on a door and she would wash him and prepare him for his funeral the following day.

Maria sat on a stool beside her dead husband. The tears ran down her face as she looked at the shrouded body. The memories of all the good times they had spent together during their married life flooded back to her. Their first night, when both of them had been fumbling, innocent young people; then their joy when Sofia was born. Over the years they had disagreed, but never argued seriously, even when she knew Theo was gambling away the money that he owed for his taxes. The bath nights, when they had washed each other's backs and often made personal remarks about parts of each other's anatomy. Never again would she feel his hand in hers or the squeeze he would give to her shoulders, the kiss he would place on her cheek just before he turned on his side to sleep.

Alesandros arrived back in Kastelli. He had heard the church bell tolling when he was still some distance away and tried to make the donkey move at a faster pace. He racked his brains, there were a number of elderly people in the village and the bell could be tolling for any one of them. He recoiled in shock when he reached his house and saw the flowers laid outside. Hurriedly he tied the donkey's reins to the metal window grill and strode inside.

'What's happened?' he asked, and was relieved as Sofia came forwards, her face streaked with tears and with Maria in her arms.

'It's Pappa. He had an accident.'

Alesandros placed his bag on the table and opened his arms to her. For once she did not ignore his invitation and walked into them. He held her gently as she cried, not remonstrating with Maria as she tugged at his moustache. Finally he moved her away from his shoulder and went over to the dresser. He took out three glasses and a bottle of raki, pouring a generous measure for each of them.

Alesandros handed a glass to Maria. 'Drink that, Maria. It will steady your nerves.' He handed another glass to Sofia. 'You also.

You've obviously had a terrible shock.' Alesandros downed the raki in one mouthful and poured himself another. 'Tell me exactly what happened.'

Sofia took a sip of raki and wrinkled her nose. She wiped her nose on her sleeve. 'I took Maria for a walk up to the orchard. We were going to collect vine leaves as we walked back.' Tears began to run down her face. 'Pappa was lying on the ground and there was blood and flies everywhere. He wouldn't speak to me and I ran to get Theophalia. She said he was dead,' added Sofia in a whisper.

'How did it happen? Did he have a fall?'

'Theophalia said he had cut his leg with the scythe. She said he had cut through the big artery and all his blood had come out. All of it!'

Alesandros shuddered. When an animal was slaughtered the artery in the neck was cut and death was immediate. Poor Theo would not have had any chance of survival even if Theophalia had been standing next to him at the time. He poured a third glass of raki for himself.

Throughout the remainder of the evening the villagers arrived to give Maria their sympathy and light a candle for Theo. Maria sat by his side unmoving. Sofia moved around, automatically feeding her daughter and preparing a sparse meal for Alesandros. He insisted she ate also and Sofia tried to persuade her mother to join them. Father Constantinus arrived and declared he would spend the night sitting beside Theo's body along with Maria. He hoped that once he was left alone with the grieving widow he would be able to comfort her with prayer and persuade her to go to her bed and get some rest.

The entire population of Kastelli attended Theo's funeral, all dressed sombrely in black. They had followed the sad procession to the church lamenting loudly, their cries rising to a crescendo as Theo's body was finally placed in the hurriedly dug grave. Wine, bread and olives had been provided after the service and Father

Constantinus had accompanied the family back to their home where he said a final prayer and joined them in a meal. Sofia had cooked the fish; there had been no bad smell from it so she assumed it was still fresh enough to eat.

Alesandros sat and spoke kindly to his mother-in-law. 'Maria, we are all hurting due to your loss. Would it help if I collected the rents for you each week? I feel it is the least I could do for you.'

Slowly Maria shook her head. 'If you do that I won't know if they've paid me all they owe.'

'I would write down what each person paid. You could see for yourself.'

Maria gazed at him scathingly. 'Figures written on a piece of paper would mean nothing to me. No, I'll collect them myself. I know how much is put in my hand.'

'What will you do with the money?'

Maria gave him a puzzled look. 'Put it in the box under my bed, of course.'

Alesandros smiled. 'Provided you keep it safe. Remember you will need it to pay the olive tax for the villagers and any personal expenses.'

'Personal expenses?'

'New boots, wool for your weaving, the presents you give when a couple get married or a child is christened.'

Maria nodded. She had always relied on Theo to deal with the finances, however inefficiently. 'I'll have enough,' she said wearily.

Alesandros shrugged. He had initially made the offer with the intention of being helpful and then realised that if she agreed it could be to his advantage. It would give him a certain amount of control over the properties and he could have refused on her behalf to pay for all the unnecessary repairs the villagers claimed.

Sofia realised she was no longer pregnant. She had looked at her soiled clothing in relief. Obviously the shock of finding her father had affected her internally as well as mentally. She found herself trembling uncontrollably during the day and she would wake in the night, her cheeks wet with tears. Alesandros would sense her distress and hold her gently until she went back to sleep again. For once she welcomed the comfort offered by Alesandros's arms.

Father Constantinus was genuinely sorry about the death of Theo, but he also realised he could use the sad situation as a furtherance of his ambitions. The Sunday after the man's funeral he reminded his congregation of the generosity of the dead man.

'I know how much every single one of you misses Theo Angelakis. He was respected in the village for his common sense, his willingness to help and his generosity. We will all remember him in our hearts. Before he died he had given me twenty drachmas to purchase pencils and paper for the boys to attend classes where I would teach them to read, write and calculate their numbers. I cannot return that money to him now. Let us show how much we respected and admired him by sending your boys to me for some schooling during the winter for the education that Theo believed would be useful to them.'

Alesandros remembered Theo being quite scathing about the idea of education and he noticed that the priest would not meet his eyes. The village men who had been adamant that their boys needed no education felt guilty. If Theo had thought it a good idea then maybe they should agree to send the boys along for a few weeks and see how they progressed.

Stratos paid his monthly visit to his grandmother and was shocked when she told him that Theo was dead.

'I wondered why so many people were wearing black arm bands. How did he die? A heart attack?'

Olga shook her head and related the details of Theo's fatal accident.

Stratos shuddered. 'That's awful. Poor Miss Sofia. It must have been a terrible shock to her when she found him. I'll have to visit and say how sorry I am. Mr Theo was such a good man. If he hadn't given me a chance to mend my ways I would still be making a nuisance of myself in the village.'

Olga looked at her grandson. He was not the bad boy the village had thought. He still had his pointed chin and prominent ears, but the skinny little boy had filled out and was becoming a muscular young man.

'Do you have a lot of work?'

Stratos nodded. 'There's always someone who needs an outhouse properly repaired or a new wall built. Mr Benediktos is a specialist when it comes to repairing cisterns and I'm learning from him all the time. Mr Benediktos says if I continue to work hard I'll be able to take over from him when he's too old to work anymore. He only has two girls so they can't do the work. I've a corner to sleep in and I eat the same food as the family. What more could I ask?'

'You keep your eyes and hands off Mr Benediktos's girls or you'll soon find you haven't a roof over your head and a job of work,' remarked Olga grimly.

Stratos grinned. 'I'm not that stupid, Grandma. There are plenty of girls around in Neapoli. It's not like here. Tell me what else has been happening since I last visited you, then I'll call on Mrs Maria and Miss Sofia on my way back to Neapoli.'

Autumn 1915

Sofia was definitely pregnant and she knew it would not be very much longer before her child was born. Her father had been dead over a year now and the annual memorial service had been held. Once again she had moved out the dresser whilst cleaning before Easter, but this time the child had stayed firmly inside her and she knew Theophalia would not be willing to give her any medicine that might move it. She was a married woman, already a mother, and there was no reason why she should not have more children.

Alesandros had been overjoyed when she told him and touched her stomach gently. 'A little boy this time, please.'

Sofia shrugged. 'You'll have to accept whatever I give you. Provided the child is strong and healthy you can ask for nothing more.'

Maria had accepted her daughter's news with a tear in her eye. 'Your Pappa would be pleased. He doted on your Maria.'

It was the first time her mother had spoken about her father since the day of his death. Each day Maria sat at her loom, weaving steadily from morning to night. The only exceptions were on a Saturday when she went around the cottages and collected her rents and Sunday when she visited church. She no longer shed tears, but Sofia could tell by the set of her mouth and the sadness in her eyes that Theo was never far from her thoughts. She held her mother tightly to her.

'I miss him too, Mamma. If this little one is a boy I shall insist he is called Theodopolous.'

Fotini arrived into the world without a problem for Sofia. She had woken during the night with the first warning signs and by mid-day she was holding her baby in her arms. Maria was curious and Sofia tried to explain to her daughter that Fotini was her new baby sister and must be touched gently.

Maria had finally stopped her incessant weaving to attend to her daughter, new grandchild and little Maria. Sofia was not sure if she was relieved to no longer hear the shuttle going backwards and forwards with regular monotony. Suddenly the house seemed quiet. She knew Alesandros was downstairs, but she did not want his company. He had admired his new daughter, kissed Sofia's forehead and immediately said he hoped for a boy the next time his wife conceived.

Sofia lay back, she felt exhausted and Theophalia had ordered her to rest and try to sleep.

'It will help you to regain your strength. You'll no doubt be awake in the night with Fotini. You must stay in bed until I've visited you tomorrow, then if all is well you can go downstairs for a short while. Join your family for a meal and then back to bed to continue to rest.'

Sofia began to make plans in her head as she drifted off to sleep. The room across from the one she and Alesandros shared would have to be cleaned out. It was no problem to have the two little girls in their room at present, but when they became older it would not be suitable for them all to share the one room when there was another available. They were not villagers, living in a two room cottage where bedding had to be fitted in wherever there was a space to accommodate the children. Her last thought before she fell asleep was that she would talk to Alesandros about the room tomorrow.

The arrival of Fotini seemed to have triggered a positive response from Maria. She no longer sat at her loom all day, but insisted she did the cooking and cleaning. Now, for the first time since her husband's death, Maria would prepare their meals whilst Sofia dealt with her children, her first job always to make the bread dough and take it up to the baker and collecting it later when the loaf was baked.

Sofia was grateful for the help her mother was giving to her. Once she had settled Fotini she would leave her in her mother's care whilst she walked with Maria to the shops, allowing her daughter to carry the empty basket and once there help to choose the produce. Maria always picked up the first tomato or onion and Sofia would make her look at it and see if there was a tomato that was firmer or an onion that was larger.

When Alesandros arrived home Maria would run to him and clutch his leg, saying 'Pappa, Pappa.' Alesandros would stroke her hair and then walk over to look at Fotini in her cradle. He seemed far more at ease with his second child than his first.

Sofia had discussed her idea of turning the storage room into a bedroom for the girls when they were older and Alesandros was enthusiastic. At present they were no inconvenience, but once they were older they would no doubt ask for an explanation of the strange noises they heard some nights.

Maria no longer slept after their mid-day meal and once again Sofia would leave Fotini in the care of her mother and take Maria out for a walk or sit and play exclusively with her. She did not want her older daughter to feel that the new arrival was receiving all her attention. Often she would walk up to visit Tryphaine, who doted on Sofia's small girl. She and Nikos had still not had any success with starting a family and Tryphaine was in despair.

'What can I do?' she asked Sofia. 'What do you and Alesandros do?'

Sofia felt embarrassed. 'Nothing different from any other married couple.'

'Do you enjoy it?'

'Not particularly. It's a husband's right so I tolerate it.'

'Does he hurt you?'

'No, never. Does Nikos hurt you?

'Oh, no. How long do you take?'

Sofia felt her face redden. 'That depends. Sometimes it takes Alesandros longer than other times.'

Tryphaine frowned. 'How long is longer?'

'I don't know. Sometimes he is satisfied within a few minutes, other times it seems to go on forever.'

Tryphaine sighed. 'I wish Nikos would go on forever, just occasionally. One moment he is there and then he's gone.'

'Have you talked to Theophalia and asked her advice?'

Tryphaine shook her head. 'I've asked her for medicine to help me, but it doesn't seem to do any good.'

'Maybe it is Nikos who needs some medicine,' suggested Sofia.

'Do you think that could be the answer?' asked Tryphaine eagerly.

Sofia shrugged. 'I don't know. You would have to ask Theophalia.'

Tryphaine considered Sofia's words. Could Theophalia give Nikos some medicine that would help her conceive? She would pay her a visit tomorrow and ask her advice.

Theophalia listened to Tryphaine patiently, asked her some very intimate questions and shook her head.

'I don't think there is any medicine I could give to Nikos. He has a problem that affects many men. They get over excited and cannot control themselves. The sperm ejects against your leg. You'll never become pregnant that way.'

Tryphaine left Theophalia feeling thoroughly miserable and intensely angry. If the medicine woman was right she would never have a child. Why had her parents arranged for her to marry Nikos? There were other boys in the village who would have been equally as suitable and who obviously had no trouble siring children. She walked through the village and along the path towards Neapoli, averting her eyes as she passed the orchard where Theo had met his death. She felt too unhappy to return home and prepare the family meal; that could wait until she had spent some time alone and accepted that she was going to be childless and no doubt everyone would say it was her fault.

'Hello, Phaini, where are you off to?'

Tryphaine raised her eyes from the path and saw Stratos standing before her.

'Just walking,' she said dully.

'I'm on my way to visit my grandmother. We could walk back together.'

'I'm not ready to go back yet.'

'What's wrong, Phaini?'

Tryphaine shrugged. 'Why should anything be wrong?'

'You look upset. What's happened? Have you and Nikos had a row?'

'No.'

'Have you found out he's seeing someone else?'

'Why should he be?'

'Well,' Stratos hesitated. 'You've been married quite a while now.'

'Have you heard that he's seeing someone?'

Stratos shook his head. 'I was just wondering if that was why you looked so miserable.'

Tryphaine gave a deep sigh and felt her eyes filling with tears.

'Come on, now. It can't be that bad. Come and sit down over here and tell me what the problem is. I'll help if I can.'

Tryphaine stiffened. Stratos had offered to help her if he could. Was that the answer? Nikos would never need to know that he was not the father. She ran a trembling hand across her forehead. Dare she ask Stratos?

'I want to be a mother,' she said in a low voice.

Stratos nodded. 'Most women have that desire.'

'Would you help me?'

'Me? You're asking me?' Stratos could not believe his ears.

Tryphaine nodded. 'You said you would help me if you could. Nikos isn't able to – to do his duty and I'm desperate.'

Stratos whistled between his teeth. 'But if Nikos isn't able to, well, perform, what will he say if you become pregnant? He'll know it isn't his.'

'Nikos doesn't realise he has a problem. He'll believe the child is his.'

'Why are you asking me, Phaini?'

Tryphaine shrugged. 'Why not? Besides, you don't live in the village. If I do have your child you won't be forever looking at it and wishing it would call you Pappa.'

'Are you sure you want this, Phaini? I don't want you to start accusing me of raping you.'

'I'm quite sure, Stratos.' Tryphaine lay back on the grass verge and Stratos shook his head.

'Not here. Follow me.'

Stratos led Tryphaine away from the main path and behind a clump of bushes. He looked at her again.

'Are you quite sure?'

Tryphaine nodded and sat down on the ground, pulling her skirt up to her waist. Stratos shrugged. He would be a fool to turn down the invitation. If Tryphaine accused him of any wrong doing he would deny ever having met her that day.

'Am I pregnant now?' asked Tryphaine. She had never had such a satisfying and exhilarating experience from Nikos.

Stratos grinned at her as he straightened his clothing. 'I don't know. I've done my best. You'll have to wait and see.'

'If it hasn't worked this time can we try again?'

'No reason why not, but we'll have to be careful. You don't want Nikos finding out that you're meeting me.'

'When are you planning to visit your grandmother again?'

Stratos considered the situation. 'I'm going back to Neapoli now. You go home. That way we won't be seen together. I'll visit my grandmother next week.'

'How will I know you're in the village?'

'I'll whistle loudly as I walk past your house. Give me a few minutes then make your way up here. I'll make a quick call on Mrs Maria and join you as soon as I can.'

'Suppose it's raining?'

'Then I won't be walking from Neapoli to Kastelli. No point in getting soaked when I can visit another day.'

Tryphaine pulled her skirt down and tied her headscarf firmly back in place. Whilst the weather held she determined to go for a walk every day and call in on a friend as she returned until the villagers accepted her routine and thought nothing of it.

Tryphaine met Stratos on four more occasions and at their last meeting she had kissed him on the cheek.

'Thank you, Stratos. I wanted you to know before I told anyone else. I'm pregnant.'

'Really? Well, that's good news.' Stratos felt both relieved and disappointed. He had been worried that someone in the village would see them and word would get back to Nikos that Tryphaine was being unfaithful to him, but he had also relished his meetings with the desperately receptive young woman. 'You won't need me any more now.'

'I may. If I lost this one I'd want to try again.'

'No reason why you should lose it provided you're sensible. If that should happen tell my grandmother. I always ask her for the gossip when I visit. She'd be bound to tell me. I'll whistle as I pass your house the next few times I visit, but I won't expect to meet you up here. If all is well I'll no doubt see you walking around in a couple of months or so proudly showing off a bump.'

Tryphaine gave a little giggle. She was ecstatically happy and longing to tell everyone her good news.

Theophalia was surprised, but genuinely pleased, when Tryphaine called on her and said she was certain she was finally pregnant.

'You obviously sorted your problems out, then.'

Tryphaine smiled contentedly. 'Yes, I found a way.'

Nikos was both proud and delighted. When Tryphaine told him she was pregnant. He had begun to wish that he had married another girl from the village as Tryphaine appeared unable to bear him any children. Now he could hold his head up and boast to his companions that he too was going to be a father.

Spring 1916

Stratos had avoided any contact with Tryphaine once she had told him she was pregnant. When he visited his grandmother he would still whistle as he walked past Tryphaine's house and if he saw her in the village he would raise his hand to her, but not stop to speak. She had continued to go for a walk each day, saying that provided the weather was not too inclement the exercise was good for her.

Tryphaine's little boy was born during the middle of the night with very little assistance needed from Theophalia. She held him to her with a satisfied smile on her face as she looked down on the red and wrinkled face, all that was visible from the soft cloths that swaddled him.

'What will he be called?' asked Theophalia, as she bundled soiled cloths into a sack.

'Nikos wants to call him Timotheos, after his father.'

'A good choice as his Name Day will be in May.'

'That's what I thought,' agreed Tryphaine, although she did not mind what her child was called. Having successfully become a mother the name of the child was immaterial to her.

Stratos sat with his grandmother. 'So what is the news in the village?' he asked.

'Nothing that would interest you. Tomas has made some bee hives and placed them up in the orchard near the carob trees.

He's hoping a swarm will come, but at present there's no sign of a queen arriving. Tryphaine's had her baby. The girl's over the moon. She's so proud of him you'd think she'd made him all by herself without any help from Nikos. Walks up and down the village street whenever she has the chance showing him off. Shame about his ears, though; apart from those he's a fine boy.'

'His ears?'

'They're rather large and stick out. Didn't notice when he was all wrapped up but they're becoming obvious now.' She looked pointedly at Stratos.

'Oh,' Stratos tried to pass the comment off lightly. 'I thought for a moment you were going to say he was deaf.'

'Shouldn't be with ears that size.'

'No doubt they'll be less noticeable as he grows. Now, I have some news for you, Grandma. I'm working on my own next week. It's only a small job, constructing an outhouse, but Mr Benediktos says I'm in charge and can keep all the money for myself. If I do well he says he'll allow me to do more jobs on my own. I wish Mr Theo was still alive so I could tell him.'

Stratos passed his grandmother some drachmas and she shook her head. 'I've plenty left from the last time you visited. You ought to start saving your money. You'll need it when you decide to marry and settle down.'

'I'm not planning to do that for a while, besides, I've not met any girl who's taken my fancy.'

'Leave it too long and you'll find all the nice girls are already married. There's only Olympia here in the village who isn't wed and it isn't likely she'll find a suitor.'

'I think she has her sights set on Father Constantinus.' Stratos grinned impishly.

Olga pursed her lips. 'That's not a suitable thing to say about a man of the cloth. She's just happy to sit and polish silver and brass all day long and that suits him.'

'How is his school coming on? Are the boys attending?'

'Most of them went along during the winter. Used it as an excuse to be inside in the warm, no doubt.'

'I wish he had been here when I was younger. I'd have liked a bit of learning.'

'You?' Olga looked at her grandson in surprise.

'Mr Benediktos had to teach me how to count. He would say "fetch me ten bricks" and I had no idea how many he needed. I can read a few words now and write my name. I told my Pappa when I saw him last week and he wouldn't believe me until I showed him.'

'So what good is being able to write your name?'

Stratos shrugged. 'When Mr Benediktos pays me each week I don't have to put an "S" on a piece of paper now.'

Olga sniffed. 'I know my name starts with "O" and I use that as my mark. Everyone knows it's me.'

'Yes, well, times have changed, Grandma. Mr Benediktos says that soon everyone will be able to write their name and do their numbers.'

'What's the use of that? Better for the boys to know when to plant and harvest their crops and the girls to be taught to cook and sew.'

'There's a school in Neapoli where the boys go every day. They'll end up working in an office or being a tax collector like Mr Alesandros. They couldn't be farmers as they live in the town. Someone has to be able to do other jobs and for those they need to have had schooling.'

Olga sniffed again. 'You'll be getting ideas above your station in life very soon; just because you say you can write your name.'

Stratos felt disheartened by his grandmother's scathing response. He was proud that he knew the letters that made up his name and he could write them down. 'Yes, well, I'd better be going. I have to be up early tomorrow to start building that outhouse.'

Olga did not try to detain her grandson. She was proud of the success he was making of his life, but could see no benefit in him being able to write his name.

As Stratos walked past Tryphaine's house he whistled as usual and was surprised when she opened the door and greeted him with a smile.

'Hello, Stratos. Been visiting your grandmother?'

Stratos nodded. 'She tells me you have a little boy.'

Tryphaine looked down at the baby in her arms. 'He's made all the difference to my life.' She turned the little boy so that Stratos could see him. 'We've called him Timotheos.'

Stratos looked down at the wrapped infant and a pair of quizzical grey eyes looked up at him, making his stomach turn over. He was the only man from the village who had grey eyes, having inherited them from his mother who had claimed Athenian descent. How long would it be before the villagers looked at Tryphaine and began to wonder if Nikos was the biological father of her child?

'He's a fine boy,' he said. 'Look after him well.' Stratos raised his hand to her and walked away. He hoped the boy's eyes would darken as he grew older and that his ears would not be as pronounced as his grandmother had said.

Sofia was happy that her friend was a mother at last but she thought Timotheos an ugly little boy. She was pleased that both her girls had been pretty babies and were showing every sign of growing into good looking girls with the promise of being beautiful when they finally matured.

Alesandros was proud of his two daughters. He would sit with Fotini on his knee and Maria beside him whilst he read to them from the Bible on a Sunday afternoon. His mother-in-law and wife would sit respectfully silent, their hands folded in their laps whilst he read. Fotini often fell asleep in his arms and he would hand the Bible to Sofia and continue to hold his little girl, whilst

Maria would wriggle away from him and resume playing with her rag doll.

Alesandros had tried to persuade Sofia to have another child, obviously hoping for a boy, but Sofia had held him off with the same excuses as she had used after the birth of Maria. Once she was no longer able to refuse his attentions she would have to visit Theophalia and ask for the medicine again. She knew it would only delay the inevitable, but she was not a village woman to produce a child each year and hope they would survive. She wanted time to spend with her daughters, to bring them up with a sound knowledge of cooking, sewing and weaving so they would be good wives eventually. She had no idea how you would bring up a boy.

Summer 1920

Sofia enjoyed the time she spent with her daughters. She was teaching Maria how to cook and the little girl would willingly fetch a bowl, spoon or the ingredients her mother asked for. Fotini would sit on a stool beside them and would be permitted to stir the mixture or be given a biscuit to sample when they were cooked.

The dreaded third child had not materialised, much to Sofia's relief. Alesandros had finally sensed her reluctance and did not approach her as often as he had in the past. Sofia really felt she had little to complain about. Alesandros was always willing to purchase new boots or shoes for all of them, although her mother would pay him from the rent money if he made a purchase on her behalf. He gave her a gold necklace each year on her Name Day and would give each girl, along with his mother-in-law, a small present on their Name Days.

Sofia was grateful and would make her husband a well stitched shirt or embroider a waistcoat for him when his Name Day was due. This year she had also made a handkerchief and shown Maria how to embroider the letter "A' in one corner. The stitching was irregular and clumsy, but Sofia knew he would admire the child's work when she presented it to him. Fotini had insisted that she gave him one also and made some large stitches on the piece of cloth her mother had given her.

Sofia had persuaded her mother to relinquish her seat at the loom some afternoons and prepare their evening meal. That way she was able to practise her own weaving skills, although her mother would often undo a few rows later, saying they were not firm or even enough.

Tryphaine's little boy was still as ugly as ever in Sofia's eyes, his ears still stuck out despite Tryphaine binding them to his head each night, but he was well behaved and she had no objection to Tryphaine bringing him to the house to play with Fotini. Fotini was patient with him, building a tower with the irregular shaped blocks her grandfather had made for Maria and allowing him to knock it over time and again whilst he crowed with delight. Maria tended to ignore him and would ask to go outside to play. She had a special friend, Eva, who was almost two years older than herself, but seemed happy enough to have the company of the younger girl. Maria preferred to spend time with her rather than with her younger sister or Tryphaine's little boy.

Maria screamed and Sofia looked up from the weaving frame. 'Mamma?'

'My feet. My legs. The water.'

Sofia rose hurriedly and went towards the fire where her mother was sitting on the ground, screaming and wailing.

Fotini began to cry and Sofia spoke to her sharply. 'Be quiet, Fotini. Maria, keep her quiet. What's happened, Mamma?'

'The water. It was just boiling and I went to take it off the fire and it tipped over me. My feet and legs, Sofia, Do something.' Tears were running down Maria's face as the pain from her injury increased.

Sofia hurried into the scullery and soaked a cloth in the pail of water, returning and placing it over her mother's scalded legs. The action brought forth more screaming from Maria and she pulled the cloth away. Sofia looked around helplessly. She was alone in the house with her two small girls 'I'll go for Theophalia. Girls don't you dare to move. You stay where you are.'

Fotini began to cry even louder and Maria joined her. Both girls were frightened and now their mother was leaving them with their grandmother screaming and sobbing.

Sofia ran up the road as quickly as she could, calling Theophalia's name as she went. The villagers looked out of their windows and doors curiously. What had happened now?

Theophalia was at the door as Sofia arrived, having heard her frantic cries. 'What's wrong?'

'My mother,' gasped Sofia. 'She's tipped boiling water over her legs.'

'Cold water is the best treatment,' said Theophalia firmly.

'I put a cold wet cloth on her legs and she pulled it off. Please come, Theophalia. I must get back. I've left my girls there alone with her.'

Sofia turned and began to run back down the road with Theophalia following at a more sedate pace. Both girls were still sobbing when Sofia entered and rushed to her, clinging to her skirt.

'Hush, girls, there's no need for you to be crying. It's Grandma who is hurt, not you. Theophalia is coming and she will make her better very soon.' Sofia stood with her arms around both the girls whilst Theophalia looked at her mother's feet and legs.

'How did it happen?' she asked Maria.

'I don't know,' sobbed Maria. 'I was just lifting off the pot when it tipped all over me. Do something Theophalia. I'm in agony. My legs are burning inside.'

'Sofia did the best thing, covering you with a wet cloth. I'm going to do the same and you are not to pull it off. Bring me a bucket of water, Sofia.'

Sofia left her children and hurried into the scullery where there was a fresh pail of water. She grabbed an armful of clean cloths and placed the bucket and cloths on the floor beside Theophalia. Each time Theophalia placed a dripping wet cloth on Maria's legs she screamed and sobbed anew.

'Stop all that noise,' commanded Theophalia sharply. 'You are frightening the children.'

'I can't help it. My legs are on fire.' Maria continued to sob and moan.

'Take the children outside,' Theophalia directed Sofia. 'None of you can do anything useful here.'

Sofia took another look at her mother. She was obviously suffering. What a shame the accident had happened in the summer when she was wearing only a thin skirt and her clogs. If it had been the winter she would have been wearing at least two skirts and a petticoat along with her boots.

'We'll go and look for Pappa,' she said to the girls and took their hands. 'We'll walk up the road towards the orchard where he leaves his donkey.'

By the time Sofia returned to the house with her daughters her mother had quietened considerably. Theophalia had bandaged her legs and feet and managed to move her to her bed. She lay there shivering and moaning.

Theophalia took Sofia to one side. 'She has some very nasty burns. By the morning her legs will have blistered. I'll come along and take her bandages off. Try to make sure she doesn't pull them off herself or her skin will come with them. She's very shocked – scalds do that to you more than an accident where you break a bone. I've given her some poppy extraction. It will help her pain and also to sleep. I'll leave some with you and you can give it to her before you go to bed.'

Sofia shook her head. 'I'll not go to bed. I'll stay down here with her. She may need something in the night.'

'Make yourself up a bed in the corner. That way you can get some rest. You'll hear her if she wakes in the night and needs you.'

Maria had moaned in her sleep most of the night and Sofia had slept in snatches and arose feeling worried and exhausted. She heated some water for Alesandros to shave and then some more to wash her daughters. She mopped her mother's feverish face and hoped Theophalia would arrive as soon as Alesandros had left for the day.

Theophalia unwrapped Maria's legs carefully. In places the

blisters had burst and the weeping liquid had stuck the bandage to her leg. With the help of warm water and a cloth she teased the cotton away carefully, dropping the bandages on the floor and examined Maria's damaged legs. Many of the blisters were almost as large as the bowl of a spoon and the skin was stretched taught across them.

'I'm going to burst the rest of these blisters,' said Theophalia. 'She'll feel more comfortable when the skin isn't stretching. Afterwards I'll apply a herbal salve and that will help her legs to heal and stop the bandages sticking to her skin.'

Taking a needle from Sofia's sewing basket Theophalia proceeded to pierce the skin of each blister, mopping away the clear liquid from inside with a cloth. Once finished she smeared the salve on Maria's legs and Sofia wrinkled her nose.

'That smells horrible,' she remarked.

'You'll get used to it and it's worth a nasty smell if it heals as it should.' Theophalia wiped her hands on the cloth she had used to mop Maria's open blisters and proceeded to re-bandage the woman's legs with the same bandages as she had removed earlier.

'Is she running a fever?' asked Sofia anxiously, looking at her mother's flushed face.

Theophalia placed her hand on Maria's forehead. 'I'll give her some more poppy juice before I leave. Give her some broth or milk this evening and if she doesn't settle you can give her a little more poppy juice to help her sleep.'

Two days' later Sofia managed to get her mother off her bed and onto a chair. 'Would you like to sit at your loom, Mamma?'

Maria shook her head. 'My legs,' she moaned.

'They won't hurt any more if you sit and do some weaving than sitting still in a chair.'

Maria rocked herself backwards and forwards, her eyes closed and groaning intermittently. Sofia looked at her in concern. She was sure Theophalia had done her best, but she would certainly ask the doctor to look at her mother's legs when he visited the village next week.

Doctor Andrianakis waited whilst Theophalia unwrapped the bandages from Maria's legs. He was horrified. Where the blisters had formed earlier there were large, angry looking, red areas with a yellow and slightly green crusting at the edges. Maria's legs were obviously infected.

The doctor listened to Maria's heart and it was beating far too rapidly for his liking. On her arms and hands there were red spots and as he moved her limbs she cried out in pain. He straightened up and looked at Theophalia and Sofia.

'The blisters where she scalded her legs have become infected. I will give her something to help her discomfort.'

'How long will it take for her to recover?' asked Sofia.

Doctor Andrianakis shook his head. 'I cannot say. Her blood is poisoned. I'll make a special journey to Kastelli next week to see if by any chance there is any improvement.'

Sofia looked at him in horror; tears formed in her eyes and ran down her cheeks. 'What can I do?'

'There's nothing you can do. You may find she becomes very confused and disorientated. Just spend time with her when she becomes distressed and try to comfort her.'

Theophalia placed an arm around Sofia's shoulders. 'I'll ask some of your neighbours to help. They could look after your girls for a while each day whilst you sit with your mother.'

Sofia nodded. She felt numb. She had expected the doctor to give her a more effective salve to apply to her mother's legs and within a few days the ugly wounds would have healed.

Each day Tryphaine collected Fotini and looked after her whilst she played with Timotheos and Eirene would take Maria to spend the day with Eva. Theophalia came every day to check on Maria's progress, wash her and change her bandages. Sofia insisted on inspecting her mother's legs and it was obvious to her that the infection was getting worse. Alesandros was sympathetic and even offered to stay in Kastelli and not go out collecting the taxes, but Sofia refused his offer.

'I appreciate it, Alesandros, but there really is nothing you can do. I will do my best to have a decent meal prepared for when you return, but if I fail I hope you will understand.'

Doctor Andrianakis called as he had promised and shook his head when he looked at Maria's legs. 'There is no improvement. I think you have to prepare yourself for the worst.'

'No, oh no,' wailed Sofia. 'There must be something you can do. You're a doctor.'

'Doctors are not miracle workers, my dear. I have done my best.'

Sofia had difficulty in controlling her emotions when Maria asked where her grandmother had gone.

'She's not in her bed, Mamma. Are her legs better?'

'Poor Grandma, her legs were so painful that God decided to take her to Heaven where He could take her pain away.'

Maria smiled. 'That's good. Can I go and visit her?'

Sofia shook her head sadly. 'No, I will take you and Fotini up to the church and you can kiss her goodbye. Come here and let me put your new blouse on. I made it especially for you to wear when you go to see Grandma.'

'Has Fo got one too?'

'Of course.' Sofia did not add that the blouse Fotini would wear was the one that Maria had worn previously when her grandfather had died.

Sofia felt totally drained. For the last three nights she had sat with her mother as she either lay motionless, her breath coming in gasps interspersed with moans of pain, or hallucinating.

'I must get up and make a meal for Theo,' she kept repeating. 'He'll be home soon and want his supper.'

'It's all ready,' Sofia had continually assured her. 'He can have it as soon as he arrives.'

Alesandros had insisted that he sat beside Maria one night to enable Sofia to get some sleep.

'You are totally exhausted,' he admonished her. 'I will sit beside your mother and if necessary I can come and wake you.'

Reluctantly, but gratefully, Sofia had agreed. Alesandros reported that her mother had spent a quiet night; he did not tell Sofia that Maria had continually mistaken him for Theo and told him that their baby must be born soon as the pains were getting stronger. She had asked him to get the tin bath down from the hook on the scullery wall so they could take their weekly bath, saying she would scrub his back the way he liked. It was harrowing for him to listen to her having an imaginary, but intimate conversation with her dead husband and he had no intention of telling Sofia how distressing he had found the night.

Sofia sorted through her mother's clothes, putting aside anything that she would be able to unpick and make into a serviceable blouse or skirt for herself. She wrapped each of her mother's necklaces in a separate cloth and placed them in a box. She would ask Alesandros to put them on the top shelf of the cupboard when he returned. She would also ask him to take down his box of photographs and place the ones he had taken of her parents on the dresser amongst those of herself and the two girls.

The box of rent money she retrieved from under the bed and placed it on the table. Alesandros would have to be responsible for the cottages and collect the rents now.

Hesitantly Sofia asked for some recompense for Tryphaine and Eirene. 'I feel they should be given some payment. They looked after our girls whilst I was dealing with my Mamma. They fed them each day, brought me a fresh loaf from the baker and often a meal saying they had cooked too much.'

'You would do the same for them,' stated Alesandros.

'Of course.'

'And you would not expect payment for a kind deed.'

'No, but we have considerably more than they have. To continually feed an extra person, even a child, was probably a drain on their resources. If you don't want to give them money I'm sure they would appreciate not paying their rent for a week as a way of showing our gratitude.'

Alesandros grunted. The doctor's visits had been paid for from Maria's money, along with Theophalia's ministrations. After deducting the amount due to him for his mother-in-law's funeral there was very little left. At least he had not had to take any money from his secret store. It was growing steadily. When he visited the farmers he insisted that the money owed to him from the produce of the trees owned by him was paid first. This often left them with insufficient to pay their tax and ensured they had to accept another loan from him.

Alesandros looked at the box that held Maria's necklaces. 'We could sell those,' he suggested.

Sofia looked at him in disgust. 'They were my Mamma's. They are to be kept and given to the girls when they are older.'

Alesandros had the grace to look abashed and turned his attention back to the box of money.

Sofia tried to sort out a workable routine now she no longer had the help of her mother. Each day she tried to do a little additional cleaning so that Alesandros could not accuse her of neglecting the house. Once the evening meal had been prepared she sat down at the weaving loom where her mother had spent so many hours. They were always in need of cloth, either to make their clothes or just to use as food covering or cleaning rags.

Both the girls were growing rapidly, continually needing to have their skirts let down or a larger blouse made for them. Each evening having cleared away the dishes from their meal she would sit and sew by the light of an oil lamp until her eyes began to close. She would tell Alesandros that she was taking the girls up to bed and once having settled them she would lay down herself and Alesandros would find her asleep, often still fully clothed, when he finally mounted the stairs to enquire about her absence.

'We need to have a serious talk,' Alesandros announced as Sofia picked up her sewing. 'We will move downstairs to sleep,' he announced and Sofia pursed her lips and looked at him. She had stripped her mother's bed and it stood unmade in the corner.

'It makes sense,' he continued. 'It is warmer and more convenient to sleep downstairs. The girls can stay in the bedroom they are familiar with and you will not need to turn out the other room. Their mattresses can be placed in the storage room and they can use our old mattress. That will give them more space. You can prepare yourself for bed when you wish and once you feel too tired to stay awake during the evening you will only have to put away your sewing and climb into bed.'

Sofia knew her husband was being practical, but she was still loath to sleep in the bed that she still considered to belong to her parents. 'The girls are still very young to sleep alone,' she demurred.

'Maria is of an age where she can put herself to bed and help Fotini if necessary,' answered Alesandros firmly. 'I expect you to talk to them and explain that as from next Sunday they will have the bedroom to themselves.'

'Suppose they are frightened to be in the room without us?'

'Why should they be frightened? They have always slept in that room and they will know we are downstairs. We need separate sleeping quarters from them. Maria is certainly getting too old to share a room with her parents and hear activities that are unsuitable for her age or understanding. We discussed earlier the need for them to sleep in another room. I did not mention it whilst your mother was ill as you had enough to do tending her. All you will need to do now is make up the bed and move the girls' mattresses.'

'Alesandros, if we are having a serious discussion I would like you to help me with some of my chores.'

Alesandros raised his eyebrows. 'Are you asking me to cook and clean the house?'

Sofia shook her head. 'Of course not. I would appreciate your help with the oil lamps. My Pappa always kept the wicks trimmed and filled them up. I am never sure if I have trimmed the wick properly or filled them sufficiently. There is also the firewood. Pappa always chopped the wood. Mamma and I managed between us to ensure there was enough prepared for the winter, but it is not a woman's work. The amount I am able to chop in one day would be burnt in half a day.'

Alesandros frowned as Sofia continued.

'There is also the outhouse. That needs to be cleaned occasionally, along with the windows and the shutters. I am unable to manage to do all the necessary work each day. You do not like finding me asleep when you come up to bed, but I am truly too tired to stay awake.'

'What are you suggesting?'

'Either you chop the wood, do some cleaning and attend to the lamps or you pay someone to come and help me as Kassianae used to come to help my mother. You will have the rent money coming in now and there should be more than sufficient to pay for some daily help.'

'Me? Chop the wood and do cleaning?' Alesandros looked at his wife in horror.

Sofia nodded. 'Alesandros, you do not understand how time consuming it is to collect water, make the bread, shop for food and prepare a meal. I have to ensure the girls do not get into mischief and I have to do the washing and keep the house clean.'

'I'll think about it,' conceded Alesandros.

'Thank you, but please do not take too long thinking or you will find there is no wood for the fire and you will be shaving in cold water.'

Alesandros gave Sofia a sour glance. 'I suppose you want that Kassianae to come back to work here.'

'I really do not mind who helps me.' Sofia bent her head over her sewing. Once again she had managed to get her own way by agreeing to Alesandros's request and then making a demand of her own.

Alesandros spoke to Perpetua and arranged that she would help Sofia each morning. Perpetua was grateful for the extra money as she had been a widow for eight years and was being very frugal. The bread she baked on Monday would last her through Tuesday and Wednesday, despite being stale and hard by then. For six days each week she ate a meal consisting of vegetables and only treated herself to a small portion of meat on a Sunday.

Sofia explained her duties to her; she would expect wood to be chopped until the store was full ready for the winter months. Once Perpetua had finished replenishing the wood store Sofia would expect her to take the bread to be baked each day along with general dusting and cleaning. It would also be her responsibility to ensure the oil lamps were filled and the wicks trimmed as necessary.

Every week the yard should be swept, more often if it had been windy, and the front doorstep scrubbed each day. Every morning she must bring two buckets of water from the well. Once each week the living room floor must be scrubbed and the bedroom occupied by the girls must have the floor mopped over. Every other week the windows and shutters must be washed and Sofia might ask Perpetua to collect extra water on a day when she was doing the washing.

Perpetua smiled. She was not being asked to do anything that she was unused to doing for herself in her own cottage. 'I'll work hard for you, Miss Sofia, but I'll not chop wood all morning for weeks on end. At the end of a week I doubt if I'd be able to lift the axe. I'll do some each day until there is sufficient to see you through the winter. I'll not want your girls near me whilst I'm chopping. Sometimes splinters can fly and I wouldn't want them to be hurt.'

'I'll make quite sure they stay well away from you and I'll also leave it up to you how much you chop each day. As soon as your arms begin to ache you can stop and do one of the other jobs.'

Summer 1921

Alesandros asked Father Constantinus to visit him after the service on Sunday. The priest sat easily in the living room and Sofia brought in wine and biscuits from the scullery. Fotini sat on the rug before the fire playing with a doll until she saw the plate of biscuits. She then scrambled to her feet.

'Mamma, may I have a biscuit?'

'Visitors are always served first,' Sofia reminded her daughter. 'Offer the plate to Father Constantinus and then you may take one.'

Shyly Fotini offered the plate of biscuits to the priest, who accepted and smiled at the little girl. 'Thank you. Your name is Fotini, I believe. I saw you in church this morning. You were very quiet and well behaved.'

Blushing, Fotini returned to the rug, a biscuit clutched in her hand and pretended to be feeding her doll in between each bite that she took.

'So Alesandros, what can I do for you that you felt it necessary to ask me to call upon you?'

Alesandros leaned forward in his chair. 'I want my girls to have a bit of schooling; to be able to read and write. I'd like my Maria to join in the class with the boys, Fotini also when she's a little older.'

Father Constantinus frowned. 'None of the other girls from the village attend.'

'That is no reason to deny the facility to my daughters. In

Agios Nikolaos and Neapoli girls attend the local school along with the boys.'

'Girls do not have the same kind of brains as boys.' Father Constantinus shook his head sadly.

'Rubbish,' snorted Alesandros. 'They are just not given the same opportunities to use them.'

Father Constantinus spread his hands. 'I will do my best, but do not be surprised if I come to you and say I am wasting my time.'

Alesandros looked at the priest. 'I expect Maria to receive the same attention as you give to the boys. I do not want to find that in six months time she is still unable to write her name. She is not a stupid girl.'

'Are you thinking of a career for her?'

Alesandros shrugged. 'I've not thought that far ahead. If she expressed the desire to become a nurse or a teacher her schooling will have been invaluable to her. They are both being well trained by their mother in household duties, but I don't want either of them married to any of these village louts and be expected to work out in the fields in all weathers.'

Father Constantinus nodded understandingly. The farmers were hard working, honest labourers, but the work was gruelling. Most days they were out in their fields from day break until nightfall where the summer sun baked them and the winter rain soaked them to the skin. Their wives were expected to work alongside them for part of each day as well as cooking, cleaning and rearing the children.

'Well, if you are so set on the idea I'll not refuse. Your Maria can come two afternoons each week. If she can catch up with the boys she can come more often.'

'And Fotini?'

'Let's wait and see how your Maria gets on.'

With that Alesandros had to be content. He found it frustrating that his wife was unable to read or write and could barely count to ten and he did not want his daughters to be in that position.

Shopkeepers would take advantage of their ignorance and cheat them out of their change.

Despite having the help of Perpetua each day Sofia insisted her daughters also completed their own chores and did not sit idle or spend all their time with the other girls in the village. Maria was expected to bring down and empty their night bucket whilst Fotini would straighten their bedding. Once they had washed they were sent to the well to fetch more water for their mother to use throughout the day and Maria would struggle back with the buckets half full whilst Fotini skipped along by her side. If Despina had delivered the milk by the time they returned they would be given a bowl and dip their rusks or stale bread to sustain them until their mid-day meal. Whilst Sofia rinsed the dishes they were sent back up to their bedroom to lift the rugs and sweep the floor before being dispatched to the village shops to purchase whatever their mother wanted in the way of fresh vegetables or fruit.

Once these daily duties were completed they watched their mother making the dough for the bread and after she had placed her mark on the side they would carry it carefully to the baker and ask him to place it in his oven. Whilst the bread baked they were allowed to spend some time playing together out in the yard before returning to the baker.

Having had a mid-day meal of freshly baked bread, olives, cheese and tomatoes they were expected to rinse the dishes whilst Sofia took her place at the weaving loom. If it was raining Maria and Sofia would sit and watch her weaving skills until she decided that the final preparations for their evening meal should be completed. If Sofia decided to make biscuits, cakes or cheese both girls were expected to watch so they would know the method for later when they would need to make their own.

During the summer months they would be allowed to spend the afternoon meeting the other girls from the village, most of whom had spent the morning in a field picking the ripe produce or expected to remove weeds from the ground. As soon as they saw their father ride through the village on his donkey they returned home with alacrity, knowing they would have time to wash their hands and face before he walked through the door and expected them to be there to greet him.

Now Maria was attending the school run by Father Constantinus two afternoons a week Fotini felt deserted. She would wander disconsolately through the village, hoping the older girls would allow her to join them. Without Maria by her side they tended to ignore her and she would return home to sit with her mother and ask for help with her embroidery or be shown how to mix the stuffing for dolmades or make the béchamel sauce for a moussaka.

Maria began to enjoy attending the school. She would return home and sit at the table in the living room writing her letters or numbers over and over again whilst Fotini looked on enviously.

'May I try and write some letters?' she asked tentatively.

'You're not old enough to know how to write,' Maria answered smugly.

'I am.'

'You're not.'

Fotini's eyes filled with tears. 'Please, Maria, show me how to write the letters and tell me the sounds,' she begged.

Maria sighed. She did not want to admit that although she could write most of the letters to Father Constantinus's satisfaction she could not always remember the sound they made. Copying their shape was easy.

Sofia spoke without looking up from her weaving. 'There's no harm in you showing her, Maria. She'll be attending the school also at the end of the summer.'

'Why should I have to wait until after the summer?' asked Fotini truculently. 'Couldn't Pappa tell Father Constantinus that I want to go to school now?'

'It will be more beneficial to you to be out in the fresh air during the summer afternoons than cooped up inside.'

Fotini sighed heavily. 'It is only *two* afternoons.'

Maria applied herself assiduously to the tasks Father Constantinus set her and by the time the summer was over and Fotini joined her she was able to write and name the sounds of all the letters of the alphabet and had learned which letters had to be written together to make an entirely different sound when spoken; she could write her own name correctly from memory and count to thirty. Despite having had help from Maria to form her letters Fotini was considerably behind the other members of the class, but determined to catch up. Each evening she sat with her father and asked him to point at the letters she had written and ask her to tell him the sound they made. Once she had mastered the alphabet she found the exercises Father Constantinus gave them were not so difficult.

Alesandros was proud of both his daughters and spoke to Father Constantinus about their progress after church that Sunday. The priest agreed that both girls were learning as fast as the boys and in one or two cases they were ahead of them.

'I'm proposing to teach them to read during the winter,' announced Father Constantinus proudly. 'We will start with the first verse of Genesis and when they have mastered that we can move on to the following verses. Once they can read the whole chapter they should be able to read any part of the Bible.'

'I could give you the newspaper I bring back from Neapoli or Agios Nikolaos each week,' offered Alesandros.

Father Constantinus smiled thinly. 'I don't think there is any need for them to be able to read a newspaper. To be able to read the Bible is far more important.'

Autumn 1922

By the time Maria had attended the classes for a year she was well able to write a simple and intelligible sentence, although her spelling was often awry. Father Constantinus was both surprised and pleased with her progress. There were only two boys amongst the small class who were more proficient. He wished she had been a boy. He could then have proposed that she tried to enter the teaching profession, but in his eyes it was not a suitable occupation for a girl. Their place was in the home.

Both girls were becoming excellent needlewomen under the tutelage of their mother. Maria particularly enjoyed sewing pieces of woven cloth together to make their clothes or embroidering a handkerchief ready for her father's Name Day. Sofia was now teaching both girls how to knit and Fotini was fascinated by the way the stitches held together and the length of the wool grew.

Fotini was longing to be knowledgeable enough to knit the woollen undergarments that they wore beneath their blouses in the winter to keep them warm. She had decided she would do one for herself first and then it would not matter is she had dropped a stitch or one side was a little longer than the other. Once hers was completed she would make one for Maria, then her mother and lastly her father. She knew it would take her a long time to make his undergarment as he was a big man.

Fotini confided her ambition to her mother who smiled gently at her eager daughter. 'It is a lovely idea, Fo, but I think it may take you so long to complete all four undergarments that it will be the summer before you have finished. Why don't you make them for yourself and Maria and knit Pappa a warm scarf to wear.'

'Would he like a scarf?' asked Fotini anxiously.

'I am sure he would. He could place it across his chest beneath his coat or wrap it around his head when it is really cold and windy and it will keep his hat in place.'

Fotini frowned. 'I ought to make Pappa his scarf first. I don't know how long it will take me to knit undergarments.'

Sofia nodded, relieved that she would not have to continually unpick rows of knitting to correct Fotini's mistakes. At least a scarf would be a piece of straight knitting and if the girl dropped a stitch that could be easily remedied.

Alesandros thanked Fotini for the knitted scarf that she had finally finished and presented to him; promising to wear it every day when he rode off to the villages to collect the taxes that were owed. He had negotiated settlements with the farmers in the area and was making a handsome second income from the interest they had to pay him when he settled their tax bills with a loan from himself, but Elias and Marina annoyed him. Each time he called Elias had an excuse and despite having relieved them of most of their orchard their debts were mounting again. If they paid their dues on time it would save him a weekly journey to their outlying farm in the hope of extracting a few drachmas from them.

As he rode up the path leading to their cottage his donkey stopped abruptly, nearly throwing him to the ground. Her ears pricked and then flattened back against her head as she brayed loudly. Alesandros patted her head to calm her. A flock of birds rose from the bushes and wheeled noisily overhead and a rabbit, followed by a number of others rushed across the path ahead of him causing the donkey to buck violently and this time Alesandros was unseated.

He landed in an ungainly heap on the hard ground, his hat falling off and his head hitting a stone. He scrambled to his feet and looked around warily. The sky was clear and there was hardly any wind. He felt certain that somewhere an earth tremor had occurred to startle the wildlife and provoke the reaction in his donkey. He took her reins and walked the remainder of the way and without protest she ambled on as the birds settled back in the bushes.

Marina opened the door and invited him in, wiping her nose on her sleeve as she did so. She looked at his dishevelled appearance. He was usually so immaculate.

'What has happened? Have you had a fall?'

'I think we've had an earth tremor. My donkey reared and threw me. Your path needs attention before you have a bad accident.' Alesandros pointed back to the irregular stones that stuck up from the muddy track.

'I have told Elias and he says he'll do it when he has time. Come inside Mr Danniakis. Your head is bleeding. Let me clean it for you. I was just about to put some lunch on the table, but that can wait.'

Alesandros nodded. He thought he had timed his arrival to coincide with a meal. It would probably be no more than bread and olives, but it would save him having to stop at a taverna and buy something to eat.

'Have you got a cold?' asked Alesandros.

'We've both had colds. They've near enough gone now.' Marina sniffed and wiped her nose again.

Elias's eye was half shut and it watered as he looked at Alesandros. 'I got rid of my head cold and it seems to have turned into a cold in my eye,' he grumbled.

'Is it painful?' asked Alesandros.

Elias shook his head. 'No, just a nuisance. It will probably be gone by next week.'

Alesandros sat at the table whilst Marina heated some water and produced a cloth. She parted Alesandros's hair carefully and dabbed at the wound.

'It isn't deep,' she assured him. 'It should heal in a few days. I've put some cobweb over it.'

'Let me see,' said Elias. He bent over and squinted at Alesandros's head, the discharge from his half open eye dripping into Alesandros's hair.

Alesandros felt a drip from Elias's eye or nose fall on his head and he put up his hand to wipe it away.

'No, don't touch it,' Marina admonished him. 'If you start to poke it around you'll make it bleed again.'

Alesandros was grateful for the glass of raki that Elias produced whilst he sat at the table waiting for Marina to bring in the plates and a freshly baked loaf, wiping her nose intermittently on her sleeve. She held the loaf against her arm where she had been wiping her nose and cut a thick slice that she handed to Alesandros.

He drizzled some olive oil over the slice and sprinkled it with salt. 'Apart from having had a cold how are things with you, Elias? Was the apple crop good?'

Elias sighed. 'You've come for your money I presume.'

Alesandros nodded. 'I'm due my share from the apple crop and it would be beneficial to you to pay off some of the interest you owe me.'

'Tell me how much is owing and I'll see what I have when we've eaten.'

Alesandros helped himself liberally to their food and accepted two more glasses of raki. His fall had unnerved him and it finally occurred to him that he should return to Kastelli as quickly as possible to ensure that his family were safe. When Elias finally counted out the amount owing for the apples and added a small amount to reduce the interest he owed Alesandros did not try to coerce him into paying any more.

'Thank you for the meal and your attention to my head,' he said to Marina. 'I must hurry back to Kastelli now I feel completely recovered. They may have suffered some damage from the tremor.'

Elias and Marina made no attempt to detain him. Elias smiled broadly as he watched Alesandros ride carefully down the uneven path.

'His accident and the tremor were beneficial. He didn't stop to argue with me about the amount I gave him or ask for anything more in lieu of the outstanding tax.' Elias wiped the watery discharge that was running from his eye on his sleeve and Marina used her hand to wipe away the drip that had formed at the end of her nose.

Alesandros had almost reached Kastelli when the donkey stopped again and this time he thought he could feel the slight movement of the ground. It was too close for comfort and he urged his donkey on, anxious to return to the village and ensure that all was well.

As he rode into the village street people were clustered outside their houses, looking anxiously at their roofs to see if the chimney was still safe and testing their walls to ensure they were not going to fall.

'Did you feel it?' called out Panayiotis.

Alesandros nodded. 'There was a tremor whilst I was out in the countryside, then I felt another that seemed stronger.'

'Hopefully it happened out at sea. We don't seem to have any damage here.'

Alesandros rode on and found Sofia and the two girls standing in the middle of the road. He drew a breath of relief, they were safe enough. He slipped the donkey's reins over the metal grill before the windows and strode over to them.

'Pappa!' Fotini rushed to him and he placed an arm around her.

'There's no need to be frightened. It's over now.'

'It made the house shake.'

'That was because the ground shook. The house is safe enough.' Alesandros looked up anxiously at the roof and balconies.

'We came outside, just until we were sure we were not going to have any more scares,' smiled Sofia. Earth tremors happened occasionally, but so far the village of Kastelli had not suffered damage to the same extent as some of the other villages.

'Quite right,' agreed Alesandros. 'I'll go inside to make sure there is no problem.'

Sofia looked askance at the donkey that was tethered to the rail. She still did not trust the animal. 'Couldn't you take the donkey up to the orchard first?'

Alesandros shook his head. 'She'll be safe enough there for a while.'

Sofia sighed; it was not the donkey's safety she was worried about.

Perpetua came along the road, holding her arm, her face white and her eyes frightened. 'Miss Sofia, will you come to Theophalia with me? My chimney came down and hit me. I would have been safer inside.'

'Of course. Girls you are to stay out here until your father says you may go back into the house. Maria, tell him I have gone to Theophalia with Perpetua as she has been hurt.' Sofia went to take the woman's injured arm and Perpetua pulled away.

'Don't touch me. It hurts too much.'

'You're probably badly bruised. It must have been very frightening for you when the chimney came down.'

'Who's going to put it back up for me? The house will be full of smoke.'

'I'm sure we'll find someone to help,' Sofia soothed her. 'At the moment it is more important for Theophalia to treat your bruises.'

Theophalia helped Perpetua remove her bolero and blouse, Perpetua wincing with pain as her right arm was moved. Once exposed it was evident that her arm was fractured just below the elbow, a piece of bone sticking up and causing a bump in the skin.

'This is going to be very painful, Perpetua. I have to press that piece of bone back down into place and then I will have to bandage your arm until it has healed,' explained Theophalia. 'I'll give you some poppy extraction; that will help with the pain. Sit down here and rest your arm on the table. Sofia will hold your shoulders firmly.'

Theophalia bustled around, giving Perpetua a strong draught of the poppy sedative before making sure she had her bandages to hand. Perpetua's eyes began to close and she relaxed back into the chair. Theophalia nodded to Sofia. 'Hold her tight,' she ordered.

As Theophalia pressed the bone back into place Perpetua screamed, her eyes opened and she struggled to move away. 'All done,' announced Theophalia. 'I just need to bandage you up.'

The sweat was pouring down Perpetua's face and Sofia wiped it away with her apron.

'Help her over to my bed,' said Theophalia. 'She can stay here for a while until the effects of the poppy have worn off. I'll see her safely home afterwards.'

Thankfully Sofia let herself out and walked back to her own house. The villagers had returned to their homes and Maria had taken it upon herself to heat some water for her father to wash his hands and face whilst he took the donkey to the orchard.

'We had no damage,' declared Alesandros and Sofia looked pointedly at the dresser where two plates had fallen down, one of them smashed.

'What has happened to Perpetua?' asked Fotini.

'She has a broken arm. Theophalia has bandaged it for her, but tomorrow you are to take her some water and ask her if there is anything she needs. I'll cook enough for her to share our meal and make an extra loaf of bread.'

'I thought she worked for us, Mamma,' said Maria with a pout.

'She cannot work with a broken arm and even looking after herself will be difficult for a while. I'm sure many of the other villagers will help her also. I would like to think they would help me if I found myself in that position and did not have you two to look after me.'

Alesandros nodded in agreement. 'Marina and Elias helped me today.'

Sofia looked at her husband in surprise. 'How?' This was the first mention Alesandros had made of his own accident.

'When the first tremor came the donkey threw me. She was spooked by the birds coming up out of the bushes and a rabbit running in front of her. Their path is full of stones and I hit my head. Marina cleaned it up for me and insisted I stayed for a meal with them until I felt better.'

'Let me see.'

Alesandros removed his hat and bent his head dutifully.

'I'll not touch it. It has bled onto your hat. I'll make you a cap to wear in bed tonight so you shouldn't aggravate it by rubbing your head on the pillow.'

'Shall I wash Pappa's hat?' asked Fotini.

'Just the inside where it is marked. Don't soak it through as your Pappa will need to wear this one again tomorrow. I can make another but it will take me a couple of days.'

Fotini placed her arms around her father. 'Poor Pappa. I'll wash your hat and then give you a cuddle to make you feel better.'

To Alesandros's disgust he found he had caught the cold that Elias and Marina had been suffering. If he had not fallen from the donkey and been forced to allow Marina to attend to his head he need not have stayed in their cottage with them for so long. His nose seemed to be dripping continually and he kept a rag tucked into the waist of his trousers to wipe it. Sofia and Maria were not affected, but Fotini caught it from him and Maria regarded her sister scathingly.

'You should have kept away from Pappa until his cold had gone.'

'I didn't think that giving him a cuddle before I went to bed each night would mean I would catch it. It isn't like a proper cold. I'm not sneezing. It's more like you get sometimes when the grass in the orchard is cut.'

'I'll make sure I sleep with my back towards you,' announced Maria. 'I don't want you breathing your germs on me.'

Spring 1923

Perpetua insisted that she should return to working for Sofia. Her arm no longer gave her any pain, but she was unable to use it fully. It stuck out at an odd angle and it was difficult for her to pick anything up in that hand. Sofia welcomed her back, but it became evident that there were a number of jobs that were impossible for her to complete with only one hand.

Sofia did not complain. She gave the two girls some extra duties and tried to give Perpetua the easiest and lightest of jobs. She could still clean the windows and scrub the floor by using her left arm, but sweeping or mopping, where she needed both hands was much more difficult and she was certainly unable to carry two buckets of water or chop the wood.

Sofia, with the help of Perpetua, began to clean the house in preparation for Lent, even the storage room had to be cleaned. By Clean Monday everywhere had to be spotless and they would not eat any animal products until Easter Day. Perpetua's inability to work as she used to became evident and she approached Sofia in tears. Gradually she was losing the use of her damaged arm.

'I cannot manage, Miss Sofia. I can only beat the rugs using one hand and my back and shoulders ache so much afterwards that I am unable to sleep. I will have to leave and you find someone else who is more capable than me to do the work.'

'Suppose you just had a rest for a few weeks?' suggested Sofia. 'Maybe you returned to work too soon after your accident. You could spend Lent cleaning your own house and resting whenever you felt you had done enough. After Easter you could come back to work for me.'

Perpetua shook her head. 'No, it's better that I leave and you find someone else to help you.'

No amount of persuasion on Sofia's part would make Perpetua change her mind. Finally Sofia accepted the woman's decision. She knew it would be useless to try to find someone to take her place until after Easter. All the women would be too busy cleaning their own houses and preparing the Easter food.

Sofia explained the situation to Alesandros and asked him if he would help by taking down the rugs from the walls for them to beat. Everything else she could manage she declared as the girls were old enough to be helpful, and Alesandros wondered why he was paying a for a village woman to come in to help his wife if she was capable of doing the work herself.

Alesandros stood on the chest and reached the poles that held the rugs easily. As he stepped down the pole swung round and as he dodged it his hat fell off. He and Sofia both bent to pick it up at the same time.

'Alesandros, your head has still not healed properly.'

Alesandros clapped his hat back on his head. 'It is much better than it was.'

'Why don't you ask Theophalia to have a look at it and give you something to complete the healing.'

'There's no need to trouble her,' replied Alesandros firmly. 'Unfortunately I am beginning to lose my hair. That is why it is noticeable.'

Sofia dyed the hard boiled eggs red and polished them until they shone and finally made the margiritsa soup. Although she had insisted that both girls helped her with sweeping and dusting she had beaten the rugs herself, washed the floors and windows and moved the furniture unaided. All was now in readiness for the

Easter celebrations. She was longing to return to her weaving, which never seemed like work to her.

Once the Easter celebrations were over Alesandros regarded his wife with concern. She continually admitted to feeling unwell with headaches and dizziness. Rather than sit at her weaving loom each day she would rest on the bed, leaving her daughters to amuse themselves with the other girls in the village. After not seeing any improvement in her for a week Alesandros decided it was time to ask Theophalia to call and give her advice.

Theophalia talked to Sofia about her symptoms, and Sofia confirmed that she was certainly not pregnant. Her course had finished a few days ago, although earlier than she had expected and her loss was not as great as usual. Theophalia smiled knowledgeably.

'You are suffering from exhaustion.' Theophalia pricked Sofia's finger and a small drop of blood appeared. 'There,' declared Theophalia triumphantly, 'your blood is not red enough. You need to rest, eat red meat and drink red wine. Once your blood has improved your headaches and dizziness will disappear.'

Alesandros was relieved by Theophalia's diagnosis. 'You obviously worked far too hard before Easter. As Perpetua is no longer able to help you why don't you ask Kassianae to return?'

Sofia leaned back in her chair, a glass of red wine in her hand that she sipped at slowly. She was also relieved that there was nothing seriously wrong with her. 'I will speak to her tomorrow, Alesandros.'

Kassianae shook her head. 'I'll not work for your husband. Not after the way he made your father get rid of me and then took my mother's cottage and forced her to come to live with me.'

Sofia flushed with embarrassment. 'Please, Kassianae, he had his reasons. He was not doing it to be cruel.'

'If he wanted me to work here why did he ask Perpetua to come after your mother died? Why didn't he ask me to come back then?' Kassianae shook her head. 'I've said no. I'm too old anyway to do heavy work. My daughter might be willing. Do you want me ask her. I don't mind looking after her children whilst she comes here.'

Dimitra seized the opportunity to work at the big house eagerly. It would provide her family with a little extra money and you never knew what else they might decide to give you. She thought that Maria and Fotini should be made to help their mother more, rather than going to the school and getting ideas above their station. She and her husband, Panicos had managed well enough without being taught how to read and write. Panicos could judge by eye if the length of a piece of timber was right for the job he was doing and she could tell by the weight of the spoon is she was adding enough flour to her cooking.

Sofia explained to Dimitra the cleaning and other duties she would expect her to undertake and agreed that two hours each day should be sufficient. Once Dimitra was familiar with her work Sofia could either cook or sit and weave; she also needed to continue educating her daughters in the art of cooking, weaving and needlework.

Within a few weeks Dimitra was complaining vociferously about Sofia's daughters. They left finger marks on the windows after she had cleaned them, they had not swept their room thoroughly and she had found dust beneath a rug, the night bucket, although it had been emptied it had not been rinsed out. Sofia listened patiently.

'I'll speak to them and say they must be more conscientious.' she said mildly.

Dimitra sniffed. 'There's another thing, when I've mopped their bedroom they are not to come upstairs immediately and leave dirty footprints everywhere. They should remember whatever they want and take it down with them.'

'I'll remind them,' promised Sofia.

'It's the same whenever I've just mopped or scrubbed the living room floor. They walk across it without any regard and I often have to do it a second time. They stand on the step talking and scuffing it with their boots. They are thoughtless.'

'You have to remember they are still young.'

'If they are not taught to be considerate when they're young when will they be? They need to show respect for a clean house or they will end up a couple of slatterns.'

'I'll speak to both of them whilst we are preparing our evening meal. I'm sure they don't realise they are being inconsiderate to you.'

Sofia sighed. Perpetua had never complained about either of the girls. She had an idea that Maria disliked the woman and was being deliberately annoying and encouraging Fotini to follow suit.

Fotini looked suitably contrite when her mother asked her to be more thoughtful whilst Dimitra was working in the house, but Maria tossed her head scornfully.

'Surely she is a servant, Mamma. She should not be telling us what we can and cannot do.'

'She is still entitled to respect,' replied Sofia sternly.

Maria fumed inwardly. Dimitra had no right to complain about her or Fotini. Perpetua had laughed and joked with them, whilst she worked whereas Dimitra regarded them grimly with her dark, beady eyes.

As Dimitra began to move the furniture in the living room prior to sweeping and mopping the floor Maria settled herself at the table with her writing book and began to copy out sentences assiduously. Finally Dimitra asked her to move and Maria shook her head.

'I am at class this afternoon with Father Constantinus. I need to make sure I know how to spell the words he gave us in our last lesson.'

'You should have done that yesterday,' replied Dimitra brusquely.

Maria shook her head and smiled. 'I was not able to do it yesterday. Mamma said we had to leave you alone in here to scrub the floor.'

Dimitra glowered at her. 'Lift your feet,' she commanded and proceeded to sweep beneath the table, banging Maria's ankles as she did so.

Maria cried out as if in pain and Sofia hastened into the living room. 'What has happened, Maria?'

'Dimitra hit me with her broom.'

Dimitra shrugged. 'I did not hit her on purpose. Maria says she has to do her school work and I asked her to lift her feet so I could sweep under the table. I banged her ankle accidently.'

'It still hurts, whether it was an accident or not.'

Maria collected up her books and with an exaggerated limp walked to the stairs. 'I am going to my room. I need to make sure I know how to write some words ready for my class this afternoon.'

'I've only just finished mopping your bedroom floor,' protested Dimitra.

Maria raised her eyebrows. 'Mamma, is there nowhere in the house where I can sit quietly and make sure I know how to spell the words Father Constantinus gave us to learn?'

'Sit at the table, Maria. Dimitra can leave mopping the floor today and just scrub the front step. The floor cannot be that dirty as it was scrubbed yesterday.'

Maria limped back to the table and placed her books down with a flourish. She smiled sweetly at Dimitra. 'Schooling is so important so that you know how to read and write by the time you are grown up,' she proclaimed smugly, knowing that Dimitra was unable to do either.

Fotini tried to reason with her sister. 'I know you do not like Dimitra, but Mamma needs her to help in the house. Just keep out of her way whilst she is here.'

'I don't like her and I don't trust her. If Mamma is talking to one of us in the scullery she stops what she is doing to listen. The same when Despina comes with the milk. Mamma chats to her and Dimitra listens. What we talk about is none of her business.'

Maria kept out of Dimitra's way for the following two weeks. She could not always claim to need the table to complete work for Father Constantinus, but she deliberately licked her finger and ran it down the window pane in her bedroom and when challenged by her mother she appeared contrite.

'I may have left a mark on the window, Mamma. Sometimes I have to push it quite hard to ensure it opens.'

'Try to be more careful in future. You should not push on the glass. If it broke you would be badly cut; always push on the wooden frame.'

Maria opened her eyes wide. 'Goodness, Mamma, I hadn't thought about being cut.'

Maria waited until she heard Dimitra scrubbing the living room floor. She walked downstairs quietly and as she passed Dimitra she deliberately kicked the bucket of water over, soaking the woman's skirt and petticoat. Maria's hand flew to her mouth.

'Oh, Dimitra, I am so sorry.'

'You did that deliberately,' shouted Dimitra. 'Look at me. I'm soaked.'

Sofia appeared from the scullery. 'What has happened?'

'Your daughter deliberately kicked my bucket over.'

Maria looked at Dimitra scornfully. 'Of course I didn't kick it over on purpose. I just didn't realise how close it was to my foot.'

Sofia looked at her daughter sternly. 'You should be more careful, Maria. Dimitra, go home and change your wet clothes. Whilst you are gone Maria can go to the well and fetch two more buckets of water.'

Maria looked at her mother mutinously. 'Why should I be punished for an accident?'

'You are not being punished. It is a way of apologising to Dimitra for your carelessness.' Sofia sighed. 'When you return you can go to the shops for me. That will keep you out of Dimitra's way for a while.'

'Can Fo come with me?'

Sofia nodded. It could be better to send both the girls out of the house on errands whilst Dimitra was there. When it became cold or rained she would keep them in the scullery with her and show them how to cook or give Dimitra other work to do and she and her daughters could sit by the fire and sew.

Maria was pleased that when Dimitra was working at the house her mother sent her and Fotini to the shops or they were told to go into the village and amuse themselves. She wished Father Constantinus held classes every day as she was enjoying learning and trying hard to be as proficient as Yiorgo and Costas. She longed for the praise they received from the priest. Whenever she considered that something important or interesting had happened she recorded it in her diary and planned to show it to Father Constantinus to prove her diligence.

Dimitra was also pleased that the two girls were out of the house whilst she was cleaning. She needed to prove to Sofia that her services were indispensable as she knew that in about five months' time she would need to ask for a few days or even a week to spend at home. She wanted to ensure she would have the job to return to as another mouth to feed would be an additional burden. She did whatever Sofia asked of her without question. When Sofia said the girls could sit at the table in the living room as she and Dimitra were going to remove the rugs from the walls to be beaten Maria pulled a face. That meant their bedroom would be cold for a few days until her father replaced them.

Dimitra did not hesitate to climb on the chest as Sofia instructed and reach up to remove the wooden pole from the bracket and pass the end to Sofia where she would take the weight whilst Dimitra removed the other end. She did not know how she came to slip, but she landed heavily, banging her stomach against the side of the chest and the heavy rug covering her whilst the wooden pole hit her head. Sofia tugged the rug away and insisted she must not move.

Sofia called to Maria to bring a glass of water up immediately, as Dimitra's face had gone white and Sofia was concerned that the woman was going to faint.

'Put your head down between your knees. Are you hurting anywhere?'

Dimitra drew a ragged breath. 'Of course I'm hurting. The pole hit my head.' She took the glass of water and sipped, but her colour did not return and she continued to sit on the floor for some minutes. 'Help me up,' she finally commanded.

Sofia and Maria helped her to stand and Dimitra leant against the wall. She pressed her hand to her stomach and gave a little gasp of pain. Sofia was concerned, she knew the woman was expecting. She should never have asked her to stand on the chest to remove the rugs.

'When you have recovered sufficiently go home and rest, Dimitra. You can always beat the rugs tomorrow.'

That afternoon Sofia sent Maria and Fotini to enquire if Dimitra was feeling better. Maria returned to say that she was lying on her bed and Mr Panicos seemed to be very cross. Sofia sighed. She wished she had never mentioned taking down the rugs.

It was over a week before Dimitra had recovered sufficiently from her miscarriage to return to work. Maria and Fotini had been given extra jobs to do, along with beating the rugs. Now that Dimitra had returned they had regained their freedom. At first they had wandered around the village aimlessly, then Maria decided it would be amusing to visit the villagers and their children who were working out in the fields. They would stand and talk to the boys, laughing and joking until Maria decided it was time she found Eva and spent some time with her.

Fotini was concerned. 'Should we go to the fields and talk to the boys?' she asked.

'Why not? We talk to them if we meet in the village. We are not alone with them as their parents are working nearby. Besides, we don't just talk to the boys. We talk to the girls as well. Come on, let's find Eva.'

They sat and watched for a while whilst Eva pulled onions, placing them in a box, every so often she would straighten up and rub her aching back.

'Shall I pull some for you?' offered Maria.

Eva looked at her friend in surprise. 'Would you?'

'I'll probably not be as fast as you, but I don't mind doing some whilst you have a rest. Come on Fo, let's finish pulling this row.'

Fotini looked at her sister doubtfully. She did not think either of their parents would approve if they knew they were pulling onions for one of the farmers, but she followed her sister's lead.

It soon became a matter of routine for the two girls to join Eva at some time during the morning and help her collect whatever produce was ripe and would be taken to the market in Neapoli after the local shop had been supplied.

Sofia remonstrated with her daughters. 'Dimitra tells me you are spending time in the fields with the village boys. Is that so?'

Maria shrugged. 'It passes the time. We talk to the girls also. It just depends who is around. It's really no different from when we collect the apples or olives. We talk to them all then.'

Sofia frowned. It was quite true that when the whole village joined together her daughters mingled with both the girls and boys whilst they worked. 'I've also been told that you've been helping Eva do her work.'

Maria nodded. 'I don't mind pulling onions or picking peas for a while. It means she can have a bit of a rest. We can stop whenever we feel we've done enough, besides, I'm teaching Eva how to count.'

'Are you?' Sofia looked at Maria in surprise.

Maria nodded. 'I could teach you, too, Mamma. I could teach you to count and how to read and write.'

Sofia smiled. 'I think I'm a little old now to think about reading and counting. Do you want to be a teacher, Maria?'

'Not particularly. When I'm married and have my children I'll teach them and I enjoy helping Fo, but I'm not sure I'd want to have a whole class of children like Father Constantinus does.'

Fotini looked anxiously at her sister the following day as they walked towards the fields. 'Maybe we shouldn't go and talk to any of the boys,' she said timidly.

Maria tossed her head. 'I've told you, there's no harm in talking to them. Dimitra is just trying to make trouble for us. Dimitra is the village gossip. She should be pleased that we are willing to go out whilst she is there. When it's cold and wet we certainly won't be going to the fields. We'll insist that we spend our time either cooking with Mamma or sitting at the table doing our lessons for Father Constantinus. I've started to write a diary,' she declared to Fotini.

'What's a diary?'

'It's a book where you write everything you have done that day.'

Fotini looked at her sister sceptically. 'What is the point of doing that? You'll write the same thing each day.'

Maria shook her head. 'No I won't. I'll write about important things that happen, like Easter and Christmas and our Name Days. I don't have to write in it *every* day.'

'What will you do with it?' asked Fotini curiously.

'I'll show it to Father Constantinus and ask him to read it and tell me if I have spelled the words correctly. It will be like doing homework for him, but more interesting than just copying out words to learn or some paragraphs from the Bible.'

Summer 1929

Sofia watched her daughters maturing. Maria had become a woman over a year ago and Sofia agonised over how much she should tell her about her physical development. Should she explain how a child was conceived? Her face had become hot at the thought of describing explicit sexual details and she was relieved that Maria accepted the scant information she gave her without any further questions. Finally she decided that detailed explanations could wait until the girl was betrothed.

'Look, there's Eva. She's talking to Mikhaelis. Hello, Eva, hello Mikhaelis,' called Maria.

Eva spun round angrily as Mikhaelis walked away. 'Why did you call out like that?'

Maria shrugged. 'I was only saying hello to you both.'

'Yes, well don't do it again if you see us alone together.'

Maria raised her eyebrows. 'Do you like Mikhaelis?'

'Of course we like each other. We're betrothed, but we're not supposed see each other without one of our parents being around.'

'That's silly. What do they think you're going to do?'

Eva gave Maria a withering glance and did not answer. On the few occasions they had managed to spend a few minutes alone they had kissed and touched each other intimately, both longing for the time to pass so they could be officially married.

Maria thought about Eva being betrothed and wondered if her parents had a young man in mind for her. She considered each of the village boys and discounted them all. They were uncouth and ugly, except for Yiorgo and now he was working in Aghios Nikolaos for a shipping company as a clerk. She hoped he would not decide he liked a girl from the town and began to think how she could attract him when he returned to Kastelli each weekend to visit his parents.

Dimitra noticed that Maria and Fotini were always waiting at the end of the village street when Yiorgo returned on a Friday evening from Aghios Nikolaos. They would walk with Yiorgo to his house and then wander back to where there was usually a group of girls gathered and spend some time with them. She was convinced the girl was not behaving in a ladylike manner and determined to speak to Sofia.

Sofia listened to Dimitra's concerns and shook her head. 'It is natural for a girl of her age to begin to notice the boys. Whenever Maria goes out she always has Fotini with her so I don't think there is anything to worry about.'

Dimitra pursed her lips. She was sure Maria was meeting Yiorgo on a Sunday afternoon and she had overheard the conversations between the two girls. She made certain that when they were up in their bedroom she was sweeping the yard just below the open window. From what she had heard Maria say to her sister the girl was far too knowledgeable for her age.

Although Sofia would not have admitted it to Dimitra she was concerned that Maria was becoming too interested in the local boys. Maria insisted that she and Fotini went for a walk each Sunday after they had helped their mother clear away after lunch. Most Sunday afternoons the boys gathered together and usually ended up playing a game of football.

'I know we went out to church this morning, Pappa, but that was only a short walk up the road. Fo and I are used to going out every day and we just feel stifled if we have to stay in. We won't be very long.'

'If you were out like me in all weathers you'd be only too pleased to stay indoors' Alesandros commented.

Sofia watched as the girls put their boots on and picked up their cloaks. 'Where exactly are you going girls?'

'Shall we walk up as far as the turn for Driros?' asked Maria and Fotini nodded. She knew she would be told to walk as far as the turn off to give Maria and Yiorgo time alone together.

'We'll only go as far as the turn off, Mamma. We won't go on to the village,' Maria assured her mother, anxious that she should not be forbidden to go out after all. 'We'll look to see if the herbs are sprouting and if we find any mushrooms we'll bring them back.'

'Do you want a basket?' asked Sofia and Maria shook her head.

'If we find any we can put them in our apron pockets.' Maria closed the front door behind her and drew a breath of relief.

Sofia waited until Alesandros decided he had read enough of the Bible for one Sunday and spoke to him tentatively.

'Alesandros, Maria became a woman some time ago and I understand from Dimitra that her interest in boys has awakened. She says she hangs around where the boys are and pushes out her chest to attract their attention. The boys look at her and whisper amongst themselves.'

Alesandros raised his eyebrows. 'Has she got her sights set on anyone in particular?'

Sofia shook her head. 'Not that I know of.'

'Have you asked Fotini?'

'I asked what they did when they went out and she said they just walked and talked to anyone they happened to meet. I think we should consider getting her betrothed to someone suitable.'

Alesandros nodded and wiped his nose. 'I'll give it some thought,' he said. 'There may be someone working in the tax office who would be suitable for her. This annoying cold seems to have returned. When I visited Elias and Marina they complained they were suffering again and they think it must be to do with the pollen seeds at this time of year. Elias's eye is virtually shut. He has a lump developing on his forehead as well, one of those cist things I imagine. I said he should speak to the doctor the next time he is in the village but Elias just shrugged and said it was nothing.'

'How is your head? Has it healed completely?'

Alesandros was still wearing the night caps that Sofia had made for him and had taken to placing a piece of cloth on his head so his hat would not become soiled with the discharge that came from the wound on occasions.

'More or less.'

'Take off your hat and let me look at it.'

Alesandros shook his head. 'There's virtually nothing to see now.'

'How would you know? You cannot see the back of your head.'

'I've managed to look in my shaving mirror.'

Alesandros did not admit that he had only been able to see a small area of his head in the shaving mirror. He had lost a considerable amount of hair in the region and could see that the cut had not healed. There was also a small lump on his scalp and he surmised it was one of those annoying sebaceous cists. He did not know if they eventually burst, but he would certainly wear his nightcap in case it should burst during the night. He was so self conscious of his hair loss that he had taken to wearing his hat continually, even whilst in the house, saying that his hair was thinning and a hat kept him warm.

'Besides, I've other more important things to think about. Perpetua says she cannot pay her rent. I've told her she can have two weeks to find the money and if she still can't pay she will have to go elsewhere.'

'Where will she go?' asked Sofia in concern.

Alesandros shrugged. 'That is not my problem. She has a son in Fourni. She could go and live with him.'

'You cannot turn her out, Alesandros. She has always lived in the village. I think she was born in that cottage.'

'That doesn't give her the right to live there rent free. If I allowed her to do so everyone else would be claiming they couldn't pay their rent. I'm not a soft touch like your father was. He believed any hard luck story a villager told him.'

Sofia compressed her lips. Her father had been the village philanthropist, never refusing to make a repair to a cottage or wait for a week or two until the occupant could pay rent arrears, often accepting produce instead of cash. "One is as good as the other" he used to say.

Maria looked flushed and her eyes were sparkling when she and Fotini returned.

'Where did you walk to?' asked Sofia.

'To the Driros turn off,' answered Fotini, not mentioning that she had been alone on the walk, leaving her sister and Yiorgo together.

'We may go a little further next week,' announced Maria. 'It really took no time at all.'

Fotini bent to pull off her boots. It was lonely walking along the country lane without her sister for company and she hoped that when the weather became colder or it rained that Maria would no longer want to go out to meet Yiorgo.

'Eva and Mikhaelis are getting married soon,' said Maria, hoping to divert attention away from herself. 'Eva is getting really excited. I believe her Pappa is coming to speak to you.'

'What does he need to see me about?' Alesandros frowned. Was Eva's father going to say he could not afford to pay his rent as he had to provide his daughter with a wedding feast?

'She didn't say.' Confident that she had turned the attention of her parents away from herself Maria climbed the stairs to her bedroom. She would write in her diary all that had passed between her and Yiorgo during the time they had spent together.

Eva's father arrived that evening and stood hesitantly before Alesandros, twisting his hat in his hands.

'Mr Danniakis, I believe you know my daughter is to be married in the autumn.'

Alesandros nodded. As he had surmised the man was going to ask for a loan of money to pay for the celebrations.

'I understand that Perpetua is having a problem paying her rent now she has lost the use of her damaged arm.'

'Most unfortunate for the poor woman. She has a son in Fourni; no doubt he will look after her.'

'Perpetua does not want to leave Kastelli. The village has always been her home.'

Alesandros frowned. Was the man going to beg him to allow Perpetua to stay in her cottage rent free? He was certainly not prepared to have her living for nothing in one of the cottages, even a reduced rent was unacceptable to him.

'I wanted to ask if you would consider renting her cottage to Eva and Mikhaelis once they are married? Perpetua could come and live with us.'

Sofia looked up hopefully from her sewing. If Alesandros would accept Vassilis's proposal it would certainly solve the problem.

'Can Mikhaelis afford to pay the rent each week?' asked Alesandros abruptly.

Vassilis nodded. 'Mikhaelis has been saving and Perpetua said she would leave all her kitchen items for them. She would have no need of them if she came to us. Eva has made sheets and hopes she might receive a blanket as a dowry present. They would have no immediate expenses.'

Vassilis stood there, uncertain whether Alesandros was going to decide immediately or having made his request he should leave.

'I'll think about it. Come back next Sunday.'

'Thank you, Mr Danniakis. Eva and Mikhaelis would be very grateful to have their own cottage.'

Vassilis backed towards the door and once having left the house he gave a sigh of relief. He had dreaded that Alesandros would turn his request down out of hand. He certainly did not want a newly married couple living with him and his wife, whereas Perpetua would be no trouble.

Sofia smiled at Alesandros as Vassilis closed the door. 'Well,' she said, 'that problem seems to be solved for you. Now all you have to deal with is finding someone suitable for Maria to marry.'

Winter 1929

Maria overheard her parents discussing a suitor for her and she was distraught. She made her way to Eva's cottage, intent on confiding in her and asking if there was any way she could refuse to be married. Eva was brimming over with happiness and Maria listened to her extolling the virtues of Mikhaelis and saying how wonderful it was to be married and be able to spend time as much time as they wished enjoying each other, rather than having to snatch odd moments when they hoped no one would see them.

When Maria questioned her more closely Eva explained to her exactly how their union had been consummated, even before they had taken their wedding vows. Eva had smiled complacently.

'Now we're married we can think about having babies.'

Maria left Eva deep in thought. She wanted to marry Yiorgo. If they did as Eva and Mikhaelis had done surely her father could not then make her marry another man? She determined to ask Yiorgo when she saw him on Sunday if he really wanted to marry her. Provided he swore she was the only woman he would consider marrying she would give her body to him without reservation.

Fotini found it cold sitting inside the sheep shelter, despite wearing her cloak and wrapping herself in the old blanket Yiorgo had placed there. She shivered and rubbed her hands together. Finally, unable to bear the cold any longer she walked out and began to jump up and down. She could not help seeing that her sister's skirts were pulled up to her waist and Yiorgo was moving up and down on top of her. She turned away, embarrassed and also worried. She was certain that if her parents knew they would certainly not allow Maria to go out just in the company of her sister in future.

When they were in the privacy of their room Fotini asked Maria nervously if she was going to become pregnant. Maria had answered her scornfully.

'Don't be silly. Eva says you can't have babies until after you are married. It is just Yiorgo and I saying that we love each other and will get married.'

Fotini shook her head. 'I don't think you should do it.'

'If you dare to tell Mamma or Pappa I'll cut your hair off whilst you are asleep,' threatened Maria. 'I'm not prepared to marry any old man that Pappa knows.'

Alesandros returned from Neapoli feeling thoroughly disgruntled. He had spoken to Lefteris and suggested the man should meet his daughter with a view to becoming betrothed the following year. Lefteris had refused, saying he was already betrothed and a date for his wedding had been set. Now he would have to look for someone else who was both suitable and available for his daughter. Added to that his hands and feet were cold and he had a headache. He hoped that once he was home and warm again he would recover quickly.

Maria overheard her father relating his news to her mother and was elated. He was going to look around to see if there was anyone suitable in Aghios Nikolaos. Maria clasped her hands together. Yiorgo worked in Aghios Nikolaos and her father and Father Constantinus had both thought highly enough of him to recommend that a shipping firm employed him as a clerk. Maria prayed fervently that night that her father's eye would alight on Yiorgo.

Two weeks later Alesandros stood before the fire, rubbing his cold hands together. 'I think I have found the ideal man,' he declared to Sofia. 'Christos has an unmarried son who works as a teacher. I met him today and he seems pleasant enough.'

Sofia stopped weaving and gave her full attention to Alesandros. 'How old is he?'

'Christos says he's nearly thirty.'

'Why has he not married before?'

'I didn't ask. Many men do not wish to get married until they are older. I had no thoughts of marriage when I was that age.'

'If Maria married him,' Sofia continued 'would she be expected to live in Aghios Nikolaos?'

'Of course.'

'Would we ever see her again?'

'She could ride up here with me on the donkey some Fridays and return on the Monday. That way she could have the weekend with us. I could always take you down in a morning and bring you back in the evening.'

'I'd like to meet him before anything is settled and so should Maria,' said Sofia firmly. 'I would not want her married to anyone whom she found repugnant. I trust your judgement, Alesandros, but sometimes a woman can see things that a man has missed. Are his eyes straight?'

Alesandros looked at Sofia in surprise. 'I didn't notice anything wrong with them.'

'Does he have a temper?'

'How would I know?'

'I would like to make sure he would not mistreat Maria if he was angry. She would not have the strength to defend herself against a grown man.'

'Well,' Alesandros shifted a little closer to the fire. 'I'll see what more I can find out from Christos next time I go down to the town.'

Sofia sighed and turned back to her loom. It was such a risk to allow an unknown man to marry your daughter. If only they had had relatives and a betrothal could have been arranged when she was a child there would be no problem now.

Maria had been in tears when she met Yiorgo on Sunday afternoon and between her sobs and sniffs she told him her father had found a suitor for her.

'You are quite sure you want to marry me?' he had asked.

'Quite sure, Yiorgo. I love you,' she had assured him

Yiorgo had wiped away her tears and kissed her. 'Then we will have to make sure we can be married,' he had said as he lifted her skirt.

Christmas came and Yiorgo was given leave to stay in Kastelli until the New Year. At first Maria had been delighted, then she realised that during the festivities it would be unlikely they would be able to spend any time alone. Yiorgo would be expected to spend the time with his family and her mother was insistent that she helped with the baking.

'Fotini could help you,' grumbled Maria.

'You can both help me,' Sofia answered firmly. 'You will both want to eat whatever I have cooked so it is only right that you should both help me.'

Maria walked around looking miserable and Fotini tried to cheer her up. 'You don't usually see Yiorgo during the week. It will soon be Sunday.'

Maria looked for any excuse to visit the shops for her mother and dawdled over the purchases, hoping Yiorgo would arrive on an errand. She was pleased when she saw Stratos walking down the street and he waved to her. If Yiorgo saw her talking to him he might well come and join them.

'Hello, Stratos; visiting your grandmother?'

Stratos nodded. 'I thought I should come and tell her I'm getting married next year.'

Maria beamed at him. 'I'm pleased for you and I know Mamma will be also.'

'I'll call in on my way back to Neapoli and tell her.'

'Who are you marrying? Anyone we know?' asked Maria, racking her brains to think of a village girl that Stratos may have been visiting at the same time as his grandmother.

Stratos shook his head. 'Mr Benediktos's youngest daughter.' He waved his hand and began to walk on his way. 'I'll see you later, Maria, when I call on your mother.'

Maria walked slowly down the road to her house. There was no sign of Yiorgo and she had no excuse to stand around in the village street during the cold weather hoping he would appear. She hoped it would not snow on Sunday and she and Fotini would be forbidden to go for their weekly walk.

She placed her purchases on the living room table and Sofia cast an eye over them to ensure Maria had bought the flour and extra spices she had requested to make the Christopsomo. 'You were gone a long time,' she admonished.

'I met Stratos on his way to visit his grandmother. He said he would call in here when he left. He said he's getting married next year to one of Mr Benediktos's daughters.'

'Really? He's done well for himself,' Sofia admitted, recalling the little boy standing in front of the fire whilst she fetched her old boots. As she pictured him Timotheos came to mind with his large ears and her hand flew to her mouth. Surely not!

'What's the matter, Mamma?' asked Fotini.

Sofia shook her head. 'Nothing. I was just wondering if had some lemonade to offer him, and then I remembered he is a grown man now and would probably prefer a glass of wine.'

Sofia regarded Maria anxiously. The girl seemed preoccupied and she often had to speak to her a second time before she received an answer.

'Is something wrong, Maria?'

Maria shook her head. 'No, I was thinking about Eva. I'll walk down and speak to her later and see how she's feeling. She was so excited when she told me she was expecting a baby.'

Sofia smiled. 'We could do with some more young people in the village. There's Dimitra's daughter, but she's near enough two years old now. The other children are older and soon there will be no one for the youngest to play with. I hope Eva is looking after herself properly, resting and eating as she should.'

'I thought I would weave a small blanket for when the baby arrives, if you'll allow me to use the loom, Mamma.'

'I could do it for you.'

Maria shook her head. 'It wouldn't be a gift from me then.'

'I thought you wanted to get on with your embroidery?'

Maria shrugged. 'I do, but it won't take me very long to make a small blanket. Your sewing is much neater than mine; maybe you could make a little nightdress whilst I'm weaving.'

Sofia gave her daughter a searching look. Had she overheard her parents discussing a possible betrothal? She had asked permission to take a new sheet from the trunk and was busy embroidering the top hem with scarlet flowers, saying she should begin to think about making herself a dowry.

Two weeks later the girls returned from their Sunday afternoon walk accompanied by Yiorgo. Fotini immediately went upstairs to her bedroom, whilst Yiorgo stood nervously in the living room, holding Maria's hand. At first Alesandros had been furious when Yiorgo asked permission to marry Maria and confessed that she was pregnant due to him.

'I ought to beat you,' raged Alesandros, rising from his chair.

Yiorgo stepped forward. 'No, sir. I couldn't let you lay a finger on Maria. I would have to defend her and without any disrespect I am younger than you and probably stronger. I would not wish to hurt you whilst I restrained you.'

Sofia laid a placating hand on her husband's arm. 'I understand how cross you are, Alesandros, but that won't change the situation. We have to accept that Maria has been very foolish.'

'We love each other, Pappa,' protested Maria and her father

promptly sent her to her room where Fotini tried to reassure and comfort her sister.

It was more than an hour later when Sofia called her daughter and said she was to come downstairs. Maria stood before her father, her lips trembling. She was relieved to see Yiorgo was still there and her father had not thrown him out of the house.

'I have made a decision,' announced Alesandros. 'You and Yiorgo are to be married as soon as I can make the arrangements with Father Constantinus. Until such time as you are legally wed there are to be no more illicit meetings between you. After you are married Yiorgo will come here each weekend when he returns from Aghios Nikolaos. Fotini will sleep in the storage room when it has been cleared out and cleaned. I am still disgusted by your loose behaviour. The whole village will know why you have been married so hurriedly, but at least having a husband will go some way to restoring your reputation,'

'Yes, Pappa. Thank you, Pappa.' Yiorgo took Maria's arm as she swayed on her feet and guided her into a chair.

'Thank you, Mr Danniakis,' said Yiorgo and he meant the words sincerely. Had Maria's father decided his daughter should go and live in his parent's house they would have been forced to have a mattress in the corner of the living room where he had slept since he was a boy. 'If you will excuse me I must go and speak to my parents. I will then need to return to Aghios Nikolaos.'

Alesandros made no attempt to detain Yiorgo. He sighed heavily. He would now have to visit Father Constantinus and listen to his condemnatory words about his pregnant daughter. The only consolation to him was that Yiorgo was not a farmer and his daughter would not be expected to work out in the fields in all weathers.

Sofia waited until Alesandros had left to go up to the church, then she called Maria to her.

'How are you feeling, Maria?'

'Very relieved and thankful, Mamma.'

'I meant physically.'

Maria blushed. 'I don't feel very well first thing in the morning when I get up.'

'Hopefully that will soon pass. How far are you?'

Maria looked puzzled. 'How far?'

'Yes, how many months do you think you are? How many courses have you missed?'

'Two courses.'

'What possessed you to be so foolish?'

'Yiorgo and I wanted to be promised to each other so Pappa couldn't insist that I married someone else. Besides, Eva had told me that you didn't have babies until you were married. I thought she meant you couldn't.' Maria hung her head.

'Why didn't you tell me you wanted to marry Yiorgo?'

Sofia looked at her daughter. Despite having to confess to her father and spending some time weeping in her room, Maria looked ecstatically happy. No wonder she had been coming back with starry eyes and a dreamy expression on her face after her Sunday walks. The girl was obviously in love with Yiorgo and Sofia felt a pang of envy. How she would like to know how it felt to love someone so much that you wanted to give yourself to them, rather than seeing it as a wifely duty. She had loved her parents and she loved both her daughters, but the love between a man and woman was something special and it had been denied to her.

Maria spoke contritely. 'I am truly sorry, Mamma. Not about having a baby, because it means Yiorgo and I can be married, but because I didn't tell you. I thought you would agree with whatever Pappa said. I know he wanted me to marry a school teacher that I had never even met. I cannot marry anyone but Yiorgo; we love each other so much.'

'You silly girl. I know how to get my own way with your Pappa.'

Maria looked at her mother in surprise. She had never heard

her contradict or argue with her father. 'How do you do that?'

'I talk to him. He is a reasonable man,'

'Do you love him, Mamma?'

Sofia felt uncomfortable. This was not the kind of conversation she thought seemly to have with her daughter. 'I have become very fond of him over the years. There are no problems between us. Now, you had best go up and tell Fotini that she is going to have a bedroom to herself in a few weeks. Dimitra can clean it and we will get out some rugs and hang them to keep out the draughts.'

Dimitra smirked when she was asked to clean out the storage room ready for Fotini to occupy it once Maria was married. She looked pointedly at Maria's stomach. There was only one reason why a marriage was arranged hastily without a betrothal announcement with the marriage taking place some months or even years later. Sofia should have listened to her when she said that Maria was trying to attract the boys. She was thankful that her own son was too young to have been the object of her intent.

Sofia began to make a white skirt and blouse ready for Maria's wedding day. 'It's too big for me, Mamma,' complained Maria. 'I don't want it to fall to my ankles whilst I'm standing before Father Constantinus with Yiorgo. It would be so embarrassing.'

'If I make it to fit you now you'll probably not get into it in a couple of weeks. You'll be losing your waist by then. If it is too large on the day I can always put a few stitches in to make it smaller.'

'Can't you make it smaller now? I don't feel at all comfortable in it at the moment.'

Sofia sighed. 'Very well. I'll put a tuck at each side and unpick them if necessary.'

'I'm sure it won't be,' Maria answered confidently.

By the time the day of Maria and Yiorgo's wedding day arrived Sofia was nervous. She had needed to place an insert into the waist of Maria's skirt and the girl complained of feeling nauseous every morning. Sofia just hoped she would be able to get through the marriage service without disgracing herself in any way.

As Sofia walked down the aisle to take her seat at the front of the church she saw Dimitra whispering behind her hand to the woman next to her and felt a flash of anger. How she must have enjoyed spreading the news around the village that Maria was pregnant. Sofia knew Maria had seen Dimitra's actions also as she tossed her head and smiled. Maria would not let the woman spoil her special day. She was going to enjoy dancing and feasting and being the centre of attention, and then when it was all over she and Yiorgo would be able to enjoy themselves.

Spring 1930

Sofia eyed her daughter anxiously. In the weeks after her wedding she appeared to have ballooned out and already Sofia had needed to cut the waistband of Maria's skirts and attach ties so she could wear them. Sofia wondered if her daughter had missed more than the two courses she had originally admitted to.

Maria had cried when she saw her stomach extending. 'I don't want to be fat, Mamma. I shall look like Olympia soon.'

'Don't be so silly,' replied Sofia brusquely. 'You are not getting fat. You are growing bigger to accommodate the baby inside you. Once you have had the child you will go back to looking the way you were before. Look at Eva. She is just as slim now as she was before Sotiria was born.'

Sofia sat beside Maria as she lay on her bed. Theophalia had warned her that she must expect to lose the child. She could not hear a heartbeat and Maria had not felt any movement for almost two weeks. Maria lay there listlessly. Her head ached and she had woken in the night to find that she was bleeding profusely. The pains in her stomach were now so bad that she drew up her legs and groaned. Finally she threw back the sheet that was covering her and went to use the bucket. Sofia stood behind her daughter so she could lean back on her as she gasped and strained, the sweat pouring down her face and mingling with her tears.

Sofia helped her daughter back onto the mattress, had a quick glance in the bucket and gave a satisfied smile. By the look of the contents the miscarriage had taken place. She covered the bucket with a cloth and put it in the corner of the room. She would leave it there until Theophalia had confirmed that Maria's ordeal was over.

Alesandros had grunted when Sofia told him Maria had miscarried. If only that had happened three months ago there would have been no need for the hasty wedding. Now he was committed to having Yiorgo living in his house, although he insisted the young man paid for his share of the food he ate at the weekends.

'I do wish Yiorgo could have been with her. I think he would have been able to comfort her more than I was able to,' sighed Sofia.

'I offered to take a message to ask him to come back to Kastelli.'

'I know you did and Maria said not to bother him. I know it concerns her that he walks back each weekend, whatever the weather. You know about these things, Alesandros. Could you arrange for him to have a donkey to ride the same as you do? He often arrives here on a Friday evening quite exhausted.' Sofia bent her head back down over her sewing. If her husband did not produce a donkey for their son-in-law in the near future she would have to mention the subject again.

'He'd have to buy it. I can't afford to give donkeys away as presents.'

'I'm sure he wouldn't expect you to give it to him. If you bought it he could pay you back from his wages each week.' Sofia continued to sew without looking up at Alesandros.

'You seem to think he's made of money. He has to pay for his lodging in Aghios Nikolaos, his weekends here and he is responsible for Maria and her expenses now.'

'But if he had a donkey he could ride back to Kastelli every evening after work. He wouldn't have to pay for his lodgings in Aghios Nikolaos and could use that money to pay you back.'

'He'd have to pay extra for the days he lives here,' argued Alesandros.

'Of course,' agreed Sofia. She did not admit to Alesandros that most weeks she gave the money Yiorgo had paid back to Maria. It cost very little more to add to a dish and feed an extra mouth. Her main expense was an extra loaf of bread.

'I'll think about it.' Alesandros finally conceded. He was annoyed. He had held his shaving mirror above his head and realised that his head was not healing as he had expected. He had lost his hair from around the wound and his scalp showed white and lumpy. It was unsightly and he would have to ask Sofia to make him some more nightcaps and hats.

Maria insisted on being down in the living room to greet Yiorgo when he arrived on the Friday evening. His eyes took in her white face and the fact that her stomach no longer protruded beneath her skirt.

'Have you had the baby?' he asked, looking around for a crib.

Maria shook her head. 'According to Theophalia the baby died inside me. She said that usually happens if there is something wrong with it.'

Yiorgo took his wife in his arms. 'I'm so sorry, Maria. How do you feel?'

Maria gave a shaky smile. 'Just a little weary. It was not a pleasant experience.'

Yiorgo kissed her forehead. He felt incredibly guilty. Each week since they had married Father Constantinus had looked directly at him when he reminded his congregation that the sins of the fathers were visited on the children. He had sinned with Maria; was this retribution?

'Shouldn't you be in bed?'

Maria shook her head. 'I'm not ill. Theophalia said everything came away.' Maria flushed as she said the words. A woman did not usually discuss any of her bodily functions with her husband. 'She will ask Doctor Andrianakis to visit me the next time he comes to the village.'

Alesandros arranged the purchase of a donkey for Yiorgo. He was becoming a very respectable son-in-law. Twice he had been promoted at work and he and Maria obviously adored each other. Whatever either he or Sofia asked of him he never refused and when it had been particularly cold with snow on the ground in the winter he had made numerous journeys to the well, bringing back water for the household and also for his mother.

'You should not be out in this weather,' he had admonished Maria when he saw her putting on her cloak and picking up her basket. 'Tell me what your mother needs from the shops and I will go on your behalf.'

Maria agreed thankfully. She did not enjoy the cold weather and hated the snow which seemed to penetrate through her cloak and chilling her to the bone.

'Would you like me to collect the rents for you, Mr Danniakis?' offered Yiorgo. 'It would be no trouble whilst I was out.'

Alesandros shook his head. 'Thank you, but I'm sure I can manage, despite my arthritis playing me up. The villagers would probably give you all sorts of excuses for not paying. They know I will not accept any of their pleas of poverty.'

The villagers spoke truly when they said they had no money for their rent due to various reasons. You could not expect their children to go around only half dressed during the winter: they needed woollen undergarments and a cloak and boots and these had to be made or bought. The ground was often too hard for them to pull all but the most meagre crop so they had nothing to take to the shops or on to Neapoli to sell. Even if they had been frugal during the summer and also saved any payments made to them for their fruit or olives, with nothing coming in each week their savings were soon eaten up.

Yiorgo nodded; twice already he had paid the rent for his parents' cottage as Despina found getting milk from her goats during the winter was difficult as the sustenance they usually

258

foraged for was not available to them. Manos complained that his chickens stopped laying eggs and there was no point in wringing their necks when the villagers could not afford to buy one to make a meal. He would leave them to peck at whatever they could find and by the time the villagers were able to purchase them again they would be old and the flesh stringy, but that was not his fault.

'You will be careful, won't you, Alesandros? It may be slippery in places and you don't want to fall over.' Sofia regarded her husband anxiously. He had recently taken to using a stick when he walked to church, saying his arthritis was painful.

'I'm sure I'll not have a problem.' Alesandros was not prepared to admit that the arthritis he was suffering from left him without any feeling in his toes and made him feel very unsteady on his feet. When he rode his donkey to the outlying villages to collect the taxes he would flex his fingers regularly. No doubt it was holding the reins of the donkey over the years that had caused them to stiffen up. He sighed. It was no pleasure becoming old.

Maria was enjoying herself. During the day, having helped her mother, she was free to amuse herself with her sister as she pleased. They took to taking a walk around the village each day and Maria noticed that Fotini was trying to attract the attention of the boys much the same as she had done before she married Yiorgo. Fotini had brushed the accusation aside, declaring there was no boy in the village who interested her.

When they went to the orchard to help pick the annual apple crop Maria could not help noticing that Fotini seemed to single out Costas, trying to work close to him and engaging him in conversation when he brought over his basket of apples for her to sort. Fotini was so busy looking at Costas that she did not notice that Nikos had tripped on the ladder and as it fell it hit her arm, knocking her to the ground.

Both Nikos and Costas were full of apologies and helped her up, whilst Maria brushed her skirt down.

'Are you hurt?' asked Maria.

Fotini shook her head. 'Just my arm. I expect it will be bruised.'

Maria looked at her sister's arm; the sleeve of her blouse was torn and her arm was covered in mud and bleeding from a cut. 'We're going home for Mamma to see to your arm. It needs to be cleaned and bandaged.'

'I'm sure it's nothing to worry about.'

'You must get the mud off and cover the cut. You don't want to get dirt in it or it will become infected. Come on, Fo, don't be silly. We can return to the orchard afterwards.'

Reluctantly Fotini accompanied her sister back to their house. Sofia heated some water and sent Maria for an old rag to wipe the dirt away. The lining from one of Alesandros's hats was on top of the pile of laundry that her mother had been intending to wash that morning. Maria picked it up and returned to the living room, whilst Sofia insisted Fotini removed her blouse.

Sofia swabbed the dirt away and examined the wound. It was quite a deep cut and still bleeding. She held the pad on Fotini's arm until the blood was no longer oozing out and wound a clean bandage tightly around Fotini's arm.

'That will keep it clean. Put your blouse on the washing pile and I'll do that along with the other blouses and your Pappa's shirt. I'll see if I can mend it later.' Sofia threw the dirty cloth into her rubbish.

Fotini's arm felt tender, but she was determined to return to the orchard and continue helping with the apple harvest.

Maria had resisted Yiorgo's advances for as long as possible before consenting to try for another child and now she was pregnant again. She had consulted Theophalia who assured her there was no reason why she should not carry a healthy child the full term, but nagging at the back of Maria's mind was the possibility of another miscarriage. Now she was fat and waddling around in imitation of Eva who produced another child each year

Sofia fussed over Maria, ensuring that she ate and rested properly, lifted nothing heavy and did only the lightest of housework. Fotini did not complain about any extra chores she was asked to complete, only Dimitra looked at Maria with scorn. Dimitra had worked hard each time she had been pregnant, and apart from the one miscarriage due to her fall, she had come to no harm. In Dimitra's opinion far too much fuss was made of the girl.

When Maria gave birth to her son she had a difficult time. Sofia was distraught at her daughter's condition and urged Theophalia to do something to relieve the girl of the pain she was in. Theophalia was also beginning to be concerned that the baby would suffer from foetal distress and after thirty six hours considered sending for Doctor Andrianakis to see what he recommended. The girl had narrow hips and the baby was large; that was the problem. If she needed to be cut open she would have to be taken to the hospital in Neapoli on a cart. Sofia and Fotini took turns in sitting with Maria, trying to comfort her and sponging her forehead, both of them drawing a breath of relief when the boy was finally born.

Within a couple of days Maria had recovered physically from her ordeal, but did feel incredibly tired. The baby would wake in the night and demand sustenance although her milk had not arrived. Maria dreaded feeding him; he clenched his gums around her nipple so hard that she had thought at first that he had been born with teeth. Theophalia assured her this was natural and she would soon become used to the sensation and it would no longer be painful.

Yiorgo was delighted with his son and bought Maria a gold necklace. Having finally repaid Alesandros for the purchase of a donkey and not found it necessary to help pay his parents' rent he had been able to save some of his wages over the past few months.

After Father Constantinus had christened the boy, Alesandros took photographs of Yiorgo and Maria holding baby Alexandros and then allowed Yiorgo to take a photograph with Sofia holding their grandson and him standing behind her with his hand on her shoulder. Once they were developed he placed the photograph of himself, Sofia and Alexandros into the pocket of his bag so he could show it to the villagers he called on in the outlying districts. The other he placed on the dresser amongst the other photographs he had taken over the years.

Alesandros rode to Perambela. It was time Elias and Marina paid him some of the money they owed him. The last time he had called at the cottage Marina had claimed they were both unwell and would not allow him to enter. He had to admit she did look sick and also worried. He also wanted to show them the photograph of Alexandros. He was proud of his beautiful grandson and had already shown the photograph to Makkis, Christos, the various taverna owners whenever he stopped for refreshment, along with the workers in the tax offices at Neapoli and Aghios Nikolaos.

Alesandros hammered on the farmhouse door. There was no answer and he walked around to the rear of the building to see if they were working out in the fields, finally deciding they were either hiding from him or had gone to Nofalias or one of the other nearby villages for the day. Sighing in exasperation over his wasted journey, Alesandros rode down to the taverna; he would ask the owner to give them a message to say he would call again the following week.

Voukolos looked at Alesandros suspiciously as he made his request. 'Why do you need to see them?'

'I'm the local tax man and I've come to collect their debt.'

Voukolos snorted. 'You'll be lucky to get that. They're not there anymore.'

'Not there? Where have they gone?'

'How would I know? They said they were too old to work the farm anymore and were going to live with relatives.

Alesandros sat there stunned. How was he going to be repaid the money they owed him? 'What is happening to their cottage and the farmland?' he asked eventually.

Voukolos shrugged. 'I understand they only rented the place. I imagine the owner is looking for a new tenant.'

'I own the apple orchard and some of his orange trees. I need to know who to speak to so they realise they belong to me and I receive the money from the harvest.'

'You could try Father Matthias. He might be able to help you.'

Alesandros nodded. Unless Elias had left the money for the apple crop with the priest, which he doubted, it was most unlikely that he would ever see the amount owed to him.

Fotini doted on the small boy. When he cried she would take him in her arms and rock him until he quietened or went to sleep. She even enjoyed changing his soiled clothes; a job that Maria hated. Sofia chided her over her fastidiousness.

'It's natural,' she said, as Maria wrinkled her nose. 'You cannot expect a child of that age to be anything except wet. They have to learn to control their bladder and bowels. You and Fotini were exactly the same.'

Maria sighed. 'I've decided I don't like babies. When will he stop waking me in the night?'

'You have to be patient,' Sofia admonished her. 'No doubt in a year or so he'll sleep through.'

'A year!' Maria was horrified.

Fotini smiled at her sister. 'If I was able I would feed him for you during the night. He has a good pair of lungs on him so he wakes me up as well as you.'

Maria shook her head. 'I'm sorry, Fo. I try to quieten him as soon as possible.'

'I know. I'm not complaining. He's such a lovely little boy. I hope when I'm married I can have a little one just like him.'

'Do you have anyone in mind?' asked Maria.

Fotini shook her head. 'I quite liked Costas for a while, but I've heard he's marrying a girl from Fourni.' Fotini lowered her voice. 'I just hope Pappa doesn't decide to marry me to some old man I have never met.'

'Like he intended for me!' remarked Maria bitterly. 'If there is anyone you especially like tell Mamma. She said she would have been able to change Pappa's mind and arrange for Yiorgo and I to be married.'

'I'll remember,' smiled Fotini. 'Let me carry Alexandros down to the shops. Mamma only wants some flour.'

Maria placed her son in her sister's arms. Fotini shifted him onto her right arm and Maria looked surprised. 'Why do you carry him that side?'

'I find it easier.' Fotini did not mention that where the ladder had hit her left arm it often felt numb and she was frightened she would drop Alesandros if she used that arm to carry him. Despite the weather being warm she had not changed into a short sleeved blouse like her mother and sister.

Maria thought no more about Fotini's remark that she found it easier to carry Alexandros on her right arm until a few weeks later when she asked Maria to accompany her to the well each morning as she claimed she was unable to carry a bucket of water in her left hand as she had no strength in her arm.

'I have to keep going backwards and forwards. If you would come with me and carry back two buckets we could manage until Dimitra arrives.'

'Let me see your arm.'

'There's really nothing to see.' Reluctantly Fotini rolled up the sleeve of her blouse and showed her sister the ugly scar.

'Is that why you are still wearing your long sleeve blouses?' asked Maria and Fotini nodded.

'There's no need for a bandage, but it doesn't look very nice. Everyone will look at it and ask me what I have done. If I keep wearing my winter blouses they won't see it.'

Sofia finished making the dough and shaped the loaves, making her mark on the side. 'They're ready for the baker, Fotini.'

Fotini picked up a clean cloth and placed it over the tray that held the loaves. As she picked up the tray her arm gave way and it fell to the floor, the dough falling into a sticky mass on the flagstones. Sofia clicked her tongue in annoyance at her daughter's carelessness and Fotini apologised immediately.

'I'm sorry, Mamma. It just slipped. I'll clear it up.' Fotini knelt down on the flagstones and began to scoop the mess of dough into a heap with her right hand.

'Place it in the cloth,' Sofia instructed. 'It will have to be thrown away and I'll make some more. You'll need to wash the floor before I start or we'll be sticking to it.'

Fotini fetched a pail of water and dipped in the scrubbing brush, then placed it to one side whilst she mopped the floor with a cloth.

'Use both hands,' snapped Sofia. 'You'll be there all day otherwise.

Fotini scrubbed and mopped again. 'Have you hurt your hand?' asked Sofia.

'No, it was only the bread dough that suffered.'

'So why aren't you using it?'

Fotini flushed. 'It's still a bit sore from where the ladder fell on it.'

'That was well over a year ago. Stand up and let me have a look.'

Fotini pulled up her sleeve and Sofia sucked in her breath. Around the original cut the skin was white and looked dry and cracked, with small lumps that looked like boils. She remembered only too well how old Anastasia's skin had looked when the cart came to take her away to the leprosarium and watching as the old lady's cottage was set on fire before the cart had even rounded the corner.

'I think I must have got some dirt in it.'

Sofia nodded. 'I'll ask your Pappa to have a look at it tonight. He could ask Doctor Andrianakis to call in and have a look at it the next time he comes to the village.'

'It really is nothing to worry over; it doesn't hurt, Mamma,' Fotini assured her.

Alesandros, at Sofia's instruction, took Fotini into the scullery and examined her arm. He shook his head sadly. 'I want you to go to your room, Fotini and stay there.'

Fotini looked at her father in surprise. 'I have done nothing wrong, Pappa. I couldn't help dropping the bread dough and spoiling it.'

'I am not cross with you, Fotini, but I am concerned about your arm. I think you have an infection in there and I do not want you passing it on to the rest of us. I will ride to Aghios Nikolaos tomorrow and speak to Doctor Stavros.'

Alesandros had seen the lepers being transported from Aghios Nikolaos, on a couple of occasions finding himself closer to them than he would choose. He had seen the ugly disfiguration the disease had caused and had crossed himself fervently, hoping he would never have to add to their number.

'Why can't you ask Doctor Andrianakis to call? He knows us well.'

'I have my reasons. Now, go to your room, Fotini. Your mother will bring you a meal, but you are not to admit her. She will place it outside and talk to you through the door. You use your slop bucket and you can come down and empty it in the morning before Dimitra arrives. If she asks you simply say you are not feeling well and do not want her cleaning your room and disturbing you.'

Fotini's lip trembled. 'What do you think is wrong with my arm?'

'I am not a doctor and I hope I am wrong, but it looks like a leprosy infection to me.'

Fotini's hand went to her mouth and tears began to roll down her face. 'It cannot be.'

Alesandros patted his daughter's shoulder. 'I hope I am

mistaken, but until I have spoken to the doctor you must stay in your room away from us.'

Alesandros returned to the living room, his face grave. 'I have instructed Fotini to stay in her room. You may speak to her through the door, but do not enter. I believe she may have contracted leprosy.'

Maria held Alexandros to her tightly. 'How?'

Alesandros shrugged. 'Who knows how leprosy is contracted. I will speak to Doctor Stavros in Aghios Nikolaos and see what he advises.'

'Suppose he wants to see her? She cannot walk all the way to Aghios Nikolaos.'

'If he considers that is necessary I will make arrangements. You do not have to worry, Sofia. Just take up her meals and leave them outside her door. Spend as long as you wish talking to her, but make sure you have the door closed.' Alesandros wiped his nose on the rag he carried.

'What will we tell Dimitra?' asked Sofia.

'You just say Fotini is feeling unwell and staying in bed. Nothing more.'

'What about us, Pappa? Will she have given it to us? To Yiorgo and my little Alexandros.'

'It is most unlikely. I am sure you would have noticed any blemish on Alexandros's skin. I will speak to Yiorgo and impress upon him that he must tell no one of my suspicions. We do not want word getting around the village. They could refuse to allow us to purchase our food or use the well.'

'If Fo is sick, what will happen to her?' asked Maria tentatively.

'She will go to the hospital,' answered Alesandros firmly.

Alesandros returned from Aghios Nikolaos with the depressing news that Doctor Stavros was away for two weeks. Whilst Dimitra was in the house no one went near Fotini's room, but as soon as she had left for the day Sofia would rush up and ask how she was feeling and if there was anything she wanted.

'How much longer do I have to stay in here?' asked Fotini.

'Until your father has spoken to the doctor. It is only another couple of days until he returns. I'm sure he will say there is nothing to be concerned over and Theophalia can give you a cream that will help your arm to heal.'

'Can you bring me up some more knitting wool?' asked Fotini. 'It is so boring sitting here doing nothing.'

'Of course, and I'll ask your father to bring some more back from Neapoli tomorrow. What colour shall I ask him to buy?'

'I really don't mind,' answered Fotini dully.

Sofia thought about her daughter constantly. If the doctor did think she had leprosy Alesandros would have to take her to Aghios Nikolaos. He would be unlikely to want to sit the girl in front of him on the donkey's back and be in such close proximity to her for a couple of hours or more. Then there was the additional problem that if the doctor confirmed that Fotini was suffering from leprosy he would insist that the whole family was tested. There was no way they would be able to keep the dilemma hidden from the villagers.

'Alesandros,' Sofia spoke to her husband tentatively,' What do you plan to do if the doctor says he wants to see Fotini?'

'I will have to take her to Aghios Nikolaos. I do not want him to come here.'

'The only way for you to take her to the town is by cart. She cannot walk all that way and nor can you now your arthritis is bad.'

Alesandros sighed. If he had to buy a cart he would have to use the money from his savings and it could be a useless purchase if there was nothing wrong with the girl.

'Are you going to tell the doctor she is your daughter?'

'What choice do I have?'

'Why don't you tell him that she is a girl you have seen on the outskirts of Kritsa? You have given her food and persuaded her to ride in your cart to visit the doctor to ask for some treatment.'

'Would he believe me?'

Sofia shrugged. 'Provided you tell Fotini she must not call you "Pappa" and impress upon her that she has to say she comes from Kritsa or even a village that is further away, why should he not believe you? If the doctor should confirm your worst fears,' continued Sofia, unable to say the word "leprosy", 'What are you planning to tell the villagers when she is no longer around?'

'I hadn't thought about it. Let's hear what the doctor has to say first.'

'We need to be prepared. If Fotini is ill and admitted to the hospital we cannot tell them the truth.'

Sofia bought two more incense burners. She gave one to Maria and the other to Fotini with instructions to hang them in their bedrooms. That afternoon she collected wild thyme and placed a bunch in each room, even the scullery and outhouse. She knew thyme had healing and cleansing properties. Throughout the day she turned the problem over in her mind – what would they tell the villagers if it was confirmed that Fotini was leprous and admitted to hospital?

Alesandros returned from Aghios Nikolaos with a cart that he managed to manoeuvre into the yard at the back of the house. It had cost far more than he had envisaged. He had tried to bargain with the wagon maker, asking if he could hire rather than buy, but he was refused.

'If I hired it out to you how do I know that you would return it to me? Even if you did it could be damaged. No, it's a sale or nothing.'

Reluctantly Alesandros handed over the money. Once he had taken Fotini to Aghios Nikolaos and, hopefully, brought her back home, he would have no further use for the cart. Fotini could see the cart from her bedroom window and wept anew. Each time she examined her arm she imagined the unsightly blemishes had grown larger and she dreaded the impending visit to Doctor Stavros.

Dimitra looked at the cart outside in the yard. 'What's that for?' she asked.

'My husband has always wanted a cart. He is often asked to take items to the outlying villages and it can be difficult holding them whilst riding the donkey,' lied Sofia glibly.

Dimitra sniffed. It was an unnecessary expense to buy a cart. He could have bought a couple of panniers and attached them to each side of the donkey if he needed to transport anything large to a village.

Maria and Yiorgo had examined each others' bodies minutely and not found a single blemish and Maria confirmed that Alexandros's skin was smooth and soft. Not only did this relieve some of her anxiety, but gave her hope that Fotini would be diagnosed with a localised infection that could be cleared with treatment from the doctor.

Sofia had examined herself and offered to look at Alesandros to ensure he had no possible signs, but he refused.

'I have looked at myself. There is nothing on me. Fotini must have picked up some contamination whilst she was in the orchard and the ladder fell on her arm. I am going to speak to the doctor tomorrow and tell him I will try to persuade the girl I have befriended to visit him.'

Sofia's heart sank. She had questioned Fotini each day and asked if there was any sign that her arm was improving, hoping the girl would report favourably and there would be no need for a visit to Aghios Nikolaos.

Alesandros approached Doctor Stavros nervously. He did not want to be questioned too closely or have to admit that Fotini was his daughter. If the doctor decided the whole family should be examined and tested he dreaded the outcome.

He took a seat in the doctor's small consulting room and tried to appear relaxed. 'I'm a tax collector and travel around the countryside. There's a girl living near Kritsa. She's begging for food. At first I ignored her, then when I saw her a couple of weeks later I took pity on her and gave her the rusks and olives I was carrying. Since then I've given her some each time I've passed and I think she trusts me. I'm sure she's leprous. I can't think of any other reason why she should be living out in the open. If I bring her here in my cart would you have a look at her? If she's clean I'll take her to the village priest and ask him to arrange somewhere for her to live and find some work. It isn't right that a young girl should be living rough having to beg to stay alive.'

Doctor Stavros looked at Alesandros. He was not sure he believed the story the man was telling him. 'How do you propose to bring her here if she is at Kritsa?'

'I have my donkey and cart. She can sit in the back, well away from me.'

'When do you think you will bring her?'

'I have to visit Flamouriana tomorrow. I can continue to Kritsa and see if she is there and if so bring her on to Aghios Nikolaos if that is amenable to you, doctor.'

Doctor Stavros nodded. It was all very convenient for the man. 'Can you give me some details about yourself, please?'

'Me? Why should you want details about me?' Alesandros felt alarmed.

'I have to make sure you have no intimate knowledge of this girl. You understand what I am asking? If you have, then I would need to ask you to undergo tests also.'

'I assure you I have not touched the girl. I am a happily married man with a family in Kastelli. If you wish to check up on my credentials you can speak the local tax office. They have known me for over twenty years. I am sure they would vouch for my honesty and integrity.'

'I notice you have a problem with walking and use a stick.

What is the reason for that?'

'Arthritis,' explained Alesandros immediately. 'Doctor Andrianakis of Neapoli diagnosed the problem when I first went to him a number of years ago. Unfortunately as I get older the arthritis gets worse.' Alesandros made sure he kept his hands hidden. He did not want to have to explain that his misshapen fingers were also the result of arthritis due to holding the donkey's reins.

'Do you want a second opinion?' asked Doctor Stavros.

'No, oh, no.' Alesandros felt alarmed. 'I trust Doctor Andrianakis. It can be painful during the winter, but I've learnt to live with that. Is that all, Doctor?' Alesandros was in a hurry to remove himself from the doctor's scrutiny.

Doctor Stavros nodded. 'I may have some more questions for you when you bring the girl to me.'

Alesandros sat in Fotini's bedroom. He had assured Sofia he would be at no risk if he sat far enough away from his daughter and did not touch her. 'After all,' he added, 'she will be sitting in the cart behind me tomorrow.'

Fotini looked at her father in despair. 'Do I have to go to the doctor, Pappa? Couldn't I just stay here in my room?'

Alesandros shook his head. 'Sooner or later Dimitra would no longer believe you were suffering from a fever. She would demand that Doctor Andrianakis visited you and word would spread throughout the village. You have to think of the effect that would have on your mother and sister, also little Alexandros. It's better for you to see an unknown doctor and do not tell him that you come from Kastelli. I have told him that I have found you begging for food outside Kritsa and persuaded you to visit him. I am trusting you not to say anything different.'

'Yes, Pappa,' said Fotini dully.

'Your mother will bring up some clean sacks and you can pack your belongings in those. We will leave here in the early hours before the village is astir. We do not want them to see you being driven away in my cart.'

'Yes, Pappa,' Fotini said again. 'May I see Mamma and Maria before I leave?'

'Very briefly, just to say goodbye, but do not touch them.'

'You don't think I will be returning, do you?' said Fotini dispiritedly.

'I pray that I am wrong in my diagnosis and I will be bringing you back home in a few hours. It is for the best, Fotini. If you are diagnosed you will be given treatment. If you stay hidden here your condition will only worsen.' Alesandros handed Fotini his nose rag as the tears rolled unchecked down her face. He felt close to tears himself.

Sofia spent a long time talking to Fotini. She was crying as much as her daughter and the reassuring words she had planned to speak would not come. Finally she left the sacks by the door and returned downstairs where the rest of the family were sitting miserably around the table. No one had any appetite for the food that had been prepared and despite Sofia taking a bowl up to Fotini and saying her father had ordered her to eat, she had refused.

Maria took Alexandros up to his bed and waited until he fell asleep. She could hear her sister sobbing and she felt tears coming into he own eyes. Disobeying her father she pushed open Fotini's door and sat down on the mattress beside her, taking her sister in her arms and holding her tightly.

'I love you, Fo,' was all she managed to say as they clung together.

Once it was dark Alesandros collected his donkey from the orchard and tethered her in the yard. He did not want the sound of her hooves waking people before dawn and he hoped the noise of the cart would not disturb them either. Sofia and Maria clung together as Fotini climbed obediently into the cart and her father placed her sacks beside her. Tears were rolling down her face and they could just make out Fotini raising her hand in farewell as the cart rounded the corner.

Dimitra arrived early for work and confronted Sofia.

'My husband says I'm not to work here anymore. He reckons there's sickness in the house.'

Sofia opened her eyes wide. 'Sickness? There is no sickness here.'

'You told me Miss Fotini had a fever.' Dimitra pointed an accusing finger at Sofia. 'Where is she? You've had her shut up in her room for weeks.'

Sofia nodded. 'That is true. She has been confined to her room. It was on her father's orders. She had decided she wished to marry a most unsuitable man. Unfortunately even keeping her under our eye did not work. We found this morning that she had run away, no doubt with her lover. My husband is out searching for her at this moment.'

Dimitra looked at Sofia suspiciously.

'Miss Fotini's room has not been cleaned since my husband insisted she stayed in there. If you will clean it thoroughly and wash her bedding this morning I will ask my husband not to charge you rent for two weeks.'

Dimitra hesitated. She would be a fool to refuse. 'I'll go and get some more water,' she said and picked up the empty buckets from the scullery.

As soon as she had left the house Sofia turned to Maria. 'Remember, Maria, if anyone asks you tell them that Fotini has run away,' she said sternly.

Whilst the water was heating Dimitra stripped off the sheets from the bed and took them down to the scullery along with the blanket that she draped over a bush to air. She opened the windows and hung the rugs over the iron work of the balconies whilst she swept the room. Once she had washed the sheets the next container of water would have heated sufficiently for her to bring it upstairs and scrub the wooden floor.

The thought of two weeks without having to pay rent encouraged Dimitra to work hard and she scrubbed diligently, stopping every so often to recover her breath. She heard the sound of the donkey and cart returning and hurried to the window to see if Mr Danniakis had his daughter with him. Sofia and Maria rushed out to greet him and he held them in his arms.

'It was confirmed. She has been admitted,' he said.

Dimitra recoiled from the window. So there was sickness in the house. Her husband had been correct. She was tempted to leave immediately and then she looked at the floor she had nearly finished scrubbing. If she left now they would not receive the free rent. Having already done so much there could be no harm in finishing the job, but she would not return tomorrow.

Dimitra's husband knocked on the door that evening and at first refused to enter. He seemed both embarrassed and annoyed.

'My wife tells me that Miss Fotini has been taken away.'

Maria gave a gasp and Alesandros stared at him speechless. Sofia rose and smiled at Panicos.

'Our daughter has been very foolish. She allowed a most unsuitable man to take liberties with her, expecting that we would then agree to her marriage. We could still not approve the match and she took matters into her own hands. She has harmed herself internally and is in hospital for an operation.'

Panicos's mouth opened and shut as Sofia continued. 'I had hoped your wife would understand this morning and we would be able to keep this unfortunate occurrence to ourselves. I should obviously have been more explicit when I spoke to her.'

Panicos's face turned brick red with embarrassment. 'I'm sorry,' he mumbled. 'My wife must have misunderstood.'

Sofia closed the door behind him and took a deep breath. 'If anyone asks that is what we have to tell them.'

Maria looked at her mother in consternation. 'But what will

they think if Fotini doesn't come back?'

'We have to say she did not survive,' replied Sofia harshly.

1935

Alesandros examined his head as carefully as possible in his shaving mirror. He touched the small lumps with his fingers and they did not hurt, so they could not be anything to worry about. Despite the reassurance of nothing feeling painful he remembered Fotini had said her arm did not hurt. He looked at the lumps again. Surely he must be mistaken, but they did bear a distinct resemblance to the lumps on his daughter's arm. Hearing Sofia re-entering the scullery he placed his hat on his head swiftly. If his awful suspicions were true he would not infect anyone provided he kept his head covered.

Sofia hardly left the house, sending Maria to the well and village shops. Maria was well aware that the villagers avoided her, even her friend Eva being unwilling to welcome her into her house. Dimitra had spread enough rumours and suspicion amongst the villagers to make them wary.

Tryphaine, wanting to know the truth of the situation as much as the other villagers, visited Sofia.

'We are old friends,' she said. 'Can you not confide your troubles to me?'

Sofia looked at her and shook her head. 'You did not confide in me when you had problems.'

Tryphaine looked at her in surprise. 'I have no troubles.'

'Your Timotheos is a fine boy.'

'What do you mean?' Tryphaine looked at Sofia warily.

'You have been fortunate that the villagers and Nikos are not as observant as I am.'

Tryphaine's face reddened and she could not look at Sofia. 'I was desperate,' she muttered.

'I have spread no rumours about his parentage,' Sofia assured her. 'I kept your confidence when I could have caused such trouble for you that you would have been forced to leave the village. You have had to live with the knowledge that you deceived Nikos and have no doubt worried daily that the truth would be realised. That must have been punishment enough for you. I expect you to respect our troubles and not spread false rumours. Fotini was foolish and she has paid the price. That is all the villagers need to know. Malicious rumours and speculation only make our sad situation more distressing.'

'I am truly sorry, Sofia. I cannot imagine how I would bear it if anything happened to Timotheos. I will make sure that everyone knows Dimitra is just making up stories for the sake of gossip. Because she works for you people tend to believe her.'

'Thank you, Tryphaine. Obviously whatever Dimitra has said regarding Fotini leaving us will be proved incorrect with time.' Sofia sighed deeply and would have liked to cross herself.

'And you will still say nothing?' Tryphaine looked at Sofia anxiously.

'What advantage would it be to me to speak out now?' Sofia shook her head. 'No, Tryphaine, your secret is safe with me.' She wished she could confide her own fears to her friend.

Sofia had woken just as the living room became light and turned to wake Alesandros. His night cap had become untied and slipped off during the night. She drew in her breath. It could not be true. She looked again at the ugly lumps and scabs on her husband's scalp. Alesandros stirred and Sofia closed her eyes swiftly. She could feel him groping for his hat and waited until she felt him rise from the mattress before she opened her eyes again. What was she going to do?

She went through her normal morning routine, heating water for Alesandros to wash and shave, putting out the rusks and olives that Maria would wrap for her father to take with him whilst he was out for the day, all the while her hands were shaking, her mouth felt dry and she longed for him to leave the house.

Sofia drew a deep breath. She needed time alone to think. 'I'm going to pick some marjoram,' she said to Maria. 'If I see any mushrooms I'll bring those back as well.'

Maria had smiled in delight. If her mother was going out to look for marjoram she must be feeling more reconciled to Fotini's fate.

Walking along the lane from the village Sofia's thoughts were in turmoil. What was she going to do? She could speak to Theophalia and describe how Alesandros's head looked, but Theophalia would want to see for herself. If she waited until Doctor Andrianakis visited and spoke to him he would also want to see Alesandros, but would not be prepared to wait until late afternoon when he returned from collecting the taxes. She could not ask the doctor to make a special journey to the village on a Saturday when Alesandros would be at home as it was not an emergency like an accident or a woman having birthing problems.

There was the added problem that if she asked the doctor to call on them specifically the whole village would know and be curious. If Alesandros was diagnosed as an incurable he would be sent away and they would all be tested to see if they were suffering as well. The villagers would shun them, possible turn them out of their house and drive them into the countryside. She could not risk that fate befalling Maria; there was Alexandros to be considered. She had no relatives anywhere on Crete where she could beg for sanctuary.

How long ago was it that Alesandros had fallen from the donkey and cut his head? She knew it had happened when there was the earth tremor and Perpetua had damaged her arm, but how long ago was that? Sofia tried in vain to calculate the length of time that had passed and gave up. Surely she must be wrong in her diagnosis if Alesandros had been suffering from leprosy for some years and she had not caught the disease. With that comforting thought Sofia picked some sprigs of marjoram and turned back towards the house.

Alexandros seemed to sense that something untoward had happened. He would look at Maria questioningly, but no longer asked for "Fo". Maria examined his sturdy body each time she undressed him, sending up a prayer of thanks that he had no signs that Fotini might have infected him.

Yiorgo set off each day for Aghios Nikolaos with a plan formulating in his head. He had not confided in Maria, but he felt certain that Fotini would have been taken to Spinalonga. On occasions he had seen a boatman setting out with distressed passengers, his boat also loaded with supplies of food and bedding. He was not sure where Spinalonga was, but it had to be a village further around the bay on the coast.

Each day he would wander down to the quayside and look for the boatman, waiting as late as he dared before riding his donkey back to Kastelli. He had told Maria that he was busy at work and she was not to worry if he arrived home a little later than usual. Finally his efforts bore results. He waited until Manolis had moored and then approached him.

'Excuse me, may I ask you something?'

Manolis looked at the man before him. 'You can ask. I may not know the answer.'

'Do you take the sufferers to the hospital in the village of Spinalonga?'

Manolis raised his eyebrows. 'Spinalonga isn't a village. It's an island. I go out every day and take Doctor Stavros over once a week. Why do you want to know?'

'Just curious.' Yiorgo turned to go and Manolis called after him

'I'm usually around at this time of day if you have any more questions.'

Yiorgo nodded, 'Thanks,' he called back over his shoulder.

Riding back to Kastelli Yiorgo thought over his brief conversation with the boatman. Was that where Fotini had been taken? He would talk to Maria and if she wanted him to find out more he would wait around for the boatman after he had finished work each day.

Maria looked at her husband adoringly. 'You are so clever, Yiorgo. Fancy realising that the boatman was taking people to the hospital! Do you think he would remember taking Fotini? I expected her to be in a hospital in Aghios Nikolaos.' Maria frowned. 'I hope she wasn't too frightened when she had to go on a boat. You've told me the sea is so big you cannot see the end of it.'

'I'm sure the hospital where Fo was taken is only a short way along the coast. The boatman said it was on an island.'

'I wonder if Pappa would know.'

Yiorgo frowned. 'I don't think we should mention this to your parents at the moment. Your father could forbid me to talk to the boatman again.'

'Why would he do that?'

'He could be worried that someone from Kastelli would see me. I'll try to meet the boatman again and see if he knows anything about Fo.'

Maria paced her arms around Yiorgo's neck. 'Please find out whatever you can.'

Yiorgo hung around the quayside for some days before he was able to speak to Manolis again and after doing so he returned to Maria elated.

'I have seen the boatman again. His name is Manolis. He did take Fo to Spinalonga and says he left her in the care of a friend of his over there.' Yiorgo lowered his voice further. 'He said that if I wanted to write a letter to her he would carry it over for me and only charge one drachma.'

Maria's face lit up with a smile, then she frowned. 'Can you trust him? We'll never know if Fo received the letter.'

Yiorgo shrugged. 'If you want to send a letter I'm willing to pay him. He told me he buys whatever goods the islanders want and takes the money from their pension. They obviously trust him.'

'I suppose it is only one drachma. I'll start writing a letter to Fo tonight.'

Ten days later Maria handed a number of sheets of folded paper to her husband. 'You don't think he will want to charge more because it is a long letter, do you?'

Yiorgo had no idea. He had never sent a letter to anyone in his life. 'I think it needs to be wrapped up so the pages don't blow away. Find me a piece of cloth and I'll make it into a parcel. I should be able to take an envelope from work and place it inside and write Fo's name on it.'

'Suppose there is more than one person there called Fotini?'

'I'll write "Fotini D" on the envelope and add "from her sister".'

Yiorgo handed the thick envelope to Manolis who whistled through his teeth. 'That's a long love letter.'

Yiorgo was about to say that it was not from him when he thought better of it. 'If you could just make sure she gets it, please.' He placed a drachma in the fisherman's hand and Manolis grinned at him.

'Is there to be a reply?'

'A reply?' asked Yiorgo, mystified. He did not think anyone who had been declared an incurable was allowed to have contact in any way with healthy people, even members of their immediate family.

'You can trust me. Come and look for me again some time.'

Alesandros seemed to be affected most by the absence of Fotini. He would sit at the table for hours on end with his head resting on his hands and sigh deeply. Sofia could only imagine that he felt guilty as he was the one who had to take their daughter to the doctor to be diagnosed and, in all likelihood given her the disease in the first place.

'How is your head?' she asked?

'My head? It's years ago that I hurt it. It's completely healed now.'

'I'm pleased to hear it. May I see?'

'What do you need to see it for? I've told you there's nothing wrong.' He rose and walked unsteadily over to the wash stand and took his account book from the drawer. 'I've work to do. If people paid their debts on time I wouldn't have to be forever going backwards and forwards to the villages,' he complained.

'Why don't you ask Yiorgo for some help?' asked Sofia. 'He's good with numbers.'

'I'm quite capable of adding up the money that is owed.'

'I know you are. I just thought it might help if Yiorgo did the writing for you. You know you have trouble holding the pencil some days when your fingers are bad.'

Alesandros tried unsuccessfully to straighten out his fingers. 'I can manage,' he said.

'Would you at least consider letting Yiorgo collect the rents for you? It worries me when I see you walking on the rough ground. Your balance is not good.'

Alesandros did not answer her. He knew how difficult it was becoming for him to walk any distance. If he rode on his donkey Yiorgo could accompany him and knock at the cottager's doors, going inside and collecting the rent on his behalf. He would only need to climb off the donkey's back if the tenant refused to pay. All his joints seemed stiff and he could only think his arthritis was getting considerably worse.

Yiorgo had managed to wait until he and Maria were alone in their bedroom. He took the letter Manolis had given to him from his pocket.

'I saw Manolis today,' he said by way of explanation.

'Is it from Fo?' asked Maria eagerly.

'I imagine so. I didn't want to raise your hopes, but he asked if there was to be a reply when I gave him the first letter. He told me to look out for him. I'd almost given up hope as I've seen him three times and there was nothing. Today he gave me this.'

Maria clasped the letter to her. 'Mamma and Pappa will be so happy to hear from her.'

Yiorgo placed a restraining hand on her arm. 'I think you should read it before you allow your Pappa to see it. If there is any bad news in there it could be kinder not to tell them. Also your Pappa could throw it in the fire before you've had a chance to read it.'

Maria sat with Yiorgo's arm around her and by the light of the oil lamp they read the long letter Fotini had sent describing her arrival on the island.

'I'll copy everything she says into my diary; then if Pappa does decide to throw it into the fire without reading it I will be able to tell Mamma what she said.' Maria's eyes were glistening with tears.

As Yiorgo had surmised, Alesandros read the letter aloud to Sofia and then crumpled it into a ball and threw it into the fire. Sofia stretched out her hand as if she would retrieve it from the flames.

'I would have liked to keep it,' she said sadly.

'You can't read it, so what would be the point?' asked Alesandros harshly. 'It is better burnt. It could be contaminated. Heat me some water, Maria. I need to wash my hands after touching that, and you should do the same.'

'Yes, Pappa,' answered Maria obediently. She planned to have a quiet word with her mother the following day and she could read Fotini's letter to her as often as her mother requested from the copy she had made.

Sofia would look hopefully at Yiorgo each day as he arrived home from work. He always smiled and gave her a cordial greeting, but she now knew that if he winked at the same time he had a letter from Fotini with him. She would curb her impatience until Maria would produce it and Alesandros would read aloud to them the words Fotini had written before he discarded the pages into the fire.

Sofia was happier now she knew that Fotini was not languishing in a hospital ward, but living much the same as she would in any small village and Maria spent hours composing letters relating the day to day happenings in Kastelli. She reported that Yiorgo had been promoted again and was now the head of a department. He had decided to open a bank account and try to save some of his wages.

"Yiorgo says the day will come when we are old and he can no longer work. We may need the money then," she wrote. Maria described the new trousers that Yiorgo had bought in the town and the dress he had promised to bring for her. "The most incredible thing is that Pappa now allows Yiorgo to collect the rents. He goes with him, of course, riding on his donkey, but it shows that at last he trusts Yiorgo. I think it is because he has now been promoted to a manager."

Whilst they were alone in the house Sofia and Maria talked about Fotini and Maria told her mother that she planned to send a parcel to Fo for her Name Day. Together they discussed the contents that she would probably find most useful and Sofia immediately made a new skirt and blouse, Yiorgo was instructed to purchase wool and knitting needles and also returned with a bundle of candles.

Sofia insisted they told Alesandros of their plans to send Fotini a parcel, saying it could be hurtful for him to think himself excluded. Alesandros had said nothing, but the following day he had returned from Neapoli with a pair of boots and handed them to Maria.

'Fotini may need some new ones,' he said gruffly and tried to push Maria away as she flung her arms around him and cried in gratitude.

Fotini sent letters regularly, describing her life on Spinalonga and Sofia waited for them eagerly. She would sit with a delighted smile on her face whilst Maria read the contents to her time and again from her diary. They tried to picture the flying boat and shook their heads in puzzlement over its ability to land on the sea; they laughed together over the story of the smuggler who had given Fotini such a fright, but were thankful that the islanders had come to her aid. Sofia was full of admiration that Fotini was helping up at the hospital, but secretly dreaded that being in such close contact with the sick people would make her own disease spread.

When Fotini finally wrote and said that one of the men on the island had asked to marry her Sofia and Maria cried together.

'My little girl, getting married,' said Sofia. 'How I wish I could be there with her.'

'If only it were possible,' sighed Maria. She knew her father would have enjoyed Fotini's wedding far more than hers. Fotini would not have a bump beneath her skirt that she was trying to hide.

Alesandros was disgusted when he read Fotini's letter. 'She cannot get married. It is against the law for incurables to marry.'

Maria shrugged. 'Surely it is better for her to have a blessing on her union with this man than just live in his house with him? That way everyone knows they are committed to each other forever.'

Alesandros pursed his lips. He was more annoyed that Fotini had confided the truth to both her prospective husband and to the priest on the island. The priest might well think it his duty to tell the doctor she came from Kastelli and the doctor would visit the village and demand that he tested her family for the disease. He examined his head regularly: he had lost more hair and the lumps and bumps on his scalp were very evident; some of them breaking open and leaving an unpleasant yellow pus on the lining of his hat or nightcap.

Fotini wrote a long letter describing her wedding to Aristo, extolling his virtues and saying how happy she was living with him in his house; her only regret being that her family had been unable to be there with her.

Maria felt she had very little interesting news to send to her sister. Life in the village continued without weddings, smugglers or flying boats. When Fotini wrote and said that she and Aristo were expecting a child both Sofia and Maria were concerned. Sofia was worried that the child would be malformed due to both parents suffering from leprosy and for Maria it brought back the memory of the agonies she had suffered during the birth of Alexandros.

Fotini brushed their worries aside. Doctor Stavros had said there was no reason why their child should not be healthy and have no sign of the disease. One of the women on the island had worked at the hospital on the mainland and had promised to care for Fotini when she gave birth and she had a more exciting event to tell them about.

Electricity had been installed on the island and it made the night as bright as the day. Fotini described how the generator had been delivered and hauled ashore, then men had fitted up wires to the outside of the houses and then through the roof or walls where a lamp was fixed. It had made so much difference to the hospital. They were no longer dependent upon oil lamps when it became dark.

Neither Sofia nor Maria could understand how electricity worked, but Yiorgo said that some parts of Aghios Nikolaos had electric light and when he rode past on his way home he had seen the rooms lit up brightly. Sofia could see no advantage of electric light. Once it became dark you lit the oil lamps or went to bed.

Fotini's next letter held even more exciting news. They were to be allowed to have visitors to the island. Already a Karagiozis puppeteer had visited and they were holding concerts where musical instruments were played and people danced. As Maria thought about the events that Fotini described to her she wished she was able to visit and see the village for herself. Unless it was a religious feast day or there was a wedding or christening very little happened in Kastelli to break up the monotonous days.

Alesandros raged when he read the letter. 'This is utter foolishness on the part of the government to allow these outcasts to have visitors. They will bring the disease back with them and before we know it everyone will be infected.'

Yiorgo shook his head. 'The government would not give permission if they thought visitors would bring it back. I asked the boatman and he said he had been visiting the island for years and never had a day's illness. There is a priest over there who voluntarily went to the island to be with the people. He lives amongst them and has not contracted the disease.'

'Wouldn't you like to visit Fotini?' asked Maria of her father.

Alesandros gave her a scathing glance. 'I would not take the chance. If you have any such stupid idea then you can forget it. I forbid you to go to visit your sister.'

Maria set her mouth in a determined line, but did not reply.

Sofia noticed that Maria raised her eyebrows as soon as Yiorgo entered each evening and he would shake his head, resulting in Maria giving a deep sigh. Sofia was certain they were planning something. It could not be another baby or it would have been Yiorgo raising his eyebrows and Maria shaking her head. She wished her daughter would confide in her and finally had her wish.

'Mamma, Yiorgo has to go to Heraklion and he has said he will take me with him if you will look after Alesandros.'

'Heraklion?'

Maria nodded. 'It is to do with his work. He is going to ask Pappa this evening if I may go with him. I'm so excited.'

'Suppose your father says you cannot go?'

'Why should he say that? If I wanted to go to Neapoli he would not stop me.'

'You could walk to Neapoli and back in the day. Heraklion is far away.'

'Yiorgo says we will have to go to Aghios Nikolaos and catch the bus to Heraklion. We will have to stay in a guest house for two nights. That is also exciting. I have never slept anywhere but in my own bed. Yiorgo says he will show me the sea and I will not believe how big it is.' Sofia listened as Maria continued to chatter away excitedly. No doubt this was why Maria had raised her eyebrows each day when Yiorgo arrived home. She was waiting for news from him about their impending journey.

Maria and Yiorgo arrived home and Sofia could not believe how excited Maria appeared. The whole evening she talked about the sea, that it did not look like water as it was blue and stretched so far out that you could not tell where the sea ended and the sky began, or the town where there were so many people and shops selling different goods.

Maria had presented Sofia with combs for her hair, wine glasses for Alesandros and a wonderful toy cart for Alexandros. He had sat for hours on the rug, pushing it backwards and forwards, sometimes placing a rusk in the back and pretending it was a sack of vegetables that he was taking to market.

'How did you know where to buy such beautiful gifts?' asked Sofia.

'We just walked around and looked until we saw something we thought you would like,' replied Maria airily.

'And the bus journey?' asked Alesandros.

'Quicker than riding on a donkey,' answered Yiorgo and Maria added that it had been hot and stuffy with so many people on board.

Maria was relieved that her father appeared to accept that they had travelled to Heraklion, and much as she wished to confide in her mother the nature of their journey she dared not. If Sofia told Alesandros they had visited Fotini she dreaded his reaction.

1938 - 1939

Sofia noticed that Maria seemed happier than she had done for a considerable amount of time. Was this due to do with the visit to Heraklion? Sofia waited for an opportune moment to ask her daughter, but was forestalled by the arrival of a letter from Fotini. Maria was unable to contain herself.

'Mamma, Fo has had a little girl.'

Sofia crossed herself. 'Is all well?'

Maria nodded. 'I'll copy the letter and then give it to Pappa to read to you.'

'Couldn't you read it to me tomorrow whilst your Pappa is out?' asked Sofia.

'I can, but when Pappa reads it you must appear surprised, as though you did not know the news it contained.'

Sofia and Maria smiled together conspiratorially and once again Maria wished she could tell her mother the truth. Letters arrived regularly from Fotini describing the progress of her daughter and the various events that had taken place on Spinalonga. Maria did not always tell her father that she had received a letter from Fotini as her sister had begun to include phrases like "you remember meeting" and "when you met", but she would read them to her mother leaving out a line or paragraph that was incriminating.

Maria begged Yiorgo to take her to Aghios Nikolaos again and over to Spinalonga. She so wanted to visit her sister and see her little niece. Yiorgo demurred; the weather was not conducive to travelling at present. She must wait until nearer the summer and he would consider telling her father that he had to visit Heraklion again. Having extracted a promise from her husband Maria constantly reminded him, until Yiorgo finally agreed to arrange a second visit.

During the week preceding their proposed visit Maria washed all the clothes that Alexandros had outgrown, added two old skirts and a blouse of her own along with a pair of Yiorgo's trousers. Each day Yiorgo took a small parcel in to work with him so they would not be seen leaving with a large sack. They planned to buy gifts when they were in Aghios Nikolaos, but Maria felt sure that the clothes would be useful.

Sofia noticed the extra washing and asked Maria why she was taking so much trouble over old clothes.

Maria shrugged. 'I thought I could offer them to Eva,' she said, reddening. She had given clothes to Eva in the past, but now she thought Fotini could need them more.

Sofia looked at her daughter searchingly. She was certain there was something being planned again between her and Yiorgo. She wished her daughter would confide in her, but knew better than to ask Maria directly.

Returning from visiting Fotini a second time Maria longed to tell her mother that Vivi was a beautiful little girl and they were a very happy family. She wished her father's attitude was more amenable and they could all visit her sister, but when she tried to broach the subject of travelling to Aghios Nikolaos with her mother Sofia shook her head.

'I don't like donkeys and I have never ridden on one.'

'Yiorgo could use Pappa's cart,' suggested Maria. 'It just sits outside in the yard doing nothing.'

'Your father wouldn't allow it; besides I have no wish to see the town. You have described it to me and also the sea. I know what it looks like.'

Maria was tempted to add that her mother would be able to visit Fotini and meet Aristo and Vivi, but dared not. If Sofia told Alesandros that they had deceived him with the story of going to Heraklion he would certainly not allow her to accompany Yiorgo when he said he had to make the business trip another time.

Maria read Fotini's letter to her mother and sucked in her breath. 'Mamma, do you think the couple Fotini mentions were the couple who tended to Pappa's head?'

Sofia shrugged. 'I have no idea.' She did not wish to discuss Alesandros's head with her daughter.

'I'll ask Pappa when he's shaving tomorrow,' said Maria. 'He's bound to remember their names. I'll ask him to show me how well it has healed.'

Sofia was about to say that Alesandros would not appreciate the enquiry when Alexandros tumbled over and Maria rushed to him, picking him up in her arms and ensuring that he was not truly hurt.

The summer days were hot and both Sofia and Maria were pleased to be inside in the coolness of their house. When the sun went down and the air cooled Sofia suggested they sat outside their house as the other villagers did, but Alesandros would not hear of it.

'You are not a peasant,' he said sternly. 'What would the villagers think if we sat outside?'

Sofia was about to say that he parents had often sat outside during the summer evenings and no one had thought any the less of them for doing so when Alesandros looked at her sternly and she returned to her weaving.

'We sit inside as befits our station,' he said pompously.

Maria gave a heavy sigh. She could sit and sew just as well outside as in and Yiorgo could continue to read his newspaper. No doubt Fotini and Aristo were sitting outside of their house, probably drinking a glass of wine and chatting to their neighbours.

Maria placed her sewing on the table and answered the door

when the knock came. Her hand flew to her throat when she saw Doctor Stavros standing on the doorstep.

'Fo?' she gasped and the doctor shook his head.

'May I come in? I believe you are Fotini's sister.'

Sofia stopped weaving and held her breath, whilst Alesandros pushed his hands into his pockets and did not rise from his chair.

'I assure you Fotini is well, there is no problem with her or her family.'

Maria drew a breath of relief and at Yiorgo's bidding hurried into the scullery to fetch a carafe of wine and glasses. Doctor Stavros sat at the table and looked at Yiorgo.

'Father Minos asked me to call. I understand you have visited Fotini and Aristo?'

Yiorgo nodded. 'On two occasions.'

'What!' Alesandros was about to rise and then thought better of it. 'I forbade you to visit that island. How dare you disobey me?' he raged and Alexandros's lip began to quiver. He was not used to hearing raised voices.

'There is no harm in visiting Spinalonga,' Doctor Stavros assured Alesandros. 'I have been going there for many years and have no sign of infection. All visitors have to go through a disinfection process before they are allowed to leave.'

Alesandros subsided into his chair. He had refused the glass of wine Maria had offered him and Sofia added some water so she could drink it herself whilst Maria sent Alexandros out into the yard to play.

'I have actually come to visit you to talk about the child Fotini and Aristo have.'

'She's beautiful,' interposed Maria.

Doctor Stavros smiled and nodded. 'Also she is quite free from infection. That being the case she will have to leave the island.'

'Leave? What do you mean?'

'It is a government ruling that any healthy child has to leave the island at the age of two. They will then be sent to an orphanage to be brought up.'

Maria gasped. 'An orphanage? No, you can't send Vivi away.'

Doctor Stavros spread his hands. 'I have no control over the situation. A healthy child either has to be adopted by relatives on the mainland or sent to an orphanage.' The doctor waited a moment for his words to be understood. 'Would you be willing to adopt your sister's child and bring her up as your own?'

'It's out of the question.' Alesandros's face was tinged with purple his rage was so great. 'There is no way that child is entering my house.'

Tears began to run down Maria's face and she groped for Yiorgo's hand. 'In that case Pappa Yiorgo, Alexandros and I will be leaving. We will find a small house of our own where we can live and Vivi will be with us as a part of our family.'

'You do not have to decide immediately. You can have time to consider the implications and discuss the situation thoroughly.'

Sofia rose from her weaving loom and stood looking down at Alesandros. 'There is nothing to discuss. Of course we will take the child.'

Alesandros opened his mouth to argue with her and Sofia continued. 'It is the least we can do for Fotini under the circumstances. We are her grandparents. Naturally she can have a home here.'

Doctor Stavros looked relieved. 'I will tell Fotini and Aristo when I visit next week.'

Yiorgo shook his head. 'No, we will go and speak to them ourselves. The decision for us to adopt their daughter must be made by them.' Yiorgo refilled our glasses and we raised them, except for Alesandros who had no glass and sat and glowered.

Sofia waited anxiously for the return of Maria and Yiorgo from their visit to Spinalonga. Maria had confided in her mother that they had been over twice before, but both times had been during the summer months. Now it was the autumn and the weather could be unpredictable. Throughout the day Sofia glanced out of the window. The trees were beginning to lose their leaves and the dust was swirling along the path. If they had a wind in Kastelli they must have one in Aghios Nikolaos.

Alesandros returned home and poured himself a glass of wine. 'They're not back yet?'

Sofia shook her head. 'I hope that doesn't mean they've encountered a problem. I wish they were bringing the child back today. I'll be happier when all is settled.'

'You might be, but I don't want the bastard in my house.'

Sofia looked at her husband sternly. 'You have no choice, Alesandros. You heard Maria say that if you refused to have Vivi here she and Yiorgo would leave. She meant it. She's a strong willed young woman. What is more I would go with them.'

'You would leave me?'

Sofia nodded. 'I have tried to be a good and obedient wife to you, Alesandros, but I will not refuse Fo's daughter a home. If you cannot accept her then it is better that I live apart from you.'

Alesandros drained his glass of wine. 'Don't expect me to make her welcome.'

'I trust that in time you will be able to accept the circumstances of her birth and treat her as your granddaughter.'

Maria found it a relief to be able to sit and talk to Sofia about their visits to the island, describing each of their journeys to Aghios Nikolaos and travelling by boat to Spinalonga.

'Why didn't you tell me you were going to see Fo?' asked Sofia.

'I couldn't, Mamma. You might have told Pappa and he had forbidden me to go over there. It would have caused trouble if he knew I had deliberately disobeyed him.'

Sofia shook her head. 'I've told you before; I know how to manage your father Tell me about Aristo. Is he disfigured?'

'One side of his head. If it were not for that he would be handsome, as handsome as my Yiorgo or Pappa.'

'And he and Fotini are happy together?'

'Blissfully happy. They love each other as much as Yiorgo and I love each other.'

'Tell me again about the shops and the people you have met over there,' begged Sofia. 'Describe the inside of their house again,'

Sofia asked much the same questions every day and Maria was happy to comply. The previous Christmas Yiorgo had given Maria a camera of her own and she had practised, ruining film after film, until she had become reasonably proficient.

'I'm planning to go to Spinalonga every week. I want Vivi to get to know me properly. Whilst I'm there I'll take some photographs of Fo and Aristo and also their house.' Maria did not add that she also planned to take photographs of Vivi and send them regularly to Fotini and Aristo so they could watch their daughter grow, albeit from a distance.

Maria entered the house bearing Vivi in her arms. Sofia immediately rose and came over to look at the addition to their family. Vivi buried her head in Maria's neck and then peeped out shyly at her grandmother.

Sofia's throat constricted. 'She is so like Fo.'

Maria nodded. 'A little mirror image. She has been so good on the journey. I'll sit her on the rug and introduce Alexandros to his sister.' Maria opened her arms to her son and he clung to her momentarily before becoming more interested in the sack that his father had brought in from the cart.

Alesandros immersed himself in the newspaper Yiorgo had brought for him from Aghios Nikolaos and ignored the little girl, whilst Sofia sat and talked to Vivi, trying to gain her confidence.

Finally Alesandros threw the newspaper to one side. 'Load of rubbish,' he announced crossly. 'They make these stories up. Saying this man Hitler is amassing an army and intending to invade Poland. How would they know what is happening if they aren't there?'

Dimitra looked suspiciously at Vivi and it was obvious that she did not believe Sofia when she explained that Maria and Yiorgo had adopted the child.

'Whose child is she?' she asked.

Sofia shrugged. 'How would we know? When a child is adopted you are not told who her natural parents are.'

'She looks a lot like your girls when they were small,' she remarked as she carried the buckets of water into the scullery. She would certainly have some news to pass on to the villagers that afternoon.

Yiorgo's parents accepted Maria's story of adopting Vivi unconditionally; they were delighted to think they were grandparents and would have a little girl to fuss over along with Alesandros when Maria brought both children to visit them.

Eva was equally as welcoming, but Maria noticed the quizzical glances that the villagers gave her and finally Theophalia asked outright if Vivi was Fotini's daughter. With a toss of her head Maria denied it, but she was convinced Dimitra had spread the rumour throughout the village.

Tryphaine was curious. She had seen Vivi when Maria had taken the child with her to the shops and also noticed the family resemblance. The only way to find out for sure was to pay a visit to Sofia.

Vivi was playing happily with her wooden animals when Tryphaine arrived. Sofia invited her in and produced coffee and a slice of honey cake for her visitor. Tryphaine sat at the table in the living room and looked at Vivi.

'She's a lovely little girl, Sofia. Where did they find her?'

'They didn't find her. They adopted her,' replied Sofia firmly.

Tryphaine looked at Sofia, hurt that her old friend was obviously not telling her the whole truth. 'You kept my secret, Sofia. I'll not spread rumours.'

'There are no rumours to spread. She has settled well with us.

Maria is ensuring that she gives Alexandros time alone with her so he will not be jealous of the attention she needs to give to Vivi.'

At the sound of her name Vivi looked up and smiled.

Tryphaine shook her head. 'I'll not press you for details, Sofia, but a family resemblance is obvious. Remember Timotheos's ears.'

'I do. It was unfortunate that such a family trait appeared so strongly in him. I never said a word to anyone. If Vivi looks anything like us it is pure coincidence,' Sofia said firmly.

Maria was concerned. Whenever Vivi accompanied her to the village people would turn their backs on her and sometimes she heard an audible hiss. If they were unable to avoid her they would cross themselves openly before stepping to one side. Maria spoke to Yiorgo, asking if they could move to Aghios Nikolaos to live.

'We know no one there so questions will not be asked. You would be closer to your work and not have to make the long journey each day.'

Yiorgo had taken Maria's hand. 'I think we should go further away that Aghios Nikolaos.'

'You mean Heraklion?'

Yiorgo shook his head. 'I think we should consider going to America.'

Maria gasped. 'America? Why would we have to go so far? We just need to live where we are an unknown family and accepted.'

Yiorgo explained how he had spoken to the captains of the ships that docked in Aghios Nikolaos and the disturbing reports they had given him about conditions in Europe. 'They say many people are going to America. The people over there have a good life.'

'But what about Mamma and Pappa?' asked Maria.

'They could come with us. Think about it, Maria. If we were in America we would be out of danger from this man who seems intent on occupying the whole of Europe and no one would know we had adopted Vivi. I'll find out what we have to do and you can give me your decision then.'

Sofia did not understand the talk between Alesandros and Yiorgo. They mentioned territories, advances, incursions, invasions, battles, treaties, agreements, a country called Germany and a man called Hitler. Finally Alesandros appeared to be taking the newspaper reports seriously. When Yiorgo brought a wireless set back from Aghios Nikolaos Sofia looked at it suspiciously.

Whilst she was alone in the house she examined it carefully. Where was the man who spoke out of it? It was too small for a normal size man to hide in, but where did his voice come from? Both Yiorgo and Alesandros tried to explain to her how it worked, but Sofia still shook her head in wonderment and disbelief.

Every night the men would listen to the news that was coming from Europe and Yiorgo was becoming seriously worried, although Alesandros scoffed at the thought that Crete would be involved in any way with the European turmoil. Despite Alesandros's scepticism Yiorgo remained concerned.

Maria turned Yiorgo's suggestion over and over in her mind. America was a long way across the sea – the other side of the world. How many days would it take them to get there? Suppose the sea was rough and the boat capsized? Would she ever see her parents again? She would not understand what the people were saying – how would she manage to do her shopping?

Each night she asked her questions of Yiorgo, but had still come to no decision until Father Constantinus approached her whilst she was in the village. The villagers still looked at Vivi suspiciously and Maria was near to tears after Father Constantinus had confronted her and asked about Vivi's origins, suggesting that she was a blood relative.

At first Yiorgo was cross that the priest had upset his wife, but when Maria set her mouth in a determined line and said her decision was made; she would be willing to go to America; he had sent up a silent prayer of thanks.

'Leave it with me. I know we have to apply for papers giving us permission to travel. It may take some time for the arrangements to be finalised. If you feel you have made the wrong decision it is not too late to tell me.'

Sofia listened in silence when Yiorgo told Alesandros they were making arrangements to go to America and suggested that Sofia and Alesandros joined them. Alesandros immediately replied that neither he nor his wife would be leaving Kastelli. Maria did her best to persuade her mother, but Sofia shook her head.

'If your Pappa is staying then I have to stay here. Who would look after him and the house until you return?'

No amount of persuasive talk by either Maria or Yiorgo would make Sofia change her mind and Yiorgo's parents were unwilling to leave the village also.

'I'll start making arrangements,' said Yiorgo with a sigh. 'I'm sorry, Maria, but your father is not going to change his mind.'

Yiorgo returned from Aghios Nikolaos disheartened. 'I do not know if we will be able to go,' he said sadly. 'I had no idea it would cost so much. I had to pay a bribe to the man to give me a certificate for Vivi, then another so that I could collect our papers immediately rather than wait a week. Once I had the papers I went to the shipping office to see if we could book a passage and when they told me the cost I nearly fainted.'

'Couldn't you use your savings?' asked Maria and Yiorgo shook his head.

'We will need all my savings when we arrive in America. We have to pay for somewhere to stay and I have to find some work.'

'Sell your donkey,' proposed Maria and Yiorgo smiled.

'The poor beast would not fetch enough to pay for more than a week's meals.'

'My necklaces.' Maria pulled out the box from under the bed and handed it to Yiorgo. 'You could sell those.'

Yiorgo ran them through his fingers. 'I will only sell them if they will provide us with enough money for our passage. If they do not then I will return them to you.'

Maria waited anxiously for Yiorgo's return. He shook his head and handed her the box containing her gold necklaces. 'I was not offered enough. I have brought them back for you.'

Maria bit her lip. She did not relish the thought of leaving Crete and her mother to go so far away, but having made the decision she was anxious to go before she had an excuse to change her mind.

'Ask Pappa. Ask Pappa if he will lend you the money.'

Yiorgo shook his head. 'I cannot ask him.'

'Then I will.' Maria strode from their room and waited until her father had finished listening to the news on the wireless. As soon as he switched it off she stood beside him, her hands clasped before her. She explained that Yiorgo had paid for their papers and they had cost more than he had expected. The price of their passage was to be ten thousand drachmas and they did not have enough to pay. 'Please, Pappa, will you help us? Will you lend us the money?'

'No,' was Alesandros's immediate reply.

Sofia pushed Maria out of the way and stood over her husband. 'Open up your drawer, Alesandros, and take out the money you have hidden in there. Let Yiorgo count it and see if there is enough.'

'No,' replied Alesandros again.

'Would you want me to tell the village what I know?'

Alesandros quailed beneath his wife's threat, walked over to the wash stand and pulled out the drawer. He tipped the contents onto the table and proceeded to pull out bundles of notes from the cavity beneath.

'Count it, Yiorgo,' commanded Sofia and Yiorgo sat at the table counting each bundle and making a note of the amount.

'There is still not enough,' he said finally.

Maria looked at Yiorgo in despair. 'Is there no other way?'

'What about the bank?' suggested Yiorgo. 'If you were to ask for a loan and guarantee it against the house I'm sure they would agree.'

Sofia waited for her husband's reaction and it was as she had expected. 'You have tried to rob me of my savings and now you want to rob me of my house.'

'You have no right to this house, Alesandros. My father intended it for me and you continually allowed him to run up a debt to you that became impossible for him to pay. You finally claimed his house along with me as a final payment. Either you go to the bank with Yiorgo tomorrow or I will go to confession.'

Sofia stood with her hands on her hips waiting for Alesandros's answer. 'You wouldn't,' he whispered.

'I should have gone long ago. You go to the bank with Yiorgo tomorrow or I will be on my knees before Father Constantinus.'

Maria looked at her mother. Sofia had obviously spoken truly when she said she knew how to get her own way with her husband.

Sofia waited in trepidation for Maria to return from Spinalonga. What would happen if Fotini and Aristo refused permission for Vivi to be taken to America? The villagers would think it very strange if, having adopted a child, they then left without her.

Maria returned from Aghios Nikolaos with Yiorgo looking exhausted. 'It wasn't easy, Mamma. I explained our plans to Fo and Aristo and I've promised to write to them regularly and send photos of Vivi. The doctor has agreed to collect letters for her from the post office and ask Manolis to deliver them. I left the photos I have taken of Vivi with them.'

'You'll send some photos to me, I hope,' said Sofia.

'Of course. I also asked Aristo to take a photo of Fo and I together. I'll leave one with you and take another with me.'

'Do you know when you are leaving yet?'

Maria shook her head. 'It will depend upon the bank.'

Yiorgo returned disappointed from his visit to the bank with Alesandros. 'The bank is willing to lend five thousand drachmas against the house, but that still does not give us enough money to pay our passage.'

'I'll speak to Pappa again,' promised Maria, but her request when she mentioned more money to her father was met with a scowl.

'You've taken all I have.'

Sofia took the box containing her necklaces from under the bed. 'You can sell my necklaces. They are more use to you than sitting under the bed for most of the time.'

'You cannot sell your chains,' Alesandros almost shouted at his wife.

Sofia raised her eyebrows. 'I can sell them if I wish. You gave them to me so they are mine. Take them, Yiorgo, and see how much you are able to get for them.'

Yiorgo took the chains into Aghios Nikolaos with him the following day, but returned with the news that not all the chains were solid gold and he was offered so little for them that he did not sell them.

Maria did not tell her mother that many of her chains were a base metal with only a thin covering of gold. She said that even if Yiorgo had sold them they would still not have had enough money for them to pay their passage to America.

Alesandros smirked and Sofia looked at her despairing daughter. She went down on her hands and knees and scrabbled in the cupboard beneath the large bed, finally drawing out a metal box.

'Your grandmother's chains. You could sell those.'

'Grandma's chains!'

Sofia nodded. 'I was saving them to give to you and Fotini. It would be better to sell them and you and Yiorgo have the money.'

Maria frowned. 'If these were sold shouldn't some of the money belong to Fo?'

'Accept it as the cost of looking after Vivi. She is going to need new clothes as she grows and Fo won't be able to send you any money.'

1940

Maria spent most of her days washing and packing their clothes. She had no sooner filled the trunk when she decided there was something in it that they might need whilst on the ship and she removed the contents again. Finally Yiorgo shook his head.

'We cannot take everything. Fill the trunk with clothes that we are unlikely to need during the journey and make up two sacks that we can have in our cabin. Remember we will be wearing our winter cloaks and boots, so make sure the clothes we have to hand are our warm winter ones.'

'Can I take my embroidered sheets and my diaries?'

Yiorgo was adamant. 'You can embroider some more sheets and write some more diaries. We can only take essential items with us or we will be charged extra to place another trunk in the hold.'

Reluctantly Maria removed all the items from the trunk and started to pack again.

Under Sofia's stern stare Alesandros had agreed to drive them to Aghios Nikolaos in the cart. 'If you refuse then I am sure Yiorgo can manage to drive to Aghios Nikolaos and leave the cart there for you to collect.'

Grudgingly Alesandros had agreed and Maria had told Alexandros that he was going to have a treat. They were going or a drive in Grandpa's cart to a big town and he would be able to look at the sea. Then they were going on a ferry boat to a different town and after a few days they would sail on a big ship to a new country. Maria was not sure how much Alexandros understood, but he was excited about riding in the cart.

Vivi had been fractious all day and when Maria heard her father ride past the house she asked Sofia to care for the little girl whilst she walked with Alexandros up to the orchard.

Sofia was totally unprepared for Maria's return. She burst through the door, pulling Alexandros with her.

'Mamma, have you seen Pappa's head? It looks like Fo's arm, even worse. It was Pappa who made Fo sick.'

Alesandros entered and Maria turned on him immediately. 'You are a wicked man. How long have you known that you were an incurable?'

Alesandros sat down in his chair. 'There's nothing wrong with me except for my arthritis,' he stated and glared at Maria.

Maria was trembling with emotion. 'Having been to Spinalonga I have seen people suffering from leprosy. I know what their wounds and sores look like. No wonder you insist on wearing a hat all the time'

Alesandros shrugged. 'My hair has thinned and I feel the cold. I've not been anywhere to catch leprosy.'

'Yes you have; the couple who tended to your head. They have been sent to Spinalonga. You must have been infected by them.'

Alesandros seemed to shrink under Maria's malevolent gaze. 'I didn't know,' he said sadly and there were tears in his eyes as he spoke. 'I didn't realise my cut had not healed until my hair thinned and I could see the wound properly. It was not until after Fo went away that I looked at it properly and realised.'

'You should have told the doctor and gone to Spinalonga to join Fo,' replied Maria accusingly.

Alesandros seemed to have regained some of his spirit. 'If I had gone to the doctor and been sent to Spinalonga with Fo the villagers would have driven you and your mother away. It was for your sake that I said nothing.'

'Yiorgo would have looked after us.'

Alesandros shook his head. 'He would have been tested along with you and your mother. There is no way you would have been allowed to go to America.'

'We could have gone to Aghios Nikolaos. Yiorgo's work is there and Mamma could have sold her jewellery,' argued Maria.

'Very soon someone from Kastelli would have seen you. Before you knew it Yiorgo would have been asked to leave the shipping company and then what would you have lived on? You would have become beggars. No, it was better that I stayed here and said nothing.'

'And probably infected all of us!'

Sofia rose and placed her arm around Maria. 'I'm sure he has not.'

'Did you know?'

Sofia sighed. 'I realised a number of years ago. At first I was very frightened, but I have no signs and I have shared a bed with your father for many years.'

Maria turned back to her father again. 'Now I know why you did not want me to visit Fo. You knew I would see how the other sufferers were afflicted. I would realise that your shuffling gait was not arthritis. How will you excuse your condition when your toes begin to drop off and your fingers clawed?' Maria burst into tears and retreated into the scullery.

'When did you realise my head was infected?' asked Alesandros of Sofia.

'Your nightcap had slipped off one morning and I saw it then. I kept asking you to let me look at it. Now I know why you always refused.'

Alesandros dropped his eyes. 'I knew my head was unsightly, but it wasn't until I saw Fo's arm that I realised my head looked much the same. I didn't infect her deliberately. Why do you think I never approached you again?'

'I thought that was due to your age. I know you didn't mean

to infect Fo, but families should not have secrets. I wish you had been honest and shown me.'

'And you would have asked Doctor Andrianakis to examine me and send me to Spinalonga,' Alesandros's lip curled in disgust.

'As you had Fo sent,' replied Sofia bitterly.

Alesandros looked at his wife. 'So what are you planning to do now? Tell the doctor?'

Sofia shook her head. 'I am not vindictive. I could have gone to America with Maria and the children but I knew I could not leave you here alone. If the disease progresses you could be crippled. You will need someone to look after you then.'

Alesandros reached out and took Sofia's hand. 'I love you, Sofia.'

Sofia felt her eyes fill with tears. She wished she could return the sentiment.

Sofia watched as the cart rounded the corner and disappeared from her view. Her shoulders drooped and she went back inside the house and sat down at the table, her head in her hands and her tears falling freely. Now she had lost both her daughters. Maria had promised to write to tell them about their journey and their new life in America, but it would not be the same as speaking to her and hearing the children laugh.

She knew Alesandros would never take her to visit Fotini on Spinalonga and not for the first time she wondered if she had done the right thing by keeping silent over the years. To have disclosed her knowledge would not have stopped Fo from contracting leprosy, but she would have been able to accompany Maria and Yiorgo to America with a clear conscience.

The door to the house opened and Sofia looked up, having a moment of false hope that they had changed their minds and were returning. Tryphaine stood there, looking at Sofia with concern.

'Sofia, what has happened? I saw everyone except you leaving the village on the cart.' She placed her arm across Sofia's shoulders and felt the woman's shuddering sobs.

'They have gone,' she managed to say finally.

'Gone? Gone where?'

'To America,' she whispered.

'America?' Tryphaine could not believe her ears. 'Do you mean the America across the sea?'

Sofia raised her head and nodded. 'They have gone there to have a new life. Yiorgo thinks the war in Europe could spread here and we would not be safe.'

Tryphaine was not sure she believed her friend. 'Why didn't you go with them?'

'It cost thousands of drachmas.' Sofia shook her head. 'It was not possible for all of us to go.'

'But Alesandros? He has gone.'

'He is only driving them to Aghios Nikolaos. We are too old to go travelling.'

'Alesandros may be, but you are not too old.'

'I could not leave Alesandros here alone.' Sofia lifted her apron and wiped her eyes. 'I can't sit here all day. There is work to be done.' She shrugged off Tryphaine's arm and rose to her feet. 'Will you stay for coffee, Phaini?'

Tryphaine shook her head. She wanted to be the first to spread the news throughout the village.

Alesandros arrived back from Aghios Nikolaos later than Sofia had expected him. 'Was there a problem?' she asked.

Alesandros shook his head. 'I called in to the tax office whilst I was there. I am no longer a tax collector.'

'Why not? Have you done something wrong?'

Alesandros gave his wife a scathing look. He had been gradually working towards this day over the previous couple of years. He had told the farmers that the tax regulations had been changed and he could no longer pay tax on their account. They would have to settle up the amount they owed to him immediately and when their tax was due they would be responsible for paying it in full.

The farmers had complained, but Alesandros had stood firm. He did not want apple, orange or olive trees; he wanted his money. Grudgingly, one by one, they had paid their debt to him, some even being willing to purchase back the trees they had sold to him over the years. At last Alesandros felt confident that he could leave the tax office and the accounts would be in perfect order.

'I have resigned my position. I am becoming too old to be out in all weathers riding a donkey.'

'I'm pleased you have realised that, but how are we going to manage? You gave all your savings to Yiorgo and have to repay the bank from the rents.'

Alesandros shrugged. 'Don't blame me that we are now paupers. No doubt we'll manage somehow.'

Sofia had never considered that the day would come when Alesandros did not ride off on his donkey each morning and return in the late afternoon. She was not at all sure that she wanted him in the house all the time under her feet.

'Did you see Maria and Yiorgo safely onto the ferry?'

'They told me not to wait around. It could be some hours whilst their papers were checked and everything declared in order for them to sail.' Alesandros did not admit that having deposited them on the quayside he had not offered to wait with them. He had been surprised when Maria had finally thrown her arms around his neck and kissed him, but he did not want to watch them sail out of his life forever. He knew it would be many years before they could afford the sea passage to return to Crete and most unlikely that he would be around to greet them.

Sofia, despite not understanding money, realised that she would not be able to buy with impunity whatever she wanted from the shops and replenish her stock of weaving wool whenever she pleased. There was no reason why they should not grow their own vegetables; there was plenty of space in the yard. It would just be a case of taking up the flagstones and digging the hard earth that lay beneath.

To Alesandros's annoyance she had purchased a fork and spade, assuring him that the money was well spent. Once she had dug the ground over she would plant vegetables and they would be saving money.

'I also plan to keep some chickens,' she informed him. 'We can use the eggs and when they stop laying eggs we will eat the bird.'

'They'll eat your vegetables.'

Sofia shook her head. 'I'll place wire fencing around the vegetable plots to keep them off. I just need a small amount of money to get started.'

Alesandros still left her money for food on the dresser each week and by careful planning Sofia managed to save a little. They did not need very much milk now there were no longer any children in the house, and only one loaf of bread each day. Rather than making kebabs she would purchase a small piece of meat and add it to rice or pasta along with herbs and a tomato sauce. Dolmades became a regular item on the menu as she could gather the leaves when they were in season as she walked along the lane and stuff them with rice and marjoram.

Alesandros had immediately told Dimitra that her services at the house were no longer needed. She had complained bitterly to Sofia; her daughter was getting married in the spring.

'How are we to provide for them as we should if I am no longer earning any money?'

Sofia shook her head sadly. 'I'm sorry. We did not realise how much it would cost for Maria and Yiorgo to go to America. My husband gave them all his savings and also took out a loan from the bank. He no longer works as a tax collector due to his age so our only income is the rent from the cottages. We can no longer afford to pay for help in the house.'

Dimitra sniffed. It was about time they found out what it was like to live as a villager with no guarantee of putting food on your table the following day.

Sofia waited anxiously for a letter from Maria to tell her they had arrived safely in America. Finally a farmer from Kastelli was seen in the market and asked to deliver two letters to Alesandros Danniakis as they had been sitting in the post office for some weeks.

Alesandros looked at the date stamped on the envelope and opened the first one whilst Sofia waited in excited anticipation. Alesandros read it through to himself and then read it aloud to Sofia. It contained a long description of their journey from Crete to Piraeus and on to America, how different it was living in America after spending all her life in a small village.

For the first time in her life Sofia regretted that she was unable to read or write. She had to depend upon Alesandros to read the letters to her and she would have to ask him to write back to Maria when she sent them her address. She hoped she would be able to remember everything she wanted to tell her.

Sofia would stand over Alesandros as he replied to Maria's first letters and assured his wife that he had written down everything she had told him. Every sentence began with "Your mother says"

'When will you send it?' she asked.

'I'll ask one of the farmers to take it to Doctor Andrianakis with a message attached asking him to post it. I can pay for the stamp when the doctor visits the village next.'

'Why don't you ask if he would be willing to collect any letters that arrive in Neapoli from Maria?' suggested Sofia. 'He could bring them to Kastelli on his monthly visits and I'm sure he would be more reliable than one of the farmers.'

Letters from Maria continued to arrive at regular intervals, telling them more about America and the way of life over there. Each one contained photographs of the children showing how they had grown and were flourishing. She also voiced her concern over the fighting she had heard was taking place in Greece and was praying that the turmoil would not spread to Crete and her parents would be safe.

Alesandros sold both the donkeys and the cart. He had no further use for them and the money he received enabled him to pay off the loan to the bank for the next four months. To his consternation he found they were charging him interest for each day the loan was outstanding and the donkey and cart money had made very little difference to the overall amount that he owed. Now he knew how the farmers had felt when he had informed them that despite the payments they had made there was still a large sum outstanding.

Sofia found it impossible to lift the large flag stones and finally asked Timotheos for his help. Digging the hard earth was an arduous task and she seemed to make very little impression despite the time she spent out there. She wished she could have asked Timotheos to prepare the vegetable beds for her as she would have been able to previously.

Sofia realised that she was totally ignorant about farming but she was wise enough to ask advice from the local farmers. They told her which vegetables it would be practical for her to grow to provide her with a basic stock of food and some were kind enough to give her a plant or seeds and she nurtured them carefully.

When was able to pick the first of her produce she felt very proud. No longer did she have to go to the shops or a farmer to ask for vegetables. She was able to provide onions, tomatoes and cucumber to accompany every meal and most weeks her chickens gave her an egg each day. She was able to use the eggs for omelettes on two days each week and Alesandros did not complain about the lack of variety in his evening meal.

Alesandros spent his days doing very little. He would listen to the wireless and then insist the news was complete rubbish. Of course the Germans were not in Greece, and they were certainly not in Africa, that was a continent in itself and could not be called Europe.

He left the house only to collect the rents and go to church on

Sunday. Before they left he would often consult his little book of accounts and on seeing a villager he would accost him and insist that he owed his taxes. At first the farmer would argue and often become quite angry; Sofia had got into the habit of remonstrating gently with him and saying he had mistaken the farmer for someone else, slipping her arm in his and drawing him away.

The following day she would seek out the farmer and apologise on behalf of her husband. 'I'm afraid Alesandros is becoming a little confused due to his age. Please excuse him. If he approaches you again, just say you will settle the debt tomorrow. By then he will have forgotten.'

The villagers smirked behind their hands and speculated about Alesandros's senility.

'Forget his own name next.'

'Provided he doesn't forget where he lives and comes to my house by mistake.'

'Don't know how Mrs Sofia puts up with him.'

'She has no one else now both her daughters have gone.'

'I'd still like to know exactly what happened to that younger one.'

'I reckon she had a big falling out with them and ran away.'

'That's what they told Dimitra first, then they said she needed a – you know what – because she was pregnant.'

'If they insisted on that then it isn't any wonder that she never came back home.'

'She would have been the talk of the village.'

'Until they found something else to talk about.'

Father Constantinus would disperse the gossiping group of men, telling them they were no better than a lot of old women with nothing better to do with their time. 'Charity begins at home. Be charitable towards them. They have suffered due to the loss of both their daughters.'

1941

Alesandros could no longer claim that the news he heard on the wireless was a load of rubbish. German paratroopers had landed at Maleme and in the ensuing fighting had finally taken Heraklion and their troops were spreading throughout Crete. Italians had landed on the southern side of the island and were marching up to join forces with their compatriots.

Many of the younger men from the village had left the area, saying they were going to join the resistance who were fighting the invading forces.

Tryphaine was distraught. 'How can I stop Timotheos from leaving the village? He's safe here. He's not in the army. He doesn't have to go away and fight.'

Sofia regarded her friend sympathetically. 'You cannot stop him. He is a man, not a boy. If his wife could not persuade him to stay here with her then I don't see how you can. He may not be involved in any fighting.'

'It's alright for you,' Tryphaine muttered belligerently. 'Your daughter and family are safe in America.'

'I'm very thankful they are, but life is not easy for them over there. Yiorgo is packing flooring materials.'

Tryphaine sniffed. Packing flooring materials was certainly safer than joining a resistance group. 'I'm going to ask Father Constantinus to forbid him to leave the village.'

Sofia did not comment. She thought it very unlikely that Father

315

Constantinus would have any influence over the young man if neither his wife nor mother had been able to dissuade him from joining a resistance group.

Sofia noticed that many of the young men from the village had disappeared, slipping away quietly at night or marching proudly out of the village announcing their intention of helping to liberate Crete. Wives and mothers wept as they left, but consoled themselves with the assurances the men had given them that they would not be away for long. The villagers who remained behind toiled for even longer hours on their small plots of land trying to produce the same amount of food as they had before their sons had left.

Mikhaelis stayed behind. He said his first duty was to his wife and their children. There was no way Eva could farm their plot of land and look after their seven children, the youngest only a few months old. Many of the older villagers looked at him scathingly, branding him a coward, their son had gone away to fight and he should have joined them.

Father Constantinus led his depleted congregation in prayers each Sunday pleading for the defeat of the Germans and a speedy return of their sons to their families. He would accompany Sofia and Alesandros back to their house after the service and listen to the latest news on their wireless, shaking his head in both despair and disbelief as the army's progress was reported. Later he would hold another church service and would relay the latest news he had to the anxious villagers.

Despite being told by Father Constantinus that they should expect to see German troops to march through their village the arrival of Italian soldiers came as a shock. They went from house to house, rousing the occupants at dawn and insisting they gathered in the courtyard before the church. Armed men guarded them and the villagers looked at each other fearfully; were they going to be shot?

Finally Father Constantinus confirmed to their commander

that everyone was present. The commander stepped forward and in halting Greek announced that the village was now under the control of the Italian army. The people should go about their business as usual, but if anything was demanded of them they should comply immediately. The farmers would be expected to provide sufficient food for the detachment of soldiers who would be stationed in Kastelli and this would be collected from them each morning. No one was to leave the village without written authority from him.

The villagers listened in stony silence until one had the temerity to speak. 'What about taking our produce to Neapoli for the market each week? Will we need written authority from you to do that?'

'It is unlikely that you will have any surplus produce to take to a market anywhere. My men will be hungry and expect to be well fed whilst they are here.'

The villagers muttered between themselves and cast sideways glances at Alesandros. If they were unable to take their produce to Neapoli to sell how would they pay their rent?

Alesandros walked forward, leaning heavily on his stick. He looked directly at the commander, then raised his stick and shook it in his face.

'You owe me the tax for the olive crop. For too long you have made excuses and not paid me. I demand that you pay up immediately.'

At first the commander looked puzzled; then Sofia took hold of Alesandros's arm. She tapped her head. 'He is confused,' she explained. 'May I take him home?'

The commander nodded. 'You are all free to return about your business, but remember, we will be watching you. If any one of you causes trouble my men have orders to shoot.' His glance rested on each one of them.

Silently the villagers backed away and returned to their homes. With that many soldiers living in the village the population was doubled immediately. They would certainly not have any surplus produce to take to market.

The soldiers cut down the trees in the orchard, ignoring Tomas's beehives, and erected their tents as temporary shelters. They set about digging foundations and began to erect a stone building to house them permanently whilst the villagers watched in consternation; their unwelcome visitors were obviously planning to stay for a considerable amount of time.

Alesandros walked up to the orchard and raged at them for cutting down the trees. He would stand shouting and waving his fists until a villager hurriedly called Sofia and she would persuade him to return to the house. The Italians ignored him. As far as they were concerned he was the village simpleton.

Each Sunday some of the Italian soldiers would attend the morning church service. They would leave their rifles at the door in the keeping of a subordinate, entering with bowed heads and crossing themselves fervently. Sofia had no idea if they understood any of the words spoken by Father Constantinus, but they muttered prayers in their own unintelligible language.

Sofia watched Alesandros carefully during the morning service, despite being with the women on the other side of the church. To her shame, on two occasions Father Constantinus had been forced to ask her if she would accompany her husband outside as he was so disturbed; continually interrupting the service by shouting at the soldiers. Since then she had insisted they sat at the back so she would be able to leave with minimum disruption.

This week Alesandros appeared calm as he sat and listened to the priest until he suddenly rose and made his way to the door. Sofia crossed herself and followed him where she found him waiting quietly outside the church for her. She slipped her hand through his arm as she had always done over the years and began to walk slowly back to their house. She did not mention that they had left before the Blessing. She was sure Father Constantinus would understand.

Sofia went out into the yard. She hoped she would manage to find a few potatoes or an onion to add to their meal. She had boiled up the remains of half of the scrawny chicken that she had purchased at the beginning of the week and used to make a meal each evening. Had there been any flour available she would have made the final scraps into a pie, but she planned to add potatoes and a small amount of rice to thicken the liquor and hoped it would be acceptable.

She returned to the living room expecting to see Alesandros sitting in his chair, but there was no sign of him. Puzzled she returned to the yard and knocked on the outhouse door. Had he managed to walk over there without her noticing? Not receiving a reply she pulled open the door to find the outhouse empty.

Sofia looked again in the living room and called his name loudly, then she realised the front door was slightly ajar. He must have gone out. Maybe he thought she was still at the church and had gone up there looking for her. Hurriedly she removed her apron, tucked her hair beneath her scarf and wiped her hands down her skirt. He would be worried when he could not find her.

As Sofia reached the church she could see Alesandros waiting by the side of the door and sighed with relief. He had obviously forgotten that they had left together earlier. The villagers were milling around outside the church and Sofia waited. The Italians would leave last, collecting their weapons on the way, with their commander bringing up the rear. She would wait until they were out of the way before she approached her husband.

Alesandros stepped forward and levelled the old shotgun he was carrying at the commander.

'You owe me my taxes. I demand that you pay me.'

Without a second thought the Italian raised his own gun and shot Alesandros in the chest. Alesandros's eyes bulged and his hand went up to the wound that was already staining his shirt with his blood before he collapsed, his hat falling off as his body hit the ground.

At the sound of the gun shot the villagers stopped, many of them raising their hands in the air. They gasped in horror as they saw Alesandros lying on the ground, but not just because he had been shot; without his hat the condition of his head was visible to all. Slowly they backed away and the Italians marched back down to their encampment, leaving Sofia kneeling alone beside her dead husband. Now they knew what had happened to the younger daughter. The story about her running away was all lies. She had been sent to Spinalonga as an incurable, no doubt she had caught the disease from her father.

Father Constantinus hurried to Sofia's side. 'What happened?'

Sofia shook her head. 'He threatened the commander with my Pappa's old shotgun. It wasn't even loaded. I was too late to stop him.'

'You mustn't blame yourself. I'm sure commander didn't realise there was no ammunition in the gun and he thought he was defending himself.'

Father Constantinus bent to place a cross of Alesandros's forehead and paled visibly as he saw Alesandros's head.

'Did you know, Sofia?'

'Yes, Father.'

'How long has he been afflicted?'

'Many years now. I should have come to confession long ago.'

'Why didn't he consult a doctor when he first noticed the symptoms?'

'For a long time he did not realise there was anything seriously wrong; then he was frightened he would be sent away and we would suffer once the villagers knew.'

'Well they know now! I doubt anyone will be willing to carry him back to your house.'

Sofia straightened up. 'If I fetch a blanket would you help me to carry him home?'

Father Constantinus considered. 'I think, under the circumstances, it could be better if his funeral took place as soon as possible. I do not think the villagers will refuse to dig a grave.'

Sofia sat back down on the paving stones next to Alesandros and placed his hat back on his head. She felt empty and at a loss, but no tears came.

The men, at Father Constantinus request, changed back into their working clothes and made their way to the graveyard with their forks and spades. They had not planned to spend their afternoon digging a grave, particularly for a man who was so disliked.

Father Constantinus left the men at their work and walked down to the Italian camp, asking to speak to the commander. When he finally appeared he drew himself up and regarded the priest sternly.

'If you have come to complain that I shot a villager it was in self defence. He threatened me with his shotgun. I had no choice.'

'The shotgun was not loaded.'

'I was not to know that; besides, it is against the law to own a gun.'

'It belonged to his father-in-law and has not been used for many years. I came to ask if some of your men could move him to the burial ground'

'Why can't the villagers move him?'

'They are busy digging his grave. As soon as it is completed he needs to be interred and I will hold the service at the graveside.'

'What is so urgent about his burial?'

'The sooner it is over with the more quickly the villagers will forget the unfortunate incident. If they see your men are willing to aid them in carrying his body they will accept that as an apology for your action. So far the villagers have obeyed you, but this could cause them to feel threatened and could encourage them to become trouble makers.' Father Constantinus hoped fervently that the commander would agree. He was sure no one from the village would agree to touch Alesandros's body and Sofia was certainly not strong enough to move the man on her own.

The commander considered the priest's words. They contained no direct threat of rebellion or violence towards any of his men, but he certainly did not want a pitched battle to take place in the village. For all he knew all the men had shotguns hidden away and if they decided to produce them they were sure to be loaded. The cottages would have to be searched.

'Very well. I will send four men in two hours. They will place the body in the grave then even if it is unfinished. My men have other work to do.' The commander turned away whilst Father Constantinus stuttered his thanks.

Sofia stood by the hurriedly dug grave. She had returned home long enough to wash her hands and face and don a black blouse, now she and Father Constantinus waited for the soldiers to bring Alesandros's body to the graveyard. Before they arrived Father Constantinus had completed the prayers for the deceased and none of the villagers had arrived to support Sofia.

Alesandros's body was unceremoniously tipped into the hole and Sofia stifled a cry as his hat fell off again. It was an ignominious end for a man who had always been so proud. Father Constantinus muttered the closing prayer, patted Sofia on the shoulder and began to walk away.

Sofia hurried after him. 'Will the men come back to fill the grave in now?' she asked.

Father Constantinus shook his head. 'They will not come here until he is fully covered up. I suggest you make a start.'

Sofia looked after the priest in disbelief. She was supposed to fill in the grave herself? She had no tools with her and although the grave was not as deeply dug as usual it would take her some time to replace the earth. With a sigh she walked back to her house and collected her spade from the garden.

Once she had covered Alesandros completely, having left his face to the last, she did not find it so difficult to continue. Now she could no longer see him she could forget that it was a grave and consider it as just a hole. Once there was no more than a small mound of earth to show where her husband was buried she knelt down.

'I'm sorry, Alesandros. Whatever your faults you should have had a more dignified burial. At least Father Constantinus said prayers for you. If I had reached the church just a few moments earlier you would still be alive now.'

With her head bowed Sofia left the graveyard and returned home. It was finally her house, but she felt no joy in the knowledge.

It was three days before Theophalia knocked at her door. She stood hesitantly on the doorstep.

'Father Constantinus has asked me to call and examine you.'

'Examine me? What for?'

'Any marks or blemishes that could be developing.'

Sofia shook her head. 'I have nothing, I can assure you.'

'I promised Father Constantinus that I would see for myself. Could we go out to the yard? There is less chance of infection in the open air.' As Theophalia followed Sofia through the house she held her skirt tightly to her with one hand and placed the other over her nose and mouth, trying not to breathe.

Once outside she insisted Sofia stripped until she stood naked before her. Embarrassed, but compliant, Sofia stood there, raised her arms, opened her legs and turned with her back to Theophalia as she was directed. Eventually Theophalia had to confess that she could see nothing on Sofia's body that looked suspicious and she allowed her to dress.

'Take off your scarf and let me see your head. You will have to part your hair for me so I can see your scalp.'

Obediently Sofia removed her scarf and bent so Theophalia could see there were no sores amongst her thick hair. Finally Theophalia ordered her to open her mouth and she peered inside.

'I can see nothing, Sofia. That does not mean you are not infected. When the doctor comes to the village next he will have to take some blood from you and have it tested. Until he has the result you are not to go inside anyone's house or go to church.'

'Not go to church?' gasped Sofia. 'I have to go to church.'

Theophalia shook her head. 'Father Constantinus will refuse to admit you. It will only be for a short while. You look clean, but until the doctor has the result from inside you I cannot be sure.'

'If Alesandros's hat had not fallen off no one would have known,' said Sofia bitterly.

'We just have to hope that he has not infected you or anyone else in the village.'

The villagers retreated inside their cottages, calling their children to them, as Sofia walked down the road. Even Tryphaine crossed to the other side of the path before she raised her hand and waved at Sofia. The shopkeepers hurried outside as she approached and asked what goods she wanted, depositing them on the step for her, but accepting her money willingly. When she called for the rents the cottagers passed the money to her through a crack in the door and closed it again as quickly as possible.

Sofia felt sad and lonely and hoped that when Doctor Andrianakis did visit and take a blood sample from her it would prove that she also had leprosy and she would be sent to Spinalonga. At least she would have the company of Fotini once she was there. She sorted out Alesandros's clothes. No one in the village would want them and she sat and diligently unpicked the stitching on his shirts. She could make petticoats and drawers for herself with the material. His black shirt she could make into a blouse for herself, but his trousers were useless to her and she cut them up to make rags to clean the floor.

When an entirely unknown doctor knocked at her door Sofia cringed away in fright. Was she being condemned as an incurable without a single test taken?

Doctor Fokianakis removed his hat and smiled at her. 'There is no need to be alarmed. I am the new doctor who will be visiting the village. Doctor Andrianakis has decided he has become too old to make the journey to the outlying villages. He will only treat the sick people in Neapoli.'

Sofia nodded. Doctor Fokianakis looked her up and down. 'Are you feeling well?'

'Perfectly well, thank you.'

'Do you understand why I am here?'

Sofia sighed and opened the door to admit the doctor. 'Theophalia told me she would ask Doctor Andrianakis to call. She has examined my body and found no marks on me.'

Doctor Fokianakis nodded. 'So she told me. That is a very good sign, but, of course, you realise that sometimes you can be carrying the germs with no outward symptoms.'

Sofia shook her head.

'We do not know how this disease develops. It may be through getting dirt into a wound or catching a gem from the air. I am sure some people live with the disease for many years and show no outward signs. Until we have the result from your blood we cannot be certain that you are not infected.'

'When will you know?'

'I cannot say for certain, but I do not want you to worry.' Doctor Fokianakis smiled at her kindly and patted her hand. 'I promise you if your results are positive then I will make a special journey down to Kastelli to tell you before I alert the authorities and they send a cart for you. That will give you time to pack your belongings and make any necessary arrangements.'

Each day Sofia awoke with a feeling of trepidation. Would the doctor pay her a visit today? Would he have forgotten his promise and the cart arrive instead? Should she start to pack her belongings? She collected up the photographs that stood amongst the plates on the dresser, looking at each one carefully.

There she was on her wedding day, all those years ago, and again, holding Maria. Her parents standing self-consciously outside the house; her mother wearing all her gold necklaces as it was Easter. There was Fotini as a baby, then more of both the girls, usually together, sometimes with her in the photograph also. Maria's wedding day, her hands demurely clasped in front of her to hide her pregnancy, then later the photos of little Alexandros and finally a few of Vivi, taken before they left for America. She had a moment of panic – where were the photos they had sent her from America? Then she remembered, she had left them inside the envelopes along with the letters and they were in the cupboard. They were certainly not safe there.

She opened the cupboard beneath the bed and removed the metal box that had held her gold jewellery and placed the letters inside. There was not enough space to add the photographs and she groped around in the cupboard until her fingers found the box where her mother's gold jewellery had been stored. She placed the photographs inside and turned the key on both boxes. Now she could put them in the cupboard and they would be safe. If the cart did come for her it would take her only a moment to pick them both up to take with her.

The days went by and the cart did not arrive, instead Doctor Fokianakis knocked on her door, his face wreathed in smiles.

'I have good news, Mrs Sofia. Your results have been returned to me and show that you are negative. You are completely healthy.'

'Oh!' Sofia felt both disappointed and relieved at the same time; disappointed that she would not be going to Spinalonga to live with Fotini, but relieved that she was not sick.

'As I pass through the village I will give your priest the good news. No doubt he will call on you.'

'Doctor,' Sofia hesitated, 'May I ask if you have been given any letters to deliver to me? My daughter and her family are in America and Doctor Andrianakis agreed to check at the post office and collect any letters from them.'

Doctor Fokianakis frowned. 'I had not been made aware of the arrangement. I will certainly call and if there is a letter for you I will bring it with me the next time I am this way. You understand that at the moment it is very unlikely. No post is being received from overseas. You will have to be patient Mrs Sofia.'

'Thank you, doctor. Thank you for bringing me the results of my tests.'

'The pleasure was mine. I always like to take good news to my patients.' He smiled at her again. 'I hope when I call on you next I will have a letter in my hand.'

It was over an hour later when Father Constantinus knocked on Sofia's door and stood smiling benignly at her.

'Mrs Sofia, I have good news for you. Doctor Fokianakis came through the village this morning on his way to Fourni. He stopped briefly to tell me that your results had come back and you have nothing to worry about. You are quite clear of the disease. You will be welcome to attend church on Sunday,' continued Father Constantinus, 'and I will tell the village that your results show that you are fit and healthy. They have nothing to fear from you.'

'Thank you, Father.' Sofia felt limp. All those weeks of being ostracised by the villagers and forbidden the comfort of the church for no good reason. She had told them she was clean, Theophalia had confirmed it, but Father Constantinus had needed proof. She could not help but compare his attitude to that of the priest Fotini had written about who lived on Spinalonga amongst the lepers, despite not being a sufferer himself.

The villagers eyed Sofia warily when she walked into church and down to the front of the church where the women of her family had always sat. There was no need now for her to sit at the back to escort Alesandros out if he became an embarrassment. She held her head high. Her father had been the head man of the village, a position taken over by Alesandros after Theo had died, but now she was in charge of the village as her father had always intended.

Tryphaine was the first to visit her and she stood on the

doorstep, wondering at the reception she would receive from her old friend. Sofia invited her in and Tryphaine sat at the living room table nervously. Could furniture carry germs and give you the sickness?

'I would have liked to visit you before, but Father Constantinus said no one was to come near you until your test results had confirmed you were not infected.'

'I understand,' Sofia replied wearily. 'You had your own family to consider.'

Tryphaine twisted her fingers together. 'Of course, Alesandros may have had some other skin affliction. That would explain why you are not ill.'

Sofia nodded. She was convinced that Alesandros was suffering from leprosy, but if Tryphaine wished to think otherwise she would not disillusion her.

'I wanted to tell you how awful I felt when I saw that commander shoot him. It was so unnecessary. He knew Alesandros was confused. He should have spoken to him.'

'The commander was not to know that my Pappa's old shotgun was not loaded. It had not been touched for years and would have been more likely to explode in Alesandros's hands than fire a shot. I cannot blame the commander.'

'How long do you think those Italians will stay in the village?' asked Tryphaine.

Sofia shrugged. 'How should I know?'

'The farmers are complaining. They are taking so much of their produce and not paying them anything.'

'Has Father Constantinus spoken to them?'

Tryphaine shook her head. 'He says we are in the hands of God.'

Sofia snorted in derision. She had been taught to believe in a merciful God, not one who turned his back on people when they were suffering.

'Have you heard from your Maria?'

Sofia shook her head sadly. 'Doctor Fokianakis said we were not receiving post from other countries at the moment. I shall just have to be patient.'

'Does that mean you are unable to send her the news about her father?'

'If post is not coming to Crete from America it is not likely to be going anywhere from Crete,' replied Sofia quickly. She was certainly not going to admit to Tryphaine that she would be unable to write a letter back to her daughter now Alesandros was dead. 'Have you heard anything from Timotheos?' asked Sofia diverting the conversation away from herself.

To her consternation Tryphaine's eyes filled with tears and she shook her head. 'Not a thing.'

Sofia patted her friend's hand. 'I'm sure he'll send you a message if anyone is coming this way.'

'He's more likely to send one to his wife.'

'If he does I'm sure she will tell you.'

'What will I do if he doesn't come back?' Tryphaine's tears were falling now.

'Of course he will come back,' Sofia tried to reassure her. 'There's no reason why he shouldn't return to the village as soon as the Italians have gone.'

Most of the Italians did leave Kastelli, but a battalion of German soldiers arrived, their lorries and trucks churning up the earth road and leaving deep ruts. The soldiers moved into the barracks that had been erected by the Italians. A small number of Italians who served as a medical team evicted the occupants of a large single storey house and turned it into a makeshift hospital. The villagers eyed the German soldiers warily. Despite their complaints about the Italians demanding to be fed they had not been ill treated.

The German contingent was very different. They searched each house for any hidden armaments, a soldier holding the occupant at gunpoint whilst two others made a thorough search, throwing belongings to the ground regardless. Sofia cowered before them. The Italian commander had confiscated her father's shotgun after the unfortunate incident with Alesandros and she knew the Germans would not find anything more threatening than the axe for chopping firewood or a kitchen knife.

Sofia heard them moving between the two rooms upstairs. There was very little in them. The rugs hung on the walls, the mattresses lay where they had been left and the trunk only contained items of no value that Maria had left behind.

Disappointed they returned to the living room, opening the dresser doors and rummaging amongst the miscellaneous items stored in there, breaking one of the wine glasses Yiorgo had given to Alesandros. They turned their attention to her cupboards and lifted down the two metal boxes from the top shelf, being disgusted when they discovered they only contained photographs and letters.

Sofia kept her eyes downcast. She hoped the Germans would not open the drawer of the wash stand. She had placed the rent money she had collected from the villagers in there. She wondered if she could ask Doctor Fokianakis if he could take it to the bank for her or if someone from the bank would call and ask her for the money to pay off the loan that Alesandros had taken out. Her fears were realised when a soldier opened the drawer and saw the small bundles lying there. He pulled them out and gave some to each of his companions before stuffing the remainder into his pockets. Sofia would have liked to protest, but dared not open her mouth.

Finally one went through to the scullery and the other out to the yard. She heard her chickens squawking in fear and to her horror when the soldier returned he held three dead chickens in his hand and had a broad grin on his face. They had taken her money and also her food. How was she supposed to survive?

1942 – 1945

Sofia was no longer able to listen to the wireless for the latest news. Not a sound would come out of it. She did not realise there was a battery inside that needed to be recharged. She was now as dependent as the other villagers on news filtering through to them, brought by a shepherd or passing pedlar.

She joined the other women and the old men who remained in the village in their hunt for food. There was very little to be found in the shops and none of them had any money with which to buy the goods. The Germans took most of the fruit and vegetables the farmers were able to produce, they had taken any livestock they found and slaughtered them, there was not even a rabbit to be snared.

When Sofia called for her rent the occupant of the cottage shook their head. They had no money for anything. When the olives were harvested a group of German soldiers stood over them, ensuring they were unable to sneak a basket or sack back to their own house for consumption. Despite their watchful eyes the men and women would manage to drop a few into their pockets and eat them thankfully that evening.

Weeds that grew freely were collected and either eaten raw or boiled to accompany the snails that had been gathered at dusk the previous evening. Sofia, along with the other villagers, lost weight and had little energy. The children would look at their parents with large, hungry eyes, not understanding why their stomachs ached from hunger due to the meagre meal they had been given.

Olga died, followed by Theophalia and more of the oldest residents. Father Constantinus was being continually called upon to exercise the last rights and hear a confession. When his dwindling congregation gathered inside the church each Sunday he would study them and wonder which household would be requiring his services next. There were no weddings or christenings, only funerals.

During the winter months the villagers suffered even more. Inside their houses they huddled beneath blankets and wore copious layers of clothes just to try to keep warm. Each day they would go out, not only searching for anything edible, but also any wood or twigs they would be able to use as kindling

The soldiers appeared oblivious to the villagers' suffering. They were well fed, able to visit Aghios Nikolaos in one of their noisy, smelly lorries each week and return with sacks of rice, flour, lentils and pasta that had been imported. As they became more desperate the village women would wait until a lorry had been unloaded and then throw themselves on their knees begging to be allowed a sack of flour or rice to share between them. They began to know which soldier would ignore them, which one would threaten to shoot them if they did not disperse and which one would push a sack in their direction.

Sofia was truly sorry for her friend Tryphaine when Nikos died. He had been hit by one of the lorries as he crossed the road and lay in a tangled mass on the hard dirt pathway. The villagers gathered around and covered him with their jackets whilst Mikhaelis hurried to the house which had been converted into a makeshift hospital.

Despite not understanding the words Mikhaelis was saying the doctor realised that his presence was required urgently and followed him back to where Tryphaine was weeping noisily. The doctor waved the spectators back and felt for Nikos's pulse – there was nothing. He shook his head, the man had obviously died instantly.

After Nikos's death no one wandered across the road automatically as they had in the past. They would stand on the grass at the side, listening for any sound of a motor vehicle and look fearfully from left to right before they dared to step forward, scared that the same fate would overtake them.

The unhappy days merged into each other. The villagers attended the church each Sunday and prayed fervently for deliverance form their oppressors. On Saint's days, Easter and Christmas they prayed that when the next one arrived they would be free again and their sons and husbands returned. It was three and a half long years before their prayers were answered.

One by one the men returned, many with harrowing tales to tell if the experiences could be dragged out of them. Each day the women waited, some of them to be disappointed when their husband, brother or son did not arrive. They tried to cheer each other.

'He may have a long way to travel.'

'He could be waiting to travel with companions.'

'He may have married and be bringing a wife back with him. That would slow his progress.'

No one voiced the thought uppermost in their mind; he could be dead.

After some months without a sign of their men folk the women had to accept that they were the unlucky ones who would have to spend the remainder of their life without a loved one. Sometimes one who had returned was able to say when he had last seen or spoken to the man, but they had been spread out across the Lassithi Plain in small groups, often coming from many different towns and villages. Some of the men returned, searching in vain for their parents, only to find they were beneath the ground.

Tryphaine waited in an agony of suspense. Every day she spent the morning in the church on her knees praying desperately that Timotheos had been spared and would return to her. She was furious when she found he had returned during the morning and first gone to be reunited with his wife before searching her out.

'You should have come to me first,' she declared. 'I am your mother.'

Timotheos shook his head. 'I wanted to see my wife. I'm not a little boy, remember. I'm a married man.'

'You will have to think about me as well as your wife now your father is no longer with us.'

'Of course I will look after you. I was very sad to hear about Pappa. You will have to show me his grave and I will say a prayer for him. I had hoped that now I was home I would be able to make him a grandfather within the year. He would have enjoyed having a grandson to play with.'

'You don't know if you would have a son,' sniffed Tryphaine. 'You have to accept whatever you are given.'

'As I will, but I have a feeling that any child we may have will be a boy.'

The government was prepared to help and a man was sent to all the villages to estimate their losses. Despina was given two goats, Manos half a dozen chickens and Sofia a hundred drachmas for the loss of her orchard, whilst the farmers were supplied with seed and the shops sent essential basic food supplies.

Gradually the farmers were able to replant their fields and a semblance of normality returned to Kastelli. Despina pulled her cart through the village street to deliver milk, the fruit hung from the trees that had been spared by the Italians, and the weekly journeys to the market at Neapoli were resumed.

Doctor Fokianakis visited the village to check on the health of the occupants and despite them all being thin and undernourished none of them appeared ill. He paid particular attention to Sofia, but certainly could not see any outward signs that she was suffering from the incurable and dreaded disease.

Stratos visited the village. He arrived riding on a donkey, his crutches tied to the wooden saddle. On finding his grandmother's house closed and empty he limped the few doors along to Tryphaine's cottage.

'Stratos!' she exclaimed. 'What brings you here?'

'I came looking for my grandmother, but I imagine I am too late.'

'She died some years ago. Fortunately she did not suffer for as long as some. I can take you to her grave if you want. There is a wooden marker there. What happened to you?' Tryphaine looked down at Stratos's feet – he had only one, his left leg ended at his knee and his trouser leg was pinned up.

He shrugged. 'I was involved in a bit of a skirmish and came off worst. Can I come in, Tryphaine? It's tiring standing here on one leg.'

Tryphaine blushed. She had been so surprised to see the man that she had forgotten her manners. 'Of course. Sit at the table and I'll bring you a glass of wine. Would you like something to eat?'

Stratos grinned at her. 'I never say no to food. I spent many days with only a crust of bread to keep me going.'

'You were more fortunate than many of us,' remarked Tryphaine. 'By the time the war ended we had all but forgotten how to make a loaf and what bread tasted like.' She placed a glass of wine before him.

Tryphaine disappeared into the scullery and returned a short while later with a plate containing a stuffed pepper sitting beside some rice and a salad to accompany it

'So if you have lost your leg how are you able to work?' she asked.

'I'm classed as a war veteran. I've been given a periptero by the government. I sit inside a little hut all day selling newspapers, cigarettes, matches, needles, cotton; you name it, just about anything and everything to anyone who passes by. I'm better off than those who lost an arm. They are expected to walk around the town in all weathers selling lottery tickets. At least I'm dry. How is Timotheos?'

Tryphaine's face lit up. 'He's well, thank you; he arrived back without a scratch. He married shortly before the war and we did our best to persuade him to stay in Kastelli, but he would have none of it. Said it was his duty to help drive out the Italian and Germans.'

'Like father; like son.'

'Nikos did not go away to fight.'

'I wasn't talking about Nikos,' grinned Stratos and Tryphaine's face flamed.

'Nikos was hit by a German lorry and killed outright.'

'Oh, Phaini, I had no idea. I'm sorry.'

Tryphaine shrugged. She had grieved for Nikos for months as she had been genuinely fond of her husband. 'What about your family?'

'Gone. Mr Benediktos died whilst I was away fighting so there was no one to take over from him. When I returned my wife took one look at my legs and showed me the door.'

Tryphaine looked at him in horror. 'You mean she left you because you had lost your leg?'

Stratos shook his head. 'No, that was the excuse she made. She was already living with someone else. I'm not sorry. Things were not good between us.'

'What about your children?'

'We haven't any. She said it had to be my fault.' Stratos winked at Tryphaine and she felt her face reddening again. 'Tell me about the rest of the villagers whilst I eat.'

'Many of the men came back from wherever they had been fighting to find their parents were no longer alive. There are a lot of new graves. Maria and Yiorgo were the sensible ones. They went off to America a few months before the Germans and Italians invaded.'

Stratos whistled through his teeth. 'Where did they get that kind of money from?'

'According to Sofia, Alesandros gave them all his savings;

they sold their gold necklaces and also had to borrow money from the bank. I think it must be true as Sofia has been growing her own vegetables since then. She also had a few chickens until the Germans took them for their supper.'

'I bet Mr Alesandros had something to say about that!'

Tryphaine shook her head. 'Alesandros was dead by then. He had become quite senile and he threatened the Italian commander with an old shotgun and the commander shot him on the spot.' Tryphaine lowered her voice. 'His hat came off and you should have seen the state of his head.'

'Where the Italian had blown it to bits no doubt.'

Tryphaine shook her head. 'He had leprosy. Well, if he didn't have leprosy he had a skin condition that looked very much like it,' she corrected herself out of loyalty to her friend.

Stratos whistled through his teeth.

'He was buried very hurriedly, the same day in fact. Theophalia was sent to examine Sofia and said she could find nothing to indicate that she could be infected. Father Constantinus insisted that the doctor came and took tests and we were told to avoid her. He wouldn't even let her attend church until the results had come through.'

'So what were the results?' asked Stratos as he forked the last of his meal into his mouth.

'There was nothing wrong with her.'

'So she's all alone now in that big house?'

Tryphaine nodded. 'She seems happy enough and keeps herself busy.'

'The other girl didn't come back?'

'Sofia never mentions her. The villagers believe she was infected, like her father.'

Stratos raised his eyebrows. 'So she would have been sent to the island. No wonder her parents said she had run away and let everyone assume she had died.'

Tryphaine shook her head sadly. 'I wish she had told me.'

'Do you? Would you have been able to visit her and remain friends? I think you would have been as frightened of catching it as anyone else in the village.'

'I suppose so. I would have been scared that Timotheos would become infected.'

Stratos leaned back in his chair and belched contentedly. 'That was a really good meal, Phaini. Thank you.'

Tryphaine beamed with pleasure, but did not admit he had just eaten her supper. Now she would only have a few salad leaves and some bread and cheese. 'Do you want me to come with you to the graveyard?'

Stratos nodded and hauled himself upright, tucking his crutches under his arm. 'Can I leave the donkey here? I can easily walk that far. I thought the journey from Neapoli to Kastelli a bit beyond me, though.'

Stratos kept pace easily with Tryphaine as they made their way to the graveyard. Stratos tutted and shook his head over the number of villagers' names he read. When he reached his grandmother's grave he looked at it sadly.

'I'd like to have seen her one more time. I'll save up and have a proper headstone erected for her.'

'I'm sure she'd appreciate that; knowing you hadn't forgotten her.'

Stratos looked at Tryphaine reproachfully. 'How could I forget her? She cared for me until I went off with Mr Benediktos.'

'I meant forgotten her now she was dead. You were always conscientious about visiting her.'

'I enjoyed my visits.' Stratos slipped an arm around Tryphaine's shoulders and gave her a quick hug, clutching his crutch swiftly again so he did not overbalance.

'It was very wrong of me, but I will always be grateful to you, Stratos.'

'Any time,' he said airily.

Tryphaine shook her head. 'I have Timotheos. I ask for nothing more.' Tryphaine was not sure if Stratos was making a serious proposition to her or if it was his usual banter. 'I ought to get back. Timotheos usually calls in on his way home. He'll wonder where I've gone.'

As Stratos settled himself in the donkey's saddle and tied the crutches firmly to it a young man approached. Stratos grinned. There was no mistaking Timotheos, his ears stuck out even more prominently than Stratos's own ears. Timotheos looked at Stratos curiously. Somehow the man looked very familiar, but he could not recall seeing him in the village before.

'Hello, Mamma.' Timotheos nodded his head towards Stratos. 'I didn't know you had a visitor.'

'Stratos is just leaving. He lived in the village when he was a boy and came down in the hope of visiting his grandmother. I have just taken him up to the graveyard to show him where she is buried.'

Stratos leaned across the donkey's head and held out his hand. 'Timotheos, isn't it? Your mother's told me about you. Pleased to meet you.'

Timotheos shook the proffered hand. He had probably seen the man in the village if he had visited his grandmother on other occasions and that was why he was so familiar.

Tryphaine unhitched the donkey's reins and passed them to Stratos. Stratos winked at her. 'It was good to see you again. I'll look you up the next time I come down this way.' He raised his hand and kicked the donkey's side with his leg, encouraging her to start ambling off down the village street.

Stratos stopped his donkey outside of Sofia's house and hung the reins over the metal railing of the window. Having knocked he was about to remount the donkey and ride on when Sofia finally answered the door to him.

'Stratos, what a surprise.' Sofia wiped her hands down her skirt and tried to push some stray hair back underneath her scarf.

'You'll have to forgive the state of me, but I was gardening. You are welcome to come in.'

Stratos shook his head. 'I'll not disturb you. I came down hoping to see my grandmother. I spoke to Phaini and she told me she had died some years ago. She also told me about Mr Alesandros. I just wanted to call and say I was sorry.'

'That's very kind of you, Stratos. Will you come in for a glass of wine?'

'Thank you, no. I have to ride back to Neapoli and return this donkey to the owner. If I'm not back within the next hour or so he'll think I've run off with her. I said I'd only be gone a short while.'

'I'm sure Phaini will tell me all your news.'

Sofia watched Stratos ride off towards Neapoli. She would have liked to ask him how he had lost his leg, but no doubt Tryphaine would arrive the following morning and sit and gossip.

Stratos shook his head as he rode off. He had nearly said something very foolish to Tryphaine and he was thankful he had stopped himself in time. There was no way he could ever live in Kastelli with Timotheos walking around, a mirror image of himself, and he could not imagine Tryphaine being prepared to move to Neapoli. No, far better to leave things as they were and make a visit occasionally.

The villagers had begun to pay their rent to Sofia again and she was saving it carefully. She no longer placed it in the drawer of the wash stand. After the way the Germans had wrenched it open it no longer closed properly. She slit open the seam on the far side of her mattress and placed the notes inside, cobbling the seam back together with large stitches so it could be slit open again easily when she had enough to hide in there again.

She was worried. She had been expecting someone from the bank to call and demand their money. She had no idea how much they would ask for and she decided that the next time Doctor Fokianakis called she would ask his advice.

'So, Mrs Sofia, what is worrying you? Nothing to do with your late husband's problems, I hope.'

Sofia shook her head. 'As far as I am aware I am fit and well Doctor, but I need some advice. My husband borrowed a large sum of money from the bank to enable my daughter and her husband to go to America. I had a considerable amount saved until the Germans arrived. They robbed me of it. I have been saving again, but no one has come from the bank to ask me for any money.'

'Which bank did you husband use?' asked Doctor Fokianakis. 'Was it in Neapoli or Aghios Nikolaos?'

'I don't know,' admitted Sofia. 'I didn't know there was more than one.'

'There are a number of banks in the town. To make any enquiries for you I would need to know which bank I should approach if it is in Neapoli.'

Sofia sighed and shrugged. 'I have no idea. I will just have to wait until they come to me.'

'I'm sure they will eventually. No doubt they are all trying to sort out their accounts now we are no longer occupied.' Doctor Fokianakis pulled two letters from his pocket. 'I believe these are for you.'

'Oh!' Sofia's eyes lit up. 'Thank you so much.' She held the letters reverently in her hands.

'All is well with you family in America, I hope.'

'I'm sure it is. You told me I had to be patient as the mail was held up during the war.'

The doctor took his leave and Sofia turned the letters over and over in her hands, finally placing them on the table. Throughout the day she looked at them again and finally took down the metal box from the shelf and placed them inside along with the other letters she had received from Maria. There was no point in opening them; she would not be able to read the words written on the paper.

Each week Sofia cut open the side of the mattress inserted some notes and stitched it up again. She left herself a small amount to purchase any items she wanted from the shops and when the pedlar visited she bought wool to weave herself a new cloak ready for the winter. She desperately needed some new boots and she would ask Timotheos to buy a pair for her when he next visited Neapoli.

1946 – 1950

The money that Sofia hid in her mattress had grown considerably. She had needed to undo the mattress seam all the way down the side in order to reach inside and spread the notes out as evenly as she could. Still no one had come from the bank asking for the money owed by Alesandros, but she was sure they would eventually.

The village was benefitting now the occupying armies had left their shores. The cart track that had led to Neapoli for so many years had been filled in and was now a black ribbon of tarmac, some of the farmers had bought three wheeled motorised carts that could travel easily on the smooth road and made their weekly journey to Neapoli easier and quicker.

The electricity, that had only previously been available in the towns, was gradually being taken into the villages and when Sofia heard it was coming to Kastelli she raised her eyebrows in surprise.

'Why do we need electricity? We have our oil lamps.'

Father Constantinus shook his head in despair. He had met with similar opinions from the other villagers and was doing his best to convince them that it would be beneficial for everyone.

'You will be able to have light in your house by putting down a switch. There will be no need for you to fill your lamps and trim the wicks. You will no longer be in danger from knocking one over and starting a fire. If you go to the taverna in the evening you will be able to see your way home and not fall into the ditch.

You will also have a telephone.'

'A telephone?'

Father Constantinus nodded. 'If you wish to speak to one of your neighbours you will not need to walk to their house. You will be able to lift up the hand set and be asked the number you want to call. You tell the person the number and they will dial it and the telephone will ring inside your neighbour's house until they answer.'

Sofia looked at the priest in derision. 'All the time I have two good legs I do not need a telephone.' She walked away from him. What a stupid idea. It would be quicker to walk to Tryphaine's house if she wanted to speak to her; besides she would be asked in for coffee and they could sit and gossip. You wouldn't be able to do that with this new machine they called a telephone.

Reluctantly Sofia allowed the workmen to enter her house and run the electric wires down the walls. She looked at them with distaste. At least when she had replaced the rugs that hung there you would not see them. The glass bulb that hung in the middle of the room could not be disguised. She had been told she could not drape a piece of cloth over it or she would start a fire and she looked at the ugly appendage in disgust.

For weeks Sofia ignored the light switch and lit her oil lamps when it became dark, sitting in their comforting glow at her loom or sewing a new skirt or blouse. Father Constantinus was in despair over her stubbornness and finally went to the general store and asked them not to provide Sofia with any more oil for her lamps.

'It is for her own good,' he insisted. 'Once she realises the benefit of electric light she will stop running the risk of setting herself and her house alight.'

For two evenings Sofia sat in darkness and retired to her bed early. She lay there thinking. Yiorgo had said that some of the houses in Aghios Nikolaos had electric light. She was sure Fotini had written to say that her house on Spinalonga had electricity and how beneficial she had found it. Maybe she should put the light switch down and see what happened.

The other villagers had no such scruples and were delighted when they could switch on a light and no longer had to move oil lamps to strategic places in their living rooms to enable them to cook or sew. They might only be poor farmers living in a village, but that was reason why they should be ignored by the government and not have the same amenities as the towns.

The black telephone sat in the corner of the room on the floor gathering dust. She had no use for that and on the two occasions when it had rung, she had ignored it. If a neighbour wished to speak to her they could come and knock at her door.

She was surprised when Kassianae, Dimitra's daughter, knocked her door and asked to be admitted. Since Alesandros had told Dimitra that her help was no longer required in the house the woman had hardly spoken to her except to grumble when Sofia asked for her rent.

'Kassie, is something wrong?'

Kassianae nodded and sat down at the table without being invited. 'It's my mother. She's ill.' She looked at Sofia with distressed eyes.

'What's wrong with her?' It was rare for the villagers to suffer more than a cold.

'Doctor Fokianakis isn't sure. She has a bad pain in her chest and he wants her to go to the hospital in Neapoli.'

'The doctor? He isn't due in the village for another week.'

'I know,' Kassianae agreed. 'I used the telephone and asked him to come to see Mamma. She was writhing in agony.'

Sofia's eyes went to the black appliance that sat in the corner. If you could use that to call the doctor rather than have to walk to the town she supposed it could have its uses.

'So why have you come to me?'

'The doctor said he would send some medical transport for her. I'll need to go with her and have to stay up in Neapoli. The doctor says he can arrange some lodgings for me but I'll have to pay for it. Would you – could you – lend me some money?' pleaded Kassianae. 'I didn't know who else to go to ask. I'll pay you back,' she promised.

'When is the transport coming for her?

Kassianae shrugged. 'He used the telephone to arrange it and said it should be here within an hour.'

Sofia considered quickly. She was willing to lend the girl the money, but she did not want her to see that she was removing it from inside her mattress. 'Go back to your mother and make sure all is in readiness for her to leave. I'll come down as soon as I can with some money for you.'

A look of tremendous relief crossed Kassianae's face. 'I'm terribly grateful and I'm sure Mamma will be when I tell her.'

'Don't tell the other villagers or they'll all come begging at my door.' Sofia rose from the table and Kassianae threw her arms around he benefactor.

'I can't thank you enough,' she said, with tears in her eyes.

Sofia removed the notes from their hiding place and sorted them into small piles, each one equalling the amount a cottager paid as rent each week. She checked and re-checked to make sure that she was lending Kassianae the equivalent of ten weeks rent on her cottage. On a piece of paper she made ten pencil strokes and beneath each one another ten. As Kassianae repaid her she could put a line through and know when the debt had been cleared.

It was three weeks before Kassianae returned from Neapoli. When she did she was wearing a black blouse beneath her cloak and Sofia could tell immediately that the news was not good.

'Mamma died. The doctors said she had a growth in her chest. They could do nothing.'

Sofia placed her arms around the young woman. 'I am so sorry, Kassianae. I'm sure your mother was happy to have you with her to the end.'

Kassianae nodded. 'I like to think so, but I've got a problem. I had only expected to be in Neapoli for about a week and by the time I had paid for the hospital treatment I had run out of money. Doctor Fokianakis was very kind and persuaded the family I was lodging with to allow me to stay on without paying. I've promised to send the money back with him the next time he visits Kastelli.'

'That was good of him to make that arrangement for you.'

Kassianae twisted her fingers nervously. 'But I haven't any money, Mrs Sofia.'

Sofia frowned. 'So you are asking me if I can lend you some more?'

'Is it possible? If you're not able to do so I will have to ask Father Constantinus. I know he will say he has to ask permission from the Bishop and that could take months.'

'If you have no money, Kassianae, how do you propose to pay me back?'

'Could we pay you a little extra with the rent each week until it's cleared? We could manage that after we've been to the market.'

Sofia took the piece of paper with the pencil marks from beneath a dish on the dresser. 'This is what you owe me at the moment. How much more do you need?'

Although Kassianae was able to count she was not sure if she understood Sofia's accounting system. 'Two week's rent should be enough.'

'I can manage that.'

Kassianae's face lost its worried expression and she gave Sofia a grateful smile. 'I'll always be grateful to you. Even when I have repaid you the money I will still be in your debt forever.'

1970

Sofia sat propped up in her bed, whilst Doctor Fokianakis felt her weakening pulse. After Father Constantinus's unsympathetic attitude towards her when Alesandros's died she no longer had the same faith in the priest. Sofia had insisted that when the doctor visited next Kassianae was to be there and also the priest. If she made her wishes known to all three of them at the same time and made them swear on Alesandros's Bible surely they would be carried out.

'When I go, Kassianae, I want everything in the house left untouched.'

Kassianae pursed her lips. It would be wicked to leave the plates and glasses along with some of the rugs.

'I mean it,' continued Sofia. 'My husband's Bible is there and I want you to take it in your hands and swear that neither you nor any of the villagers will set foot in here after I'm gone. My daughter will be back and she will not want to find that everything has been taken.

'She is returning?' asked Kassianae in surprise.

Sofia nodded. 'I have had a letter.' She did not add that she had received the letter years earlier and never opened the envelope as she would have been unable to read Maria's message to her.

Kassianae picked up the Bible and held the heavy tome with both hands. 'I swear, Sofia. I will take nothing from the house, nor will I allow anyone else in the village to take anything.'

'Now you, Father and then the doctor. Once you have all sworn I will be able to rest in peace.'

Sofia closed her eyes and nodded after she had heard the two men confirm her wishes would be carried out. 'Just remove my body. Nothing else. That oath is binding. I have placed some money on the dresser for you Kassianae. You've earned it this past year looking after me.'

'You've been no trouble. It was the least I could do for you after the way you had helped me. I said I was in your debt for evermore.'

'You paid me back regularly and I kept it aside from the rents. All you repaid is there along with a little more. You may take that now. Father Constantinus, I would like you to arrange for me to be buried in the family vault where my parents are interred and my name added to the gravestone. Doctor Fokianakis I would like a few moments alone with you.'

Kassianae picked up the money from the dresser, hurriedly stuffing it into her apron pocket. She would count it once she had returned to her cottage. She did not want Father Constantinus to see the amount that was there or he could well expect her to give a large donation to the church on Sunday.

Father Constantinus hovered by Sofia's bed. Was her death so imminent that he should stay and give her the last rites?

'You may leave, Father. No doubt Kassie will send for you when it becomes necessary.'

Sofia waited until the priest had left, then she turned to Doctor Fokianakis, fumbled beneath her pillow and handed him two keys tied together with a piece of string.

'I want you to go upstairs. You will see the rugs that are hanging there. A hook supports each end of the pole and on one of those hooks I want you to hang these keys. Any one will do provided you pull the rug across to hide them.'

Doctor Fokianakis took the two small keys and looked at them. 'Are they the keys to your jewellery boxes?'

'I have no jewellery,' Sofia assured him. 'The boxes contain the letters and photographs from my daughter. I cannot throw them away. They are all I have left that I value.'